THAT SUMMER OF '74

Howard Rayner

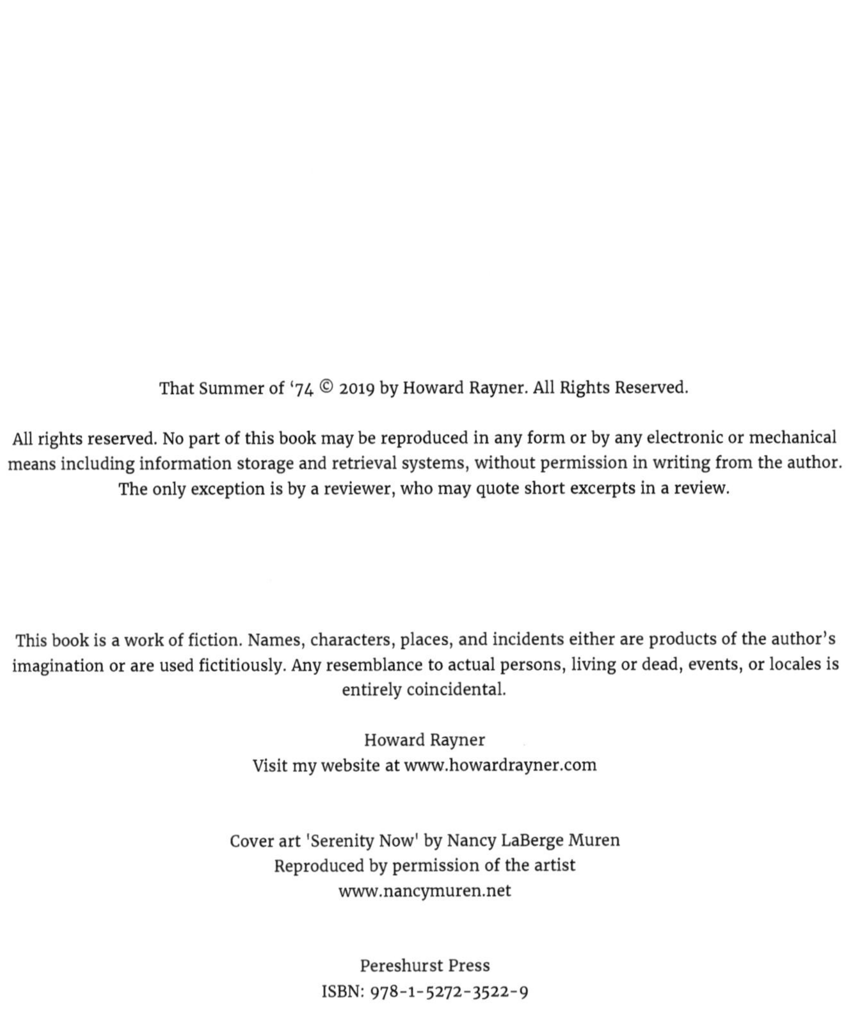

Howard Rayner
Visit my website at www.howardrayner.com

Cover art 'Serenity Now' by Nancy LaBerge Muren
Reproduced by permission of the artist
www.nancymuren.net

Pereshurst Press
ISBN: 978-1-5272-3522-9

CONTENTS

ACKNOWLEDGEMENTS

Many thanks to Anthony Lapsley for his editorial advice, colorful margin notes and unwavering patience during the writing of this book.

Special thanks to Heather Tanchuck whose knowledge of the movie industry and locations of the period in this book was of immense help in my research.

Howard Rayner

"What a strange thing is memory, and hope; one looks backward, the other forward; one is of today, the other of tomorrow."

GRANDMA MOSES

MAROONED ON RED – APRIL 1974

Alex leaned back and stared at his painting on the easel. Pretending to be a stranger to himself, he tried to appraise the work dispassionately. This latest red painting unnerved him. The way in which the artist had let the Scarlet Lake Extra run into Cadmium Red made him uneasy. The technique used to dribble the Carmine into the Ruby Lake seemed clumsy. The myriad of reds draining and uniting in a pool of blood-like Alizarin Crimson at the foot of the piece elicited despair.

Despair in his talent.

Turning away in frustration, Alex slammed down his brushes and hurled the spent tubes of red pigment into the trash. 'Get something on the canvas', was what his old professor had always said, 'you can't share feelings which remain in your head'. But if this vast, uncontrolled outpouring of reds represented his feelings, what the hell were those feelings? His work suddenly felt so pointless, so airless, such a waste of life. Perhaps he'd lost his talent? Heck, did he have any to begin with? He'd graduated from Long Beach the same year as Scotty and look at her today. She'd a one woman show coming up at the LaFonte Gallery, or so he'd heard off Hank, and was being touted as an 'up and coming' artist. Where was his career? Non-existent. His new abstract glared back at him like a child confused by its parent, their face flushed by a guilty secret's color …

Red.

This was when the beach house's isolation came in handy, it was a good place for secrets. Alex considered his other canvases propped up along the walls, his jars of thinners, his paint stained rags, his tubs of splayed brushes, his chewed pencil stubs, his palettes of crusty colors. There was a time just the smell of linseed oil, black ink and pastels filled him with excitement, but today everything associated with his art filled him with gloom. What time was it? Time for the twenty-first cigarette of the day, that's what. He cracked open a fresh pack of Kools, slipped one out and lit up. Pottering onto the verandah, he filled his lungs with Pacific ozone. The fresh air lent the Kools' menthol smoke a piquancy, and also triggered a coughing fit. Kicking this habit would be good for his health, his bank balance too. Yeah, that's what he'd do, he'd quit smoking ...

Tomorrow.

Alex contemplated the day ahead. The sun's position through the studio's frosted skylight told him it was a half hour before noon, that left five and a half hours to kill until Julie rang the martini bell at the Beachcomber. Having no shifts for lifeguard duty at the country club pool rostered, he'd been sure an entire day solely devoted to his craft would overcome the doubt that had stymied his creativity for the past few months. But even without schlepping out to earn a crust, once again he was mired in uncertainty and craving escape. At times like this in their old studio at Venice Beach, he, Hank and Scoop would write the day off as a bad vibe. They'd down tools and hang out at Barney's Beanery. The going must have been tough pretty consistently, for in retrospect they'd hung out at Barney's discussing their art more than practicing it that fall of seventy-one.

On the shoreline in front of the beach houses, the faithful congregated in board shorts and bikinis for sun worship. Alex shucked off his sneakers, perched on the edge of his deck and dangled his bare feet. The phone's shrill ring startled him. He didn't leap to answer. They must've crossed a wire when they'd installed the phone lines, as every other day he got calls for Angie. He'd gotten sick of explaining, "There's no Angie here. I've lived around here two years and don't know any Angie." He occasionally wondered if he should answer with something fresh like, "Angie can't talk right now, she's got my dick in her mouth," but he resisted. He suspected Angie was a hooker and a statement like that could whet a punter's appetite. This soon to be disappointed trick kept on ringing.

Alex knocked the sand off his feet on the upturned brush beside the front door and padded inside. "Y'ello," he muttered gruffly into the receiver. Surprisingly this caller was for him. It was Scotty, and only took a couple of words to make clear she was investigating the reason for his no-show at her party. Alex trotted out the standard excuses about feeling sick/tired/car trouble etc.

"Just checking you hadn't died," she said cheerfully.

"Your party was two days ago. If I was dead then, I'd still be dead now."

"I know, but it's been hot and I plan on coming to visit. I didn't want to turn up unannounced and find you dissolved on the floor."

"You can put away your rubber gloves, I'm still alive." Alex dragged the phone as far as the cord would allow and flopped into the sagging wicker chair by the window. "Heard on the grapevine about your exhibition. Exciting news." He realized he didn't sound excited. "Congratulations!"

After an uncomfortable silence, Scotty said, "You don't sound right. Is that beach house the best place for you? I worry about you out there on your own." The line went muffled as she covered the mouthpiece. Alex could tell Bob, her man, was saying something to her. "Sorry." Scotty came back on the line. "Bob says he's worried about you too. You've been so distant lately. Did we do something to upset you?"

"I'm in a funk, but it's not to do with you guys. I've dried up, simple as that. Maybe pop was right, the only thing I'm worthy of painting is houses. Sure I put paint on the canvas, but I'm not feeling it." Alex scuffed the wall with his toes. "I've lost my way."

"I've gone through months in the past with nothing happening. Hang on in."

"I'm struggling to keep hanging on in, and I'm sick to death of working the pool to make ends meet. As it is I can barely afford to keep this shack going. You don't know what it's like to struggle, you've got Bob to fall back on."

"To fall back on? What am I, the little woman? You've spent too much time at Barney's with Scoop and Hank. Those chauvinist throwbacks only see a woman functioning on her back or in the kitchen."

"C'mon, you've got to admit that Bob having money takes the pressure off you."

After a pause Scotty said, "I can make you a loan if that'd help?"

"No. Look, I didn't mean it to sound that way."

"Hey, how about I toss my string bikini and some good weed in the jalopy and motor down the week after next? How's Thursday grab you?"

"Cool. See you then."

"And seriously, Alex, don't give yourself a hard time."

After hanging up, Alex regretted mentioning money. Scotty's loan offer felt like pity. He hated revealing weakness to anyone, let alone Scotty. At college *he'd* been the golden boy, the one to watch, and Scotty had been his number one groupie. Boy did the tables turn after graduation. His acolyte was now riding the crest of a wave while he was languishing in the drift. Alex pushed the phone aside, went out and resumed the task of dangling his feet off the deck.

Next door on his right, Gloria Waverley had set up a sun lounger on the scrubby grass out front of her place. She lay sprawled unappetizingly, face down sunning her back. The Waverleys had only opened up their beach house a week ago, yet Gloria was already the color of mahogany. Gloria and Harry, her husband, called this beach cottage their 'retreat'. They owned a sprawling house and car dealership in Glendale, which one would assume gave them space to retreat without coming to Sunset Cove. Harry didn't appear to like the heat, the ocean, or even Gloria, which made it hard to fathom why he wanted to summer here. Gloria's motivation was clearer. She saw herself as an 'artist' and wanted to live amidst the local community to legitimately call herself part of the Laguna Beach art scene.

Alex kicked himself for inserting quotation marks around the word *artist* even just thinking about Gloria. Flicking ash off his cigarette, he cast his eyes over the Waverleys' beach house. They'd bought the lease four years ago in the wake of some undisclosed family crisis. The house's original resident, a sculptor called Zoltan, had grown too infirm to live independently and gone back east to end his days with his sisters. The Waverleys had spent plenty of dough on the place, making his and the Pipers' houses look pretty shabby in comparison. There was no doubt the Waverleys' was the slickest of the three houses on this end of the beach. Slickness wasn't Sunset Cove's attraction, he reasoned. 'Real' artists don't care about living in fancy places, all they need is a space in which to create and a non-judgmental environment in which to live an authentic life. That was the reason his grandmother, Dora, had wound up here. On quiet nights together, after he'd escaped the hell that was Dayton and turned up in the middle of the night on her doorstep, Dora had filled him in on the backstory of how she'd settled in Sunset Cove.

Dora had been an actress in silent movies, or the 'flickers' as she jokingly referred to them. She'd been a stunt double for Lillian Gish and had played a bit part in *Drums of Love*. Whether this was true or not was debatable without a séance to contact D.W. Griffith. However, her embryonic acting career went belly up with the talkies. Never one to linger on failure, Dora waved goodbye to her movie dreams and took up painting. One weekend, a girlfriend who worked at the studios had invited her down here to paint, drink hooch and swim in the nude. This hidden cove had become a haunt for Hollywood's art department workers. Some of them built tin shelters or wooden huts on the beach in order to stay all weekend. The rocky cliffs, golden sand and colorful wildlife provided inspiration for their art in daylight hours - the nude bathing and booze provided inspiration for their night time activities. Within a few years, the rough shelters turned into solid houses and the place became a semi-respectable artists' colony.

After spending increasing amounts of time in Sunset Cove indulging her artistic passions, Dora gave up her old life in L.A. and her marriage. She didn't make the decision lightly because they had the kid to consider. She'd wanted to bring their daughter to live at the beach, but the soon to be ex-husband wouldn't countenance it. Although he'd never visited the place, he'd heard tales of 'goings on' and deemed it unsuitable for a youngster. He was determined to take the kid to live with his folks back in Dayton, where she could be raised in a God-Fearing manner. Dora hated conflict, so she gave the kid the choice of going with poppa or coming with her - the kid was five after all. The kid chose to go with poppa. Dora understood. After all, she'd loved the man too, she just didn't anymore. Not wanting to poison the air with acrimonious court cases, she'd let them skedaddle. Dora had never set eyes on her daughter, Alex's mother, ever again.

Alive that was.

Despite resistance from the Dayton side of the family, Dora had made the trip east to attend her daughter's funeral ten years back. That was when she'd met her grandson, Alex, for the first time. Much to the family's annoyance Dora and Alex hit it off immediately, possibly due to their mutual love of art and a similar gentleness in their natures. Dora always regretted that her daughter became a stranger but found joy in Alex, a stranger who became her grandson. Alex could never understand why his father's side of the family was so dead set against Dora. However, Dora never shut the door on them, always believing reconciliation was possible. She maintained that the heart's never still by necessity, it must be in constant motion to sustain life and so it was only natural the heart's desires would be in constant motion too.

Alex rested his head on the deck's wooden railings with their cracked green lead paint. He didn't know where he'd be if Dora hadn't left the beach house to him in her will. The tides of change would eventually wash away this swathe of cream, green and blue beach houses clinging to the scrubby hill between the highway and the sea, but he hoped that day was a long way off. A car door slammed and a few moments later Mrs. Piper came around the front of her cottage on his left. "Morning, Alex!" she called over, lugging a brown sack of groceries. "Looks like another rare day, don't it?"

"Sure does," Alex called back.

Mrs. Piper set her groceries on the bench beside her front door, rubbed her back and walked to the edge of her verandah. "You hear that storm last night? A real fierce nor'easter."

"Must've slept through it."

"Ah." Mrs. Piper's eyes crinkled in a smile and her silver curls fluttered in the breeze. "You made your way home from the Beachcomber mighty late last night. Perhaps you could do with an early night for once?"

"You know the Sunset Cove saying, 'Every night's Saturday night and every Saturday night's New Year's Eve'."

"I also know the saying that if you burn a candle at both ends, you'll have no light to paint by on a dark night."

Alex nodded in grudging acceptance of her point. Mary Piper had been a lifelong friend of Dora's. After Dora's death, Mrs. Piper had taken on the responsibility for his moral welfare. Just who he needed living next door, Jiminy Cricket in comfort slacks.

"You missed a treat of nature, it was quite some storm! Your roof was rattling to high heaven, sounded ready to blow right off."

"Well, it didn't wake me, but thanks for letting me know. I'll get the ladder and check it out."

"Make sure you do. Today's a rare day, but you never know when another storm's going to blow in." Mrs. Piper gathered her groceries and went inside.

The last thing Alex needed was a repair bill, or worse a new roof. The only way he could raise cash for that would be to sell the car. And losing his car would be like having his legs cut off out here. He didn't have to make rent, but he still needed to eat and drink, and he'd gotten used to luxuries like electricity and piped water. Yeah, he needed to make some real money, real soon. This realization called for another cigarette.

A couple of noisy kids were kicking a red and yellow beach ball in the surf. Two gaudy green and orange sunshades had gone up at the water's edge, their tacky artificial colors clashing hideously against the cove's natural tones. The creak of metal and canvas alerted him to Gloria Waverley turning to fry her other side. Out of the corner of his eye, Alex saw Harry come out carrying a margarita. Unnoticed by Gloria, Harry set the drink next to her lounger and whispered something in her ear. Lifting her head minimally, Gloria muttered, "Nothing makes it better." Harry went back into the house. Gloria glared at the closed door. She picked up the glass, emptied its contents into the sand and hurled the glass at their front door, where it smashed with an explosive crash. The Dodgers could use a pitcher with such a right arm. There was no doubt the Waverleys were a mystery - one Alex didn't want to get involved with solving.

More bathers were setting up on the beach, spreading towels and erecting parasols. The Pina Colada scent of Hawaiian Tropic wafted on the breeze. Amidst the trunks, bikinis and crop tops, one person on the beach stood out - a preppy guy who'd dressed himself in a white polo shirt, beige Bermudas, white ankle socks and white sneakers. Pausing at the water's edge, the guy shielded his eyes and gazed at the horizon. A yacht, its sails full of wind, slid across the azure bay. Mr. White and Beige remained immobile, staring out to sea. His stillness mesmerized Alex. Just when it felt as though the guy was never going to move again, he abruptly strode towards the rocky cliffs at the head. Alex wondered what the guy had suddenly found so interesting, there was nothing up there except a hazardous climb.

Stretching the tension from his neck, Alex was troubled by that nagging ache in his shoulder again. Perhaps some exercise would get his head in shape? A run on the beach would also kill some time until the martini bell. Hauling himself to his feet, he went up to his bedroom. After peeling off his paint splashed jeans and t-shirt, he slipped into a pair of blue running shorts and a white tank. Going outside, he discovered Gloria had rolled onto her back.

Gloria dipped her sunglasses and gave him an approving once over as he jumped onto the beach. "Howdy stranger! How you keeping?" she shouted over.

"Good, thanks!"

"How's the work going?" Gloria awkwardly raised herself to a sitting position, then tugged her bikini top down into place.

"Great. Yours?"

"Great too." Gloria tucked a strand of straggly peroxide blond hair behind her ear. "I got a new piece going. I'm calling it *Winsome Flotsam*. Isn't that a great title?"

"A doozy. You've a real knack for merging your titles with your vision," he said, momentarily amazed by his facility to spout bullshit.

"Drop by later and I'll give you a peek." Gloria adjusted her bikini, not in the right direction.

"Sounds fun. I'll see how I feel later."

"Just give me a shout." Gloria prepared to flop back into prone sunning position, then added, "If you're swinging by the store could you pick me up a head of lettuce?"

It was not totally surprising Gloria considered bare feet, short shorts and wife-beater a suitable shopping outfit. "Nah. I'm taking a run up to the cliffs."

"Hey!" Gloria called after him, "If you see any, grab some black shells for me!"

"Will do!" Alex called over his shoulder, knowing full well he wouldn't.

Jogging along the surf was his favorite exercise. A naturally active metabolism and lack of funds for food kept him lean. Years of crewing on the yachts had developed strong muscles in his chest and back, and chin-ups around the pool to fill the long hours of lifeguard duty kept his veiny biceps and forearms toned. His wavy brown hair was shoulder length, outdoor life having sun bleached the tips. His year-around tan made the hair on his legs, arms and chest glisten gold against his skin. However, he took his good looks for granted and spent not a second of the day gazing in the mirror. The ocean foamed refreshingly around his ankles and the tide shifted the sand underfoot, kicking his calves and thighs into action. He was just finding his rhythm when a soggy golden retriever bounded out of the water. Swerving to avoid it broke his stride and he nearly tripped as the dog tangled around his legs.

"Watch it bud! Careful of my dog!" yelled the red-faced owner with white pork pie hat and a chain leash draped around his neck. The panting dog splattered water as it shook itself off, then raced away on some urgent errand.

Getting back into his stride, Alex spotted Mr. White and Beige in the distance. The guy was picking his way up the head's rocky incline. He'd either not seen, or ignored, the warning sign, 'UNSTABLE CLIFFS! DANGER OF DEATH - KEEP OFF'. Three months back someone had fallen off and been smashed to pieces on the rocks. Reaching his regular turning point at the end of the cove, Alex caught his breath. Resting in the surf, he watched the guy scrambling up the cliff. A flurry of shale landed in the scrub as the ground crumbled under his footfall. It didn't deter the guy, he carried on up. This darned fool was liable to kill himself. Alex cupped his hands and yelled, "Hey, you! You up there! The cliffs are dangerous!"

Mr. White and Beige glanced down at Alex like he was an annoying bug. Alex made an urgent 'come down' movement. The guy was intent on ignoring him, however, and disappeared over the peak. Great, now the guy was out of sight Alex knew there was no reason to keep watch. If Mr. White and Beige was intent on hurling himself onto the rocks or slipped because he'd ignored the warning sign that was his own lookout. Alex turned to run back to the house.

Shit.

He couldn't walk, or rather jog, away with a clear conscience. Leaving the water, Alex approached the cliff. Cursing his lack of footwear, he gingerly trod around the rock pools and small boulders. After the painful pricks of dried grass and saltbush in the scrub at the cliff's bottom, stepping onto the rock face was almost a relief. Sweat dripped from his hair, ran along his neck and trickled down his back into his shorts. This ad hoc mountaineering wasn't what he'd had in mind for a workout. Nearing the point where he'd be able to see over the cliff top, he wondered what he'd find; an empty space and a broken body on the rocks below? Grunting with effort as he surmounted the pinnacle, he got his answer. Mr. White and Beige was standing precariously on the cliff edge, staring mournfully down at the sea. Alex wondered how to make his presence felt without startling the guy. Fearing that the guy was about to jump, Alex coughed gently and softly said, "Hey, you should come back from the edge."

Mr. White and Beige raised his head but didn't move.

"Seriously, man, whatever you're thinking of doing it's not worth it."

The guy turned his head, dropped his aviator sunglasses onto the bridge of his nose, tossed a pebble into the sea and asked, "Excuse me? Is there a law against throwing stones off the cliff?"

Alex realized he'd been mistaken in thinking the guy was suicidal, this kid was plain stupid. "The cliffs are eroding and real unstable. Didn't you see the warning sign at the bottom?"

"What are you, some kind of beach official?"

"Hell, no," said Alex with a grunt.

"What's it to you then?" The guy tossed another pebble into the sea.

"Someone slipped off here a few months back. Do me a favor, just come away from the edge."

The guy tossed his last stone. It made a tiny distant crack on the rocks below. Taking a few steps back, he asked, "Slipped? Maybe they jumped."

"Maybe they did. Whatever the reason, their brains and guts made one heck of a mess on the rocks."

"Did you think I'd come up here to kill myself?"

"It crossed my mind, but now I'm wondering if maybe you just can't read."

The guy let out a rueful laugh. "I didn't see any sign. I just wanted a place to think, you know, alone."

"Well next time you want a place to think choose someplace other than a cliff edge. It'd be better for all our health. Be careful on your way down," said Alex grumpily.

As Alex turned to go, the guy stared at his feet. "Why aren't you wearing any shoes?"

"I was running on the beach. Rock climbing wasn't on my agenda." A chill rippled across Alex's skin as Mr. Beige and White pushed his sunglasses up onto his head. The guy's clear blue eyes roved over him like an x-ray machine. The stranger on the cliff appeared mid-twenties. He had fine, almost translucent skin with freckles scattered across the bridge of his nose. Alex was struck by the long lashes framing his crazily blue eyes with their large black pupils. Was the guy handsome, was he beautiful? Alex stopped his mind pursuing the question further.

"You mean to say you climbed up here barefoot because you thought I was going to kill myself? Me, a total stranger?"

"Yeah, it sounds kind of dumb when you put it like that." Feeling like a fool, Alex angrily turned to make his way down. He'd only taken five steps when the earth beneath his left foot gave way. His left hand flailed as his right knee crumpled. "Shit!" Alex's body twisted and his right hand lashed out to grab something, anything. He was shocked to feel someone grab his wrist. The stranger on the cliff had checked his fall and yanked him backwards. The guy landed on the ground and Alex tumbled on top of him. They lay still together for a couple of moments. Alex's heart was racing, both from his brush with disaster and feeling the guy's trim body pinned beneath him.

"I can't breathe," gasped Long Lashes brushing Alex's long hair from his face.

"Aw, sorry," said Alex watching a drop of his sweat fall on Long Lashes' cheek. Alex awkwardly rolled off the guy, trying not to put too much of his weight on him. "You okay?"

Long Lashes wiped Alex's sweat off his flushed face. "Fine," he said, raising himself to his elbows. "You knocked the wind out of me."

Alex got to his feet and helped Long Lashes to stand up. While Long Lashes brushed himself off, Alex peered down the gray crevasse edged with yellowy green bushes and the dark rocks splashed with white foam below.

"Ironic, huh?" said Long Lashes coming up behind Alex, "you climb up here to save someone who didn't need saving then fall off and kill yourself in the process. You gotta admit that'd be kind of funny!"

Alex dusted off his hands. "Truly hysterical. Remind me never to do it again." Testing the ground before him as he went, Alex began his descent.

Long Lashes followed, using his hands to steady himself on the rocks. "I really didn't see a sign, I wouldn't have come up if I had."

Once they were near the bottom, Alex asked in annoyance, "How could you not see it? Over there, in big black letters it says …" Alex realized Long Lashes hadn't been lying, the warning sign was face down in the scrub several yards away. "Last night's storm must've blown it over. Can you grab it for me?" Since he was wearing shoes, Long Lashes walked over the sharp sea grass and saltbush with no issues. He carried the sign back. Together they swung it high, slammed it into the ground and Alex gave it a swift bash with his fist.

Long Lashes squinted down the beach towards the beach houses. "Lucky you spotted me. If I'd needed saving, that is."

"You're okay, I guess that's all that counts."

"Yeah, thanks. See you around," said Long Lashes.

"Be more careful in the future. You only get one life, don't treat it casually." Leaving Long Lashes standing by the cliffs, and without glancing back to see what he was going to do next, Alex sprinted to the ocean and rinsed his feet. He checked his soles and thankfully both were intact. Alex jogged back to the house, wanting to put the whole incident behind him. Luckily no-one had witnessed him making a fool of himself up there, pretty stupid when the victim ended up having to save the lifeguard.

Back at the beach house, Alex cooled down on the deck's steps. He was reluctant to go in and face that red canvas. Finding a good reason to stay outside, he fished for his sneakers. Ambling around the side of the house, he rattled through the tangle of rusty tools in the outhouse. The ladder came free and a tin shovel and a couple of brooms clattered down. Alex rested the ladder against the wall, stuffed the tools back in and slammed the door. Time to survey the roof. He crossed his fingers that this wasn't going to reveal a costly problem.

Of the three houses on this end of beach, the Piper's was the only one with space for an automobile outside. A rough track, one vehicle's width, ran behind his and the Waverley's houses ending in a small lot up in the dunes. Only locals used this track, but an occasional tourist who'd overshot the lot off the highway would wind up here every so often.

Alex extended the ladder, positioned it against the eaves and tucked the hammer in his shorts. He'd nearly climbed to the top when he heard a voice shout, "Oh, it's you!" Alex looked down and saw Long Lashes heading his way. Up in the dunes, nestled between his forest green Chevy Impala and the Waverleys' bronze Cadillac Deville, Alex spotted a nifty red automobile, the kind of car a guy like him could only ever dream of slipping into and jamming his foot on the gas - a Mercedes 450 SL Coupé. Its hood was raised with steam billowing out. Long Lashes had trouble written right through him. "Guessing that's yours?" Alex called down.

"I only turned the ignition and the next thing I know it's about to explode. Do you know your way around cars?"

"A fair bit, but it doesn't take an expert to know you've overheated."

"For sure? But I only just started it."

"It was maybe running hot when you parked. And the sun's pretty strong today. Yep, overheating's my guess."

"What should I do?"

"Let it cool then top up the radiator."

"You got water here?"

"Sure do. We got electricity and phones too. It's practically civilized," Alex called down while examining his roof.

"You know anyone who lives round here who could help?"

"I live here."

"Seriously? You're not a contractor?"

"This is my home." Alex pulled the hammer from his shorts and ran his hand over the shingles, testing for loose ones.

"I know people with beach houses, but I don't know anybody who actually lives in one."

Finding a couple of obviously loose and raised shingles, Alex hammered them down. "What'd they do with 'em then?"

"They visit for an afternoon or weekend every so often."

"Mostly just a place to store the beach towels then." Alex stretched his hand to check as many shingles as he could reach. He hammered a few more nails down for good measure, tucked the hammer back in his shorts and backed down the ladder.

"About that water? I'd really appreciate your help," Long Lashes said once Alex reached the bottom.

Alex swept sweat soaked hair off his face in irritation. "Hold this." Alex passed him the hammer. "I'll find a jug."

"You say you have a phone? May I use it?" The guy lingered on the threshold, watching Alex rifle through the cupboards. "It's long-distance. I'll give you the cash."

Alex hesitated, "I dunno ..."

"I'll make it real short." The guy flapped his long lashes over his blue eyes.

Long Lashes didn't look like your average conman or Manson Family devotee, but how many poor saps had been lured to their doom thinking the same thing? Hoping he didn't live to regret it, Alex said, "Phone's through there," and pointed to the wicker chair by the front door.

"Thanks." Long Lashes rested the hammer on the kitchen table, flicking his eyes into Alex's studio as he passed by.

While he ran water into the jug, Alex heard Long Lashes ask the operator for an international line. After getting the connection, there followed some jabber in fluent Italian. All Alex gleaned from this was a word which sounded like 'mamma'. After more Italian talk, Long Lashes switched to English, shouting, "I didn't do it, but I can't deal with you. For god's sake, let me go!" Alex was poised by the back door, jug of water in his hand, when Long Lashes came back. "Get through to Timbuktu?"

"They're relaying my message by camel." Long Lashes didn't take the water off him but surveyed the house. Long Lashes went back into the living room, magnetically drawn to the ocean view. "The sea practically comes to your front door."

Long Lashes pointed to the doorway off on the left. "That your bedroom?"

"Nah, just a spare room. It's a mess." It had been Dora's room after she got too infirm to climb the stairs. Alex kept it closed. Too many memories.

"It must be wonderful to fall asleep with the surf in your ears."

"That's why gran loved it here. This was her house. She died a while back."

"I'm sorry."

"Thanks, she was real old. Here's the water you needed." Alex ushered Long Lashes back through the house and shoved the jug into his hands.

"I nearly forgot the phone money." The guy set the jug on the kitchen counter and fumbled in his pocket. In doing so, he squinted into Alex's studio. "Are those canvases?"

"They're nothing." Alex snappily shut the studio door.

"This should cover it." The guy handed Alex a bill. "You're an artist then. I'd love to see your work."

"I don't show things that aren't finished. Hey, how about we sort out your car? It's quite some drive back to L.A."

"I don't mind unfinished."

"I'm not happy with how they're going."

"I'm not an authority, but I do know a bit about art."

"They're not worth looking at. In fact, they may be trash and tonight that's where they might end up," said Alex.

"If you think they're trash, the worst that can happen is if I think they're trash too. And who knows, I may love your work and offer to buy them all for an undisclosed fortune. If you hide something no-one will ever know what it is. Imagine you throw them in the trash. You may have destroyed your greatest work through insecurity."

What Long Lashes said held an uncanny resonance. "To be honest, I could do with an outside eye." Alex nervously opened the door and Long Lashes entered the studio with the air of Lord Carnavon entering Tutankhamen's tomb.

After studying the current red canvas on the easel, Long Lashes went around the rest of the studio. He pored through other canvases propped against the walls, several of them other abstracts from Alex's recent *Red* series. "Very red, aren't they? Are you angry?"

"It's not quite the word I'd use," replied Alex.

Long Lashes held up one of the smaller red studies. "After this I imagine there'll be a vermillion shortage. I find them derivative of Rothko. I'm not sold on the technique either."

Alex began to combust, letting this guy in had been another of his dumb judgements. Time to put a lid on this before any more negative critical judgement was passed. "Let's get that water and send you on your way." Alex picked up the jug and marched out the house.

"You said they were trash, not me!" Long Lashes trailed behind him.

Stomping up the incline to the parking lot, Alex berated himself for dropping his guard. But maybe the guy was right? Maybe this recent work was just confused, unchanneled rage. And Long Lashes had a point about the technique. Only this morning he'd acknowledged he was out of control. The glimmer of hope these new works had merit was well and truly crushed. Alex stuck his head under the Merc's hood. Unscrewing the radiator cap, he snatched his hand away. "Shit!" Alex rubbed his palm on his sweaty tank. "Needs longer to cool. Leave the jug on the doorstep when you're done." Alex scuffed down the dirt road back to the house. He became aware of Long Lashes trailing behind him. Alex turned and snarled, "What now? Wanna kick me while I'm down?"

"I was just thinking out loud. Did you want me to lie?"

"Right now, all I want is you to be back on the highway to La La Land!" Long Lashes recoiled like a smacked puppy. Alex took a deep breath to compose himself. He knew all too well how it felt to be snapped at. "Look, that's the only work I've done in the past few months and I don't know if I have a reason to carry on."

"I shouldn't have intruded. I'll wait by my car." Long Lashes slowly walked away.

Each step Long Lashes took, the worse Alex felt. This was crazy, why did he feel guilty? The guy had burst *his* bubble. "Hey, how about a drink while you wait? I got some sodas in the fridge. And maybe a beer or two."

"Something cold would be good," said Long Lashes with a shy smile.

Once back in the house, Alex cracked open a couple of beers. "Let's go out front. The verandah catches the breeze." Alex dragged over a sagging rattan chair and offered it to Long Lashes, but he flopped onto the old gray couch which ran along one side of the verandah. Long Lashes made a puzzled face at the upturned brush by the front door. "You knock the sand off your feet on it when you come inside off the beach," explained Alex.

"Ah." Long Lashes sipped his beer. "Pretty neat place you got here."

"Nothing fancy but you can't beat the view. By the way, my name's Alex. Alex Morgan."

"Hi, I'm Rick Stradman."

"Name sounds familiar."

"Dad's a movie producer," Rick said with disinterest. "Maybe that's where you've heard it?"

"Unlikely. I know zilch about the movie industry." Alex reached for a cigarette.

"You live in L.A. No interest in the movie industry's a violation of State law."

"Put out an A.P.B. on me."

"It's kind of refreshing. What do you do for a living? You're obviously not making any money from your art."

Another bullseye. "I'm a lifeguard at the country club pool. However, I am an artist. I just haven't sold anything for a while. To tell the truth, I haven't sold a painting in over a year." Saying it out loud really hit home. "I spend all my time trying to earn enough money to live and then I don't have the headspace to paint. And then when I do have the headspace to paint, I'm overwhelmed with doubt. You know how it is." That was a stupid thing to say, the kid was clearly rich and confident. Alex guessed he knew neither of those feelings. Alex stopped himself confessing more by drinking his beer.

Rick's eyes wandered to the distant horizon. "About this place ..."

"What about it?"

"You ever considered renting it out."

"What'd that achieve? Where'd I live then?"

With the eyes of a realtor, Rick appraised the green and beige interior. "How many rooms you got?"

"Six."

"Perfect," said Rick decisively. "You could be a live-in landlord. Find a tenant who'll pay for the privilege of most of the house. That'd give you an income. You could paint all day without having to work. You'd get money for nothing and the tenant gets a beach house for peanuts."

"Who in their right mind would rent this place under those terms?" asked Alex.

Rick finished his beer and plonked the bottle on the deck. "Me. I need a break from the city. Your house is perfect. I'll rent it."

Alex's heart plunged like an elevator with its lines cut. "Well, I ..." He struggled to come up with a good reason why this was such a bad, verging on terrible, idea. "It sounds fine in theory, but ..."

Rick's energy quickened. "I'm real quiet. I'd go for long walks on the beach all day. You wouldn't even notice I'm here!"

"How'd you get to work? When the traffic's heavy it's a long drive. And there's nothing to do here, it's real dull." Alex's mind raced to find other suggestions to put the kibosh on Rick's suggestion.

"I want dull. I need dull! Look, I have money and I'll pay you well." Rick paused for a moment of reflection. "Of course, there will be a few conditions."

Oh heck, he'd said *will* not *would*. Alex realized Mr. Rick Stradman had made up his mind and moved in. What was even worse, here came the conditions. "Like?"

"I'll decorate the place to my taste. You can keep your room upstairs and the studio as your private spaces."

"Peachy, I'll make a reservation to use the john. Hold it, I need to think this over."

Rick stared at him like he was an imbecile. "You want to paint and not worry about money. The only reason you'd refuse my offer is if you don't believe in yourself. If you don't want to be an artist, then give it all up and go full time at the pool right now."

If this was the end of a heavy night at the Beachcomber and he was fueled on a haze of alcohol induced resentment, Alex feared he may have socked this arrogant prick in the jaw. It was just before five, however, and his gray cells were functioning rationally. It was a tussle, but the lure of cash in his pocket and not having to spend all day preventing rich folks from drowning won out. "We could give it a go. But if it's not working out, I can pull the plug at any time. Right?"

"As per tenants' rights I don't think you can, but let's not start by getting legal. My car should've cooled by now. I'll be back with my stuff tomorrow." Rick came up to Alex, very close, almost too close, "Thank you, you saved my life today."

Alex pulled back, "You said you weren't going to jump?"

Rick laughed. "Not on the cliff. I mean here, your beach house. It's exactly what I needed. See you at ten-thirty sharp!" Rick marched cheerily out the house.

Alex snatched the packet of Kools. Jeez, what'd he let himself in for? If he was going to receive an income from, he hated this archaic word, a patron, and a live-in one at that, he was going to have to face his demons. He'd need to prove to himself that he truly was an artist, one without inverted commas. If this chance failed it could mean the end of his borderline non-existent art career. A few more smokes afforded him time to mull it over and allowed Rick time to get on his way.

Clang! Clang! Clang!

Julie was ringing the martini bell at the Beachcomber. Five p.m. salvation had arrived. After hopping into some clean duds, Alex went out the back-door. The empty jug was on the step and Rick's car had gone from the dunes. Striding down the scrub lined track to the Beachcomber, Alex glanced back. This beach house would either be the scene of his renaissance or a double homicide.

Whatever.

He'd have to worry about that tomorrow.

IN THE OPEN AIR

Last night, after loading up on liquid courage at the Beachcomber, Alex had called the country club and handed in his notice. Fueled by one too many drinks his tone had been acerbic. He guessed from his former boss's response that if he changed his mind and wanted his job back it wasn't likely to be forthcoming. After his bravado had worn off, he worried if this Rick guy might be a crazy fantasist with no intention of making good on the arrangement. He'd definitely have to sell his car if Rick didn't turn up now that he had no job. At ten twenty-five the following morning, however, Rick's red Mercedes did crunch along the track behind the house. On hearing the Merc, Alex's dread about being broke and unemployed was replaced by a different dread - the dread of an unwanted roommate.

Overall, dread was coming out tops.

Tentatively, Alex opened the back door and watched Rick getting out of his car. After grabbing two bags from the rear, Rick came and dumped them on the step. "Wanna give me a hand? Another trip should do it."

Accompanying Rick up to his car, visions of steamer trunks and froufrou interior décor items crossed Alex's mind. Rick was travelling light, however, with only two expensive looking brown valises and a shoulder bag with a red and green striped strap in the trunk for luggage. "What are these for?" Alex asked, lifting out a couple of industrial sized cans of exterior paint.

They carried the paint and bags to the house while Rick scrutinized the green, taupe, and yellow window frames and door trims. "Your house's color scheme may have been all the rage in nineteen forty-five, but it's not so great for nineteen seventy-four." The decor had been Dora's choice and Alex guessed Rick was spot on with the date she'd chosen it. The paintwork, Tiffany lamps, shredding sunshades and light layer of grime had been in his eye line so long they'd become invisible. "While you get your groove back, I plan on doing some painting of the less artistic kind," said Rick.

"Seriously?"

"Your deck's railings will rot if you don't protect them. This is a beautiful house. Would your grandmother want you to let it fall apart?"

Alex suspected it would be easier to give Rick his head than to argue. He set the paint cans by the back door and picked up Rick's luggage. "Better get *your* bags into *your* room then." Steeling himself, Alex strode through the house and opened up Dora's old room. The drapes were closed. Her bed, with her crocheted bedspread still on it, nestled in the crook of the windows. The memory of her last days was not good. She'd struggled to carry on her daily routine for as long as she could. Alex had sat and held her hand on that last night ...

"Go up to bed, pudding," Dora had whispered, struggling to breathe. "You need your rest. Leave me down here with the waves."

Lying upstairs in his bed, Alex had hung on the erratic ins and outs of her breath until they'd merged with the sea. The next morning he'd found her head tilted back, her mouth open - her life gone ...

"Coming through!" Rick bustled into the room and swished open the drapes. Light entered the room, dimmed by years of salt spray clouding the windows. Rick picked up the crocheted bedspread like it was nuclear waste and passed it to Alex. "I brought my own bedding."

"I'll leave you to settle in." Alex carried Dora's blanket up to his room, placed it reverentially on the foot of his unmade bed and went down to his studio. With the door firmly shut, it was hard not to keep imagining the cause of the noises coming from the front of the house while Rick did whatever he was doing. There'd be silence for ten or fifteen minutes, followed by five minutes of scraping, dragging and banging.

During the silent periods, Alex got into his stride. He stacked the *Red* paintings on one side of the room. There were around thirty of his other pieces leaning around the walls. He took stock of each as he put them into order. There were several from his *Mendocino Cliffs* series. A few more of these were stowed in the loft. Hank and Scoop had been outspoken in their contempt of figurative art, considering it old fashioned and pedestrian. He'd secreted these older works away with a sense of shame. He recalled the key piece from the *Cliffs* collection which had garnered much attention at college. Scotty even going as far as to liken it to Hopper's Maine paintings, which was over the top but a nice ego boost.

Having put things in order, it was time to start afresh. Alex picked up a frame and set about stapling fresh canvas over it. He softened the bristles of a new brush between his fingers. There'd been a protracted period of silence before he heard the not totally unexpected tap on his door. "Yeah?" he asked, opening the door a crack.

Rick rattled an empty coffee canister in his face, tipping it upside down for added emphasis. "Got any more?"

"Aw sorry, I'm low on provisions. I wasn't expecting company."

"But I *need* coffee," sighed Rick.

"I'll swing by the store and pick up stuff later."

"What am I meant to do until then?"

"We could go to the Beachcomber. They open at eleven and serve coffee." Alex hoped that was true. He'd never ever been there this early in the morning.

"Cool. Wanna see what I've done with the old room?"

Alex followed Rick. He saw that Rick had cleaned the room's paneled windows inside and out, and they served as a perfect frame for the sparkling ocean. He'd remade the bed with cream sheets and a cotton waffle bedspread, switched around the dresser and chest of drawers and taken one of the Tiffany lamps from the living area to put on the nightstand. He'd also appropriated some scatter cushions off the sagging sofa to dress the bed. "Nice work. Looks good," said Alex.

"We moved a lot when I was a kid. I got good at making places look like home in a hurry."

"This room gets chilly at night. Sure you don't want to keep Dora's blanket?"

"I'll be fine, but if I don't get coffee I'll die."

"We can't risk that. After you." Alex gestured to the front door.

Out on the verandah, Rick asked, "Aren't you forgetting something?"

"I've a couple of dollars in my pocket."

Rick swung the creaky front door to and fro. "A little thing called locking the door?"

"We don't do that around here. Besides I've nothing to steal."

"I do."

Alex wasn't certain where the door key had got to. It took a few minutes of scrabbling in random drawers to find it. The lock was rusty, the door warped, so Alex had to wrestle with the key until it finally turned and clicked. "Happy?" He dropped the key into Rick's breast pocket and patted it over his surprisingly firm pectoral.

"Got another? I'd hate to lose this and get locked out." Rick jumped off the deck to follow Alex.

"No problem. The back door's open." Hearing Rick's gasp of annoyance from behind was quite delicious. "Yeah, and all the windows too." Rick let out another sigh, a mix of exasperation combined with a laugh this time.

About fifty yards down the beach they hit the pale green shack with gray gabled roof that was the Beachcomber bar. The weathered deck out-front held an eclectic mix of rustic chairs and tables of varying heights, all shaded by blue and white striped umbrellas. They passed through a peach door with a lattice grille and went inside. The interior was pale wood. Fishing nets dotted with sea shells were draped behind the bar and ferns in macramé hangers dangled from the rafters. A girl with a perfect Californian tan and a tumbling mass of blonde hair was wiping down the melamine counter.

"Yo, Julie!" called Alex.

Julie lifted her head, tossing her mane of sun streaked hair off her face. "Hey, early bird! What can I do you for?" Julie smiled brightly at Alex and leaned across the counter, her denim halter shirt straining against her golden cleavage.

A barrier injected itself between Alex and Julie. "Coffee," Rick said tersely. "Black."

"Make that two," added Alex.

"We'll take them outside. It's kind of oppressive in here." Rick handed Julie a bill.

"I just opened and can't break a fifty. You got anything smaller?"

Rick pulled out his bill fold. There were more notes in it, but Alex figured they were all fifties as Rick didn't offer an alternative. "I'll get this. You grab a table on the deck, Rockefeller," Alex said to Rick.

Rick shoved his wallet into his pants and went outside.

Julie watched Rick go. "Who's your friend?"

"Not friend. Lodger. Can you put this on my tab?"

"This one's on the house," Julie said with a wink, "Arnold's not in yet." Julie reached across the counter and took hold of the carved greenstone pendant dangling around his neck. Tugging it, she drew him close. "How about a shot in yours?"

"You know me so well."

"How about him?" Julie jerked her head in Rick's direction.

"I don't think he's the type."

Julie let go of Alex's pendant and went to the coffee machine. Glancing over her shoulder, she looked at Rick outside wiping the table with a napkin. Julie took two cups off the shelf behind the bar. "You go sit. I'll bring them."

Alex went out and flopped at the table opposite Rick. "Cute, isn't she?"

"Perky. Young. Stacked." Through the peach lattice door, Rick squinted at Julie behind the counter. "Dead ringer for my current step mom."

"On the bright side, that means you have someone your own age to play with at family gatherings," joked Alex, but Rick failed to see the humor in his comment.

Julie came and put the coffees on the table. "Anything else for you guys?"

"Thanks, we're good," said Alex.

"Cool. Have a great day." Julie pivoted and sashayed inside.

Rick stirred his coffee, took a sip and wrinkled his nose. A couple of minutes passed in silence. Alex cracked his knuckles, then said, "Your dad's remarried then. Does your mom still live in L.A.?"

Rick dropped his sunglasses and stared over the top of them before answering succinctly, "No."

"I heard you speaking Italian on the phone, is she in Europe?"

Rick's expression hardened. "She's dead."

Alex wished he could rewind the conversational gambit about the mother. "Sorry."

"Don't be. She had something wrong with her heart. It shriveled to the size of a walnut. The symptoms went unnoticed for years." Rick pushed his sunglasses back in place.

Alex thought it was a pity Julie had only put the one shot in his coffee. In fact, she could've skipped the coffee and gone with straight whiskey. Whether it was his mention of the dead mother or Julie's resemblance to his step mom, a frost had descended over Rick. There was no sign of a thaw back at the house. Without further small talk, Rick took himself out onto the verandah with sandpaper, a tin of white paint and a paintbrush.

Alex sequestered himself in his studio. He needed to work. He needed a clean start. He banished every shade of red from of his mind and let his heart guide his hand. Using a wash of turquoise blending down to an ochre, he broke the virgin surface. Wandering into a world of his own creation, he filled in detail. The turquoise became sky and the ochre the sand. Where the two met, about a third of the way up, he sketched in a rocky outcrop. Lost in his work, it was a while before he became aware of someone breathing. Rick was watching from the doorway.

"I did knock," said Rick.

"Didn't hear." Resting the brush on the palette, Alex shook out his hand.

"May I?" Rick indicated a desire to look at the canvas.

There wasn't much to comment on, so it felt low risk. "Go ahead." Since this felt like a natural time for a cigarette break, he left Rick in the studio and grabbed a pack of Kools. "Hey, what you doing?" shouted Alex. Rick wasn't looking at the canvas, he'd picked it up, along with the easel, and was carrying them out of the studio. "Where the hell are you going? Get back!" yelled Alex, but Rick took no notice. He'd already crossed the verandah, gone down off the deck and was onto the sand. "You can't just take off with my work like that!" Alex chased after Rick, who was striding towards the cliffs. Alex cursed his easy offer to let Rick move in. This morning's mood swing had escalated into a full-blown psychotic episode. Sunbathers grabbed their towels and dodged out the way of 'angry guy' in hot pursuit of 'crazy guy'. "You need to stop!" Alex shouted as he dodged from side to side in front of Rick to block him. Rick, however, dodged equally adeptly out of his way. "You can't go around pulling crazy ass shit like this!" Once he'd reached the cliffs, Rick slammed on the brakes and plonked the easel with its embryonic painting in the scrub.

"What's up with you, man?" gasped Alex, nearly crashing into him.

Rick put one hand on his hip and rested the other on the easel as he got his breath back. "Stand in front of me. Look at the canvas from my point of view," demanded Rick, "like you were seeing it through my eyes."

General advice was to accede to the demands of crazies and so Alex warily took up position in front of Rick, hoping the next thing he felt wasn't Rick's hands around his throat. Turning his back on the guy made for an uneasy sensation. Alex's unease ramped up when Rick's hands descended on his shoulders.

Rick leaned close and murmured, "Plein air."

"What?"

"En plein air. You know, painting outdoors from observation."

"I know what en plein air means, thank you very much!" snapped Alex. Jeez, did the guy think he was dumb? His snappiness shut Rick up. The panicked knot loosened in Alex's stomach. He looked at the canvas. He looked at the sea beyond. Rick must have recognized his sketched composition resembled the cove from this viewpoint.

"I've a gut feeling you should get out of the studio. I noticed some cliff studies when I was looking at your work yesterday. They were excellent. Beautiful, yet kind of sad."

"Would have been nice if you'd mentioned that at the time," said Alex with a snort.

"I didn't have the chance before you bit my head off. Just a thought." Rick removed his hands from Alex's shoulders and walked back to the house.

Needing time to take stock, Alex stayed put. Left alone with his canvas, he mulled over what Rick had just said. He'd never considered plein air work before, which was odd since Laguna had a long heritage of it. He done the Mendocino paintings from sketches and photos, not life. Hank and Scoop always considered plein air to be chocolate box art, maybe that had blinded him to considering it as a style to try. On reflection, working in his studio lately had felt like being in a prison. Hot, internal, trapped. Being out here on the sand, with the sun casting interesting textures on the cliffs and ocean, made the idea of working in the open air feel liberating. A fire to translate what his eyes were seeing and his heart was feeling ignited in his belly. Cradling his easel and canvas, Alex arrived back at the house to find Rick had finished painting one side of the deck's railings. The balustrade's clean whiteness was uplifting. He caught Gloria casting her eyes over from her window next door. She pointed at the newly painted railings and gave the thumbs up. She motioned to his easel and canvas and threw up her hands in a 'what's that about?' gesture. Alex mouthed 'later' in reply. This satisfied her and she sank back into the darkness of the interior. Alex came up on the deck, studiously avoiding the wet paint on the handrails. Rick hadn't been as successful. A streak of white paint ran across the bridge of his nose, ending in a smudge on his left cheek. Alex found it amusing to see Mr. Perfect so besmirched. Alex put his equipment back in the studio. He opened the refrigerator. They were down to the last two beers, fresh supplies were definitely called for. "Beer?"

"Sounds good!"

Alex knocked off the bottle tops. Rick was working the last of the white paint off the brush into the wooden rail as Alex handed him the bottle. "Here."

"Thanks." Rick rested the brush on the paint tin then scratched his right cheek. There was still paint on his hand and it left a white streak on the other side of his face. He looked like the negative of a football player wearing eye black. "What's the story with that woman next door?" asked Rick as he took the beer.

"Gloria's one of our artists in residence. Well, in residence from Memorial to Labor Day. Why'd you ask?"

"She came over to ask you something."

"Checking you out more like." Alex plonked himself on the saggy gray sofa. "I'm amazed she wasn't over like a shot when she saw me just now."

"No need. She's dropping by for drinks later."

"That's rich of her. You mean she just invited herself over?"

"No, I invited her."

Alex took a sharp intake of breath. "I get on okay with the Waverleys, but from a distance. I'd prefer to keep it that way. I don't want Gloria feeling she can drop by here anytime she likes."

"Oh, well. Too late now."

Alex nodded appreciatively at the railings and deck. "The paint looks good." Glancing at the white smudges on Rick's face, he stifled a smirk. "What you said about the plein air work was a good call."

"I shouldn't have just taken off with your stuff like that. I ought to edit myself. But that's me, impetuous." Rick contemplated his beer bottle and noticed the white fingerprints on it, checking his hand he saw the wet paint. "Aw, shit." He looked for something to wipe his hand on.

Alex grabbed a paint rag and tossed it over. Rick grimaced as he wiped his hands and the bottle. "You missed a bit," said Alex.

"No, I got it all." Rick studied his hands.

Alex indicated Rick's face.

"What?" Rick touched his cheek. Taking his finger away he found specks of white. "Why didn't you tell me I'd got paint all over my face? I must look like an idiot!" Rick jumped up and rushed to the bathroom.

"Correct!" said Alex with a grin.

A few minutes later Rick returned, all cleaned up and his face still slightly moist. He picked up his beer. "So you'll give it a go? The plein air?"

"Could be an interesting exercise. My set-up's not very portable as it stands though."

Rick picked up a frosty green pebble off the table and ran it through his fingers. "You could work from on the deck to begin with." Rick held the pebble to the light. "What kind of stone's this?"

"Here." Alex held his hand out and Rick tossed the pebble over. Alex rubbed some condensation off his bottle over the rock. Holding the stone up to the light again, the frostiness had disappeared and it was smooth and shiny. "Broken bottles on the beach after people have had parties are real dangerous. But if the shards get picked up by the sea and wash back and forth in the tides long enough, the sharp edges get worn down. This isn't a stone, it's glass."

"Glass is made from sand, right?" Rick's gaze drifted to the beach. "Kind of poetic. The full circle." He gestured with his beer bottle to the Piper's. "Do artists live next door too?"

"Yeah, some of the first to settle here. Mr. Piper used to sculpt. Mrs. Piper was a painter like gran. And before you keep referring to Gloria as an artist, you ought to see her work."

Rick finished his beer. "Okay. One more set of railings to go."

"Try getting more paint on them than you this time." Alex picked up the empty bottles. "Wanna come to the store with me later?"

"Sure."

"Um, you know we haven't discussed the rent." Alex's heart pounded. What was a sensible figure to ask? He should have spoken to Scotty before raising this issue. Hank and Scoop would be useless for advice, the only rent they were interested in was no rent; hence the Venice Beach years.

Rick pursed his lips. "How's a hundred sound?"

It sounded okay ... ish. A gallon of gas cost fifty-five cents. He'd been pulling in three bucks an hour at the club. A hundred bucks a month was not a negligible sum, but was it enough to warrant disrupting his life in such a manner?

Rick must've noted his lack of enthusiasm because he added, "A week."

Not letting his eyes light up too obviously, Alex replied coolly, "That I can live with." Four hundred bucks a month! With the thought of money in his pocket lightening his mood, Alex lost himself in preparing boards and arranging paints ready to have a bash at some plein air work tomorrow. An hour slipped by before Rick's gentle tap on the studio door jogged him back into the moment.

"I've finished on the deck," said Rick. "Is this a good time to go to the store?"

Alex swept his hair off his face and rubbed his chin. His stubble was thick, but he couldn't be bothered to shave. "Let me hop in the shower. Be with you in five."

Rick gave Alex's long, matted hair and ten o'clock shadow the once over. "Don't hurry on my account," he said.

Alex ducked into the bathroom and shut the door. He peeled off his sweaty vest, paint spattered jeans and stripy boxers. He took off the soapstone pendant around his neck and hung it on the back of the door. Leaning against the tub while waiting for the water to run hot, he observed that Rick had been busy in this room too. The chipped basin had been scrubbed, the rusty faucets polished. A row of square plastic bottles with small black labels and a bar of black soap had appeared on the shelf, along with a silver toothbrush and fancy toothpaste. After he'd given himself a quick yet thorough soaping in the shower, Alex let the water run through his hair for a few minutes. Stepping out of the tub, he realized he hadn't brought in a change of clothes. Living alone since Dora died he'd gotten used to wandering about naked. He toweled off, then slung the towel around his hips. After putting his pendant back on, he slipped out of the bathroom ready to dash upstairs. His path was blocked, however, by Rick sitting on the foot of the stairs.

"While we're at the store we need to pick up some bathroom cleaning supplies," said Rick, who was holding a pad and pen.

"Like what?" Alex raked his hands through his wet hair trying to get out the tangles.

"Like two gallons of bleach and a flamethrower." Rick watched Alex unknotting his hair with his fingers. "Don't you have a comb?"

"Combs rip the shit out of it."

Rick wrote a note while speaking out loud, "Hair conditioner. A wonder of the modern age."

Giving his hair a final shake, Alex became aware of Rick staring at his bare chest.

"What's that?" asked Rick.

After being momentarily taken aback, Alex realized Rick's eyes were on the pendant nestling in the dip where his chest hair converged. "It's the Maori symbol for eternity." Alex held out the greenstone pendant, the carving resembled a twisted water droplet. Rick took the pendant and ran it between his thumb and forefinger. "It's also meant to symbolize two people joined in undying love." Due to the cord's length, Alex had to lean nearer to Rick while he examined it.

"It's very beautiful," said Rick, his face very close to Alex's.

"Hey, we need to get to the store." Alex pulled back and Rick let the pendant drop. Clutching the towel around himself, Alex brushed past Rick and darted upstairs. He slung the towel on the floor, threw on a V-neck tangerine tee and faded jeans, then trotted back down. The creak of his footstep on the bottom tread made Rick turn around.

Rick tore a check out of his check book and proffered it. "Here."

Alex raised his eyebrows when he saw it was made out for eight hundred dollars. "Why so much?" he asked.

"Eight weeks rent." Without elaborating, Rick went out of the back door.

Accepting that Rick knew what he was doing, Alex gratefully folded the check and stashed it in his pocket. Up in the parking lot, Alex automatically got into his Chevy's driving seat. Rick glanced dubiously at the scrape on the passenger door before getting in. Alex drove along the track behind the houses. Just after the Beachcomber, the road doubled back on itself and rose past houses dotted around the hill up to the highway. The afternoon sun was casting an orange glow over the telegraph poles, electric lines and high-topped palms. Alex swung a right and headed south on Pacific Highway. On their left, white stucco houses stood proudly on hills between soft clumps of green trees. On their right, the ocean glittered behind gray roofs of properties on secluded coves and beaches. The turnoff for the shopping center appeared and Alex turned inland. Kids played on barren plots of land in between plots with new homes under construction. A sign declared, 'BLUFF HILL SHOPPING VILLAGE'. An array of low concrete bunkers didn't fulfill the image the sign conjured up.

"Not exactly what I'd call quaint," Rick commented archly.

"Laguna's the place for rustic charm. You'll find what you need here."

"They better have decent Beluga caviar."

Alex shot Rick a sidelong glance as he checked over his shoulder to reverse into a space.

"Joking," said Rick.

"Hey, you know what you want," said Alex, not totally convinced Rick was joking about the caviar. "What say you stock up on provisions and I'll meet you back here in twenty? I need to swing by Miguel's garage around the block."

"You want me to pick you up anything in particular?"

"Just some beers. And seeing how you've invited Gloria in, you'll need to go to the liquor store for wine as she likes a drink or five. Oh, and get me three packs of Kools." Alex hesitated. "I don't have any cash on me. But I can settle up with you after I've banked your check, if that's okay?"

"Yeah, we can sort that out later," said Rick with a smile.

After Rick had got out, Alex drove around to his garage. The car was due for an overhaul. He checked that they were still okay for it and assured Miguel, the garage's owner, he'd soon be able to settle last month's bill.

Miguel ran his finger along the scrape on the door. "You wanna that I give this a panel beat and respray?"

"Um, no. Leave it for now."

Miguel shrugged. "A no problem. Is a up to you."

No point spending recklessly, thought Alex. Better to eke out Rick's cash for as long as possible. Two months could be one hell of a long time if they didn't get on. Besides, Rick could take off as suddenly as he'd decided to move in. He found Rick waiting on a bench out front when he got back to the center. They loaded the brown sacks into the car. On their way to the parking lot's exit, Rick asked, "Would you show me around? I don't know this area at all."

Running out of gas with mister fancy pants on board would be mortifying. Alex checked the fuel gauge. The arrow said the tank was half full, so hopefully it would last until he had a few spare hours to queue for gas. The higher Alex drove into the hills, the sparser and larger grew the houses. Hitting a good viewpoint, Alex pulled up on the dirt shoulder and killed the engine. A fresh breeze rustled the foxtail ferns and bald cypresses. Alex grabbed his cigarettes and lighter from the glove and they got out. Alex leaned on the corrugated metal crash barrier and lit up.

Rick surveyed the view. "It's quiet here." As if to prove him wrong a sports car roared around the bend. He grinned, then added, "Quietish."

"Tempted to leave the big city for good?"

"Maybe," said Rick thoughtfully. "L.A.'s crazy. Every day you hear that someone's been mugged, or shot, or burglarized. People with money are moving into gated communities."

"Or to the beach." Alex exhaled a cloud of menthol smoke. "That what you're getting away from? Crime?"

Rick stuffed his hands in his pockets and stared over the swaying trees. "Other things."

After Alex finished his smoke, they ambled along a trail. Crickets chirped wildly and lizards, startled by their footfalls, slithered across their path.

Back at the house, they carried the groceries inside. Alex began to help Rick put everything away, but Rick shooed him out of the kitchen. Apparently he was no longer master of his domain, so he sloped off upstairs for a doze. Through his half-sleep the opening and closing of cupboard doors morphed into the rattling of pots and pans which in turn morphed into ...

Clang! Clang! Clang!

Julie was ringing the martini bell. In a Pavlovian reflex, Alex's eyes shot open. He was about trot down and head south when a voice from out back shouted, "Knock, knock?" Muffled dialogue followed. The voice grew louder, entered the house and came into focus as Gloria Waverley. Bad timing. Five minutes later and he'd have been in the sanctuary of the Beachcomber. He took a deep breath, coughed a little, and came down.

Gloria was in the kitchen, opening and closing drawers. "Rick can't find the corkscrew. Where've you hidden it?"

Yep, here she was in his kitchen - larger than life in a vivid pink kaftan and matching head band. Alex jiggled the drawer by the sink. He foraged in the jumble of rusty implements and withdrew the corkscrew which he slapped into Rick's hand. "I take it you've done the introductions."

"Oh, yes. Rick and I are getting along just fine." Gloria watched Rick intently as he opened the wine. "By the way, Alex, your deck looks great!"

"If you ask nicely maybe Rick will come over and paint yours?"

Out of Gloria's eye line, Rick shot Alex a dark look as he sloshed a generous red wine into a tumbler and passed it to Gloria. "Can I tempt you?" Rick held the bottle out to Alex.

"Alex doesn't need asking twice," Gloria chuckled. "He's a fixture down at the Beachcomber."

Wine wasn't his cup of tea, but anything alcoholic was required to get through this social event from hell. "Hit me," said Alex.

"Bottoms up!" Gloria winked at Alex and raised her glass.

Rick filled Alex's glass and one for himself. "Up yours." Rick raised his glass to Gloria with a salacious wink. Gloria guffawed and her pink muumuu rippled.

They went through to the living room and Alex flopped on the faded orange couch by the foot of the stairs. Gloria was waxing lyrical about sticking sea shells and random detritus onto reclaimed beach wood. To avoid listening, Alex scanned the room for Rick's home improvements. He'd done a good job. The room was comfortable in a way it hadn't been since Dora died. Rick and Gloria's inane conversation wafted over him like the sea breeze through the open door and windows.

"...and then I finish off with a light layer of varnish."

"I'm looking forward to seeing your work," said Rick appearing sincerely interested.

"Anytime." Gloria drained her glass. "Anytime Harry's out that is. He doesn't like me talking about my art."

Gloria's comment made Alex warm to Harry. A man of good taste.

Rick topped up Gloria's glass. "You say you make regular sales. Do you sell to friends?"

"Oh no!" Gloria pulled her chin back. "I've a professional dealer."

Alex's gullet burned. Maybe from the wine. Maybe from Gloria.

"You can't call yourself an artist if you don't make money from your work," said Gloria decisively.

"Impressive." Rick leaned close. "Is this dealer a local?"

"Marianne Deveraux. She owns a gallery in Laguna. She also has contacts in resorts and hotels who commission work for their interior decor."

As Rick carried on asking questions, it dawned on Alex that he'd invited Gloria in on a fact-finding mission. Getting her tipsy and flattering her was a precursor to plying her for information. The boy was an operator. And Rick must be doing it to help him as he didn't have any art to sell for himself. It was quite sweet in a Machiavellian way. The info must have dried up. Gloria was still talking, but the shutters had rolled down behind Rick's eyes. Rick glanced at his gold watch. "My how the time's flown. Seven-thirty!"

Alex was surprised. It felt much later.

"Lord, I must run. Harry gets tense if we haven't said Grace and begun to eat by eight." After multiple goodbyes, Gloria wobbled out of the back door.

Once she'd gone, Rick asked. "You hungry?" He'd put something together earlier and left it bubbling on the range while Gloria visited.

"I could eat," said Alex. Whatever Rick had cooked smelled good. They sat at the table to eat, something Alex hadn't done for a long time, usually eating on the hoof. Rick's dinner tasted as good as it smelled, if not better. "What is this?" asked Alex helping himself to more.

"Chicken with something or other. Nonna was a genius in the kitchen. Italian grandmothers can make a meal out of an old boot if needed. I think in World War One mine did once. I learned to cook from watching her in the kitchen."

Alex's stomach hadn't felt this full in a long while. His bank balance *and* waistline would both be expanding thanks to Rick. He wiped his plate clean with a hunk of bread while Rick emptied the leftovers into a faded Tupperware container. When he'd finished eating, Alex opened a fresh pack of Kools and lit up. "I don't mean to be rude ..." he said after blowing out a smoke ring.

"Which means you're going to be."

"Why are you so interested in helping me? Thanks for the rent, the cash will really help, but quizzing Gloria to find galleries for me. What's that all about?"

Rick rinsed the cooking pot under the faucet. He picked up the dish towel and came to the table drying his hands. "I'm hopeless at running my own career. Helping someone else is a good distraction."

"You have a career?"

"Don't sound so surprised. You think I'm unemployable?"

"No. I just wonder what job you could have that lets you just drop off the map. Hope you're not in air traffic control. A jumbo jet could be in an endless holding pattern thanks to you."

"I act on T.V."

"Sounds exciting."

"Lots of things sound more exciting than they are."

"I imagine there's a lot of competition. You must be good to get work."

"I guess." Rick went to pick up Alex's empty plate.

"Leave that. I'll finish clearing." Alex stubbed the cigarette out on his plate.

"I'll turn in then." Rick hung up the dish towel and disappeared into the bathroom for twenty minutes.

Alex had cleared away and left the kitchen ship shape by the time Rick emerged. "Night. See you in the morning," called Alex as Rick went to his room.

"Yeah. Goodnight." Rick called back and shut his door with a click.

As Alex brushed his teeth he contemplated Rick's skin care regime on the bathroom shelf. Black soap? Combined with the mysterious potions this must be the source of his facial glow.

Alex contemplated his own face in the mirror. He really did need a shave and a good night's sleep. Those dark circles under his eyes did not look healthy. Once upstairs, he lay naked on his bed, savoring being alone in his own space. He flicked off the lamp and began to doze. The creak of the stair's bottom tread startled him awake. Rick was coming up. Alex pulled up the sheets in a panic, urgently covering his nakedness.

"Alex?" Rick called gently from the stairs. "You still awake?"

Alex's abdominal muscles clenched in apprehension as Rick appeared in the room. He was naked except for a small pair of white briefs. The moon's silver light glanced off his tautly defined torso.

"I need something."

"What?" asked Alex nervously, flicking on the lamp.

Rick's eyes dropped to Alex's bed. "You were right." Rick stepped forward. "I got cold down there by myself."

Alex tensed as Rick's eyes looked deep into his, he tensed more as Rick came towards the bed.

Rick leaned forward and picked up Dora's crocheted blanket. "I did need this after all. Night." Rick wrapped the blanket around his shoulders and padded back downstairs.

It took a few moments for Alex's pulse to return to normal. He wondered what had made his heart race like that. Was it the stupidity of letting a total stranger come and live in his house? For all he knew Rick could be a killer on the run. Or was it something else that had rattled him so. Alex fumbled on the nightstand, found Rick's check and stuffed it in the drawer. He flicked off the lamp and lay in the dark. Tomorrow, he'd drive into Laguna and bank the check.

Eight hundred bucks.

That was the only reason he'd chosen to let Rick live in the house. The money.

Wasn't it?

AN ILLUSION OF MOVEMENT

The morning after Rick moved in, Alex had experimented with some plein air work from the deck. He'd set himself the task of painting exactly what he saw. Three sunshades were up on the beach out front. They were three of the most hideously colored ones he'd ever laid eyes on. A brutal red, a bilious green, and a jaundiced yellow. The sun's angle accentuated their artificial colors against the shore. He'd worked fast, using watercolor for the background and acrylic for the umbrellas. His speed and lack of commentary imbued the work with an immediacy, a documentary feeling if you will. Maybe it was a nothing little picture, but he'd got immense satisfaction from starting and finishing a painting within a few hours. And he liked it.

This positive foray into plein air work inspired him to make the most of his trip into Laguna to bank Rick's check. He'd swung by Pacific Art Supplies and invested in a field easel, a portable paint box and telescopic diffuser umbrella. Over the next few days he'd paid off Miguel's garage, settled his tab at the Beachcomber and dealt with several other outstanding bills. Kicking off the shackles of debt was akin to being reborn. This newfound optimism showed in his work.

The new portable equipment enabled him to complete two or three studies a day. Meandering up and down the beach with his field easel, he stopped and set up wherever a view caught his fancy – he enjoyed this freedom. He didn't set out to include figures in his paintings, but if someone visually interesting was in his eye line then he put them in. All of his studies investigated a jarring element of the scenery; an aggressively shadowed rock, a tidal mark resembling a fissure in the earth, or a leaf with an edge as jagged as a serrated blade, anything to harden a potentially 'pretty picture' scenic view.

Returning unexpectedly from an early painting session along the beach, Alex had come across Rick in his studio. He'd been going through Alex's old works and jumped guiltily. Alex's immediate response was intense anger, and he'd had to hold his tongue to prevent issuing Rick his marching orders on the spot. He'd prudently restrained his temper as kicking Rick out would mean having to pay back his upfront rent. Rick had apologized and departed chastened. Several times after that though, he'd again caught Rick going through his paintings in the studio. He noted Rick was moving them around, putting one to the fore and then another - like he was curating an exhibit. Rick always apologized for his intrusion and left without comment. Alex couldn't figure out why, but Rick's silence fed his growing self-worth more than any amount of gushing approbations.

Despite Rick's occasional overbearing nature and odd dark mood, he was easy enough company. When he wasn't cleaning, painting woodwork, or sorting out the kitchen, Rick spent most of his time in his room reading yellow spined Italian paperbacks or watching Dora's ancient portable T.V. Sometimes, when Rick was deep in thought and unaware, Alex couldn't help himself staring at Rick. He possessed a pleasing profile and a magnetically mysterious quality. Rick gave out very little personal information, this evasiveness lending him the air of a fugitive. Every so often Alex got a niggling worry if Rick was on the level, but as it was unlikely a criminal psychopath would have such a stringent skin care routine he put his doubts to the back of his mind. After a week and half passed, Alex had not only got used to having Rick around but also getting up early to work. He was already out on the beach when Rick yelled, "Coffee?" from inside the house.

"Sure, be with you in ten!" shouted Alex in response.

"It's six-thirty," said Rick coming out onto the deck and rubbing the sleep from his eyes. Wrapping his silk dressing gown around his waist, he leaned over the railing and watched Alex concentrating on a new plein air study. "You were actually up before me this morning."

"I wanted to catch the early light. Everyone paints sunsets along the coast, but the dawn over the sea's interesting too, don't you think?" Alex continued working as he spoke.

"You want coffee or not?"

"Nearly finished. Put it on."

Rick's bare feet padded into the house.

Reaching a point in his work where it was suitable to break, Alex put his brush in the jar and went inside. After they'd finished the breakfast and bathroom shuffle, Rick disappeared into his room, and Alex went back to the beach to finish his study. He was deep in concentration when the distant crunch of tires along the back road distracted him. What day was it? Shit! Thursday!

Alex grabbed the wet board and paint box and darted into the house. "Go fetch my field easel and bring it in. Quick!" he urgently said to Rick as he stashed the board and paints in his studio. He spotted tell-tale splashes of wet blue paint on his black t-shirt.

"What's the big rush?" asked Rick.

"Don't ask questions!" Alex heard a car door slam up in the dunes. "There's no time to bring it in. Just fold it up and stick it out of sight. Anywhere!" He put the right amount of force in his voice to propel Rick into action with no further questions. While running upstairs, Alex stripped off his paint splattered t-shirt. He grabbed the nearest garment to hand, a tie dye yellow tank, hurtling back downstairs as he pulled it on. Gathering his breath, he slammed the studio door and arranged his face in a casual expression while waiting for her knock.

"Is something wrong?" Rick asked nervously coming in off the verandah.

Alex sensed the agitation he'd transmitted to Rick, so felt compelled to explain. "It's Scotty, an old friend from art college. I heard a car and guessed it was hers. I'd completely forgotten she was coming today."

"Maybe it was a tourist taking the wrong turn at the Beachcomber?" Rick was on tenterhooks too, even though he had no real reason to be. They were both now waiting for a knock but still nothing happened.

"I'll go take a look," said Alex opening the back door. Scotty stood on the other side of the track, about ten feet from the back door, staring at the house. "You okay?" Alex approached her with concern. "You look like you're in shock."

"I am." Scotty gestured with an elegant hand towards the house. "Your garbage cans aren't overflowing, your windows are clean and your back door's been painted. I was concerned you may be being held hostage by a militant homemaker."

"Not quite."

"I wondered if I ought to call and check we were still on, but I thought you'd tell me I was fussing. You hadn't forgotten I was coming had you?"

"As if I could forget." Slinging his arm around Scotty's shoulder, Alex drew her inside. "See, coffee's on ready and waiting."

"God, no wonder you've been so quiet. Look what you've done to the house!" Scotty's eyes fell on Rick and she stopped in her tracks. She flicked her gaze awkwardly at Alex, "I didn't realize you had company."

"He's not company," said Alex hastily. "I mean he's not a guest. He's Rick, my new roommate." Alex wondered why his cheeks were flushing hot under his stubble.

"I'd no idea you were even looking for a roommate." Scotty wriggled free from Alex's arm around her shoulder.

"I wasn't ..." Alex paused, sensing Rick and Scotty weigh each other up like strange cats coming face to face in a narrow alley. Rick was giving Scotty a thorough once over. Scotty's below shoulder length black hair was tied back in a low ponytail. She wore a brown silk shirt tucked into a pair of form fitting navy pants. Her tortoiseshell sunglasses were pushed back on her head, a diamond in her watch glinted in the light. Scotty, meanwhile, appraised Rick.

Rick was wearing a white t-shirt and frayed blue jeans with bare feet. His hair had grown into a shaggy, sun-bleached blond and his tan had deepened to burnished gold during his week and a bit at the beach. "Hi, I'm Rick," he said coolly.

"Scotty. Nice to meet you." She turned to Alex. "If you weren't looking for a roommate then how come you have one?"

"Um, Rick was out here at the beach and ..." Alex fumbled for an explanation, the truth about his climbing barefoot up a cliff to rescue a stranger who didn't need rescuing sounded beyond stupid. Rick thankfully continued the story for him.

"... and I took a wrong turn off the highway and wound up here. Then I ran into car trouble and Alex came to my rescue."

Scotty took Alex's arm and patted his firm bicep. "That's my Alex, he's a helpful kind of guy."

"Anyway, I fell in love with Sunset Cove," continued Rick, "so I persuaded Alex to rent me his house for the summer."

Scotty scrutinized Rick. "Don't I know you from someplace?"

Rick backed off. "Hey, I'll get out of your hair. You guys must have stuff to catch up on."

"I've seen you on T.V." Scotty snapped her fingers, struggling to make the connection.

Rick suddenly lifted the pot. "Coffee?"

"Great, black for me." Alex stepped in.

"And you?" Rick proffered the pot to Scotty.

"Cream with Sweet'n Low if you have it."

"We've neither," said Rick.

"Black's fine then ... I got it! You had a guest star spot on *Eddie's Girls* last season." Scotty clenched her fist with satisfaction. "You played a French guy, an Olympic athlete who wanted to defect or something?"

"I need to sue that dialect coach. My accent was meant to be Russian." Rick concentrated on pouring the coffee and awkwardness pervaded the small hot room.

"How about we take these out to the deck?" Alex made a move to leave the kitchen, hoping Scotty would follow.

Scotty didn't take the cue and carried on talking at Rick. "I guess I wasn't concentrating. When the show's on in re-run I'll watch it properly."

"I'd appreciate that," muttered Rick, "excuse me, but I have to go."

"You're not joining us for coffee?" Scotty asked in dismay.

"I got errands to run in Laguna." Rick grabbed his car keys and billfold then shucked on his sneakers from by the back door.

"Before you dash, let's make a date. Next week, you and Alex come to me and Bob for dinner," blurted out Scotty with a tinge of hysteria.

"I'll check my diary." Rick darted out of the back door like he'd been stung.

After Alex had maneuvered Scotty out onto the deck, he said, "Nice to see you after all this time."

"You too. You're looking good," said Scotty taking a sip of coffee. "Quite some turnaround seeing how the other week you were in such a dark place. You'd lost faith in your work and were worried about money. I guess the roommate's solved the money issue, how about the other?"

Should he tell her he'd got his creative energy back and, moreover, really liked the work he was doing? Alex decided not to. He didn't want anyone else getting into his head, even if they meant well. "Still nothing doing on the creative front, but I took your advice and I'm not stressing."

"At least you've been doing some sort of painting. Good to see you can still wield a brush." Scotty ran a glossy fingernail along the fresh white railings.

"I can't take credit for that. All Rick's work."

"Roommate *and* decorator. What a treasure." Scotty folded her arms and shook her head. "Really, you could have warned me. I mean he's the last person on earth I'd have expected to find living here. And you're telling me he just turned up out of the blue?"

"He did some bit part on T.V. What's the big deal?"

"You seriously don't know who he is?"

"He's some producer's kid, that's as much as I know."

"You've got to be kidding me. Well, let me fill you in ..."

Alex wondered if he should feign disinterest but knew that wouldn't stop her. And, to tell the truth, he was more than a little intrigued to find out more about Rick. Letting Scotty divulge what she knew would also distract her from wheedling to investigate his studio, which he sensed she was dying to do. "Let's take a walk on the beach."

Scotty shot a reproachful glance at the ocean. "I'm not keen on sand."

"It's better to talk away from the house in case he comes back suddenly." Alex's point made sense to Scotty and so she reluctantly agreed to the beach walk. He kicked off his sandals and jumped down. Scotty grudgingly slipped off her pumps, rolled up her navy slacks and gingerly went down the steps to the beach. Alex decided they'd walk along the shore to the sloping green hills on cove's south rather than his usual tack to the cliffs at the north. "What's the story on Rick, then?" asked Alex.

"His father's Sid Stradman, the movie producer." A strong wave crashed in, Scotty skittered back to avoid getting wet.

"It's only seawater."

"I don't want salt stains on my Jax pants! They cost forty dollars."

"Forty dollars? You can buy a pair of pants for five bucks."

"A pair that looks like they cost five bucks," said Scotty edging back from the surf.

"His dad's some producer, so what? We're in L.A., that's not so unusual."

"The father's not the parent of interest. It's the mother who is." The wind whipped Scotty's pony tail around. "Luisa D'Onofrio."

"Should that mean something to me?"

Scotty brushed her hair from her face and mouth with annoyance. "Can we walk the other way? This wind's getting on my nerves." They u-turned and walked towards the cliffs. Putting her discomfort of the beach aside, Scotty resumed her story. "In the late forties Sid wanted to make his mark as a classy producer, so he went to Europe on a talent hunt. He was hoping to find the new Ingrid Bergman, but instead he discovered Luisa. She'd been working in pictures in Italy, low budget but classy stuff. Anyway, he brought her back to the U.S.A. with fanfares and ballyhoo. He lined up a string of movies for her to star in, but as soon as she finished shooting the first she fell pregnant."

"To Sid?"

"Correct. He was a hands-on producer. *Very* hands-on. Being a good Catholic girl she insisted on marriage. He did the honorable thing and married her. They postponed her next movie until she'd had the baby. Before shooting started on the second, however, her first picture came out. It was bad timing because her debut movie bombed big time. The critics laid the blame squarely on Luisa, calling her hard and unappealing. Everyone got cold feet and Sid's backing collapsed. Luisa was labelled box office poison and the slate of movies lined up for her got canned. Luisa was livid and took her vitriol to the press. She called the American film industry a sideshow for morons, denouncing Hollywood as a pit of vipers in a cultural desert. The industry turned its back on her. It effectively ended her movie career."

Rick's disenchantment with the dead mother kind of made sense to Alex after hearing this. She sounded somewhat of a spitfire.

Scotty continued, "Luisa blamed Sid for everything and took off back to Italy with the child, Rick that is. They had a big ugly court battle over custody. The kicker was that she didn't need to work for the money as she was wealthy in her own right, daughter of a Count or something. Once back in Italy she renounced acting and publicly dedicated herself, on the steps of the Uffizi no less, to *real* art."

"How come you know so much about her? You take a course on her or something?"

"They did a feature on her in last month's Art Press."

"I must've missed the last couple of issues. Maybe something to do with my not reading magazines written in French."

"She's now on the board of four galleries in Italy and one in Austria, has three galleries of her own and is about to open another. She's considered the most influential woman in the European art world."

"*Is*? You mean was. She's dead."

Scotty stopped. A wave washed around her ankles. The wind blew her hair in her face. Turning to Alex, disbelief written large across her face, Scotty declared, "She's not dead. She's in Venice."

"Venice, Italy?"

"No, Venice Beach. She turned her back on European high society to shack up with Scoop and Hank." Scotty couldn't disguise the irritation in her voice. "Of course Venice, Italy. They're calling her the next Peggy Guggenheim." An incoming wave headed their way, a big wave. The water slopped around her calves, right up to her knees. Resigning herself to salt stained pants, Scotty resumed walking beside Alex in the surf.

"Rick told me she had a heart condition. He said she was dead."

"If she is then it's happened in the past couple of weeks. She was alive and kicking last month. My God, you've got Luisa D'Onofrio's son living with you. The woman's art royalty." As they carried on walking, Scotty moved away from Rick's background and segued into the issues surrounding her upcoming exhibition, her insecurities, her glories and a roll call of the rich and famous with whom she was rubbing shoulders.

Alex found it hard to concentrate. His mind kept drifting to Rick's lie about his mother's death. If a man could lie so easily about that, he could lie about anything. There was no sign of Rick when they got back to the house and Alex sensed Scotty's disappointment.

"Don't forget my dinner invitation. Promise you'll ask Rick again," were Scotty's last words before she drove off mid-afternoon.

After retrieving his field easel from under the deck where Rick had hidden it, Alex still had time to work in the late afternoon light. He was distracted, however, and not in the right mindset to paint. So as not to lose an entire day's work, he set about framing some of his studies. He was experimenting with strips of bleached driftwood as a mount for the beach umbrella watercolor when the back door creaked open, it was followed by the metallic clatter of Rick tossing his car keys on the counter. Rick opened the studio door a smidge and asked, "She gone?"

"A while back. Get all your errands done?"

Rick rested his head on the door frame. "Didn't have any."

"Sorry what she said about your acting. Scotty talks without thinking at times."

"Like when I dished out that Rothko criticism to you. I was shooting my mouth off in the same way. Sorry."

A ripple of warmth towards Rick ran through Alex. That was a nice thing to say.

"That wasn't the reason I ducked out," sighed Rick. "I didn't want to be the fifth wheel. You two were an item once, right?"

Alex's spine spontaneously stiffened. "Whatever put that idea in your head?"

"She had a proprietorial air about you."

Sweeping his hair off his face, Alex leaned away from the painting he was framing. "Scotty has a proprietorial air in general. It's her way."

"I must have got the wrong message then. Anyway, I didn't waste my time in Laguna. I checked out the gallery that sells Gloria's work."

"And?"

"A few nice pieces but mostly tourist tat. You'd make some money there for sure, but I don't think it's the best showcase for you."

"Hey, what do you think of this?" Alex pointed to the framed painting.

Rick cocked his head. "Don't you think the reclaimed wood frame's too sentimental? A little too *Driftwood Dreams*?"

"Are you saying something hard would be better? Like steel?" Alex leaned his head alongside Rick's to mimic his viewpoint as much as possible. At that same moment Rick raised his own head and a loud crack ensued as their skulls collided.

"Ouch! You play rough," laughed Rick while rubbing his head.

"Gran always said I needed a bang on the head to knock some sense into me."

Rick went to the kitchen and opened the refrigerator. "I take it Scotty does well as an artist."

Alex picked up his cigarettes. "How'd you mean?"

Rick took a whole chicken out the refrigerator. "Does she sell much?" After slapping the chicken on the counter, he slid a sharp knife out of the block.

"Not a great deal. But she's got a one woman show coming up at the LaFonte Gallery and she gets commissions." Alex lit his cigarette and opened the back door.

"She's well connected in the art world then?" Rick manipulated one of the chicken legs, felt for the bone inside, then pressed the knife's tip into the fleshy joint.

"She knows the big gallery owners and vice versa. Like I said, she's getting a name, but she's a long way off the big league as yet."

Rick stabbed the knife into the chicken flesh. With a few deft slices he detached the leg. Alex exhaled, waving the smoke out of the kitchen door with his free hand. Rick dropped one chicken leg into the pot. He poised the knife and removed the other leg as he said, "About that dinner invitation. I checked my diary and I'm free. We should go."

The smoke caught in Alex's throat. "You sure?" he said with a cough. Stubbing out the cigarette, he picked up a tumbler and went to the faucet. "It's a long drive."

"We're in L.A., everything's a long drive." Rick slit the knife down the chicken's breast. White bone appeared beneath the pink flesh as Rick finished deconstructing the chicken. "Yeah, call and tell her we accept."

Guzzling down the water, Alex watched Rick rinse chicken blood off his hands. One thing was for sure about Rick's eagerness to accept Scotty's invitation, he wanted to find out something from her as much as she wanted to find out more about him.

♦ ♦ ♦

The subtle shifts of light during the day and seeing familiar views through fresh eyes became Alex's daily painting exercise and his meditation. The regular en plein air work was not only a balm to his mind but also a sharpening of his technique. Feeling more confident when working outdoors, he'd expanded his range beyond the local vicinity. Early one morning, preparing to drive down to Emerald Point, he'd loaded his painting gear in the car and turned on the ignition. A horrible noise erupted from under the hood. Having paid off all his garage debts in cash Alex was now one of Miguel's favorite customers. Managing to get the Chevy to limp to the garage, Alex asked if

Rick would follow in the Merc to give him a ride home in case the job was going to take time. It was a good call. After a quick examination, Miguel had traced the fault. It was an easy fix except he needed to source a part, so the Chevy had to stay in the shop for a few days. The drive back to Sunset Cove was Alex's first time as a passenger in Rick's car. In fact, it was the first time he'd been a passenger in anyone's car since being a kid. His eyes kept flicking to the rearview mirror. "Someone coming up behind on your right," Alex offered helpfully.

"Yep, I saw," said Rick tersely while checking the mirror and switching lanes.

Alex noticed that when Rick talked while driving he looked at the person he was talking to. Then, with his eyes off the road, he'd veer to the edge of the lane. Looking back at the road he'd make a swerving correction into lane. Due to this unsettling tendency, Alex decided it advisable not to instigate conversation from the passenger seat.

"You were quiet on the way home," said Rick as they walked to the house. "You got a problem with my driving?"

Alex wondered how to put it tactfully. "Not really, but you could benefit from a little more spatial awareness and lane discipline."

Rick's eyes widened in a scandalized affront. "I'll have you know I've driven down the Amalfi coast and those roads are literally on the edge of the cliffs. I didn't have any spatial awareness or lane discipline problems then!"

Alex was relieved to have missed that trip, particularly if Rick had a lot to say to his passenger. "I guess I just find it hard not being in the driver's seat. Call it a control issue. Forget I said anything." Further discussion was curtailed by an obviously anxious Mrs. Piper turning away from their back door. "Something wrong? Is it, Mr. Piper?" asked Alex, immediately worried he might be having heart problems again.

"No, nothing like that, he's fine." Mrs. Piper glanced over her shoulder, as if she feared being overheard. "Jim noticed a stranger's been watching our houses. I wanted to warn you that it may be worth locking your doors. Who knows what can happen these days with the terrible things going on. Can't be too careful."

Rick appeared uneasy once inside the house.

"Probably just a curious tourist," said Alex reassuringly.

"Yeah. Most likely," agreed Rick without meaning it.

Rick said no more, but Alex kept catching him peering through the kitchen blind's slats when he was near the sink. Alex put things into perspective. Who cared if a psycho killer was on the loose? He had worse things to worry about - Scotty's dinner party.

"I should take wine," said Rick on the morning of the dinner date. "What does she like?"

"Red. She won't drink white. She read somewhere that white wine's loaded with sulphites. It's colored her perception."

Rick's trip into Laguna to buy wine provided a window for Alex to phone Scotty. Once he'd got the pleasantries out of the way, he said to her, "Do *not* mention the mother!"

"Still sticking to the story that she's dead, is he?"

"Rick's had no need to stick to it because I haven't brought it up. And I'd appreciate it if you and Bob didn't either."

Scotty reluctantly agreed. After he'd hung up, Alex pondered Scotty's if displeasure was that the most powerful woman in European art was an out of bounds conversation topic.

A powerful sense of foreboding consumed Alex on the drive to Scotty and Bob's. His Chevy was still in the shop and he was in the Merc's passenger seat. Fate nearly put him of this misery when Rick changed lanes without checking the mirror and narrowly missed clipping a trailer truck. If the fifty-five mile an hour speed limit hadn't been introduced due to the oil crisis, Rick's misjudgment could have taken them out. Ironic that the Yom Kippur war had obliquely prevented a nasty accident.

While he drove, Rick needled for background on Scotty and Bob. First he asked about the Los Feliz house. Although

Scotty called it 'their' house, it was totally Bob's house. Further questions, with limited replies from Alex so as not to take Rick's eyes off the road, ticked the boxes of Bob's job - entertainment attorney in a huge firm of which he was a partner. Bob's income - stratospherically high. And Scotty and Bob's relationship status - as good as married but not.

After hanging a left off Los Feliz Boulevard, Rick navigated the twisting roads up into the hills finally pulling up outside a Moorish pile at the top of Chislehurst Drive. Falling dusk was the sprinklers' cue to hiss into life, reviving night blooming jasmines and lantanas. Bob's house sat on a large plot which sloped down the hill. The path to the front door was like a bridge, a sturdy iron railing guarding the deep drop on one side.

Standing before the walnut door set into the white stucco wall, Alex pressed the gold doorbell. Sonorous chimes echoed deep in the manse. Seconds passed before the light above their heads switched on. Prolonging the drama, it took a few more moments before the door slowly opened. Scotty appeared in the curvature of the door frame, the overhead porch light hitting her face at a perfect angle. "Alex. Rick. I trust your trip up the coast wasn't too arduous." Scotty's high cheekbones and swept back black hair gave her the air of a young Jackie Kennedy. "Welcome, welcome." She toyed with a ruffle on her apricot blouse.

Scotty made small talk while taking them on a needlessly circuitous route through the formal living room, the formal dining room and the casual living room. Alex hadn't visited here for some time, and he'd forgotten the elegant furnishings, the intricate Moroccan cornices and the sheer scale of the house - it was BIG. Spotlights illuminated bold art works on Spartan walls. Scotty flung open the double doors leading onto an ivory terrace. A marble staircase trailed down to an underlit swimming pool with expansive views of L.A. "Please, do join me on the terrace." Scotty dropped her eyes in reverential hospitality.

Alex couldn't believe the *Miss Manners and The Art of Elegant Entertaining* shit Scotty was shoveling. A twinkle in Rick's eye led him to assume Rick found it equally amusing.

"I hope you don't mind my asking, but why do people call you Scotty?" Rick asked while following Scotty down the steps.

Beside the swimming pool, a conversation area of rattan was set up around a low table with appetizers and white napkins. "My full name's Fionnuala Saoirse Scott. Bit of a mouthful, don't you think?" replied Scotty with a laugh. "Back in Chicago the kindergarten kids gave me the nickname Scotty and it's stuck ever since."

"Don't believe a word!" boomed a voice from the top of the steps. "She adores Star Trek. When we're in bed she fantasizes that I'm Spock." A bear of a man with a salt and pepper brush-cut came striding down the steps whilst opening a bottle of champagne. He timed his descent perfectly, gently popping the cork on arrival at poolside.

"Rick, let me introduce you to Bob," said Scotty and as an aside added, "and just for the record, that Spock thing's not true."

"Aye, aye Scotty," laughed Bob extending a paw to Rick. "Hello young fellow. Welcome to our humble abode." Bob pumped Rick's hand vigorously then clapped Alex roughly on the shoulder. Alex winced slightly, his shoulder had been sore before Bob's welcome.

"Hi," said Rick, discretely shaking out his hand after Bob had let go. Rick took in the glittering city view. "Cute little place you got here."

Bob passed a glass of fizz to Rick. "It's primitive but we manage. Did Scotty give you the tour?"

"Oh Bob, they've only just arrived. Have a drink and relax."

"Damn!" gasped Rick. "I left the wine in the car. I'll run and get it."

"There's no need, we've plenty," said Scotty.

"I made the trip into Laguna to buy it specially." Rick darted up the stairs.

As soon as he was out of earshot, Bob whispered, "That's the Stradman kid, huh?" Bob rubbed his chin thoughtfully. "I caught him on a couple of shows."

"Any good?" asked Alex.

Bob shrugged. "Not embarrassing, not great. He was prettier than the rest of the cast of *Eddie's Girls* but then the broads on that show *are* getting long in the tooth!"

Scotty swatted Bob in mock annoyance. "I'll have you know that Danielle Brown's only a couple of years older than me!"

"What's your point?" guffawed Bob. "Are we still pretending not to know who his mother is?"

"Yes, please keep away from anything controversial tonight," replied Alex.

"Fine, we'll stick to Nixon's impeachment and the Palestine situation."

Laughter was curtailed as a police siren cut through the early evening air. "That's coming from our street," said Scotty with concern. "Rick's out there."

"I'll go check on him." Bob put down his champagne and jogged up the stairs.

"I'll join you," said Alex.

Rick had left the front door swinging open. Blue and red lights reflected around the white lobby as Bob and Alex went out to investigate. They found Rick coming towards the house with a bottle in each hand. A police car was parked at the foot of the drive opposite. Scotty had come up too, peering over Alex and Bob's shoulders she asked, "What's going on?"

Two officers got out of the police car. The female officer switched on a flashlight and examined the perimeter fence. The male officer walked up the sloping driveway.

"For a moment then I wondered if we'd invited a known felon for dinner and the cops had caught up with you," said Bob pulling Rick inside. "You guys go enjoy your drinks. I'll hop over the way and see what Adrienne and David have been getting up to."

Down by the pool, Scotty continued serving champagne and appetizers but couldn't help glancing anxiously at the house. "Dinner's ready. We should be eating by now."

"I'll see what's keeping Bob." Alex stroked Scotty's arm to reassure her. "Let's go in."

Coming into the house off the terrace, they found Bob had just arrived back. "Did you see Adrienne and David?" Scotty immediately asked. "Are they okay?"

"David just got back from Palm Springs to find they've been burglarized," Bob said somberly. "He's pretty shook up."

Scotty's questions kept coming while they took their seats around the marble table in the dining room. "But how could they get robbed, Bob? They have security?" Scotty repeated for the fourth time as she served the Beef Wellington.

"Honey, I don't know. Let it go. Now what do we have here?" Bob examined the label of one of the bottles Rick had brought in. "Château Lafite Rothschild? Lucky you didn't run into those crooks! They'd have gunned you down for these!"

"Does David know what the robbers took?" asked Scotty. "Beans?" She passed the serving dish to Bob.

"He thinks they took all Adrienne's jewelry and some cash." Bob served himself with beans, then passed the dish to Rick. "And he can't find his gun."

Scotty paled. "Bob, that's awful"

"Stuff like this happens every day. Have a drink." Bob filled a fresh glass with the red wine and pushed it to Scotty. "I only buy you cheap jewelry. See the benefit of having a skinflint as a lover?"

"What if David or Adrienne had been home? Or even the maid." Scotty passed the carrots.

"Darling, I won't allow this trivial incident to monopolize our dinner conversation. Rick's been in our home for over an hour and we've hardly heard a word from our guest." Bob filled Rick's glass with a hefty serving of the Lafite. "Time to put young Rick on the spot!"

Alex's knuckles instinctively clenched, fearful of where Bob was heading with this.

"So, Rick," Bob said intently across the table, "what are your feelings about the L.A. Rams this season?"

All eyes focused on Rick. He may have been expecting all sorts of questions, but this one caught him from left field. As it turned out, Rick had a rudimentary knowledge of sport, enough to give a few not totally inept opinions about the Rams' line up and scores at least. After exhausting sport, they moved on to discuss popular new movies. Alex sat this round out and listened. Their consensus was *The Great Gatsby* had terrific visuals but was essentially superficial, *Blazing Saddles* had a lot of laughs but was overly vulgar, and *Man on a Swing* was intriguing but too dark to be a hit. The conversation lulled during the overly rich dessert which Alex declined. They moved on to Scotty's favorite subject ... celebrities. In his comfort zone too, Bob couldn't help regaling them with one showbiz anecdote after the other. "...anyway, the director yells over the loudhailer, in front of the entire crew I may add, 'It's all in the playing! Play it the way I told you!' Paul fires back fast as lightning, 'Actually, it's all in the contract. Call Bob Swanson at C.F.A.' and storms off set." Bob chuckled at the memory. "That little altercation cost the studio three million to settle."

Scotty wrinkled her nose. "This talk about contracts and money makes every artistic relationship sound like a deal."

Opening the second bottle of Lafite, Bob went to top up all of their glasses. Alex covered his. The wine may have cost a bomb, but he'd rather have had a beer. He noticed a cloud of concern pass Scotty's face, most likely still fretting about the robbery. He knew a surefire way to snap her out of it and asked, "Scotty, are you going to reveal your new works in progress?"

"Yeah, honey! Don't hide your light under a bushel." Bob squeezed Scotty's hand. "Not only her exhibition at LaFonte's but a new commission too. And not just for anyone. Tell them who it's for."

"Bob, don't make it sound like a big deal," said Scotty.

"But it is big deal!" Bob got conspiratorial. "Marvin threw a big party the other week and I ran into R.J. and Natalie. It was her first time out after having the baby. Anyway, they're moving in to a new house and she's all excited about picking color schemes and art for the place. R.J.'s singing her praises, saying what a great eye she's got. Scotty mentions she's an artist and tells them about her exhibition. They were fascinated, weren't they honey?"

Scotty nodded modestly.

"Luckily Scotty had Polaroids of her new flower pieces in her purse. She showed them the gardenia one. It turns out Natalie's crazy about gardenias and fell in love with Scotty's work on the spot. Well, Natalie's getting tired from the standing so she goes sit. Then R.J. drags me away on the pretext of getting another Scotch. That's when he says he wants a surprise for Natalie's birthday. They've got three yards of wall space to fill in the remodel of their master suite. He thinks Scotty's work would be perfect and commissions a piece on the spot!"

It honestly didn't mean much to Alex. "I've no idea who you're talking about."

"R.J. is Robert Wagner. He's married to Natalie Wood," explained Rick to Alex.

"And what a swell couple they are. Honey, take the guys down to your studio." Bob topped up Rick's glass with the last of the red.

Scotty sighed with an 'If you insist' eyeroll that she didn't really mean. She led them down to the floor below, the level of the pool and bedrooms. Turning the corner, she opened another arched door set into an alcove. Behind this door a circular staircase ran to the lowest level. Rick stumbled on the winding stairs but caught himself without spilling any wine. Reaching the bottom, Scotty opened another dark wooden door and pressed a switch. After a momentary flicker, bright lights illuminated the studio. Rick took another slug of wine and blinked as his eyes adjusted.

A series of intensely vibrant plant studies were hanging on the pure white walls. All the pictures were on a grand scale, approximately five or six feet square. Each was of a single bloom in mega close-up. Orchid, lily, strelitzia, gardenia, rose - around fifteen different flowers in total. What set Scotty's work apart from the ordinary was they all had a three-dimensional representation of the flower, fashioned from twisted and woven wire, springing out from the painting. The bent wire lattice hovering in front of the picture gave the impression that the flowers were swaying as you walked past. Simply moving your eyes over the largest pieces created an illusion of movement.

"When did you master this wire work? The technique's incredibly fine." Alex studied one of the pieces up close.

Scotty picked a piece of twisted wire work off a bench. "I found an amazingly talented student at U.C.L.A. to do it. I'd never have achieved this finesse myself." Rick paced back and forth in front of Scotty's work, wine in hand and that x-ray look in his eyes. "What do you think?" Scotty twisted her hands nervously.

Rick took a swig from his glass and rolled the red wine over his tongue. Alex and Scotty stood immobile, breathlessly awaiting his reaction. Rick shook his head. Alex actually heard himself swallow, fearful of Rick's reaction. If he was harshly negative, perhaps in retaliation for Scotty dishing his accent on the T.V. show, this could prove embarrassing.

"Georgia O'Keeffe on acid," said Rick.

Scotty let out a nervous laugh. "Is that a good thing?"

"Most certainly." Rick got closer to the study of the strelitzia. Noting that Rick was a little woozy, Alex casually took the glass from him. Rick peered at the wire and painting amalgam.

"My next step is taking them farther into three dimensions." Scotty went to the trestle table covered with clay sculptures and plaster moldings of flowers. One of the plaster casts had been diced into cubes and was in the process of being reassembled in a disjointed manner. "I'm going to suspend them from the ceiling on stems like mutant anti-flowers," said Scotty.

Rick went to look at the works on the trestle table. "You sculpt as well?"

"Suzy from Long Beach helped with these. She's such a talented sculptress. You remember Suzy, don't you Alex?" Scotty asked.

"She the one with the coffee addiction and a birthmark shaped like North Dakota?"

Scotty shot Alex a withering glance. "No."

"Not who I was thinking of then."

"Impressive work, congratulations Scotty." Rick retrieved his glass. "I'm not au fait with the L.A. gallery scene. Is LaFonte a big player?"

Scotty tipped her head. "Not the biggest but he vibes with new artists and's one of the few who's interested in women's art. He gave Tina Seattle a one woman show last year."

"Who'd you classify as the most influential then?" asked Rick. "I mean, which galleries can really make an artist's name."

Rick's praise had relaxed Scotty and she spoke freely. "The Koenig Gallery undoubtedly. If Koenig likes you then you've got it made. Copley Van Sant's rumored to be the new Ferus, very cutting edge. Yumi Mihara's about to open a new space. She's more commercial than the others, but she's got a nose for what sells and gets big bucks for her stable." Rick took all this in, hanging on Scotty's every word. "It's wonderful to talk to someone with a deep interest in art. Have you studied?"

Rick stifled a yawn. "Interested amateur."

"Thanks for looking at my work. I appreciate your feedback." Scotty toyed with pieces of the deconstructed plaster sculpt. "I love the finish on this plaster. Doesn't it feel great?"

Scotty handed Alex one of the flower plaster casts. As he rolled it around in his hand, Scotty turned her attention back to Rick. "The galleries here are excellent, but I'm not sure the L.A. art scene's taken seriously outside America. I'm honored to have people in this town who champion me, but I wonder how my work would be received in Europe. I'd give my right arm to get my pieces in front of a curator for one of those great European collections. I mean, one of the big names in Paris, Milan, or Venice ..."

Crash!

The plaster cast smashed on the floor in an explosion of white dust. "Oops," said Alex raising his hand. "You were right about the smoothness of that finish. Darn thing slipped clean through my fingers."

"It's just a work in progress," said Scotty, somewhat humbled.

Rick's eyes had drooped closed.

"Hey buddy, we should be hitting the road." Alex jiggled Rick's arm. "Sorry about that," he said to Scotty while glancing at the pile of plaster and dust on the floor.

When they got back upstair, Bob was looking out of the front door. "Natalie's going to love one of those, don't you think?" he asked on seeing them.

"I'm sure," replied Alex, "who wouldn't?"

"It was a pleasure to meet you," said Rick swaying slightly.

"You're not driving, are you?" Bob wrinkled his brow at Rick.

"Stay over?" Scotty offered. "We've plenty of space."

Rick looked at Alex but couldn't quite focus. "Are you sober?"

Alex nodded. "As a judge."

"Great." Rick pressed his car keys into Alex's hand. "I'll let Jesus take the wheel."

"Thanks for a fun night." Alex kissed Scotty on the cheek. "Dinner, drinks and a crime scene."

"We may rustle up a murder for entertainment next time!" guffawed Bob.

The police car was still parked across the street. Rick steadied himself against the Merc, red and blue police lights glinting off his face. "Okay, Cinderfella, pumpkin time," said Alex as he slid into the driver's side. Reaching over, Alex unlocked the passenger door and Rick slowly climbed in the car. It took Alex a little time to assess the controls. The ignition was straightforward, but his first attempt at finding the headlights actually switched on the wipers. After some unproductive fumbling, Rick leaned over and hit the lights for him. From there on in, it was plain sailing. The Mercedes handled sweetly, hugging the curves down Chislehurst. Alex had never driven an automatic transmission before, it was surprisingly relaxing. Within ten minutes they'd hit the freeway.

Rick's eyes slowly opened and closed as he struggled to stay awake. "How long's Scotty been with Bob?" he asked.

"About four years," answered Alex keeping his eyes on the road. "She was selling her paintings, or rather trying to sell her paintings in his building. There was a temp on reception who mistook her for a client and directed her to Bob's office in error. He was in middle of a hectic morning, and the last thing he needed was some flake showing him her etchings."

"I'll guess what happened next." Rick slumped in his seat. "He loved her work and bought everything."

"Actually, he thought her work stank but didn't want to hurt her feelings and took her out to dinner."

"Similar thing happened to Renoir."

Alex snorted a laugh. "I was blown away by her flower works. She's some artist."

"A three-yard wall to fill? More like a glorified interior decorator if you ask me."

"That's harsh. She's had help with technical aspects of the work, but that's not uncommon. It's her vision that counts, isn't it?" No response. Alex glanced over and saw that Rick had fallen asleep. Since this car practically drove itself, Alex let his mind wander while cruising Pacific Highway. It was hard to deny he felt competitive with Scotty, but he didn't like hearing Rick put her down. What was harder, if being brutally honest, was that he agreed with Rick. He flicked on the radio. After jabbing a couple of buttons it locked onto a mellow jazz station. Passing over an intersection, the taillights and headlights of the traffic flowed with a fluid quality, like rivers of quicksilver melding with the notes from a clarinet.

It was just after two when Alex swung the Mercedes around the back of the beach house. Sunset Cove was silent except for the surf. Stars crowded the night sky, the blinking lights of a jet passed before a distant constellation. "Bud, wake up. End of the line. Everybody out." Rick was groggy and immobile. Alex wondered if he should let him sleep it off in the car but decided that was too mean. Some shoulder jiggling and cajoling finally aroused Rick into a semi-conscious state, enough to manhandle him out of the car and get him on two feet at least.

"Where am I?" slurred Rick loudly.

"Shh!" Alex hissed. "You'll wake the neighbors."

"Where you taking me, mister? I want to go to San Jose. You said you knew the way."

"Shh!" Alex dragged Rick to the back door. Keys? Where were the keys? Mrs. Piper's warning had made locking the doors the new norm. "You got the keys?"

Rick giggled loudly. "Keys?"

Alex dipped into Rick's jacket pocket. Nothing. The key must be in his pants. It was difficult to slide his hand in while facing Rick. He twizzled Rick around and, with his face pressed against the wall, managed to delve deep into Rick's pants.

"Why you putting your hand in my pants, mister? I got my cab fare," blurted Rick.

Alex felt around in Rick's pants pocket. It was an odd sensation, his fingertips tracing the dip of Rick's groin then his firm thigh. That's when he touched it, the key. "Don't move." Alex opened up the house and, slinging his arm around Rick's shoulder, half walked and half dragged him inside. "Bedtime for Bonzo," said Alex propelling Rick towards his bedroom. Rick let out a strange groan. Afraid he was going to throw up, Alex halted. Bending to look at Rick's face, he saw that he was crying. "What's this about, bud?"

"Where am I?"

"At the beach. I just drove us home. Remember?" Alex spoke soothingly, gently patting Rick's shoulder to calm him.

Rick pivoted his head to look at Alex, rather like a ventriloquist's dummy, and squinted though his tears. "I know you. You're the painter."

"Got it in one." Alex set Rick's legs into motion again and entered his room. Steadying Rick against his hip, he threw back the covers. Rick wobbled and then tumbled onto the bed, his momentum dragging Alex down with him. "There we go," said Alex extricating himself from Rick's arms. He took off Rick's shoes. "Let's get this off too." Alex managed to remove his jacket. He was about to take off Rick's shirt and pants but thought better of it. He was picking Rick's jacket up off the floor when Rick's hand snaked out and grabbed his wrist.

"You're not a painter." Rick pulled Alex close, so close their noses were nearly touching, then slurred, "You're an *artist*." Rick rolled over and promptly passed out.

After hanging Rick's jacket on the back of the chair, Alex pulled the covers over him, shook out the crochet blanket and spread it on top. He needed to chill before going to sleep. Having gently closed Rick's door, he dug his stash from the art deco vase on the mantel and rolled a joint. Opening the front door, he peeked out to check no-one was about. The beach was deserted, as it should be at this time of night, so he peeled off his clothes and slipped onto the verandah. He crashed on the gray couch, letting the breeze fan his naked skin. That's when he remembered he'd left Rick's car blocking the track behind the house. What the hell, he figured it could stay there until morning. With a deep drag on the joint he reflected on the evening. From the burglary across the road to Scotty's attempt to channel Princess Grace, everything about the night had been off kilter. What was Scotty thinking? That Rick would grant her wish to have her work shown in Europe by giving her an entrée to his mother's world? The mother he told people was dead? And what was behind Rick's acceptance of Scotty's invitation tonight? Was he testing how much people knew about him? Both their motivations were unfathomable.

The smoke quieted Alex's mind. In his mellowness, the fluid images of the traffic on the drive home swirled like multi-colored eddies in an ocean. Alex carried on smoking until the colors became mind-blowingly intense and the constellations danced in dizzying patterns. Alex stubbed out the joint and walked unsteadily inside. The bottom step creaked as he started up to his bed. Pausing, he came back and softly opened Rick's door. Naked, he stood on the threshold watching Rick sleep. He decided to leave Rick's door open. He thought he'd sleep better if he could hear Rick breathing during the night, just in case he woke up in a panic and disturbed the neighbors.

PROVENANCE

Honk!

An insistent car horn roused Alex from a dry-mouthed sleep. He prized his eyes open and discovered it was light, painfully light. Through the fuzz of half sleep he slowly pieced last night together ... shit! He'd left Rick's car blocking the lane. Sitting bolt upright, throbbing pain coursed through his brain. He immediately dropped back into a horizontal position. That late-night joint had not been a good idea.

Honk! Honk! Hoooonk!

Each toot of the horn was an ice pick in his eardrums. "Hold on!" he yelled. His voice's vibration in his skull was agony. Dragging himself out of bed, he wriggled into the nearest pair of boxers to hand. "Coming, I'm coming!" Raised voices, horn honking, his heart pounding in his ears; the combined noises reached a painful crescendo as he got to the back door. Shielding his eyes from the sun, Alex went out to find Rick and Gloria standing on the track beside Rick's Mercedes and an irate Harry sitting behind his Cadillac's wheel, pounding the horn. "Sorry, I meant to move the car last night."

"Morning!" said Rick brightly upon seeing Alex bumble outside in his full bleary eyed, hairy chested glory. Rick was fresh as a daisy, hair washed, teeth brushed and wearing a freshly pressed white shirt and khakis.

Alex managed a grunt in response. The sun's reflection off Gloria's shocking lilac shift, matching hair bandana and white blonde hair was propelling Alex's eyeballs to the point of explosion. He massaged his temples, hoping to stave off a stroke. "What the hell time is it anyway?" muttered Alex.

"Eight fifteen," replied Rick.

Hooonk!

"Knock it off, will ya!" Gloria hollered to Harry in a voice that could win any hog calling competition.

"Hold your horses. I'll get the keys," said Alex. Turning to go inside made his head spin. He clutched the door frame while talking himself out of throwing up.

Rick twirled the car keys around his finger. "I got this. I was just about to move it when you came down." Harry's Caddy sat nose to nose with Rick's Merc. Harry apparently wasn't willing to reverse, so Rick hopped in and backed his car down to the Beachcomber.

"We're only going to the store. I told Harry we could leave it until later, but he wasn't listening to me," said Gloria to Alex.

Honk!

Harry had stopped beside the Beachcomber and was leaning on the horn again. "Need anything from the store?" Gloria asked Alex, unfazed by Harry's urgency.

"Thanks, but we're ..." Another blast from Harry's horn cut off Alex's words.

"For Pete's sake, I'm coming!" Gloria shouted as she walked to the car and got in. Harry gunned the car and it lurched forward, spitting gravel at Rick's Mercedes and the Piper's picket fence.

Coming out of her back door, Mrs. Piper asked, "What's all the commotion?"

"My fault. I blocked in the Waverley's car," replied Alex.

"Is that all? I thought they'd announced World War Three." Mrs. Piper walked to him, kicking shale off her path on the way.

"You know how Harry gets sometimes."

"When the Waverleys have one of their spats we all know. Is everything all right with you and your new friend?"

Alex ran his fingers through his matted bed hair. "Roommate."

"Whatever he is, I'm glad you have company. It's not healthy to spend too much time alone and he's keeping you out of the Beachcomber, which is good for your figure." Mrs. Piper went to pat Alex's tummy.

Alex defensively folded his arms over his chest. Any pressure around the stomach area, however affectionately meant, was liable to induce projectile vomiting.

"I wanted to tell you there was another man hanging around your house last night, looking in through the windows and all." Mrs. Piper lowered her voice. "Jim came out and told him no-one was home and said we'd call the police if he didn't leave." Mrs. Piper glanced at Rick, who'd driven past them and parked his Merc in the dunes. He was now examining the paintwork. "You're not in some kind of trouble are you, Alex?"

"I hope not. What was he like?"

"Older man. Well dressed, gray hair, black glasses."

"It doesn't sound like anyone I know. And I don't think Rick's told anyone he's here, so I can't think they were looking for him."

"It's all very unsettling" Mrs. Piper stroked Alex's arm. "You take care. Sunset Cove's always been such a safe haven, let's hope it stays that way."

After saying goodbye to Mrs. Piper, Alex went inside and poured himself a large tumbler of water. He guzzled it down, but it didn't clear his pounding brain or wash the sour taste out of his mouth.

"Damn near scratched my paintwork," muttered Rick coming into the kitchen. "Bad trip?" asked Rick, watching Alex pour more water into his glass.

"What do you mean?" asked Alex defensively.

"I smelled the weed."

"You weren't exactly sober yourself last night."

"Yeah, thanks for getting me into bed. I admit I got carried away with the wine. It was an odd evening, wasn't it?"

Alex backed away from the sink, allowing Rick to fill the battered copper kettle. Rick's mention of putting him to bed reminded him of how he'd felt having his hand in Rick's pants and beginning to undress him. He stifled the memory. "You didn't warm to Scotty?" asked Alex.

Rick wrinkled his nose. "She's okay, just blatantly ambitious."

Alex took several deep breaths, summoning the courage to make it to the bathroom.

The tin kettle boiled with a shrill whistle. Rick tipped coffee into a mug, leaving the kettle whistling. "It's only instant. Do you want me to make one for you too?"

"No! Just turn off that fucking noise." As water hadn't felt great in Alex's stomach, the mere thought of hot coffee had him retching.

"Are those all of your paintings in the studio?" Rick asked as he turned off the gas.

"I've more in the loft behind my room. Why?" Alex rubbed his eyes, which felt like pickled onions.

"Scotty's got an exhibition coming up, what's to stop you having one?" asked Rick making the coffee.

"The fact no gallery's expressed the slightest interest in my work's a major clue why that hasn't happened."

"How can a gallery offer you an exhibition if they don't know about you? We need to get your work seen."

"We?"

"Scotty wouldn't mix in the circles she does without Bob's connections. I've got connections. I could get you seen in the right circles."

"What do you mean, get *me* seen? You mean, get my *work* seen."

Rick rolled the mug around in his hands. "Your persona's part and parcel of your work. You ought to work on your image."

"My image has nothing to do with my work. What I put on the canvas is all that counts. Can we discuss this later? My head's killing me."

"You can't walk into a gallery looking like a derelict and expect to be taken seriously. Do you own any jeans that aren't ripped or covered in paint?"

"What have my jeans got to do with anything?" In a few more moments, when he'd got himself together, Alex vowed he'd crawl to the bathroom and pass out in private.

"Just saying you could use some new clothes." After draining his drink, Rick added, "And a haircut. Even combing your hair would help. Have you used the conditioner I bought?"

Not liking the direction this conversation was headed, Alex swiftly changed the subject. "By the way, did you tell anyone you're living here?"

"Why?" Rick lit the gas and put the pot on again.

"Mrs. Piper swung by. Seems a man was hanging around the house last night. Said he was looking for someone. Pretty sure no-one's looking for me, I'm guessing it's you he's after."

"She say what he looked like?"

"Older guy. Smartly dressed. Gray hair ..."

"Black glasses?"

"Yeah."

"Oh shit," muttered Rick.

"Rick, are you in some kind of trouble?"

Rick slammed down his mug. "Fuck, fuck, fuck!"

Alex wondered what was with all the screaming and shouting this morning.

Rick slammed his fist on the counter in frustration, then pelted out of the house and onto the beach.

The kettle's whistle pierced the air. Alex hastily shut off the gas. With the room spinning like a carousel, he headed to the shower. Maybe the steam would clear his head, the creeping unease and the inconvenient boner tenting out his shorts. God, how long had *that* been going on? If last night had been weird, this morning was upping the ante in that department.

♦ ♦ ♦

Rick didn't return quickly, which was a shame as Miguel phoned to say the Chevy was ready to pick up. Alex went out and scanned the beach, but there was no sign of Rick. The nice thing about having cash in his pocket was independence. He called a cab to take him to the garage. He'd picked up the Chevy and was back home within an hour.

Still no sign of Rick.

With the vague worry of how long Rick had to be gone before he filed a Missing Person's Report, Alex contemplated the pros and cons of different mediums for the urban studies he was planning. He liked the idea of watercolors but using them presented a challenge. To produce an impressionistic blur of traffic against the solidity of concrete and asphalt, he'd have to lay the traffic blur down first and then fill in the background. This would negate the study's immediacy. He finally heard sandy feet tapping on the brush by the front door. Rick had been gone over six hours. He went straight to his room and slammed the door. Five minutes later, Alex heard the pad of Rick's feet coming to the studio.

"You busy?" asked Rick.

"Glad you're back. I was beginning to worry," said Alex without turning around.

"It's half an hour off the martini bell, but I need a drink. Wanna come with me? My treat."

Now turning around, Alex saw Rick's eyes were red and puffy. "Sure," replied Alex gently.

They walked in silence to the bar. The Star-Spangled Banner fluttered over the Beachcomber's deck. After they'd taken a corner table under a blue and white striped parasol, Rick said, "There's a possibility you're wondering why I reacted how I did this morning."

"Correct, it was pretty extreme."

"I haven't been completely honest with you ..."

"Hey guys!" Julie hopped over to their table with her pad and pencil at the ready. Beneath her bistro apron she wore white short shorts teamed with a red jersey halter top, her fluffy blonde hair scraped back into a high pony. "What's your poison?" Julie fixed Alex with her twinkling eyes while rattling the orange pencil between her perfectly small teeth.

Looking back on earlier in the day, Alex wondered why he hadn't conjured up this image of Julie when he was beating off in the shower. "Whiskey and Coke," answered Alex, which was nuts as his head had only just stopped banging from this morning's hangover.

"Make that two," added Rick.

"Doubles?" asked Julie.

"What the hell," quipped Alex. "Who needs a liver anyway?"

"Coming right up." Julie sashayed to the bar.

"When I said I wanted to move to the beach to get away from everything, I really meant everybody." Rick didn't raise his eyes as he spoke. "I wanted to drop off the radar."

"Sounds like you're back on it."

Rick absently traced the wood grain of the table with his finger for a few minutes, then said, "I've been having problems lately. Struggling with things, you know, in my head ..."

"Two whiskeys and Coke. Doubles." Julie set two condensation frosted tumblers on the table. "My hand was a little shaky when I poured so they may be larger than doubles. Oops! Don't tell Arnold," she said with a wink before going to serve the next table.

Rick agitated his ice cubes with the plastic straw. "You ever have the feeling that everyone wants a piece of you, or is telling you what to do, or expecting something from you, something you know you'll never be able to give them?"

"I live alone at the beach and have no career. Being pursued is not among my issues."

"I kind of got that the day I first came into your house. I guess I wanted that kind of peace too." Rick downed a large slug of his drink. "Lately I've had everyone getting into my head, what with Gina and dad. Then momma interfering was the last straw."

"That'd be your dead mother, then?"

Rick drained his glass and slapped it on the table. He squinted into the café and beckoned to Julie. When she noticed him he raised his empty glass and tapped it. Getting the message that he wanted another round, Julie gave the thumbs up. Rick turned to Alex and, meeting his eyes, said, "I guessed Scotty knew about me from that first moment we met."

"Why were you so keen on accepting her dinner invitation then?"

"I was teasing her, wondering how far she'd go in trying to manipulate an introduction to momma. She told you I'd lied about momma being dead, didn't she?"

"Yeah, but to be honest I still don't really know who your mother is. I'm not up on the European art scene like Scotty. She reads highbrow magazines in French. But I sensed you telling me she was dead meant you had heavy issues in that area. I told Scotty to respect that and not bring her up."

"That was thoughtful. But she couldn't resist."

"You guys are thirsty!" Julie was setting down their drinks with her usual perkiness.

"Gotta keep hydrated." Alex winked at her.

"If you begin to dry out you know where to find me," said Julie with a giggle, clearing their empties.

Suddenly a deep voice boomed from the other side of the wooden trellis surrounding the deck. "Finally, I've found you! Ricky baby, you've had me worried sick."

"Ugh, great timing." Rick threw back his head and covered his eyes.

A tall man in a crumpled white linen shirt and checkered slacks lumbered up the stairs. "It's hotter than hades down here. Jesus H. Christ!" Blinking perspiration from his eyes, the man polished his horn-rimmed spectacles with his handkerchief. Putting them back on he immediately focused on Julie's bust. "How can you people stand it?" The man lifted his eyes to Julie's face. "Say, you got a great look. You ought to be on T.V. You got an agent?"

Julie laughed shyly and said, "I'm not an actress."

"Who cares when you look like you do? Honey, get me an iced tea." The man switched his attention from Julie to Rick. "Baby, your apartment's empty, your car's gone, your phone's ringing off the hook. How can you do this to me?" The man pulled out a chair and joined them at the table.

"How did you find me?" Rick squinted at the man.

"I hired a private detective."

"I mean here in the bar," Rick said in exasperation.

"I went to that shack the private dick said you're holed up in. The blonde broad next door with skin like Naugahyde said you may be here."

"You hired a private eye to track me down? Jesus." Rick screwed up his face in disgust.

"Do you blame me with all this Patty Hearst business? Taking off without a word like you did, how'd I know you hadn't been kidnapped? Then what am I meant to think when the private dick tells me you've shacked up in the back of beyond with some hippie." The man theatrically clutched his chest. "My heart can't take this. You know how long it takes to drive down here? And this is the second time in two days. I had to see for myself that you're okay. I got a movie shooting next week. I haven't got time for this."

"Now you see for yourself that I'm not being held hostage or planning to rob any banks you can relax," said Rick unkindly.

"Your tea." Julie put a large jug of iced tea and a chilled glass in front of the man. "You guys okay?"

"Same again," said Rick rattling the ice in his empty glass.

"Okay." Julie sashayed inside. The man's eyes followed her shapely legs.

"Dad, must you do that?"

"I'm a producer. I have an eye for talent." Rick's dad poured tea into his glass.

Alex pushed back his chair. "Excuse me, I'll give you two some privacy."

Rick's dad jabbed his finger at Alex. "You're going nowhere. Sit!"

Although there was no reason to obey this stranger's demands it seemed easier to comply than make a scene, so Alex sat back down.

"Are you holding my son against his will?" Rick's dad demanded as he directed a gimlet stare at Alex.

"The fact I'm not manacled in a closet surely indicates that's not the case," said Rick like an irritated fourteen-year-old.

"Who's this bozo anyway?" Rick's dad jerked his thumb at Alex.

"Alex Morgan." Alex politely proffered his hand.

Rick's dad didn't shake it, instead he barked at Alex, "How do you know my son?"

"I'm renting his house," Rick answered on Alex's behalf. "I needed a place to think."

"I just bought you an apartment in Brentwood! What's wrong with thinking in Brentwood? Julie Andrews lives in Brentwood. Do you see Julie Andrews having a problem thinking? People can think in Brentwood! This isn't about thinking, it's about your Ricky trip of taking off on a whim and not giving a hoot about anyone or anything else. I got your agent chasing my back! The guy's about to give up on you. He's pushed to get you a reading at Universal for *McMillan and Wife*. Now they're desperate to see you and you've disappeared off the face of the earth. He's stalled them as long as he can. What do you want him to tell the casting guys? You're too busy to meet with them cause you're hanging out on the beach with a beatnik?"

"I'm not a beatnik," said Alex rationally.

"Nobody's talking to you," snapped Rick's dad.

"Dad! Don't be rude. Alex is my friend!"

"Ah, your friend now. Is that what you're doing?" Rick's dad zeroed in on Alex. "Brainwashing the kid? Luring him into your hippie commune?"

"Sir, I'm neither a hippie nor a kidnapper and I resent being called a beatnik. I was happily minding my own business when I saw your son climbing the cliffs. They're unstable and I didn't want him to hurt himself. I went up after him to make sure he was safe as I didn't want his death on my conscience." Alex got to his feet, having put up with enough of this crap. "In hindsight I regret my actions. Nice meeting you." Alex walked away.

"Wait, wait!" Rick's dad stood up, blocking Alex's path. "Is that true, Ricky?"

Rick averted his eyes from his dad and nodded shamefully.

"Any moron can see those cliffs are dangerous. Why'd anyone in their right mind climb up them? Why would he do that?" Rick's dad looked to Alex for the answer.

"It wasn't entirely his fault. The warning sign had got blown down by a storm," explained Alex.

Rick's dad's eyes softened. "You looked after my Ricky? He could've been hurt if it weren't for you going up after him?" Rick's dad grabbed Alex's hand and pumped it. "I'm Sid Stradman. I shouldn't have shot my yap like that. I've just been worried sick about the kid."

Julie was at the table again, setting down another round of drinks. "Everything okay?"

"Fine. Everything's fine," said Sid fishing out his wallet. "Honey, this should cover the check. Keep the change." Sid gave

Julie a bill. Her eyes widened when she realized it was a fifty. Sid delved into his wallet, pulled out a business card and offered it to her. "If you change your mind about Hollywood, call me."

"I don't think so ..." Julie didn't take it, but her eyes lingered on Sid's a moment too long.

"Just in case." Sid tucked the business card into Julie's apron, then turned back to Rick. "Okay, you've had your fun at the beach. You got a tan and this thinking bullshit out of your system. Time to return to civilization."

"I want to stay here, dad."

"So Mike should tell Universal you don't want to read for the part? It's a good part, Sally McMillan's kid cousin. This is a big show. William Morris ain't gonna keep batting for you if you don't play the game." Sid turned to Alex. "You're his friend. What advice would *you* give him? Turn down a good part, is that what you'd tell him? Good parts don't grow on trees. Why would you tell him to do that?"

"I don't know," stammered Alex wondering why he was suddenly involved. This was like an innocent bystander being dragged into a crime.

"I'm not going back to Brentwood. I like living here!" Rick smacked his hand on the table.

"How do I knock some sense into that fat head of yours? Take away your car? Cut off your credit? Then what will you do, huh? Come and live in Bel Air with me and Letitia? That's what you'd have to do without me bankrolling you."

"And how'll you keep me in Bel Air against my will? Lock me in the mansion? That sounds like a kidnap to me. And what will you do while you're holding me hostage? Force us all to dress in matching outfits and pretend to be the Von Trapps? Go ahead, cut off my credit! I'll just call momma ..."

"Ricky! You vowed to never take a cent from her again! Jesus Christ. You drive me nuts." Sid massaged his chest.

Alex felt sorry for Rick's dad. True, Sid had an abrasive quality but he genuinely seemed to care for Rick.

“Okay. Stay here. Play out your hippie fantasy with this beach bum." Sid shot a glance at Alex. "No offence, Dex."

Alex suppressed a smirk. “None taken.” To be insulted so frequently in such a short space of time by a total stranger was almost poetic. “And my name's Alex.”

"Whatever. Now you,” said Sid jabbing his finger at Rick, "you, young man, will call William Morris this instant! You tell Mike you had an accident, or contracted botulism, or make up some of your usual bullshit to explain why you haven’t returned his calls. You apologize to him then get your ass to Universal at two p.m. tomorrow and play the hell out of the scene."

Rick sniffed recalcitrantly. “How? I don't have the sides.”

Sid pulled a rolled up manila envelope out of his back pocket and flung it on the table. “Now you got ‘em. The part’s Bradley Hull. He’s a headstrong wisecracking pain in the ass. That part you’ll nail. He’s also meant to be extremely intelligent and studying law at Berkeley. That you need to work on. Now, you got a phone out here on Gilligan's Island or you rely on tom toms and psychic vibes to communicate?”

“We have a phone,” muttered Rick handling the envelope like it contained a tarantula.

“Gimme your number.” Sid reached over and tore off the envelope’s tongue. He fumbled in his pocket, then reached behind to Julie, who was bending to serve another table. He tapped her on the ass. “Babe, need your pencil.” Julie, with a slight giggle, handed it to him. “Shoot.” Sid quickly scribbled down the number as Rick read it out. “That's the right one, huh? Not some cockamamie made up one? You can vouch for it?” Sid focused on Alex, struggled to remember his name, snapped his fingers a few times and then settled for, “Buddy.”

Alex took it on the chin, there was no point fighting this insanity. He nodded.

“I need to be back in town by eight. I gotta get moving while the sun’s still up.”

Julie leaned over the balcony to ring the golden bell hanging from the canopy.

Clang! Clang! Clang!

Sid clutched his heart. "Where's the goddamn fire?"

"It's the martini bell," explained Alex. "They ring it every day at five."

People spilled from houses up and down the beach. Everyone was barefoot or in flip flops, dressed in frayed denim cut offs, tie dye tees, cheesecloth shirts, bikinis and board shorts. Sid surveyed the folk coming into the bar. "Sure look like a bunch of hippies to me. At least I got one thing to be grateful for, that Gina's out of the picture. I could kill your mother for that business. Bye Ricky. I love ya, kid." Sid kissed Rick's head and ruffled his hair.

"Oh, dad." Rick pushed Sid away and smoothed his hair back into place.

"But I'm warning you, blow out this reading and I'm cutting you off! I work with these people. You can screw up your life but don't make a fool out of me. Capiche?" Rick dropped his eyes and nodded. "And you." Sid jabbed his finger in Alex's face. "Thanks for looking out for him." Sid clapped Alex warmly on the shoulder, his aching shoulder. "Word of advice, Dex. Get a haircut, you look like a girl from behind." And with that parting shot, Sid sailed off into the sunset.

Julie cleared the glasses and wiped the table. "Another round?" she asked Rick.

"What the hell. Hit me," said Rick.

Alex and Rick carried on drinking as the sun went down. Alex mused on the revelations of Rick's provenance. Rick had a father and mother who were both very much alive. But who the hell was Gina and what part did she play in this family drama? Every time one mystery about Rick got solved, another one raised its head.

♦ ♦ ♦

"'Do you know a student called Sam Erickson?'" asked Alex.

"'He's my study partner. We're working together on an assignment for class. Do you remember the DiMaggio murder case? It was never brought to trial because of a legal loophole.'"

"'Only too well,'" said Alex.

"'Sam thinks he's found an overlooked piece of testimony that could get it into court,'" said Rick, narrowing his eyes in concentration.

"That's wrong," Alex interjected, "your line's, 'back into court.' See?" Alex showed the typewritten script to Rick.

Alex and Rick were sitting out on the deck later that evening, Alex reluctantly having been pressed into reading in the other parts to help Rick learn the script for tomorrow.

"Okay." Rick quickly scanned the page, pushed it back at Alex and picked up the scene. "'Sam thinks he's found an overlooked piece of testimony that could get it *back* into court. He said on the phone he'd fill me in on it when I get to college next week.'"

"Mildred comes into the room and tidies Sally's clothes, which are messily strewn all over the bed." Alex flipped the page. "Then Mac says. 'Sam was found dead on campus this morning. He'd been strangled.'" Alex made a face. "Then Sally's line is, 'Mac, do you think it could have something to do with the DiMaggio case? If the killer finds out Bradley was working on the assignment with Sam, then he could be in danger too.'" Alex snorted and rolled his eyes at Rick, "Jeez, and Sally's meant to be the bright one."

"It's T.V., the writers have to spell everything out." Rick clicked his fingers at Alex. "Give me the end of that last line again."

Alex went back to the script. "...he could be in danger too.'"

"'Perhaps Sam's murder wasn't anything to do with the assignment?'"

"Sally says, 'But what if it was? Bradley, you'll stay here with us until Mac solves this case.'" Alex flipped the page. "Mildred and Mac exchange glances, neither of them over the moon about Sally's idea. Mac says, 'But Sally, solving this case could take a long time.' Sally holds Bradley's arm protectively and says, 'I promised Aunt June we'd look after Bradley.' Mac's line, 'A *very* long time.' Sally says, 'There's no question about it. Bradley's staying with us until we know he's safe. I don't have much family left and I'm not about to lose my only cousin.'"

Rick came in with his line and said warmly, "'Thanks Sally. Mac, you won't even notice I'm here. Promise.'"

"Mac exchanges a long-suffering look with Mildred and raises his eyes to heaven." Looking up from the script, Alex quipped, "I can identify with how Mac feels."

"Quit commenting and stick to reading the script!" said Rick tetchily. "Bradley has a line to Mildred next, right?"

"Yeah."

"'And guess what, Mildred? I'm giving you the night off. I'll cook dinner tonight.'"

"Mildred hangs up the last of Sally's dresses and says to Mac, 'Can you drop me at the jewelers on your way into town?' Sally asks, 'What for?' Mildred replies, 'I may look for some earrings to go with that diamond ring. If you leave the kitchen like you do your bedroom, it'll resemble a crime scene.' Mildred wags her finger at Bradley, 'Your bill's mounting up.' Mildred leaves the room. Bradley sits on the bed as the shock of Mac's news sinks in."

Rick focused on Alex, his blue eyes intensely boring into him. "'Sam's dead? I still can't believe it. When Professor Miller gave us this case to study I thought it was going to get us great grades.'"

Alex summoned up his solemnest voice and returned Rick's intense gaze. "'By the sound of things, it could get you killed.' Off on Sally and Mac looking at Bradley, all of them coming to the same conclusion, the killer could be coming for Bradley next. End of Act one."

"And cut," said Rick, breaking the tension.

"Want to do it again?"

"I've got it down. Thanks for running the lines."

"No problem," Alex went to blow out the flickering candles in a glass bowl on the deck.

"Leave them burning. I'll sit out a bit longer and get the scene really into my head. I need to think about my character more."

"Wish I could have been more help, but I've never seen the show."

"The way you read the script made that blatantly clear," said Rick with a laugh.

Alex shook his head and swept his hair from his face. "Hey, I'm an artist not an actor."

"You're lucky. You can paint a picture and not be present when everyone looks at it. I've got to act in front of people."

"You'll be fine. You're pretty good at acting." Alex wasn't lying. Rick conveyed the character well, he was likeable and had a gift for light comedy. "In fact, I was surprised how good."

"Gee, thanks! Did you think I was going to stink up the room?"

"I didn't mean it like that. It's the first time I've seen you doing what you do professionally."

"Acting, painting, sticking sea shells on driftwood. Weird things we do in the name of art. None of it's useful, is it? Not like being a firefighter or doing open heart surgery."

"Dunno. Firefighters and heart surgeons need something to look at after they finish work. We all need something to escape into or dream about."

"I suppose. But the kind of art you do, you know painting, takes more skill than what I do. You need technique and a mastery of the medium. Acting's more like telling a lie. You must make sure what you're doing or saying, however outrageous or nuts, has enough semblance of real life to be believable. If you push it too far or don't believe in it enough then *boom*, you've blown it and get caught in the lie."

"True. Okay, I'm off to bed. Don't stay up too late. Remember you need to be up bright and early and T.V. ready in the morning."

"Oh great, you've turned into my dad," said Rick with a grimace.

"I don't want Sid's wrath on my shoulders, they ache enough as it is." Alex went into the house.

"Night, Dex!" Rick called after him.

Alex scampered back onto the deck. "Night Ricky." Mimicking Sid's gruff voice, Alex roughly ruffled Rick's hair. "I love ya, kid."

"Fuck off and go to bed," snarled Rick, but with humor while batting Alex's hand away. "See you in the morning."

Alex snickered as he went upstairs. Why was winding Rick up so much fun!

A gentle peace descended on Sunset Cove. Slipping into bed, visions of the new work Alex planned to do tomorrow mixed with contemplation of his former pieces. Hopefully his past and future work would meld into an exciting new chapter in his growth as an artist. And with that, Alex lapsed into a whiskey induced slumber.

TROMPE L'OEIL

Over coffee at the kitchen table the next morning, Rick had cajoled Alex into doing a final run of the *McMillan* script before he left for the studio. "'Sam's dead? I still can't believe it.'" Rick said the line, his eyes holding a genuine sense of fear. "'When Professor Miller gave us this case to study I thought it was going to get us great grades ...'"

Alex was off the script for Commissioner McMillan's final line, "'By the sound of things, it could get you killed.'" He stared intensely at Rick. They held the scene for the imaginary camera zoom in leading to the act break, then they held the eye contact for an unnecessary beat longer. Alex broke away first, dropped the script on the table and pushed it to Rick. "You were *real* good this time. You were doing something with your voice. It sounded different." Alex got up from the table, ready to clear up the morning pots.

"Susan Saint James' voice has a slight husk. I figured if Bradley's her cousin there should be something to link them as a family. It's the first time we've met this character and there isn't much in the script to establish their relationship, so I thought I'd mimic her speech patterns."

"Why'd you make out you're not into this acting thing? You're good at it. A natural."

"What can I say? I'm screwed up." Rick stood up and ran his hands over his pants. "Would a law student wear these clothes?"

Alex turned from the sink and appraised Rick's khaki pants, deck shoes and button-down collar blue shirt. "Bradley's a disruptive element in the McMillan house. What you're wearing's very sensible. It'd help the character if you loosened the look, you know, more like a student."

Rick's eyes fell on Alex's frayed jeans. "I need your pants. Quick, take them off."

"Not so fast. I've more. Many, many more. Remember?" Alex darted upstairs. Within moments he was back in the kitchen. Rick had already stripped off his khakis and stood waiting in his skimpy briefs and socks. Alex handed over a pair of his ratty jeans. "Take off your socks too. The deck shoes are wrong."

Wriggling into Alex's old jeans, Rick asked, "What should I wear on my feet then?"

"Do these fit?" Alex slung over a pair of his beat-up wicker sandals from the pile by the back door.

Rick fastened the jeans' fly buttons then shoved his feet into the sandals. "Better?"

"Perfect student attire. You look ready to start campus unrest."

"Okay, here goes. See you later."

"Good ..."

Rick rushed up and clapped his hand over Alex's mouth to stop him finishing the sentence. "Never wish an actor good *you know what*!"

"You're superstitious?"

"No. Bye." Rick left the house.

Phew. Peace and quiet and no more running lines for some dumb T.V. show. All night long Alex had dreamed of doing en plein air studies of L.A. traffic and he was itching to get on with some work. He'd earmarked an intersection near Newport Beach for today's set up. The police would likely move him on for setting up camp there, so he'd have to work fast. En plein air work, however, was fast, he'd just have to work faster than the cops. Alex felt excitement building, he was going to be doing some *guerilla* painting!

The back door rattled. Rick burst in and tossed his keys angrily onto the counter. "My car won't start."

"For sure? Let me take a look."

"There's no point! Something's really wrong with it. It's not like last time."

"You mean there wasn't something really wrong with it then?"

"Back then it was overheated. This is different. It won't turn over at all. I'll call William Morris to say I can't make the casting." Rick strode to the phone.

"Wait." Alex tossed the Chevy's key to Rick. "Here!"

Instinctively, Rick swung around and made a good catch.

"Mine's back from the shop and running like a dream. Take it."

Rick toyed with the keys, his expression unreadable. "Thanks."

"Goodbye. And good ... *you know what*." Alex hustled Rick out of the back door, giving him a jokey kick in the pants to send him on his way.

This meant a change of plan for his painting day, but even without his car he could still trek up the hill and set his easel up by the highway to experiment with the traffic idea. He was preparing his paint box ready to leave, when the door creaked open again.

"It's a stick shift! Your car's a stick shift," gasped Rick with annoyance.

Alex shrugged. "And?"

"I can't drive a stick! This reading just isn't meant to be. I'm calling to cancel." Rick went to the phone.

Alex tussled with himself. Was Rick finding excuses to blow out the reading? He didn't want Sid's blame to fall on him if Rick was a no-show. Okay, he'd just have to write off painting for today. "No problem!"

With phone in hand about to dial, Rick replied, "What's not a problem?"

"I'll drive you."

"But ..." Rick's mouth moved but no words came out as he struggled to find another excuse.

"It's eleven. You need to be there at two." Alex slipped his billfold into the back pocket of his jeans. "Which means we'd better get going. Let's roll." Rick put down the phone. With a resigned expression, he trailed Alex to the Chevy.

The drive to Universal was silent for the first hour. They were making good time on the 405 when Rick blurted out, "Take Sunset and Laurel."

"I was going to join the 101 over the hills. We could get stuck in traffic on Laurel. It's twelve fifteen and you need to be there at two."

"I want to go via Laurel. If I was driving, that's the way I'd go."

Was Rick trying to be late? "You're the boss," said Alex taking the right lane. Beige concrete walls rose at their sides as they came off the highway. Alex drove up Sepulveda and swung right onto Sunset. The greenery and undulating bends did make a nice change from the highway's monotony. The banks beside the road grew lusher and higher as Bel Air rose on their left. The traffic clogged around North Canon. Once they'd passed that snarl, the road cleared and the landscape grew more mundane. Billboards of new movies jostled with dealership signs above sprawling lots of dusty used cars. It was just after one when Alex turned into Laurel Canyon. After they'd twisted and turned through the hills, Alex hung a right into Studio City.

"We need Gate 2 off Lankershim," said Rick.

"You need to guide me. This is alien territory." Alex hadn't been to the Valley for years, but why would anyone go there unless they had to? Rick barked directions. After some last-minute lane switching and a couple of terse interchanges, Universal's yellow lettering appeared above the entrance gate. Tan mountains dotted with green rose in the distance behind the soundstages. Alex pulled up in front of a security booth set into the black railings.

A uniformed guard ambled up to the car and leaned into the driver's window. "Can I help you guys?"

Alex noted the guard's attitude. It was evident the man thought they'd taken a wrong turn or were up to no good. But before Alex could respond, Rick spoke across him. "I'm Rick Stradman. I've an appointment with Mr. Epstein."

The guard pondered a few seconds before he said, "Wait here." He ambled back to the gate house and fished out a clip board. Ambling back to the car, while running his pen down the list, he peered into Alex's open window. "What was that name again?"

"Stradman," said Rick across Alex, with a 'don't you know who I am' tone to his voice. "Rick Stradman."

"Got ya." The guard squinted at Alex, then directed his attention back to Rick. "I only got one name on the list. Nothing about a guest."

Rick fixed the guard with an icy stare. "He's my chauffeur."

The guard tipped his cap back on his head. "He don't look like no chauffeur."

"His uniform's at the cleaners," responded Rick tartly.

"Along with his limousine?"

Rick glanced at his watch. "My appointment *is* at two."

Considering his options, the guard responded, "I need to make a call. Stay there." He retreated to the gatehouse.

Alex folded his arms and gave Rick a sidelong glance. "Chauffeur?"

"I was improvising."

"Other choices may have included assistant, neighbor, brother ..."

"Put a sock in it, he's coming back," snapped Rick.

The guard leaned in and addressed Alex, "Take a right. You want the M.C.A. Building. Can't miss it, it's the big black tower. Parking's right beside it. Drive slow, give way to pedestrians, buggies and studio trams." He handed a personal pass for Alex and a parking pass through the window. "Keep this on you. Stick the other one on your windshield. Have a great day." The guard went back to his booth and raised the barrier.

Alex drove onto the Universal lot. His dirty green Chevy stuck out like a sore thumb among the studio's smart automobiles and white buggies. He found a space in the lot beside the black tower and killed the engine.

"You want to come in with me?" asked Rick getting out of the car.

"Nah, I'll hang out here. Stretch my legs," said Alex. If he felt they'd attracted attention in the car then they pulled even more focus after getting out of it. Both of them were in faded ripped jeans and sandals. Alex had on the black tee and paint stained neck rag ready for his painting adventure. A smartly dressed executive on the way to his Lincoln recoiled at the sight of them and swiftly switched his attaché case to his other side.

"Don't make any sudden moves," warned Rick darkly, "the guards may be armed."

Alex guessed Rick was joking but wouldn't like to put it to the test. Once he'd seen Rick actually go into the black tower, thus removing any possibility he'd find some reason to back out of the reading, Alex wandered off the parking lot. Never having set foot in a movie studio before it became clear that the real thing was very different to how movie studios are portrayed in movies. There were no Roman Centurions on bicycles or showgirls in feathers to provide background color. There was no razzmatazz, just the industrial buzz of carpenters and electricians at work, punctuated by an occasional golf cart or studio tram trundling between the stages. Alex wandered aimlessly, engaged by the contrasting visuals of the drab concrete stages against the clear blue sky.

Turning a corner, he was startled to come face to face with a couple in torn clothing covered with dust. The woman had blood streaks down her face and the man had a bandage around his head. She was smoking a cigarette and leaning on Stage 12's sidewall while chatting to the man.

Alex's shocked expression caught the woman's eye. "Tough day at the office," she said to him with a chuckle between puffs on her cigarette.

The man patted his head wound. "Hope I don't heal before they finish the shot."

"Looks nasty," said Alex pausing from his walk. Make-up and wardrobe had done an excellent job on these two, they looked exactly like they'd been involved in a nasty accident. "Guess you guys aren't working on a musical."

"Don't make 'em anymore," said the woman with a rueful smile while stubbing out her cigarette. "The movies are all death and disaster these days."

"Planes crashing, ships sinking, buildings burning, burning planes crashing into burning buildings. You name it, they're doing it." The man jerked his head at the stage. "This movie's about an earthquake hitting L.A. The big one. Kind of sick considering we live here, but what the hell, it pays the bills."

The woman took in Alex's outfit and hair. "What picture are you working on?"

Alex realized she'd mistaken his clothes for a costume. "I'm not. I'm just looking around."

"This part of the lot's off limits if you're not on a tram." The woman's attitude cooled and she shifted uncomfortably.

"It's okay. See?" Alex flipped out his studio pass and showed it to them. It was a bit rich having to explain himself to two people who out on the street would be taken directly to the Emergency Room, but he didn't want to cause trouble.

"Can't be too careful." The woman relaxed and added, "Too many kooks and weirdos around these days."

"Is there some place I can get a cup of coffee?" asked Alex, relieved they weren't about to call security.

The woman pointed and said, "Commissary's just across from the black tower."

Alex excused himself from the bloodied couple and wandered back. He'd hit the no man's land between lunch and dinner and so the commissary was pretty empty. He bought a coffee, swilled it down and headed back just in time to bump into Rick coming out of the black tower. "Hi. How'd it go?" Alex asked with sincere interest.

Rick's face was a mask of pure thunder. "They liked me! They really liked me," he spat as he stomped towards the car.

"How awful," said Alex following him. "I can understand why you appear so devastated." As usual, Rick's reactions followed no discernable logic.

"Their office is on this side of the building." Rick glanced reproachfully up at the black tower. "They saw a beat-up car pull up and a couple of hippies get out. They were about to call security when they realized I was one of them. They had a good old chuckle about that. We read the scene and they went off for a conference. After they came back and gave me a few notes, they got me to read the scene again and were all smiles. They liked my *free spirit* and *rebellious* nature. I've got the sinking feeling they're going to make an offer." Rick got in the car and slammed the door.

"And that's bad because ...?" said Alex getting in the driver's side.

"Because I'll have to take it! How can I tell dad they made me an offer and I turned it down?"

"Why didn't you do a bad audition if you don't want to get the job?"

Rick began to chew the edge of his nail but stopped himself. "I didn't want to not get the part because I was bad. I just wanted to not get it because I wasn't right."

"Before we set off you were thinking about how your character should talk and look. You've been learning your dialog from the moment you got the script. You could've made yourself, how can I put this? Less right."

"Knock it off. I don't need the third degree. There's only one thing can take away this feeling of overwhelming doom."

"Booze, drugs?"

"Shopping. I need to go to Rodeo Drive."

Alex shot him a look.

"Please, just for an hour," said Rick cajolingly.

Reluctantly, Alex started the car and retraced their journey through Laurel Canyon. Once he'd hit Beverly Hills it was a simple turn from Sunset onto Rodeo Drive. They cruised past low white stucco buildings with store names like Gucci, Vidal Sassoon, and Van Cleef and Arpels. The names meant nothing to Alex, but they clearly catered to the very wealthy judging by the glossy people strolling down the palm lined street. Rich people didn't appear terribly happy though, they wore dissatisfied expressions which made spending wads of cash appear to be a tiresome chore.

Once in sight of the Beverly Wilshire Hotel, Rick murmured, "Giorgio."

Alex cocked an eyebrow. "A message from the other side?"

"There's a parking space. Quick, don't let anyone steal it!" Rick pointed at a maroon Chrysler Imperial pulling out on Dayton Way. Following orders, Alex rapidly hung a left and maneuvered into the freshly vacated spot. Rick only had large bills but fortunately Alex had a few nickels in his pocket to feed the meter.

Giorgio's yellow and white striped awnings shaded the store's windows from the late afternoon sun. They walked through the front doors and were enveloped by the heady scent of money changing hands. Rick's energy had been low but entering the store charged him with excitement. While running his hand along a rail of soft, understated clothes, Rick said, "Alex, you should have a tuxedo."

"Excuse me?" asked Alex, his eyes widening.

"No honestly, Alex. If you go to any evening functions you'll need to dress well. New conservatism's the name of the game. The Giorgio tuxedos are incredible. All the movie stars and executives wear them."

"I'm neither of those things," said Alex. "And the only evening function I'm likely to attend is last orders at the Beachcomber."

Rick wasn't in any mood to let logic intervene. "They're wool and mohair with satin lapels," said Rick beckoning a sales assistant.

A striking woman with chiseled cheekbones and maroon bobbed hair raised her eyes. She beamed when she recognized Rick and stalked over. "Mr. Stradman, how nice to see you again. We thought you'd left for the East." The saleswoman appeared genuinely pleased to see him. Most likely an out of work actress putting her thespian skills to good use. "May I show you something?"

"A tuxedo for the gentleman." Rick motioned towards Alex.

The woman looked Alex up and down. Although he was in torn jeans and tee she didn't bat an eyelid other than to determine his size. "Let me find you a forty-two." The saleswoman ran a long red nail along the rail, then selected a garment. "Would you care to slip it on, sir?" She took the jacket off the hanger and fluffed it out behind Alex.

Alex hesitated. "I really don't want a tuxedo ..."

"Let's see how it looks on." Rick was not letting go of this.

With a weary expression, Alex relented. Moments later he stood resplendent in wool and mohair with satin lapels. Never in his life had he worn something like this. Checking himself out in the mirror, he had to admit the tuxedo jacket looked sensational. Over his tee, neck rag and tattered jeans, its sophisticated tailoring was fucking cool. Straitening his posture, Alex noticed various other customers glancing over. He experienced a thrill he'd never felt before. The thrill of being admired.

Rick studied him with his x-ray eyes. "Wow, you look the part, Alex."

"Oh, yes sir. Truly handsome," said the saleswoman vigorously agreeing with Rick.

"I'd buy anything from you dressed like that," said Rick.

"Terrific, I'll get a job as a used car salesman," said Alex. He had to nip this ego inflation in the bud and get out of the store before he got used to feeling like a pin-up boy. It was too late, however, Rick had found his feet. With the saleswoman in tow, Rick propelled them through the store selecting other items for Alex despite his increasing protestations. A pair of butter soft suede trousers and a sleek black silk shirt were added to the cache. When Rick chose a white tailored linen jacket for him, Alex drew the line with a definite "NO!" The only occasion he'd possibly wear such an item would be selling ice creams on the boardwalk. Playing Rick's Ken doll was a debilitating experience, so Alex extricated himself and sidled off to the store's Oak Bar. Now having a bar in a store was a terrific idea, these rich folks had got one thing right at least. Alex hopped on a stool and grabbed a beer. After another thirty minutes of aerobic shopping Rick finally got the shopping bug out of his system and wound up at the cash desk. As assistants rustled tissue paper around his purchases, Rick charged them to Sid's account. Amidst a flurry of goodbyes and genuflections from the sales team, a dashing male assistant helped them across the road with the bags. This assistant didn't bat an eyelid at Alex's ramshackle automobile either, even shooting Alex a cheeky wink as he slammed the trunk. These guys apparently never judged anyone other than by the color of their money. As Alex maneuvered out of the parking space Rick told him a funny story. The wife of a big-time producer had her credit card stolen, but the husband didn't report it. Why? Because the thief spent less than she did.

They were heading back to Sunset Cove when Rick gasped. "Shit. I need to phone Mike. I should have made the call back at the store. You hungry?"

"Kind of," said Alex.

"Go back up to Sunset," commanded Rick. At the top of North Rodeo, Rick issued further directions. "The entrance is over there on the corner."

"The Beverly Hills Hotel?"

"The Polo Lounge has phones at the table. Here, now. Turn now!"

Alex swung into a palm and foliage line driveway. A pink palace of a building with a solid green facade bearing the hotel's name in white script appeared ahead. A parking valet approached and opened the driver's door. "I'll take that for you, sir," said the valet. Alex put on the brake but left the motor running as he got out. The valet slipped behind the wheel, giving a cursory glance over the controls.

"You have to jiggle it into second," said Alex helpfully.

The valet smiled. "No problem. My grandfather has one like it."

Thanks, thought Alex, nice to have his car made to sound like a museum piece. By the time the valet had handed Alex his claim tag, Rick was already marching up the red carpet shaded by a green and white striped canopy. Feeling like he was about to set foot on Mars, Alex followed Rick into the hotel.

Although the Polo Lounge was casual their rough jeans and sandals were a bit *too* casual. Rick knew the Maître D' and, after exchanging a few discrete words, surreptitiously slipped him a couple of bills. Moments later a waiter had magicked up a sports jacket to cover Alex's paint stained t-shirt. The Maître D' came back and ushered them into a dark green booth. Another waiter passed them menus and flapped open a large napkin which he used to discretely cover what was still visible of Alex's jeans.

"Get me a phone," said Rick to the waiter, "and a martini."

"For sir?" The waiter dipped his head to Alex.

"What's the time?" asked Alex, unable to see the sun and judge the time.

"A quarter after five, sir," replied the waiter.

"Make that two martinis, please." After the waiter had gone, Alex took out his cigarettes and said to Rick, "Swanky place yet no martini bell. The Beachcomber ranks superior on that front."

"And no Janet to ring it."

"Julie," corrected Alex.

"Sir." A bellman arrived with a pink phone on a silver tray. He placed the phone on the table, then plugged it into a socket beside the table.

Rick picked up the phone and said, "Give me an outside line."

Alex fished a book of matches out of a bowl on the table. He lit up and relaxed into the leather booth. He'd fallen down a very odd rabbit hole. Here he was in a borrowed sports coat at The Beverly Hills Hotel drinking twenty-dollar martinis all because Rick needed to make a phone call.

It took a couple of minutes for Rick to get through. "Hi SuAnne, Rick Stradman here. I need to speak to Mike, he still in the office? I'll hold." The waiter placed a couple of pink coasters on the dark green table cloth and set the martinis on them. Rick swirled the olive on a cocktail stick and took a gulp. He quickly put down the glass. "Mike, hi. Yes, it's Rick. Yes, much better thanks. I made the reading okay. Have you heard anything back?"

Alex sipped his drink and watched Rick's face as he listened to Mike on the other end. Rick was deep in concentration, thoughts rippling across his face like tremors before a quake.

"Fine. I'll wait to hear. Maybe they will go another way. Thanks." Still deep in thought, Rick hung up.

"So?" Alex prompted Rick.

Rick leaned back in the booth. "There's someone else in the running for my part. A *big name*. But they're keen on having a major guest star for Professor Miller."

"Is that good or bad?"

"Depends on your point of view. They don't have a huge budget and big name's cost big bucks. I'm not well known so I'm a cheaper option. And they just found out Saint James is pregnant again. Mike thinks they could get the Bradley character to recur and slot him into scripts if she can't work due to the pregnancy. His character's similar to hers, so they could pass the over dialogue without too much re-writing. If that's the case a big name wouldn't be a good choice as they wouldn't want to commit to multiple episodes for not a huge fee."

"Sounds like it could be a big break for you." Alex rested his cigarette on the ashtray and took a drink. Damn, that was some fine martini! Maybe money can't buy happiness but it sure could buy a great martini.

"God, if they offer it to me I'll have to do it. Let's hope they go for the *big name*."

Alex picked up his cigarette and thought about Rick while he inhaled. Then he said, "You've got the possibility of a part in a major T.V. show, yet it feels like you'd rather hang out in a backwater like Sunset Cove kicking your heels. Are you for real?"

Rick swirled the olive around his martini. "I'm an okay actor but I'm not a great actor. Remember what Scotty said? I couldn't even get the accent right in *Eddie's Girls*. I don't think I'll ever be as good at anything as I'd like to be." He bit the olive off the stick and signaled to a waiter they were ready to order food.

"Scotty's not right about everything," said Alex. "And you have to keep doing things to get better at them. I don't know anything about the T.V. industry but these people wouldn't be considering you for the job if they didn't think you were any good, would they?"

"You forget my novelty value. Surely Scotty filled you in on momma? I'm the son of the woman who scorned Hollywood. That could get them some column inches. And then there's dad, the producer of some of Hollywood's crummiest high grossing movies. That's a talking point too. You see, I never know if people want me for myself or my provenance." Rick smiled. "That's why I like you. You don't have the slightest interest in any of that shit."

"Sorry to keep you, sirs. What may I get you?" asked the waiter arriving at their table.

Suddenly realizing that they hadn't eaten all day, Rick and Alex got down to the serious business of ordering food and another round of drinks.

After a relaxed dinner at the Polo Lounge they enjoyed a chilled drive to Sunset Cove. Back inside the beach house, Alex flicked through the mail as Rick tried to hand him the two Giorgio Beverly Hills carrier bags. "It was wrong of me to play along with your game this afternoon," said Alex pushing them back. "I'd need to sell a hundred paintings to repay you. And I'll never wear those clothes. What possible event would I wear them to? Take them back and get a refund."

"This is a gift for helping me out today. I'm putting them in your room and will not let you refuse." Rick took the bags up to Alex's room.

Well, just putting them upstairs didn't mean they had to stay there, thought Alex as he carried on sorting the mail. Bills, bills, letter from pop, well that could go straight to the trash, Book of the Month junk, and finally a glossy envelope addressed to Rick. A few moments later, Rick came downstairs. "Something for you," said Alex flipping the envelope to him.

Rick tore open the envelope and took out a card. He grinned knowingly. "What possible event would you need something smart to wear to, you ask me?" Rick handed the card to Alex, "Invitation to the Jerry Weir showing at the Koenig Gallery."

"For you?"

"For us."

"Us?" asked Alex, unsure how he felt about being an 'us'. "How come?"

"Because I rang the gallery and left a message asking for one. Koenig's wanted momma to attend his openings for years."

"I didn't think she was in the country?"

"She's not, but Koenig doesn't know that."

This didn't sit well with Alex. It was only the other night Scotty had brought up Koenig's name and now here was an invitation from him in the mail. "You asked Koenig for the invitation? When?"

"Last week."

"So when you were quizzing Scotty about important galleries, you'd already asked for this?"

"I needed to check where Scotty placed Koenig in the table of importance and she put him right at the top. Bingo!" Rick waved the invitation triumphantly. "Good contact, huh?"

"Was that why you were so keen to accept Scotty's dinner invitation? To validate the strength of your contacts?"

"Why am I the bad guy in this? Didn't you say Scotty only invited me in the hope of ingratiating herself with my mother?"

A sick, manipulated feeling rose in the pit of Alex's stomach. Had Rick faked the car problem? And then made up an excuse about not being able to drive a stick shift to lure him into offering the ride to Universal that in turn led to the shopping trip? Had today been part of a deception to 'change his image' ready for this social event? Alex tossed down the invitation. "Seems you got my career plan under control. Want to try painting for me too?"

"Momma's a millstone around my neck, but if people who hold her in esteem can further your career is it so wrong of me to ask?"

"I'm an artist!" shouted Alex angrily. "Not some brand of soap being advertised in the commercials on a T.V. show!"

"You paint pictures. Good pictures. But you paint them in a backwater people only come to by mistake! Who the hell's going to see your work if you don't promote yourself? You've been good to me. I wanted to do something to help you. I believe in you as an artist and I want other people to see how good you are." Rick's mouth set into a hard line as he looked away and said bitterly, "But if that's how you feel I'll call and cancel."

Alex processed what Rick had just said. If he removed his suspicion that Rick had made up the car problem then Rick hadn't been manipulative, all he'd done was ask for an invitation from a family friend. That wasn't such a bad thing, was it? "Jerry Weir?" Alex reached for the invitation.

Rick grudgingly handed it to him.

"I've met Jerry a couple of times. Hank knows him. He's good."

"You'll be supporting a fellow artist. Isn't that what it's all about, the L.A. art community?" asked Rick, his composed tone accentuating Alex's sudden hysteria.

Letting his anger subside, Alex considered the situation realistically. Maybe he did need to start making new connections? "Okay, I'll go with you. But make this the last time you use your family connections on my behalf. I'm uncomfortable with it, however well intended."

"I promise not to intrude, interfere or direct you again. Cross my heart and hope to die."

"Good, thanks."

"Now don't take this the wrong way, but we need to do something about your hair."

"My hair?" Alex dragged his hand through its matted density.

"You look like the wild man of Borneo! Can I get someone to have a look at it? Please?"

"I guess so," said Alex. He had to admit his hair did need more attention than his infrequent chopping of it with the kitchen scissors. "But I won't have it cut short, no way."

"Of course not short, just tidied." Rick poured himself a glass of water. "I'm off to bed." Before going into his room, he looked back and said, "I'd never intentionally upset you, please believe that." Then Rick went into his room and closed his door.

Alex lingered in the kitchen. Dangling on the hook by the back door, the keys of Rick's Merc caught his eye. The red mist of suspicion overwhelmed him. Quietly, ever so quietly, Alex lifted the keys off the hook. To avoid any creaks he carefully opened the back door and stealthily walked to the lot in the dunes. After furtively glancing over his shoulder, to check Rick hadn't heard the door and followed him out, Alex unlocked the Mercedes. He got in the driver's seat and put the key in the ignition. If the car started it meant Rick had been lying and today had been one huge manipulation. If that was the case it would mean the end of everything between them and, damn the consequences, he'd throw Rick out on his ear without further ado. Feeling his anger rising, thinking every bad thought in the world about Rick, Alex turned the key.

PENTIMENTO

Nothing.

Alex turned the key again. Still nothing.

The Merc was as dead as the proverbial Dodo. Rick hadn't lied and hadn't made a fool out of him. The rising anger that had been thumping in Alex's ears dissipated. Guilt overwhelmed him for having harbored such mistrust and getting so wound up over nothing, mere suspicion. He got out of the Merc, locked it, and slipped back into the house. He'd only just hung Rick's car keys back on the hook, and was closing the door, when Rick came out of the bathroom.

"I heard you go out. What did you go for?" asked Rick.

Covering his momentary flinch, Alex dug in his pocket then waved his cigarettes. "Left them in the car."

"Oh," Rick stared at the counter. "But you've got two more packs in the house."

"I didn't want to break into a fresh one."

"Okay. Night then." Rick went to his room and sharply closed the door.

Alex was relieved that Rick hadn't seen him hanging up the Merc's keys, but then he noticed they were still swaying slightly on the hook. He wondered if Rick had spotted that. The suspicion Rick had been lying had made him angry, but now he was being deceitful to Rick. It wasn't a good feeling. Alex opened the bourbon and poured a generous slug. Taking his drink up to his room, he considered the Giorgio carrier bags Rick had deposited on his unmade bed. Certain now that he'd actually come to Rick's rescue today, he decided he could accept Rick's extravagant gesture of thanks. Looking around his room, Alex realized it was a shambolic mess. Worn out pants, t-shirts, boxers and board shorts were strewn across the credenza and floor. This wasn't a grown man's room, it looked like a teenager's.

Alex opened the carrier bags. He'd never had nice clothes before. They'd been wrapped with reverence at the store, that promoted his care in hanging them up. Dora's brown wood wardrobe, which she used to call her chifforobe, still had her sturdy wooden hangers rattling around inside. He used them to hang the tuxedo, the silk shirt, and the suede trousers. He found a further item in the second bag. Unwrapping the tissue, he discovered it was the white linen jacket; Rick had ignored his protestations and bought it for him anyway. Actually, if studying the jacket like a piece of art, its pristine lines were beautiful. Although he'd never wear it in a million years, Alex hung it up. His fine new clothes hanging neatly in the wardrobe compelled Alex to tidy the rest of the room. Between slugs of whiskey, he folded t-shirts, organized underwear and shorts in the chifforobe's drawers, picked up everything off the floor and threw worn out stuff to go to the trash. He smoothed the sheets and made his bed, folding neat tucks in the corners as Dora had taught him. Stepping back, he admired how he'd overpainted the mess in his room with order.

With that thought in his mind, what Rick had said about his hair struck him. He couldn't recall the last time it had been cut professionally. His long hair was a badge of honor, an overt rejection of conventional society's standards, a declaration of freedom from the stifling confines of that cramped house in Dayton and pop's oppressive presence. His long hair was his ultimate finger in pop's eye. Wiping dust off the credenza's mirror, Alex took stock of his face. Fine lines were multiplying around his eyes, his formerly shiny skin was rough and flaking, his jawline's firmness starting to sag. Yep, age was catching up with him.

Facing his reflection, Alex also faced the fact that life doesn't last forever and isn't full of endless possibilities. Earning money to support yourself, paying your taxes, getting a sense of satisfaction from tidiness, cutting your hair - all part of growing up. Alex figured it kind of sucked but knew he had to conform to some societal norms if he wanted to make something of himself. He shut the chifforobe's doors, took the bags of trash downstairs and began to formulate a plan for the next stage of his life.

♦ ♦ ♦

Rick had called Miguel to come take a look at his Merc. Miguel had discovered a small leak on the radiator hose, which explained the overheating when he'd first come to the beach. Over time the leak had shorted out an electrical circuit, that was why it wouldn't start the other morning. Miguel quickly repaired the fault.

Rick being independently mobile again was a blessing to Alex, unless he happened to be in the passenger seat. The golden hues of dusk filtered through the smog on La Cienega as Rick turned the Mercedes into the narrow alley beside the Koenig Gallery. Rick spun the wheel while Alex sat white knuckled in the passenger seat. The alley was at a sharp right angle and Rick came within a whisker of scraping his offside wing. Alex summoned all his restraint not to comment. Luckily, he'd had practice at restraint earlier in the day.

Rick had booked him into the Vidal Sassoon on Rodeo Drive to sort out his hair. Jeez, talk about feeling like a pampered pooch - the place was ever so rinty-tinty. The staff, however, had been polite and professional and obviously knew their stuff. The head stylist, while doing the initial consultation, hadn't even telegraphed his shock on attempting to run a comb through Alex's matted locks. "Fine head of hair, sir," was his only comment before dispatching Alex to the shampoo girl. She'd taken her time with the first shampoo and used the second to untangle his hair with a wide tooth comb – which was a challenge. She'd finished with a deep conditioning treatment, left on for a generous half hour. Back in the chair, Alex had been impressed by the stylist's precision, he even asked Alex to uncross his legs as it threw off the balance of the line while he was cutting. Alex felt comfortable because this smacked of art. The stylist did exactly as Rick had instructed, took off four inches of split ends and levelled everything to below chin length with an impressive edge. There was no messing about with product or finishing, Alex simply swept his hand smoothly through his hair and it fell back into place.

After he'd got up from the chair, Alex experienced that new feeling again. The girl in the yellow mini skirt and white go-go boots, the woman in the purple two-piece, the bearded guy in the beige turtle neck - all heads turned his way. People were looking at *him* and they liked what they saw, their expressions revealing a mix of interest and desire. Alex had thanked the stylist and strode back to reception to find Rick flicking through a glossy magazine. As a gesture to Rick's generosity, and from the guilt of misjudging him, Alex had put on the suede trousers Rick bought him. He'd tempered their butter soft richness by pairing them with an orange tie dye tank and denim jacket. The receptionist reclaimed his denim jacket while Rick had paid the bill. Alex shuddered to think what his Barney's buddies would think if they saw him stepping onto the sidewalk from Sassoon's with glistening hair. But then again, Hank and Scoop were unlikely to be taking a mid-afternoon stroll on Rodeo Drive.

Alex maintained his tight-lipped restraint in the car as Rick performed numerous irritating maneuvers to park behind the Koenig Gallery. Breathing a sigh of relief once Rick had finally lined up in the space, Alex got out. He paused, waiting for Rick to lock the car, then they edged through the lot back onto La Cienega. A discrete sign by the gallery's front door, simply read *KOENIG* in black letters. Alex swung open the tinted glass door and heard the hum of conversation and clinking glasses. He stepped back, holding the door for Rick to go in first, but Rick demurred and held the door for him. An unsmiling blonde girl in black polo neck and mini-skirt greeted them. Although 'greet' was a generous term. She stared blankly at Alex and asked, "Name?" Alex was about to give his own name, then remembered Rick had asked for the invitation and said, "Stradman."

The girl checked her list and handed over two catalogs. "Go through." The girl switched her attention to an older woman in a long plaid taffeta dress and short fur jacket.

Alex and Rick entered the throbbing gallery. Vivid matrons in expensive primary colors mingled with undernourished guys in thrift shop neutrals. Everyone had a drink in their hand and was talking. Accepting a glass from a passing tray, Alex went to take a close look at Jerry's work. The exhibition was titled *Burn* and consisted of charcoal sketches, all created using charcoal from trees destroyed in the Kitchen Creek Fire. Alongside the charcoal studies, Jerry had also used fumage to create a further twenty pieces. Fumage being the technique of using flame to burn an image out of the paper. The fumage studies of the wildlife killed in the fire were poignant; there was something of the phoenix in using fire to create an image of a creature fire had destroyed. Alex was engrossed in Jerry's work and lost track of Rick. Draining his glass and looking for a passing tray, Alex came face to face with Scotty.

"Alex? What are doing here" said Scotty stepping back in surprise.

Shaking his newly pliant hair off his face, Alex said casually, "Rick got invited."

Scotty looked Alex up and down, her eyes taking in his glossy locks and suede pants. Turning her attention back to Jerry's picture, she said, "Nice work."

"Yeah. Very fine." Alex looked in the same direction as Scotty, although neither were focused on the picture.

"I'm sorry about the dinner party the other night," said Scotty without looking at him.

"Yes, it was disturbing. But you couldn't help the house across the road being burglarized," said Alex.

Rick suddenly re-appeared beside Alex. "Is this exhibition called money to burn?" he asked archly while taking a sip of wine. Looking to Alex for a response, Scotty entered his eye line. There was a moment in freefall as Rick and Scotty noted each other's presence.

"Oh, thank God." Scotty broke the tension by reaching out to Rick. "Thank goodness to see some real friends here!" Before Rick could respond, Scotty recognized a face in the crowd. "There's June Felsen, she never stays long. Excuse me, I must quickly say hi before she dashes off." Scotty made a bee line for a woman with highly arched eyebrows wearing a paisley shawl fastened with a dramatic pin on the shoulder.

"Thought I'd lost you," murmured Alex to Rick.

"What a surprise to see Scotty here," said Rick fanning himself with a catalog.

"I'm sure she's equally surprised," said Alex, "considering you gave her the impression you knew no-one in the L.A. art world."

"Oh, I see him, that's Koenig," said Rick, ignoring Alex's comment and locking onto his target - a tall man with slicked back hair and studious glasses. "Follow me." Rick shouldered his way through the room with Alex trailing at a suitable distance. Waiting for a pause in the conversation, Rick hovered behind the man's shoulder. At an opportune moment, Rick cut in and said, "Walter?"

Koenig took a beat before turning. His irritated expression changed to delight upon seeing Rick. "Excuse me," Koenig made his apologies to the men he'd been conversing with. "Ricardo! Ciao, bello," Koenig grabbed Rick's shoulders and greeted him with a kiss on both cheeks. "Where's Luisa?"

Rick averted his eyes. "You know momma, something came up."

"What a shame. Nevertheless, it's delightful seeing you after so long. When was the last time we met? Was it Florence?"

Rick wrinkled his nose in thought. "Verona. The opera gala at the arena."

Koenig nodded. "Ah yes, that rather dull Nabucco. Well, thank you for coming. I hope you tell Luisa about Jerry's work. I know she has an insatiable passion for new talent."

"Of course, I'll spread the word," said Rick. Noticing Koenig was becoming restive, Rick quickly added, "Speaking of new talent, may I introduce a friend of mine, Alex Morgan."

Taking Rick's cue, Alex extended his hand.

"Walter Koenig." Koenig shook Alex's hand. "So, Alex, you from L.A. or Italy?"

"L.A.," answered Alex.

"And how do you know Ricardo?" asked Koenig glancing away to the side.

Rick answered, "I'm renting Alex's beach house at Sunset Cove for the summer"

"Ah, summer on the beach. What fun, although I'll leave the surfing to you youngsters." Smiling at Alex, Koenig said, "You have a house on the beach, then?"

"It was my grandmother's."

Koenig got a faraway look. "Must be wonderful having nothing to do all day."

Alex resisted laughing. Despite expensive clothes and hair styling, Koenig still instantly had him pegged as a beach bum.

Rick zeroed in on Koenig. "Alex is an artist."

Koenig asked Alex, with a hint of challenge, "Will I have seen your work anywhere?"

"It's not likely," said Alex honestly.

"Alex is a very fine plein air artist," Rick popped in.

Koenig's eyes glazed behind his spectacles. "The landscapes can be very picturesque along the coast."

Escape seemed to be on Koenig's agenda and Alex's mind raced. One of the biggest gallery owners in L.A. was about to indelibly stamp him as a beach bum who painted tacky sunsets, he had to do something to change that. Alex fixed Koenig squarely in the eye and said, "I'm currently experimenting with the plein air technique for urban studies. I mean, why can't there be beauty in an intersection or an off ramp? Why's a sunset intrinsically more beautiful than a traffic jam or abandoned building? There can be beauty in dereliction, don't you think?"

Koenig's interest was piqued, and he asked, "How's it going?"

Alex averted his eyes. "Excellent."

"Kudos if you pull it off," said Koenig.

"Walter!" Scotty scurried up to them. "Sorry to run off like that," she said to Rick, re-establishing herself as part of their group. "June thinks they've found space at Century City for the Institute. Isn't that wonderful?" Scotty directed that to Koenig.

"We'll see," said Koenig cryptically. "It's nice to see you, dear. I hope Guy LaFonte gives you the support you need and deserve. The wonderful thing about art is always the chance for progression." Koenig stepped back, ready to move on, and said to Rick, "I'm sorry your mother didn't make it. Give her my regards." Then he said to Alex, "Your work sounds interesting. Anytime you're passing, bring something in for me to see."

Scotty watched Koenig blend into the art lovers. "That was a little damning with faint praise, don't you think? What did he mean the 'support I need'?" asked Scotty as she sipped her red wine. Then, turning to Rick, she said, "What a small world. So Walter knows your mother? Has she some connection to the art world?"

Rick held up his hands to Scotty in surrender. "Luisa D'Onofrio's my mother. She's not dead. In fact, quite the opposite. The moment we met I sensed you knew who I was and therefore who she is. I played a silly game the other night. It was unfair and rude of me. I hope you and Bob forgive me. Alex, I shouldn't have lied to you about her in the first place. I apologize unreservedly to you both." Rick placed his hand on his heart and bowed his head.

Scotty waved Rick's apology aside. "I wasn't exactly subtle in my questioning about Venice and that other stuff. And as for you butterfingers, you owe me one plaster cast," Scotty said jokingly to Alex.

Now it was all in the open, Alex wondered how long it would be before Scotty was angling for a meeting with Luisa. Alex was pondering this when a vision in puce chiffon swept towards them.

"Who's she?" hissed Rick to Scotty.

"Monica Aigner. Big collector, deep pockets," Scotty hissed back.

"Scotty!" boomed Monica giving her an air kiss. "How delightful to see you."

"Monica, lovely as always," said Scotty after returning the air kiss.

"One tries. You and Bob were sorely missed at my fundraiser for the new wing. I'll simply not let you turn down my next invitation." Monica stroked the chiffon cladding her bust. "Jerry's pieces are stunning. Unexpected, poignant, masterful. Who knew fire could be so exciting?" Monica emitted a horsey laugh.

Scotty winked covertly at Alex, as if to say, 'Let's have a bit of fun.'

"Monica," Scotty said, "you must meet a friend of mine, Rick Stradman."

"Stradman?" Monica tilted back her head. Her top lip recoiled to reveal a set of horse like teeth to match her horse like laugh. "Are you related to Sid Stradman by any chance?"

Rick nodded and laughed apologetically. "Correct. That is I. Rick, son of Sid."

"And Rick's mother is Luisa D'Onofrio," added Scotty.

Alex felt Rick squirm as Scotty playfully got her revenge for his deception.

Monica's eyes popped. "How wonderful!" Monica gazed at Rick as if he were a gigantic diamond or a talking dog. "I only know of her by reputation, but she's highly regarded in Europe. Are you in the art world like your mother?"

Scotty chipped in with, "No. Rick's an actor. Didn't you see him in *Eddie's Girls*?"

"It's not a show I generally watch," said Monica, "but I'll look out for the re-runs!"

Scotty hadn't introduced Alex to Monica and he was feeling fine about that. He was about to peel off when Scotty drew him into the circle and, after introductions, brought Monica up to speed about his work. Scotty went overboard, waxing lyrical about his Mendocino studies and their Hopper quality. Monica listened politely, but she was clearly enamored with Rick, and as soon as it was polite resumed quizzing him about his acting work. Inadvertently, Rick mentioned the possibility he could be on *McMillan and Wife*. Monica nearly dropped her glass. "I simply adore that show with the gorgeous Rock Hudson! I'll pray nightly to the T.V. gods that you get the role!" Monica grabbed Rick's arm. "I must introduce you to my dear friends. They'll find you fascinating too."

Alex had to laugh to himself, Rick's face was a picture of discomfort as Monica dragged him off to meet her clique. Left alone, Alex and Scotty slunk off to a quiet corner.

"You do look great, by the way," said Scotty. "Was the haircut your idea?"

"Oh no. I seem to have become Rick's new project."

"I take it you're wearing those suede pants ironically."

"What? Don't you think they're *faabulous*?" said Alex with a grin.

"This from the man who pays five bucks for his pants."

"Yeah, no need to rub it in." Alex sipped his drink and studied one of Jerry's fumage pieces of a Mountain Quail. Its body and stripes were formed by being burned out the paper, the trails of soot created its crest.

"If Rick started the project then you've taken the baton and run with it. Koenig doesn't invite everyone in town to show him their work."

"He liked my idea of en plein air work in an urban setting."

Scotty switched her attention from the art to Alex. "I guess you've found your new direction then? Urban plein air. Can't wait to see it."

"Me too. It's in my head, I just need to get it on canvas."

"What did you think of my flower pieces?"

Alex paused before answering. "Very attractive. They'll sell without doubt."

"But not great art?"

"They've beauty, they have technique. They delight the eye."

"But not the soul?" Scotty didn't push further.

They were silent for a few moments and then Alex spotted Rick being trundled around the room by Monica. As Rick caught Alex's eye, unseen by Monica he mouthed the word 'help'.

"Shouldn't you go save him?" asked Scotty.

"Fuck him. Let him suffer a bit longer," muttered Alex. "Boy, he can be a real pain in the ass at times. I've no idea why he's taken such a shine to me."

"Maybe he likes your work? I might have too if you'd have let me see it. I'm not a fool, Alex, I knew you were hiding something at the beach that day. I saw the field easel thrown under the deck. Look, Rick's made a break for freedom." While

Monica was clasping Jerry Weir to her chiffon clad poitrine, Rick had backed into the crowd and was headed their way. Scotty said with a sigh, "I guess we all need someone to believe in us. Maybe it's less complicated when it's a stranger."

"Monica Aigner's a force of nature," said Rick breathlessly. "She's pushy, bombastic and will not take no for an answer."

"Reminds me of someone not a million miles away." Alex cocked an eyebrow at Rick. "Someone by the name of Ricardo?"

Rick rolled his eyes. "Trust Walter to let that cat out of the bag. Yes, revel in it. The full splendor of my name being Ricardo Ettore Durazzo Stradman. Now may we never speak of it again. I detest being called Ricardo."

"Should we stick to Ricky then?" asked Alex with a smirk. "Or maybe we ought to call you Ricky Ricardo?"

Rick clenched his jaw. "This is exactly why I don't give away too much information."

"We better not upset Ricky Ricardo or he won't let us be in his show," teased Alex. Scotty giggled along with the merriment.

"Knock it off," said Rick grumpily, but with a glint in his eye. "Monica's invited us to her fundraiser next month. She asked if you'd contribute something to her auction."

"She asked?" Alex wrinkled his brow.

"I suggested it and she agreed. So will you contribute something?"

"I guess ..."

"Darling, Ricardo! Where did you disappear to?" Monica homed in on him again. "For goodness sake, don't stand there like a wallflower. Or you, Alex," Monica took Alex by one arm and Rick by the other. "I want you both to meet the rest of my lady friends. They're passionate for art." Monica laughed, "and artists!"

As Monica pulled him and Rick away, Alex felt Scotty's eyes boring into his back. He wondered what on earth she could be thinking.

Oh, why was he kidding himself? He knew exactly what she was thinking.

THE GOLDEN HOUR

A truck roared past, only inches from his ear, but Alex barely noticed. The location he'd chosen on the highway's shoulder near Newport Beach was precipitous, but its view of the interchange below was ideal. He'd organized himself to get out of the car quickly, erect his easel and do an hour or two's work before the cops showed up. He'd chosen to work around dawn in the hope the highway patrols were on breakfast break.

Alex was aware of Kuntz's work in the early sixties. He'd painted L.A.'s concrete canyons using oils and his work had a hard graphic quality. Alex desired lyricism in his view of the same subject and therefore was using watercolor and soft strokes.

Morning commuters and tradespeople began gearing into action. The traffic grew denser, obscuring the highway's architectural lines, which combined with a siren's wail was Alex's cue to finish. Carefully placing the wet work on the rear seat, he slammed everything into the car and sped off. Good timing, as just after that a police car flashed past on the opposite carriageway. "Hey, Rick!" Alex shouted, bustling into the house with his gear. "You awake, man?" No answer. Wondering if Rick was still asleep, Alex took this new work into his studio. The sound of sandy feet tapping on the brush beside the front door let him know Rick hadn't been in bed but out on the beach. "Yo, early start!" shouted Alex poking his head into the hallway.

Rick came in from the verandah, drying himself with a beach towel. "Nearly Memorial Day and the water's fucking freezing!"

Alex stepped out of the studio. "Jeez, man. You been outside wearing those?" Alex didn't consider himself easily shocked, but Rick was sporting the tiniest turquoise swim trunks known to man. They left little to the imagination.

"What's wrong with them?" asked Rick bending to towel his legs.

Alex couldn't help noticing Rick's butt, perfectly firm and rounded like a peach. "How can I put this? They're rather skimpy."

"They're European."

"They're pornographic!"

"What would you prefer I wear? A woolen one piece?" asked Rick sarcastically.

Since it was very much on display, Alex let his gaze rest on Rick's beautifully defined body. Slim, elegant, and with statue of David proportions. Lifting his arms to towel his hair, a vein gently pulsed in the hollow where his neck dipped into the clavicle. Alex wasn't normally drawn to the human figure as a subject, but seeing Rick practically naked, with a sheen of seawater and sweat glistening on his skin, made him toy with asking Rick to pose for a life study. Alex stopped himself. Why'd he let such a crazy idea enter his head? What would Rick think if he asked him that? Averting his eyes, Alex said, "When you've dried off come take a look. Need your thoughts."

Trailing after Alex into the studio, Rick contemplated the new work on the easel. After a few moments, he said, "The concrete against the trees is good. The traffic blur doesn't work. Not in daylight anyhow. How about trying it at dusk? Maybe someplace with the ocean behind the highway for contrast?"

"That could work." Alex mused standing beside Rick. He must've used sun cream for the aroma of vanilla and coconut emanated from Rick's damp skin. "Would you go out with me tonight ..." asked Alex, quickly adding, "to paint. I'll need someone to hold the torch if I'm working at dusk."

"Sure." Rick knotted the towel around his waist and meandered over to Alex's other new studies from the past few days. The watercolor paper was still stretched around the wooden frames making them easy to handle. "I like this," said Rick picking one up. The subject was an unfinished off-ramp amidst the highway construction. "I love how the incline ends in a sheer drop."

The phone rang. When Rick didn't move, Alex asked, "Aren't you going to go answer that?"

"It's your phone," said Rick.

"True, but no-one ever calls me. And now you've had words with Bell we don't even get calls for Angie the whore anymore." Unable to bear its ringing any longer, Alex brushed past Rick, picked up the phone and said, "Y'ello?" He held out the phone to Rick. "As suspected, for you."

With a trepidation usually reserved for handling poisonous snakes, Rick took the receiver. "Hello?" Rick listened intently, giving the occasional, "Uh huh," and, "yep." He wound up with, "Thanks, Mike. Appreciate it." He whipped the towel from around his waist. "I'm off to take a shower. You need the bathroom?"

"No. So did you get the part? Did they go for a name? Did they do a psychological evaluation and rule you out because you're insane?"

Rick provocatively dropped the beach towel at Alex's feet.

"You despise wet towels on the floor! What's up with you, man?" asked Alex picking up the towel in annoyance.

"Getting into character. It's between me and the big name for the role of Bradley Hull," said Rick with a cheeky grin. He went into the bathroom, slammed the door and Alex didn't see him for the next two hours.

♦ ♦ ♦

"Higher, get it up," said Alex urgently.

"I'm losing the feeling in my fingers," whined Rick.

"Another ten minutes." It'd been going so well, Alex didn't want Rick wimping out and spoiling it. "Just swallow it, man. Keep the torch high"

They'd driven down towards Laguna and Alex had found a rough track off the highway running up into the hills. After parking at the foot, Rick helped Alex carry the equipment up. Alex erected his field easel amidst the bent grass and salt bush. Everything was in place and he'd been able to start work just before the sun set. This location had a perfect view of the highway with the ocean as a counterpoint backdrop. The setting sun's refraction through herringbone clouds made for textural lighting. Headlights and taillights began flaring into life as the day faded. Alex deftly captured their red and white streaks against the black asphalt with his brush. The moody sky, rolling ocean and verdant headland behind the highway made for a pleasing composition. He normally wouldn't use pure white in a dusk plein air study, but he needed it for the headlights in this piece as they were not of the natural world.

"My arm's about to drop off," moaned Rick,

"Nearly there," said Alex filling in the last parts of the sky. "You gotta keep the torchlight on the palette and the canvas or I can't judge the color balance." More water, more pigment, more vital strokes. Alex was impressing himself with how detailed his work had become; working at lightning speed had improved his technique immeasurably. The sun's last embers disappeared in a red flare. Night had begun and Alex said, "Done!"

Rick dropped the torchlight, then flexed his fingers and wrist with a sigh.

"Thanks, buddy. Great assistant work. How about I buy you a beer at the Beachcomber as payment?"

"Terrific. And a couple of physiotherapy sessions wouldn't go amiss too." Rick rubbed his bicep and shoulder.

"Wuss," muttered Alex with indulgent humor.

Rick helped Alex pack his kit and then lit their way down the dark hill with the torch. Back at the beach house they sifted through Alex's works of the past few weeks and assessed the qualities of each. With that fresh in mind, they walked up the beach and ensconced themselves at a corner table on the Beachcomber's deck. Memorial Day was around the corner and the bar was getting crowded. "Plan of action," said Rick, very business-like with pad and pen in hand, "now I – "

"Wow, this looks serious, guys!" exclaimed Julie arriving at their table to take their order. Under her tiny bistro apron tonight she was wearing cut-off jeans as hot pants, teamed with a denim shirt casually tied in a knot under the bust. "Your usuals?" asked Julie with an extra twinkle as Alex tossed back his mane of newly glossy hair to look up at her.

"Yeah, thanks Janet," replied Rick without looking at her at all.

"Yeah, the usual. How you doing, Julie? It's getting busy here," said Alex warmly.

"Summer folk beginning to arrive. Thank goodness I get off at ten. I can leave Arnold to deal with the night owls. Boy, I'm looking forward to my bed tonight," said Julie rubbing the back of her neck provocatively. "I'll be right back with your drinks." Julie smiled at Alex then went to the bar, his eyes following her hot pants.

"Anyway, like I was saying ..." Rick impatiently tapped his pen on the pad.

"Yeah?" Alex turned his attention away from Julie and back to Rick.

"I spoke to Koenig's assistant and she told me he'll be at the gallery tomorrow. I propose you take the off-ramp. That one's in the mold of what you spoke to him about. And, although it's practically still wet, the one you did tonight's fantastic. I really love it," said Rick making notes on the pad. "Two's not enough. What other new work shows off your current style?"

"The beach umbrellas. It's not urban but the acrylic against the watercolor's interesting, don't you think?" Alex noticed Rick didn't immediately reply, so he obviously didn't agree. Maybe it was a nothing little picture, but he liked it. "Yes, the beach umbrellas."

Rick made a note. "That settles what you'll show Koenig then. What do you propose for Monica's charity auction?"

It was a tricky question. Alex closed his eyes to consider the response. When he opened them he found Julie had delivered their drinks and he hadn't even noticed. Taking a gulp of whiskey and Coke, Alex racked his brain. What represented his best work? Could he define himself? Did he have anything he truly felt was worth auctioning?

"Monica will be inviting all the big guns. Whatever we put into that auction will be their first impression of your work. The piece must make its mark."

Alex pulled out his cigarettes. "My Mendocino paintings still hold water. It wasn't a great time for me and I think that lends a depth to the work. Scotty liked them, but Hank and Scoop were so negative I lost faith."

"You said there was one in particular that Scotty raved about. Is it one of those in the studio?"

Alex struck a match and lit his cigarette. "No. It's the one with a figure on the cliff. It's in the loft behind my room. What's left of my older work's up there too."

"What's left? What happened to the rest?" asked Rick.

"Hank and Scoop got hyped up on a performance idea. It was about how an artist's work is an extension of themselves and to lose part of it is like experiencing your own death. They decided that we'd all take a year's worth of our work, good or bad was immaterial, and lay it out on the roadway. Then, at midnight, they hired a trailer truck to drive over it. The piece was about how reality destroys dreams and the fragility of art in the face of commerce. Anyway, Scoop filmed the piece. It created a real buzz for a while."

"Hank and Scoop sound kind of dumb," said Rick,

"No, no. They were just deep into performance art at that time. The piece Chris Burden did in seventy-one had captured

Scoop's interest in particular. It was the one where Chris had a gun and shot himself in the arm."

Rick doodled on the pad. "Short performance."

Alex allowed himself a small laugh. "Give me time to think about the auction. Maybe we should see how Koenig reacts to my work tomorrow?"

"I guess." Rick reached for Alex's cigarettes and slipped one out. "Light?"

"Since when did you smoke?" asked Alex striking a match. He held the flame to Rick's tip.

Rick dragged on the cigarette and then said with a gasp, "What the fuck are these things? Mint cigarettes?"

"Menthol."

Rick made a disgusted expression and stubbed it out. "They should recommend these to people who want to give up smoking. Yuck!"

"I'm glad you don't like them. I don't want Sid to accuse me of leading you into bad ways."

They carried on chatting about art in general and Alex's work in particular. The conversation was easy and time slipped by. After finishing up their drinks, Rick slapped a twenty on the table. As they left, Julie was hanging up her apron for the night. She waved vigorously at Alex, but he didn't notice.

The next morning, Alex wrapped up the three paintings they'd decided he should show Koenig and loaded them into the Chevy. After a hazy drive in light smog, Alex pulled off La Cienega into the alley beside Koenig's gallery. Why did he feel so nervous? Taking the paintings out of the trunk and carrying them around to the entrance was underscored by his heart pounding in his ears.

Alex entered the gallery. Three people were wandering around inside bemusedly looking at Jerry's work. Blondie in the short black skirt and polo neck approached him like an automaton. With zero expression, she asked, "You care for a catalog?"

"I came to the opening."

Blondie stared blankly at him. "You don't want one, then?"

His new haircut and smartened appearance were definitely wasted on this girl. "I've come to see Walter Koenig," said Alex.

"Do you have an appointment?"

"We were chatting at Jerry's opening the other night and Koenig said I should drop by to show him my work. You see, he knows my roommate," said Alex. Blondie stared at him like she was focusing on something ten feet behind his shoulder. "Just tell him Rick Stradman's artist friend is here to see him. Oh, better tell him Ricardo."

"You're Ricardo?" asked Blondie allowing her deadpan expression to slip enough for a slight furrow to appear on her brow. She glanced at the paintings under his arm.

Alex suddenly wished he'd left his work in the Chevy until he knew for sure Koenig would meet with him. "It's my friend that knows Koenig who's called Ricardo. I'm Alex, he might not remember my name."

Blondie vacillated, then for whatever reason, decided to allow him over the threshold. "I'll see if he's available." The girl walked very slowly through the gallery. She turned and disappeared behind a floating wall at the rear.

Alex shifted uncomfortably as he waited. Rick had offered to come with him, but he'd declined as he didn't want Koenig thinking they were joined at the hip. Without Rick at his side he felt vulnerable, however, and vulnerable was an adjective he never, ever wanted to apply to himself again.

A few minutes later, Blondie re-appeared. She walked very, very slowly back, leaving it until she got to him before saying, "He can give you a half hour. Go through."

"Thanks." Alex smiled warmly at Blondie but got nothing in return. Oh well, maybe she was a riot at parties after a few drinks. Alex left her and went behind the sleek floating wall at the gallery's rear, then through the corrugated door it concealed. The rolling metal door led to a large storage area filled with cellophane wrapped paintings and sculptures. The place smelled of damp and kerosene. One roped off corner housed giant resin casts of geometric shapes in primary colors; the backroom's other corner housed a glass walled office with spotlights on metal wires jutting from its ceiling. Behind the glass wall, Koenig sat at his desk poring over a pile of documents. Koenig raised his eyes and, on seeing Alex wavering outside, beckoned him in. Koenig opened the glass door. Swallowing hard, Alex approached. "Hi, we met the other night."

"Ah yes, Ricardo's friend. Come." Koenig held the door, allowing Alex to carry in his work. He extended his hand.

Alex dithered where to put his paintings to respond to Koenig's greeting. He awkwardly leaned them on a chair and fumbled the handshake. Heat rose on the back of his neck.

"What have you brought to show me?" asked Koenig cutting to the chase.

Alex unwrapped the first of his paintings and said, "Some of my recent work."

Koenig took a turquoise and lime abstract off the shelf behind his desk. After putting it on the floor, Koenig reached across the desk.

Doing all he could to stop his hand shaking, Alex passed over his beach umbrellas painting. Koenig rested it on the shelf. The angled spotlights lit the painting mercilessly. Alex had framed *Beach Umbrellas* in simple stainless steel. Folding his arms, Koenig stared at the painting. Although looking at his painting, Alex felt so exposed it might as well have been him standing naked in front of Koenig. After a few minutes, Koenig took down the painting and put it on his desk. He held out his hand expectantly. Alex took this as his cue to give Koenig the *Off-*

Ramp painting. Koenig went through the same procedure, lining up the painting under the spotlights, considering it wordlessly and then taking it down and reaching for the next. The last piece Alex handed over was the headlights and taillights at dusk. He'd named this one *Homeward Bound*.

Once he'd considered the last piece, Koenig left it in place. "Ideally I like to see six or seven pieces of a new artist's work. Do these represent you?"

Alex gathered his thoughts. "My early work was in the realist mold. Then I switched to abstract expressionism. I recently experienced a crisis of direction and that's why I've gone back to my roots. I'd gotten too much into my head with the abstracts. The plein air work's put me back in touch with myself. And it's also put me back in touch with the world." After a pause to fully reflect on the question, Alex said, "So yes, they represent me at this point in my life."

Koenig steepled his index fingers and knocked them against his bottom lip. "You made a wise choice not to show me a variety of styles. Artists who experiment with different styles often do that. Why'd you choose to show me your most recent work?"

"I don't know how I feel about my earlier pieces at the moment. Right now, I like what I'm doing and I feel confident with it."

"Will these paintings sell?"

"If someone comes along who likes them, they may."

Koenig gave a knowing grin. "I admire your humility. And honesty." Koenig spun in his chair to look at the painting again, then spun back to Alex. "I can't take any of them."

"Fair enough," said Alex evenly.

"Your work's not for this gallery. My clientele wants cutting edge. Unusual techniques. Edgy. Modern. You know?"

"I appreciate you seeing me anyway." Alex rose, wishing he was all of those things. He had started to pack up the paintings when Koenig came around the desk.

Koenig perched on the desk's edge and glanced again at *Homeward Bound* still under the spotlight. "Wait a moment with that." Koenig reached out to stop Alex packing. "Would you entrust your work to me for a couple of days?"

"Sure, but why?"

"I've a meeting with Yumi Mihara coming up. She's opening a new gallery and she covers a very different area of the market to me. Are you okay if I let her see them?"

"Of course."

Koenig picked up the *Beach Umbrellas* painting and replaced the *Homeward Bound* one with it under the spotlight. "Yes, leave them with me and let's see what she thinks. You deserve more than one opinion, and I trust Yumi's judgement."

♦ ♦ ♦

For Alex, Memorial Day triggered memories of patriotic parades and somber neighbors. The grownups talking in hushed tones of fathers, sons and brothers lost in World War Two. They whispered their gratitude over ragged black and white photographs of those who'd given their lives for freedom. Alex recalled being smacked hard for fidgeting during the church prayers. Fearful of even breathing after that, he'd sat still as a rock compressed between mom and pop while the faithful raised their eyes to God. The priest declared that to forgive was to be forgiven and by dying they would awaken to eternal life. They'd prayed for peace on earth and love between men, then the congregation murmured 'Amen'. Back when he was a kid that was.

The body count, however, continued to rise through the fifties and sixties. Korea, Vietnam, Laos and Cambodia confirmed prayer's futility to him. Once he got to college though, a new mood was sweeping the nation. The young were making love not war, painting flowers on their faces, organizing sit-ins and love-ins and rebelling against The Establishment. But still the nation stumbled into one war after another to make the world a safer place. Grief fatigue set in.

The change to celebrate Memorial Day on the last Monday of May, instead of always the thirtieth, had only occurred a few years back. Parades and prayers were being replaced by blow out sales and barbecues. There were no long faces on the beach today, only happy ones enjoying the beginning of summer and a Sunday without work tomorrow.

Not having regular jobs meant the pleasure of the long weekend was totally lost on Alex and Rick. With neither having anything in particular to do, Alex had asked Rick to help him once more and return to the spot off the highway where he'd set up the other night. Rick eagerly agreed. They'd arrived at the same place and the same time as before, but the weather was radically different; the herringbone sky was replaced by a crystal clear one and the mottled sea by one as smooth as glass. More traffic was headed towards Laguna and less to L.A., making the balance of headlights and taillights completely different too.

Once he was halfway into this piece, it struck Alex he should mount this picture next to the earlier one as a diptych. The same view at the same time on different days. How illuminating it would be to look at similar moments in one's life side by side, he thought. How would it feel to relive the moment someone said 'I love you' for the first time alongside the last time they ever said it to you? Would the same words have the same meaning after everything that had gone on in between? But maybe he'd never hear those words from anyone anyway.

Alex stopped intellectualizing and lost himself in his art. He allowed himself to feel the earth rotating as it whirled through the Milky Way. Even standing still, he sensed the tangible world hurtling through space and time. He smiled at the memory of Dora reminding him the human heart must be constantly in motion to sustain life. Nothing stays still. Nothing stays the same. He allowed himself to be a conduit. He wasn't painting a view. He was painting this moment. This mood. These ideas. His soul. His inner being travelled down his arm, through his hand, along the brush and transmuted the pigment suspended in water into images on the canvas.

♦ ♦ ♦

Memorial Day dawned with aquamarine skies and a fresh breeze. As the day rolled on a layer of low cloud moved in. The sunbathers in front of the beach house began to pack up mid-afternoon. Seagulls folded their legs underneath themselves and took up residence in the bathers' place. The air grew still and humid and an indolent mood settled over the beach, even the gulls were reluctant to fly.

It was late afternoon and Alex had gone to his studio to seal the piece he'd done the night before. Rick was dozing in his room. That's when the ugly voices of a heated argument shattered the placid atmosphere. Wiping lacquer off his hands, Alex went to investigate. He bumped into a yawning Rick shuffling out of his room to do the same thing. They went out and stood on the verandah, listening to the continuing row. Rick glanced at the Waverley's house and asked, "Should we do something?"

The noise abated. "It happens from time to time. It's passed," said Alex turning to go in. Before he got inside though, the shouting started up again, louder and uglier than before. An ominous thud was followed by Gloria yelling, "Get away from me!"

"Should we call the police?" asked Rick.

A muffled smash in the Waverleys' house was followed by another bang.

"Perhaps we better had check what's going on in there," said Alex reluctantly. They went to the back door. Alex opened it just in time to see Gloria run out of her house. Her cerise kaftan tangled around her legs causing her to stumble and fall. Brushing gravel off her knees, Gloria got up and staggered towards them. "What's up?" asked Alex calmly.

"That bastard tried to strangle me!" yelled Gloria extending her arms to Alex.

"Take it slow, Gloria." Alex used soothing tones as he reached out to her.

Gloria took Alex's hands. Then, on hearing her back door open, she swung around. Harry stormed out of their house, his face contorted with rage. "Fuck you! You crazy ass bitch!" With the back of his hand he wiped the four bloody scratches on his left cheek. He sprinted to the parking lot and threw himself into the Caddy.

"Don't you dare walk out on me!" Gloria shouted at Harry as she pulled away from Alex. Her white blonde hair streamed behind her as she darted towards the car. Harry hit the gas, but Gloria threw herself into the car's path. Harry slammed on the brakes. Gloria pounded on the hood. "You can't run away, damnit! Don't pretend it never happened! Don't pretend he never existed!" Harry whacked the car into reverse letting Gloria fall forward. Twenty yards back, Harry stopped and put the car into gear. "You want me dead too? Then kill me! Come on. Get it over with!" screamed Gloria getting to her feet. Harry sped towards her. Alex dived out and pulled Gloria back, Harry's car narrowly missing them both. After braking momentarily by the Beachcomber, Harry took off up the hill with a squeal of tires. "Why's it like this?" asked Gloria brushing a strand of blonde hair out of her eyes. "Why does he make me act this way?"

Alex stroked Gloria's arm. "Let's get you home. I can call one of your kids if you like?"

Gloria shook her head. "Why ruin their lives too?"

"Call if you need anything," said Alex half helping, half pushing her into her house.

"No one can give me what I need," said Gloria swallowing a sob.

Alex felt bad but shut her in the house and left all the same. What could he do if he stayed? Back inside, he found Rick at the kitchen table leafing through the T.V. Guide. "They've had rows before but this one was a doozy," said Alex as he flopped on the couch in the living room. "If that's marriage, include me out."

The phone began to ring.

"Does Gloria have our number?" asked Rick coming into the living room. He stared at the phone, uneasy and inert.

"Yeah. But it'll be for you. It's always for you. Why don't you answer it?"

"If Gloria has this number it could be her. And if it's her I won't know what to say. I don't handle conflict well."

"It could be your agent."

"On Memorial Day? Mike will be on his yacht."

Alex resignedly got up and answered. "Y'ello." He was poised to pass the phone over to Rick, however he heard the person on the other end ask for him. "Yes, this is Alex." Feeling Rick staring at him inquisitively, Alex covered the mouthpiece and mouthed 'Koenig'. Rick came and knelt on the couch, craning forward to glean any information. "I totally understand. I'll wait to hear from her ... Yeah, I'll swing by and pick them up ... Thanks. I'll pass that on. Appreciate your help, Walter. Bye." Alex hung up. "Koenig told me to make sure you send your mother his warmest regards."

"And?"

"He said hi to you too."

"Yeah, yeah, lovely. What about Yumi Mihara? Did he show your work to her?"

"He did. She's interested."

"What does that mean?"

"Interested. I guess I'll find out when, or if, she makes contact."

"She's going to phone you?"

"Koenig said she'd be in touch. He didn't specify the method, but I'm guessing a phone call's more likely than a carrier pigeon."

"But she's interested! It's not a no. That's great! Isn't that great?"

"It's not a no but it's not a yes. And I'm not going to count chickens. I've got a headache from the varnish fumes and Gloria Waverley. I'm going for a run on the beach." Alex ran upstairs and stripped off his painting duds. Fiery red, rose pink and hot orange refracted through the arched window of his bedroom as he changed into a tank and shorts. He jogged downstairs and trotted barefoot out to the verandah.

"Wait," said Rick darting into his room.

"What for?"

"I'm coming with you." Moments later, having changed into a t-shirt, board shorts and sneakers, Rick jumped outside.

Compared to the skimpiness of Rick's turquoise trunks, Alex felt this beach attire was akin to a three-piece suit. "Why? You've never come with me before when I took a run."

"I don't want to be here by myself if Gloria comes around. Like I said, I'm not good with conflict."

"Join me if you like, but I'm not hanging around if you're slow. And ditch those sneakers, they'll weigh you down when they're wet."

"Wet?"

"We'll be running in the surf. It's better exercise that way. Come, if you're coming!" Alex bounded down the steps and sprinted towards the shore. Rick reluctantly kicked off his sneakers and ran after him. Alex set a strong rhythm running along the shore. He glanced behind and saw Rick struggling to catch up. Over his shoulder, Alex taunted Rick. "Can't keep up? Get with the program, G.I. Joe!"

"I can keep up too!" Rick shouted back, pumping his arms to gain momentum. He splashed through the tide and caught up with Alex. Pushing himself, he overtook Alex and cockily yelled over his shoulder, "Who's the slow poke now!"

"Where's your stamina though, city boy!" yelled Alex powering past him. They carried on running, each trying to get the lead over the other. Rick and Alex's pounding through the waves disturbed the gulls resting on the beach. The flock wheeled into the air creating a cloud of shrieks and flapping wings. Nearing the cliffs, Rick's energy began flagging. Overtaking Rick, Alex shouted, "Give up?" Now in the lead, Alex yelled, "First one to the cliffs is the winner!"

"You never said this was a race! This means war!" Rick's competitive nature gave him the extra push of energy he needed to power past Alex. "And in war one uses any means to win!" Rick swung around and stuck his leg out in front of Alex.

Alex's shin hit Rick's outstretched leg, throwing him off balance. To make sure he brought him down, Rick gave Alex an extra shove and he tumbled into the surf. "You little bastard!" spluttered Alex. Laughing merrily, Rick sprinted to the cliffs. Getting to his feet while spitting out seawater, Alex put on a spurt of speed to pursue Rick.

"I beat you!" shouted Rick panting for air only a few yards from the cliffs.

"Not yet, you haven't!" Launching himself into the air, Alex flung his arms around Rick. His flying tackle dropped them both into the surf.

"Unfair!" giggled Rick struggling to break free from Alex's clutches.

Alex held Rick tight, pressing him into the wet sand with his body weight. The surf washed over them in showers of white foam. "All's fair in love and war!" spluttered Alex through the sea spray. They rolled and wrestled in the breakers. First one on top and then the other, both gasping for air from the physical exertion and hilarity of their horseplay. Alex forced himself on top of Rick and straddled him. Taking one of Rick's wrists in each of his hands, Alex spread-eagled Rick and pinned him to the sand with his hips. "Give in?" asked Alex lifting his chin away.

A wave rolled over them, covering Rick's face. As the wave broke, Rick shook water off his face and, struggling for breath, shouted, "Never!" The backwash swept Alex along with it. Losing his grip on Rick's wrists, Alex dropped his whole body onto Rick, wrapping his arms around Rick's torso to hold him down. Alex felt Rick wriggling underneath him. A moment later Rick had slithered down out of his t-shirt. Laughing hysterically, Rick ran to touch the rocks. Jumping up and down and waving his fists in the air, Rick yelled triumphantly, "I win, I win!"

"You cheat, you cheat!" Alex romped out of the surf and whipped Rick's butt with his wet t-shirt.

"Last one to the beach house buys the drinks!" Rick's wet heels kicked sand up behind him as he scooted diagonally across the beach back to the houses.

Determined not to let Rick have the final victory, Alex summoned his last energy reserves to win this race. Nearing the Waverleys' house, Alex gave one final spurt to beat Rick to the finish line. Rick wavered and swerved. Suspecting another of Rick's cheating ploys, Alex didn't get suckered into stopping. He overtook Rick but then heard him scream, a blood curdling scream. Alex turned to see Rick rolling on the sand and crying out in distress. Sprinting back and kneeling by Rick, Alex asked, "What's up?"

"There was glass ..." said Rick clutching his foot.

Alex saw a smashed wine bottle poking out of the sand, a pool of red liquid around it - Rick's blood. "Let me see." Pushing Rick's sticky hand out of the way, Alex examined the damage. A jagged gash ran from under the arch to the top of Rick's right foot. He must have swiped his foot against the broken glass in trying to avoid it. A closer look made Alex's head swim. The gash in Rick's flesh revealed the light layer of pink fat beneath the surface. Blood was flowing from the cut, creating a small magenta river in the sand. Nausea and helplessness overcame Alex.

"What should I do?" Rick asked nervously.

Wracking his brain for his lifeguard first aid training, the recommendation to apply pressure leapt to mind. Wringing the water out of Rick's t-shirt, Alex folded it a couple of times and wrapped it around Rick's foot.

"Yow!" howled Rick in agony. "That stings!"

"Salt water will do it good. Can you make it back to the house?"

"Yeah." Using Alex's shoulder to assist him, Rick got to his feet.

The t-shirt around Rick's foot was already bright red with blood. Alex realized standing on the foot would only make the bleeding worse; Rick needed to keep his weight off it. There was only one option, Alex put one arm under Rick's shoulders, the other behind his knees and scooped him up. "You might want to lay off the pasta," joked Alex staggering to the beach house with Rick in his arms. Using a superhuman effort, Alex took the steps up to the deck in a couple of bounds and crossed the verandah. After carrying Rick across the threshold, Alex laid him on the couch and dashed to the kitchen. "Keep applying pressure. Stay there!"

"Where'd you think I'm going?" asked Rick wanly.

Alex snatched a clean dish towel and ran back. He stripped the blood-soaked t-shirt off Rick's foot and applied the towel in its place.

"Should we call 911?" asked Rick.

"It'll be quicker if I drive you." Alex was afraid even driving Rick to the emergency room may not give him enough time.

"Alex?" Gloria was staring in through the front window. "I heard a scream," said Gloria through the glass. "What happened?"

"Rick's sliced his foot pretty bad on a broken bottle. I need to get him to the E.R," replied Alex.

"Let me see." Gloria came in and bent over Rick. Tentatively, she drew back the towel. "I need to do something to stop this bleeding." Gloria whipped off her head wrap and stretched it out between her hands. She looped the scarf around Rick's leg, just below the knee, and knotted it loosely. "Alex, get me a pen or something." After grabbing the pen from the pad by the phone, he handed it to her. "Get your car while I do this." Gloria inserted the pen to one side of the knot she'd tied in the scarf and began twisting it. She saw Alex looking puzzled and said, "It's so they can release it slowly. Go. Go!"

Alex grabbed his keys, stuffed his feet into the nearest pair of sneakers and snatched his denim jacket off the hook. He shrugged on the jacket while racing to the parking lot. He brought the car to the house and left it out back with the doors open and motor running. When he got back inside, Rick's eyes were flickering. Because he'd wriggled out of his t-shirt in the surf, Rick was bare chested and shivering. Darting into Rick's room, Alex grabbed the first thing that came to hand; a black sweater off the back of the chair. Rick's wet shorts would be too difficult to take off over the tourniquet, so they'd have to stay. "Put this on." He tossed the sweater to Rick.

"But it's cashmere," murmured Rick with a pout.

"Great, it'll be warm. Just put it on," barked Alex, this was not the time for fashion statements. Rick pulled on the sweater and Gloria tugged down the sleeves. Carefully, Alex lifted Rick off the couch, then he carried Rick to the car and placed him on the rear seat.

"Keep that foot raised!" Gloria ordered Rick as she slammed the rear door shut. "I'll call St. Joseph's and warn them to expect incoming!"

"Thanks, Gloria." Alex got in the car and wound the window up. He set off carefully, but once he hit the highway he pressed the pedal to the floor. Fifty-five mile an hour limit be damned, this situation called for full speed ahead and damn the consequences. Rick was in bad shape and didn't have a moment to lose.

♦ ♦ ♦

Cold fluorescent light. Hard floors. The dreadful smell that hung everywhere. Hospitals were enough to make a person sick. Alex hated hospitals. But would anybody say they loved them?

On arrival, a local anesthetic had killed Rick's pain while the medics stemmed the bleeding. They'd nodded their approval of Gloria's tourniquet and, although not totally effective due to the location of the injury, it had lessened the blood loss. The doctor made a final sweep for glass fragments and sand. Once he was certain the cut was clean, he gave the instruction to close. While a nurse stitched and dressed Rick's injury, Alex took the opportunity to grab a coffee. He was still in his running shorts and tank for the beach run. Luckily the denim jacket he'd grabbed had a few nickels and quarters in the pocket. Counting them, he realized he didn't have enough for two drinks. Knowing Rick needed it more than him, Alex paid for one cup and put in a few sugars to help the shock. Carrying the coffee back to Rick's bay, he found the nurse putting the final touches to the dressing. "Thought you might need this," said Alex.

"Aw, thanks," said Rick gratefully accepting the plastic cup.

The doctor came to check the nurse's work. For some reason, he turned to Alex to inform him about care of the wound and when the stitches would need to come out. The final part of the process was paying the bill. It was this seemingly simple step which turned out to be tricky. The receptionist handed the bill to Alex. Apparently, he'd taken on the mantle of Rick's carer. Alex realized in the rush to get out he hadn't picked up his billfold or any identification, and Rick had no identification or cash on him either - not even his gold watch which he could have left as a bond. Glancing sympathetically at Rick in the wheelchair, the receptionist explained she needed more than a promise of payment from two strangers with no I.D. "Is there someone you could call to vouch for him?" she asked. Alex scratched his head, wondering if he should call Scotty.

"You got a paper and pen?" Rick asked the receptionist. After she passed them over, he scribbled a number and pushed it back. "Sid Stradman. My father." The receptionist reached for the phone. As she dialed, Rick asked Alex, "Would you speak to him?"

"Why me? He thinks I'm holding you hostage." Overhearing this, the receptionist shot them a dark look. Alex responded with a winsome smile, but she averted her eyes, unconvinced.

"Please, Alex. I'm not up to talking to him now. You know how he gets."

The receptionist got an answer. "Hello, is that Mr. Stradman? Mr. Sid Stradman? ... I'm sorry to trouble you so late. This is St. Joseph's hospital. I've a patient here who claims to be your son ... No, no. He's received treatment and is awaiting discharge but he has no I.D. and can't settle the bill. Could you vouch for him? ... I'll pass you over." The receptionist held the phone across the desk.

Rick's eyes pleaded with Alex's. Sighing reluctantly, Alex took the phone. "Hi, Mr. Stradman ... I'm here with Rick ... Yeah, me from the beach ... Look, he's lost a lot of blood ... No, not his wrists, his foot. We were jogging and he hit a broken bottle. I had to rush him to the E.R. and we left the house without any cash. They need to know he can cover the bill ... Um, he can't talk. He's pretty zonked. Anesthetic, you know ... Okay. I'll pass you back ... "Alex returned the phone to the receptionist who finished the call, filling in details on the form as she went.

"How'd he sound?" Rick asked Alex sheepishly.

"Once he'd chewed my ear off for being woken so late at night, he sounded worried. He said he'll take care of the bill and still thinks my name's Dex."

The receptionist hung up and passed the clipboard and pen over to Rick. "Sign next to the three crosses." Once Rick had made the signatures, the receptionist summoned an orderly. A stooped Mexican guy in a blue nylon tunic then wheeled him to the car.

On their way back to the beach, Alex said, "That was some night. You had me pretty scared back there."

"It wasn't a bundle of laughs for me either," replied Rick with a yawn.

Alex drove on, his mind turning over the conversation with Sid. "Your dad said something weird on the phone. He was worried that you'd hurt yourself deliberately."

Rick let out a stifled laugh. "Dad's spent too many years making potboilers. He can't help leaping to extreme conclusions."

Alex let the subject go. As the streetlights streaked by, he pondered the state of the house on their return. Much blood had been spilled there. And also out on the beach. The image of Rick's glossy red blood pouring onto the sand reiterated itself on his retinas. That would make an arresting composition, a golden beach with a mysterious streak of sanguinity.

Rick winced as he got out of the car and muttered, "The anesthetic's wearing off."

Alex was pleasantly surprised on entering the house. The floor had been mopped and the blood stain on the couch disguised with a throw. "Gloria must've cleaned up after we left."

"A regular *Mary Poppins*," said Rick leaning on the doorframe to his room.

"Don't be mean. I'll go find the painkillers."

"Wait," Rick reached out and took Alex's hand, pulled him close and hugged him. Nestling his head into Alex's shoulder, Rick said, "Thanks for looking after me tonight. Scotty was right, you are a helpful kind of guy."

Alex trembled. An odd ripple ran through his body as Rick's groin pressed against his thigh. The vanilla smell of Rick's hair against his cheek was disconcerting. "Don't mention it." Alex pulled away then patted Rick on the shoulder. In the kitchen, Alex poured a tumbler of water and dug out an old jar of Advil. Taking them to Rick's room, Alex found Rick had stripped off his clothes and flopped on the bed. He seemed to be asleep, naked and face down on the mattress. The moon highlighted the valley in the small of his back which rose to the pert roundness of his buttocks. After placing the water and jar of pills on the nightstand, Alex hastily covered Rick with the blanket. He picked Rick's clothes up off the floor, shook them out and hung them over the chair.

Going up to bed, Alex was alarmed by the stirring in his shorts. Why the hell was his cock hard and throbbing? His hand went to the greenstone pendant around his neck. Touching it brought back memories of old feelings. Those ones he'd pushed aside for so many years. He was determined not to give in to those feelings and risk being hurt like he had before. He let go of the pendant. Tomorrow he'd put the moves on Julie. A good woman was what he needed. That's what his body was telling him.

Wasn't it?

A MEMORY PAINTING

Alex spent the night in a fitful sleep punctuated by disconcerting dreams. Going down and checking on Rick, he found the painkillers open and the water glass empty. Rick was asleep. Alex adjusted the blanket over him and shut the door. After copious amounts of coffee he set to work in the studio. He was aching to get his *Blood on the Sand* vision onto canvas. This would be a memory painting, so the en plein air style wasn't right for it. He planned on using oils for the sand, sky and houses, and acrylic for the blood. The phone rang. Alex dragged himself from his work. It was Rick's agent. "Hold on, I'll check if he's home." Alex went and whispered through the door, "Rick, you awake?" There was no answer.

Alex opened his door. Rick had thrown off the blanket and was lying naked on the bed. The white dressing on his ankle contrasted with the golden tan of his bare leg. A shaft of light striped the blonde hairs dusting his thigh. "Hey man, your agent's on the horn," Alex said softly, dipping his eyes.

Rick mumbled into the pillow, "I'll call him back."

"Sounds important."

"Alright … I'm coming." Yawning, Rick huddled the bedsheet around himself like a toga and limped to the phone.

Alex took a cigarette break out on the verandah.

Rick wasn't saying much on the phone, merely interjecting the occasional response between stifled yawns. After five minutes, he said, "Cool," hung up and wilted onto to the couch.

Alex came inside. "So?"

"What, my foot? It's not great but I'll live." Rick peeled back the throw Gloria had placed over the bloodstain and winced. "I owe you a new couch."

"Forget about the couch. Did you get the part?"

"Ray Milland's just signed to play Professor Miller. I guess that means they don't have the budget to cast a big name for Bradley too so they've offered me the part. It's a one-episode contract with an option for five more."

"Wow, well done! That's amazing!" enthused Alex.

"They're sending over the script. It's a twelve-day shoot starting the week after next. They seem to have created this role to step in for action if Saint James can't do it because of her pregnancy. And now," he scowled at his bandaged foot, "I can't exactly do action either."

"It'll be fine by next week. And your part's not likely to involve tap dancing, is it?"

"Who knows with that show ..."

"Hello?" said Gloria. She was framed in the open front door, her cream kaftan and scarf fluttering in the breeze. "How Rick's doing?"

Rick tugged the bedspread over his bare chest and shoulders and leaned forward. "I'm fine. Thanks for helping me last night, Gloria."

"And thanks for cleaning up," added Alex going to the door.

"I've had practice," Gloria gave a rueful laugh, "you know, living with Harry."

"Has he come home yet?" asked Alex.

"No. Maybe he won't this time. Anyway, glad I could help ..." Gloria didn't say goodbye, just drifted down from the deck and onto the beach.

"Harry's never stayed away like this before," said Alex. He watched Gloria pacing aimlessly on the sand for a minutes, her cream kaftan billowing like a sail, then he sequestered himself in his studio. As he worked, Gloria's odd wandering on the beach played on his mind. And something else concerned him, his body chemistry had gone awry. He kept finding himself with a solid boner triggered by random thoughts of Rick lying naked on the bed. He kept overwriting images of Rick with ones of Julie in her red halter top. He was determined to pay her a visit at the Beachcomber tonight and make his move.

Around two p.m., a motorbike courier delivered the script. Rick took an hour to read it. Shortly after hearing the dull thud of Rick dropping the script on the floor, Alex heard him pick up the phone. After a few minutes of generic chit-chat, Rick said, "Your prayers to the T.V. gods have been answered ..." Conversation about Jerry Weir's showing followed. Alex joined the dots and they formed a picture of Monica Aigner. More chit-chat, then after a long silence Rick said excitedly, "Exposure like that would add to the value in auction ... Your collection's lending four Picassos and a Munch? I hope they don't catch fire ... That would be performance art on a grand scale. ... Great. I'll ask him." After a prolonged goodbye to Monica, Rick asked the operator for a long-distance number. The following conversation was fractious and conducted in agitated Italian. Alex made out the words 'Mademoiselle' and 'Vogue'. Rick repeated something in Italian over and over again, he reached a crescendo just before slamming down the phone. Rick hobbled to his room and slammed that door too.

Alex studied his work. He felt his rendering of the late afternoon sun on the sand and houses was good. He'd added a white seagull swooping down over the beach. Dipping his brush into the scarlet acrylic, he worked wet blood into the sand. After a while Alex sensed Rick watching him from the doorway. "You okay?" he asked without turning around.

"Where did you say that *Cliffs of Mendocino* painting was?" asked Rick.

"In the loft. Why?"

"There's an art gallery scene in this new film about a skyscraper fire. Monica's on the board of the museum loaning high profile works to the movie. Back at Jerry's opening, Scotty was raving about that piece you did up the coast. The art director mentioned the script has references to the Cliffs of Mendocino and Monica tossed your work into the conversation. He thought it would be a fun to have an unknown painting titled *The Cliffs of Mendocino* amongst the Picassos and Renoirs. Like a little in-joke."

"But he hasn't even seen my painting."

"It's titled *The Cliffs of Mendocino* it's hardly going to look like dogs playing poker, is it? Anyway, if they use it for the shoot it would make the painting a bigger draw in her auction. If you donate it, that is."

"I'll think it over. How's the *McMillan* script?"

Rick perched on the rickety wooden chair. "Real good. Bradley's on forty-two pages of ninety-six and he's got some funny lines."

"Will you have to go up to San Francisco to film the Berkeley scenes?"

"Nope. All on the backlot. And after we wrap Gina's coming to visit."

"And Gina is?"

"A model. They're flying her in to shoot a cover for Mademoiselle. I need to spend some time with her. Our relationship didn't end on the best of terms. She's the reason I had the big falling out with momma. You see, Gina and I were getting marr ..."

"Alex!" called Gloria, peering in through the open front door again.

Alex went through the house with Rick limping after him. "Still no word from Harry?" asked Alex when he got to the door.

"I'm going insane alone. Come for dinner tonight, you and Rick. I'll cook." Gloria extended her hands to Rick. "You need to build up your strength after last night."

"Okay," said Alex kindly, wincing as Rick prodded him in the ribs from behind.

"See you around eight." Swallowing a smile, Gloria drifted back onto the beach. Graphite clouds were gathering over the charcoal sea, a storm was headed inland.

Alex rewound to what Rick had been saying. "What was that about Gina?"

Limping into his room, Rick said, "Just that we were meant to get married. I'm going to sleep for an hour or two." He shut the door.

Alex stared at Rick's closed door, more determined than ever to go see Julie at the bar tonight.

♦ ♦ ♦

A candle flickered in the center of the circular table.

"How'd you like your coffee?" called Gloria from the kitchen.

"Quickly ..." muttered Rick.

"White for me!" called Alex brightly.

"Black!" shouted Rick shooting a dark look at Alex. Rick ran his eyes around the Waverleys' summer house again. Chez Waverley was draped with embroidered metallic fabrics and the candlelight shimmered off their silver threads. The furniture was light pine and the chairs had warm orange upholstery.

Gloria carried in the coffees on a tray, the cups rattling against each other due to her trembling hands. "Hope you enjoyed the lobster."

"Very good," said Alex. "Where'd you learn to cook like that?"

"Harry paid for me to take a cordon bleu course. I think he'd got tired of T.V. dinners."

The room fell silent again. To leaven the awkward pause after Gloria had poured coffee, Alex asked, "How old are your kids now?"

Gloria raised her head sharply. "Twenty, eighteen and sixteen. Davey would have been twenty-six in June." Gloria went to the dresser and took something out of the drawer. She returned to the table with a crinkled black and white photo of a clean-cut young man in military uniform. "He was killed in Vietnam in sixty-nine. Memorial Day always brings it back. He was your age." Gloria stared at Rick. "What did he die for?!" Gloria slammed her fist on the table. The coffee cups rattled and Alex quickly stopped the burning candle toppling over. Gloria walked away scratching her arms, lost in herself. "Now I feel the time, I feel it seeping through the pores of my skin."

"Maybe it's sunburn?" Rick whispered behind his hand to Alex.

Alex coughed to suppress an involuntary laugh and subtly wagged his finger at Rick in reprimand.

Gloria didn't notice what was going on at the table, she was staring dreamily at one of her collages. "That's why I lose myself in my art. I do it for Davey." Gloria trailed her fingers over the sea shells and starfish. "You see, the shells represent the earth. The tangible, that was Davey's mortal body. And this," she said touching the starfish, "is his immortal soul in Heaven. By making what I believe into a picture, I make it real."

Gloria spoke with such simplicity that Alex felt a wave of shame wash over himself, shame for belittling Gloria's art. He got up and went to study her work in detail. She'd arranged the shells with great delicacy and beauty, using their textures and graduated tones in the manner of pointillism. The starfish took on a dark irony in that a living creature was now an empty husk portraying an immortal soul in a piece of art. If he hadn't accepted Gloria's invitation tonight, he may never have discovered Gloria and Harry's rage was due to their inability to deal with shared grief. Alex realized he needed to look deeper and not judge so superficially, he needed to open himself up to possibilities. When Rick made a pantomime show of glancing at his watch, Alex knew he'd been overly judgmental of Rick too. He saw Rick's eyes were rimmed with red and his face had a pallor. "Getting tired?" he asked with concern.

"A little. Perhaps it has something to do with the twenty-eight pints of blood I lost last night."

Alex stifled another laugh. "Perhaps."

Gloria rested her hand on Rick's shoulder. "It's been nice having you all to talk to,"

Rick stood up and said, "I'm sorry about your son."

"Goodnight." Alex patted Gloria's shoulder and smiled warmly, she patted his hand in return.

"Boy, was that hard work!" exclaimed Rick once back in the safety of their living room.

"It does make sense of why it all blew up on Memorial Day though," said Alex with a sigh.

"You're a much nicer person than I am."

Alex wrinkled his brow, puzzled. "How so?"

"I was watching you listen to Gloria talking about her art." Rick drew close and looked deep into Alex's eyes. "You were living it with her. It really moved you."

Alex's heart skipped a beat. For the first time in his life he felt like someone saw him, really saw him. Breaking away from Rick's blue eyes, Alex said jauntily, "Hey, how about a night cap at the Beachcomber?"

"You go. I want to read the script again." Rick looked out at the beach, white gulls dotted the dark sand. "The birds have come inland. Take a jacket with you, the storm's about to hit." The wind rattled the windows and a flash of lightning ripped the sky.

"Yeah, looks like it," said Alex grabbing his cigarettes. It was late, he hoped Julie was still on duty as he walked up to the Beachcomber. The strings of red, green and white light bulbs around its deck rattled in the strengthening breeze. The umbrellas were furled and chairs stacked outside in readiness for rough weather. Alex brushed his wind-tossed hair off his face, swung in through the door and took a seat in the corner.

A dark-haired girl in pink capris and a lime halter came to the table, her white apron and pad implied she wasn't here for fun. "Hi, what can I get you?"

"A beer. Where's Julie?" asked Alex.

The dark-haired waitress let out a sardonic laugh. "She's gone."

"For the night?"

"For good. She rang Arnold this morning to hand in her notice. That's how come I get to wait on you tonight. My lucky day, huh?" The girl winked and rolled a wad of gum around her mouth. "So, a beer?"

"Yeah."

"You look kinda lonely, I get off in a half hour if you'd like company," said the girl jiggling her hip.

"I just remembered, I need to be somewhere else ..." said Alex shifting in his seat, faintly repulsed by the girl's brazen forthrightness. She wasn't Julie - lovely, sweet, perfect Julie.

"What, you got a bus to catch or something?" asked the girl, a moment of exasperation passing her face. "You want that beer or not?"

Alex brusquely got up. "No. I gotta go," he said, leaving the dark-haired waitress standing beside the table. He darted out of the Beachcomber and hurried back in the fiercely growing wind. The dry wrack and salt bush rustled like they were coming to life. A couple of giant water drops plopped on his shoulder. "The rain's started. Are your windows shut?" shouted Alex coming inside and shaking off his jacket. When there was no response, he went out onto the verandah and found Rick huddled on the old gray sofa studying his script. A roll of thunder boomed in the distance. The bay was a cauldron of white tops.

"You're back quick," said Rick putting down the script, "I had the feeling you were going to be out late."

"Turned out I wasn't in the mood," said Alex.

"Uh oh, here it comes," said Rick grabbing the script as the wind ruffled its pages. A clattering on the canopy announced the rain's onslaught. Then the lightning flashed, followed almost instantly by a crack of thunder. The sudden bang spurred the resting gulls into shrieking flight. "You hear that?" asked Rick cocking his head and clutching the script to his chest. "Is that the wind?" Above the gulls' shrieks came another sound, a woman's screams.

"That's not the wind," said Alex staring at the beach. Another flash of lightning illuminated a lone figure wading into the surf. "Shit, that's Gloria!" shouted Alex in horror. "Didn't you see her leave the house?"

"I was studying the script," said Rick tremulously.

"Oh, great," muttered Alex kicking off his shoes.

"What are you doing?"

"Going after her! She's trying to kill herself. Keep this safe." Alex pulled the rope with the eternity pendant from around his neck and handed it to Rick, a drowning person could easily strangle him with it. "Call the police, tell them we may need the coastguard too," said Alex. He leapt off the deck and raced to the shore.

"Don't be crazy, Alex," Rick yelled after him, "it's too rough out there!" Rick's voice got lost in the rain and wind.

Reaching the water's edge, Alex could just make out through the rain that Gloria was hip deep in the pounding surf. The waves crashed around Alex's thighs as he waded in after her. "Gloria, don't do it! Come back!" he shouted, but she ploughed on into the sea undeterred. A gigantic breaker roiled in. It dragged Gloria down and closed over her head. Alex's lifeguard brain took over. He filled his lungs, shut his eyes and dived in. The icy water enveloped him.

Underwater, he opened his eyes and was immediately blinded by fistfuls of sand churned up by the waves. Salt water rushed into his ears, deafening him. He tried to blink the grit and salt out of his eyes. Adjusting his senses to diminished vision and hearing, he searched for Gloria. Where the hell was she? Alex broke to the surface and shook water off his face. At that same moment Gloria rose above the surface too. She bobbed in the trough before being hit by the next incoming wave. Alex took a deep breath and dived back in, desperately swimming to catch her. The fierce tide kept pulling him back. He rose through the water, once more breaking the surface to catch his breath. He'd lost sight of Gloria completely but then heard her scream.

Fighting the current, Alex swam to her. Beating against the tide he managed to grab the edge of her kaftan, but the silky fabric slipped from between his fingers. The current kept sweeping her farther away. He kept fighting his way to reach her. Gloria's strength was dissipating, the sea was taking her. Alex lashed out and caught her wrist. The current was dragging them towards the rocks. He hauled her to him. An incoming wave lifted then dropped them both. His bare feet fleetingly touched something solid. Fighting the stormy sea, he tried to find a perch on the sand bank below. With Gloria bobbing inertly on the waves, he hooked his arm around her neck.

Alex's heart was ready to explode, pure adrenalin the only thing now preventing them both from drowning. He began a laborious backstroke with one arm to get them to the beach, all the time fighting to keep Gloria's face above the water. His lungs were bursting. Fuck those cigarettes! He rasped for air each time he got above the waves, sand and saltwater practically choking him with each painful breath. This was unlike any condition he'd ever swum through, the way the water churned one way then the other was like swimming inside a washing machine. A darkness came over him. For a split second he wondered if he wasn't going to be able save Gloria, if in fact they were both going to perish in this maelstrom of swirling foam. Then miraculously his foot struck the sandbank again. Semi crawling, semi swimming, semi walking, he floundered out of the surf, dragging Gloria as far up the beach as his strength would allow. Her kaftan had ripped open revealing her naked legs and buttocks with the dimpled white triangle where her swimsuit usually sat on her mahogany flesh.

Alex collapsed on the wet sand beside Gloria's body, retching sea water and catching his breath. Through blurred and stinging eyes he made out red and blue lights near the Beachcomber. Squinting through the rain he then saw two medics carrying a stretcher come stumbling across the sand. A police officer ran past them and waved his flashlight in Alex's face. Alex shielded his raw eyes from its painful glare.

"You okay?" yelled the cop.

"I'm fine. See to her. She's in a bad way," shouted Alex rolling away from Gloria.

Raindrops poured down the medics' noses as they bent to her. "She's breathing!" one called out loud to the other. "Pulse weak and rapid."

"What happened here?" barked the cop.

"She went for a swim and got into trouble," replied Alex.

The cop gave him a dubious look. "You know her?"

"Gloria Waverley, from the house at the end of the beach." Alex pointed through the lashing rain.

"She live alone?" asked the cop.

"The husband took off a couple of days back," shouted Alex. That answer seemed to satisfy the cop and he went to help the medics haul Gloria onto the stretcher. Then the three of them staggered back over the wet sand to the ambulance, the cop's walkie-talkie crackling into life as they went.

Alex groggily got to his feet and stumbled back to the beach house. He saw Rick, white faced and anguished, watching out for him. Alex practically fell up the steps onto the deck.

"My god Alex, you look terrible. Is she alive?" asked Rick helping Alex across the verandah.

"Barely." Alex's chest was heaving and painful. He wondered if this was what a heart attack felt like. Swimming against the tide and fighting the surf while supporting Gloria had been a heavy task. His head began to spin and his eyes lose what little focus they had. He just about heard the whoop of sirens down near the Beachcomber as the ambulance and police car pulled away when his teeth began to chatter ferociously, blanking out all other sound.

"Jesus, you're freezing," said Rick. He put his arm around Alex and pulled him into the house. Once inside, Rick slammed the front door against the howling wind and rain.

A terrible shivering consumed Alex. Spasms wracking his body so intensely he could barely breathe.

"We need to get those wet clothes off you," said Rick peeling up Alex's shirt and tossing it to one side. With trembling hands, Alex rolled down his jeans and underpants. Rick dashed to his room and hurried back carrying all his bed covers. "Here." Rick wrapped a now naked Alex inside the covers and guided him to the couch. "I shouldn't have let you go out there by yourself. I'm frightened, Alex. You don't look right."

Alex's teeth were knocking against each other so fiercely he could barely speak. "Really. I'm f, f, fine ..." he stammered, but the shivering intensified and his eyes rolled back into his head.

"Alex, you're going into shock!" cried Rick.

Alex sensed his life-force slipping away. Everything was dark and cold. He was falling. Falling into an endless sleep ... then he felt warmth return to his body. It took him a moment to regain enough consciousness to realize Rick had got inside the covers with him. And Rick was naked too. The heat was Rick's bare chest and stomach pressing against his.

"Stay with me, Alex. I got you, you're safe." Bundling the covers around the two of them, Rick pressed as much of his naked flesh as he could against Alex's bare skin.

Alex's shivering abated. His mind was clearing as the blood came back into his head.

"Forget about the country club pool, the county should employ you as Sunset Cove's personal lifeguard," joked Rick. Under the cocoon of the covers, Rick began massaging Alex's inner thighs and buttocks to get his circulation going.

Alex gulped. Rick's rubbing was getting more going than his circulation. The blood wasn't just returning to his head, it was rushing to his cock too. The erection he'd wanted Julie to go to work on was back with an insistent vengeance.

"You're an incredible man, Alex," said Rick.

Alex opened his eyes to find Rick's lovely face in front of him, his long lashes fluttering against his cheek. A moment later, Rick's lips were on his. Rick's hand slid down Alex's abdomen and through his luscious, moist bush. Rick grasped Alex's turgid cock and moved his hand up and down it in the way Alex had needed for such a long, long time. "Rick, maybe we shouldn't do this ..." murmured Alex. But his body was tingling and his nipples firming and tautening as Rick ran his hands through his chest hair.

"Maybe we shouldn't," said Rick but didn't stop wanking Alex's aching cock with fervid intensity.

What the heck, thought Alex. He was too tired, too shocked and too horny to object. He surrendered completely to Rick. And it felt great. He let Rick kiss him again. This was what he wanted and he wanted more. Alex grasped Rick's face between his hands and plunged his salty tongue into Rick's sweet mouth as they entwined around each other.

Rain lashed against the windows. Thunder and lightning raged around the house. The electric lights flickered and went out, plunging the room into total darkness.

Alex tossed off the covers, allowing passion and Rick to consume his needy body, paying no heed to the little voice in his head warning him of the complications that could arise from this.

Fuck them.

Fuck everything.

Fuck Rick.

Alex decided he'd just have to worry about the complications tomorrow.

SCALE

"Every time you look at something, see it afresh and without preconceptions. Don't let yourself fall into producing clichés of expectation."

The words of his old professor at Long Beach rang through Alex's mind as he walked into St. Joseph's hospital for the second time in two days. "She has someone with her at the minute." The white uniformed nurse in the sensible shoes who spoke to Alex was the epitome of the soap-opera stereotype. Or was it a stereotype? Perhaps that's what nurses are generally like, bright, efficient and in sensible shoes. "I'll see if it's okay for you to go in." The nurse slipped into the hospital room. Alex figured one of Gloria's kids must be visiting. The nurse came back and held open the door. "They said you can go in."

On entering the room Alex stepped back in shock, Harry was holding Gloria's hand, holding it tightly enough to stop the circulation by the look of it. Gloria didn't appear to be complaining. "Sorry." Alex felt the need to apologize for telegraphing his surprise so openly. "I wasn't expecting to see you."

"Hi, Alex," said Gloria with a weak smile.

"I needed to find out how you were," said Alex.

"We owe you a massive debt of gratitude." Harry let go of Gloria's hand and stood up. "She'd be dead if you hadn't gone in after her."

"And I could've taken you down with me," added Gloria solemnly. "I wouldn't have blamed you for leaving me. I don't know what happens when these madnesses come over me."

"How long are they keeping you in for?" asked Alex.

"Couple of days," sighed Gloria. "They say I need rest."

"And after she gets out we're taking a vacation. A long one, overseas." Harry looked to Gloria for confirmation and she nodded in agreement. "Will you keep an eye on the house while we're away?"

"Sure. It'll be quiet without you."

"You mean a goddamn relief!" said Gloria with humor.

Funnily enough Alex would miss the Waverleys. Even Rick had admitted this morning that life with Gloria was never dull, even if only for her endless stream of colorful kaftans. "Harry," said Alex, "may I have a word with Gloria? You know, just the two of us." Brushing his momentary puzzlement aside, Harry excused himself. Alex took Harry's seat beside the bed. After considering his words, Alex said, "I owe you an apology."

"What for? It was me who nearly got you killed."

"Not that. I'm ashamed of something. Ashamed I didn't treat you equally as an artist."

"Your work's exquisite. You can paint a masterpiece in a few brushstrokes. You've no need to apologize."

"When you explained how losing your son informed your work, you changed my life. Your work connects with people because you put your whole-hearted belief into it. It's the mark of a true artist."

"I'm a deluded old woman sticking shells on plywood. Harry and I made the mistake of letting Davey's death drive us apart. You've given us a second chance. You're young with so much ahead of you. I bet you haven't even thought about starting a family yet. Go, live your life and don't give me another thought."

Walking out of the hospital room, saying goodbye to Harry, getting in the car and driving back to Sunset Cove, a sense of déjà vu kept crept over Alex. Adrift in that dark sea, there'd been a moment when he thought he wasn't going to make it. It had taken all his inner strength to come through. Then there'd been another moment, back at the house, when the cold and shock overwhelmed him and he felt his life slipping away again. That time Rick had rescued him. If Julie hadn't given in her notice and Gloria hadn't decided to kill herself, last night wouldn't have unfolded as it had. Life's threads had woven a complex tapestry to bring him to this point.

Perhaps making love with Rick had been inevitable. All morning he'd kept convincing himself last night with Rick was a one off, the result of his sexual need and the elation of escaping death. But he wasn't convincing himself. That summer crewing on the yacht with Dean had been the happiest of his life. The way that summer ended, however, had left him vowing to never let himself feel that way about a guy again. Instinctively he reached for the soapstone pendant around his neck. It wasn't there, Rick must still have it. What was it about Rick that had allowed his resolve to waver? The guy was as unpredictable as the sea; you never knew what he was going to do or say next. For instance, this morning had begun with a disturbing banging. Rousing himself from a tangle of sweaty bedlinen, Alex realized the noise was Rick foraging in the loft. Scratching his balls, then his head, Alex dragged himself out of bed. He padded to the door under the eaves, leaned in and groggily muttered, "What're you doing?"

"Looking for *The Cliffs of Mendocino*," replied Rick's muffled voice. Rick's butt reversed out, followed by the rest of him. He clutched a couple of plastic wrapped canvasses.

"Um, why now? Because it's like ..." Alex squinted at the arched window to gauge the light on the sea, "...seven in the morning." He swept back his hair and rubbed his stubbly chin. It was amazing, Rick was neat as a new pin. Alex wondered how long he'd been up to get showered, shaved and smartly dressed in khaki pants and orange madras shirt.

"I want Monica Aigner to see it. If she likes it maybe she can get it into the movie. You're cool with me doing this, aren't you?"

Alex grunted inconclusively, unsure of what he was cool and uncool with anymore.

Rick peeled back a corner of plastic. "Is this it?

Alex recognized the wrapping. "Yeah, that's the one."

Rick peeled off the rest and held out the painting. It was a stunning study of the Mendocino Cliffs. There was a tiny, almost imperceptible, figure perched on the edge of the white peaks. "This is very good. Scotty was right. It's beautiful but ominous."

Alex's heart began to race. The effects of last night's rescue, numerous brandies and heavy fucking were taking their toll. He stumbled backwards and collapsed onto the bed. "Rick, we need to talk about last night. You mentioned marriage with this Gina girl, I don't want to get involved in something complicated."

Rick got on the bed and placed his hand over Alex's mouth. "I'm taking this to Monica. And Mike's asked me to go in to the office to sign the contract."

Alex pushed Rick's hand from his mouth. "But Rick ..." Alex lay naked beneath him, confused and aroused.

"We can talk later, but everything with Gina is over. It was a mistake. Maybe you'll meet her when she comes next month. If you do perhaps it'll be clear why I've done so many things I regret. Now may I take this and go?"

Lacking the willpower to discuss things further, Alex let Rick drive off with the painting. Getting out of bed again he found both of his shoulders were excruciatingly painful. He was taking a scaldingly hot shower to ease the pain when Gloria had buzzed through his mind. That's when he'd decided he had to visit the hospital to put his mind at rest. Once he'd got back from St. Joseph's though, he still walked restlessly around the house. Picking things up, putting things down, unable to concentrate. Vacillating. Unable to settle, he pulled on his shorts, grabbed his board and ran to the ocean. Sunset Cove wasn't the greatest of surf beaches, that allowed plenty of time between waves to float on his board and think. He wavered between wanting Rick to come home and hoping to never see him again, thus removing the temptation of his body.

Rick did come home around six. He didn't burst in with his usual vigor because he was limping badly. "Jesus!" said Rick flopping on the bloodstained couch. "Can you believe it? Out of a twelve-day shoot the first scene up's the one where the car tries to knock down Bradley. Then he has to chase the car!" Rick kicked off one loafer and tentatively removed the other.

"What happened with the *Cliffs*?" Alex flopped alongside Rick.

"Monica adored it. Honestly Al, she *really* loved it."

"What happens next?"

"She's meeting with the movie people about insurance for the items on loan. She'll talk to them about it then." Rick distractedly twirled a wet strand of Alex's hair around his finger. "I just signed the contract to do the show. It's real now." Rick sighed, then buried his face in Alex's bare chest. "I hope I don't fuck this up."

Stroking Rick's hair, Alex said reassuringly, "You won't. You're a good actor."

"Not the show. I mean this," said Rick patting Alex's chest. "I was so scared you were going to die last night, but I shouldn't have taken advantage of you in that state."

"I wasn't so weak I couldn't have fought you off. I guess we both wanted it."

"I nearly forgot." Rick dug into his pocket and pulled out the eternity pendant. "I kept it safe for you." He hung it back around Alex's neck. "It's pretty. Maybe I'll get one like it someday."

Something twanged in Alex's heart, Rick was such a sweet thing. They stared into each other's eyes for an overly long time, then Alex draped his arm around Rick. "I went to the hospital to visit Gloria. Harry was with her."

"For real?" Rick leaned in and traced along Alex's inner thigh with his finger.

"Funny how trying to kill herself brought them together. They're not coming back this summer, seems they're taking a trip abroad."

"Maybe I should give them momma's address so they can visit. That'd teach her." Rick laughed, then became serious again. "It gave me the creeps when Gloria stared at me after talking about the dead son. You know, saying he was my age. You ever think about the draft?"

"I got a deferment because I was into my graduate course. How about you?"

"I've dual citizenship, Italy and U.S.A. Once the dust settled from the custody battle momma and Sid patched things up. For a few years she wouldn't let me out of her sight. That was until her art empire took off, along with her sex life. Whenever she got distracted by a challenging new gallery or some sleazeball lothario, I got shipped back to Sid and the wife du jour. When I turned eighteen she billeted me to Sid to study for a couple of years to avoid the Italian call up. She obviously considered him less dangerous than guns and bombs. If my number had come up here I guess Sid would've paid them off."

"If you didn't have the means to avoid it, would you accept the call to duty or be a conscientious objector?"

"Could I take up arms and kill other men to defend my country?"

"Yeah."

"Well, if America and Italy went to war and both sides drafted me, I'd just shoot myself to get it over with quickly."

"But seriously, could you kill a man if you had to?"

Rick's finger was about to slip up Alex's shorts but stopped. "If it was a choice of them or me, I guess I could. How about you? Would you go to war?"

"Stopping the Nazis and concentration camps is one thing, even nuking Japan after Pearl Harbor I guess had some justification. But Korea, Vietnam and the others? How many had to die before Nixon pulled the troops out to rescue his popularity. And don't forget, we're still of an age to be drafted if the country got into a big new conflict. But I don't believe I could kill anyone under any circumstance."

"I read in the papers Nixon's impeachment is imminent."

"Makes you wonder who you can trust when you can't trust the President. The world's in a fucking mess," said Alex ruefully.

"They're testing nuclear warheads in Nevada, we've got heiresses being kidnapped, planes being hijacked, and we need to queue for gas. When the stations have gas, that is. You're right, the world's in a fucking mess." Rick stroked Alex's face. "Let's be the antidote to the mess. We'll make love, not war. And there's one thing you can trust, I loved being with you last night."

Alex stretched out his painful shoulders then smiled at Rick. "Yeah, me too."

♦ ♦ ♦

Monica had been true to her word about loving *The Cliffs of Mendocino* and suggested it to her contact on the movie. Her description apparently resonated with their storyboard elements and the art director was keen to view the piece. So, one Monday in early June, they loaded *The Cliffs of Mendocino* into the Chevy's trunk and headed to 20th Century Fox Studios.

Turning off West Pico onto the lot, the industrial nature of studio buildings struck Alex once more. They really were factories, albeit factories of dreams. This studio had a bit more semblance of movie magic as, after getting clearance from the white security booth with a blue roof, they had to drive along the recreation of an eighteen-nineties New York street scene to get to the stages. And it was a *whole* street, complete with tenement houses, shops, restaurants and even an elevated railroad track.

"They built this for the *Hello, Dolly* movie," explained Rick. "It cost so much to put up they couldn't afford to take it down."

"Impressive," conceded Alex.

"They build movie sets like this smaller than life to fit more detail into the camera frame which makes them look bigger on screen. Sometimes they actually use dwarfs as extras in the distance to add to the illusion of depth," said Rick knowledgably.

"Hope Snow White gets a finder's fee."

Rick laughed and came back with, "Feeling Happy's her reward."

Alex chuckled at Rick's wit as he drove down the period street set. If you limited your eye line, as a camera would, it was like stepping back in time. They'd even constructed a Gothic church tower beside the railroad station in the distance. The set's magical illusion of bygone New York was immediately dashed when they turned the corner. The quaint facades were revealed to be plywood frontages covering the soundstage and office exteriors. Alex parked beside Stage 8 and hopped out to release the painting from the trunk.

Construction equipment and random pieces of scenery sprawled outside the stage's gigantic open door. Rick informed Alex that these heavy metal studio doors were called 'elephant doors' due to their scale. They could be raised to allow in large pieces of scenery and then lowered to soundproof the stage with solid steel. Rick exchanged words with a couple of technicians lounging outside on a smoke break. They pointed to Raphael, the guy in charge of set decoration. Rick went over and introduced himself. Beckoning Alex over with the painting, Rick introduced him to Raphael, who in turn led them onto the stage, issuing the stern warning, "Mind your step. Watch out for cables!"

Inside the cavernous soundstage they saw set dressers adding finishing touches to an art gallery set. The art gallery's supposedly solid walls were wooden flats, the construction joists propping them up clearly visible around the sides. The assistants were hanging framed artworks on brown walls. A wooden easel, an antique escritoire and a mahogany chair dressed the set, giving it an old-world feel. There were gaps between paintings hung on the low angles, Alex guessed these spots were reserved for the high-profile works from Monica's museum.

Alex passed *The Cliffs of Mendocino* to Raphael. Assistants came down from ladders and gathered around to look. All were hugely complimentary. A guy in a safari jacket holding a pipe, along with a man in a pink polyester leisure suit who'd been looking at the set through a viewfinder, also came and gave the painting their seal of approval. Alex allowed himself a small moment of pride.

Rick looked around nervously. "Are they doing fire effects on this stage?"

"Don't worry," said Raphael. "The fire scenes are on the other stages. There's no chance of a random spark in here."

Exiting through the elephant door, Alex felt like he was walking out on a puppy leaving his painting behind. He and Rick got in the car. "I need to swing by Caxton's Art Supplies, if that's okay with you," said Alex starting the motor.

"Sure, no problem."

As they waited for a couple of cars to pass by on the *Dolly* street, a white studio buggy turned in next to them. The buggy stopped with a jolt. Alex saw a familiar face stare into their car. He nearly jumped out of his skin when the man leapt from the buggy ... it was Sid.

"What the hell are you doing on the lot?" barked Sid rapping on Rick's window.

Rick wound down the window. "Hi, dad. What are *you* doing here?"

Sid spread his hands in disbelief. "I'm shooting a picture. I told you I was shooting a picture! Does anybody listen to a word I say?" A frazzled woman in tweed skirt and white blouse with her hair in a bun followed Sid out of the buggy. She hovered behind him with a pad and pen. "Did I not tell him I was shooting a picture?" Sid turned to her and looked for an answer. She made a noncommittal face in response. Sid turned back to Rick. "Like I said, what are *you* doing on the lot?" Sid noticed Alex behind the wheel. "Hi, Dex."

"Hi, Mr. Stradman," said Alex.

"We're delivering one of Alex's paintings. They're using it in the movie shooting on stage 8," explained Rick in a long-suffering tone.

"You're really an artist then?" Sid asked Alex.

"Apparently," replied Alex with a half-smile.

Sid's attention returned to Rick. "Show me your foot."

"Not now, dad. We were just leaving."

"Get out of the car and show me your goddamned foot! I paid the goddamn bill and want to see what kind of job they did!"

Like a surly schoolkid, Rick climbed out of the car. Steadying himself on the open door, he raised his foot, slipped off his sneaker and rolled down his sock. Using his free hand, he displayed the ankle like a prize on *The Price is Right*. "Happy?"

Sid bent to inspect the dressing. "Three hundred and fifty dollars for that? What's that goddamn bandage made of? Spun silk." Sid turned to the woman. "Is it made of spun silk, Shirley?" Shirley made a face like she was about to say something but hesitated. Sid was back on Rick. "For that price I'd have expected them to have had to sew your foot back on! Ye gods!"

"The glass nicked an artery, dad," said Rick, putting his sock and shoe back on.

"This is the quiet life you want? This is thinking on the beach? Quiet for you maybe. Meanwhile I got hospitals ringing my phone off the hook in the middle of the night! My heart can't take this, Ricky," Sid theatrically clutched his chest.

"It was an accident, dad."

Sid let out an exasperated sigh. Then he softened and hugged Rick roughly. "As long as you're okay, Ricky. That's all that matters." Sid released Rick and held him at arm's length. "I spoke to someone at Talent Associates. They were over the moon with your reading! We're thrilled, Ricky. See that, Shirley's thrilled too. Aren't you thrilled Shirley?" Shirley smiled wanly and tapped her pen on her pad to attract Sid's attention. Sid ignored Shirley's attempt to communicate and asked Rick, "When do you shoot?"

"Next week at Universal." Rick hung his head morosely.

Sid turned to Shirley. "Is this the face of a kid who just got a part in a big T.V. show?" Shirley shrugged as Sid carried on to Rick, "You got a part in a big T.V. show, Dex got a painting in a movie and you got a three-hundred-and-fifty-dollar bandage on your ankle. We should all be so lucky!"

Shirley anxiously checked her watch and tentatively tapped Sid's shoulder. "Mr. Stradman, you really must get to set. We shoot at eleven."

"Gotta run," said Sid breaking away and striding back to the buggy, which was now causing a small traffic jam on the *Dolly* street. "Big scene coming up, lots of effects and extras."

"What's the movie, dad?" asked Rick getting into the Chevy.

"*Tornado!* ... With an exclamation point!" Sid held up his hands to emphasize the exclamation point. "Big budget, big names, big headaches! They switched on the wind machines yesterday and blew off the leading man's toupee. If the wig guys can't glue it on stronger we're gonna have to put a chin strap on it. When we're back from location I'll throw a brunch at the house. You'll come. Letitia thinks you're avoiding her!"

"That's because I am," muttered Rick in an aside to Alex.

"For Pete's sake Shirley, quit your yakking and get in the cart," growled Sid. Shirley scampered around and climbed in the buggy. "So long, Dex!" Sid yelled. "Thanks for looking after the kid. I'll have to put you on retainer as his nanny at this rate." Sid then barked at the old guy driving the buggy, "Move it, Manny! We don't got all day! Jesus, what's with you people?"

"Dad's jumped on the disaster movie bandwagon then," said Rick watching Sid's buggy trundle away. "*Tornado*."

"Don't forget the exclamation point," added Alex turning the car onto the *Dolly* street.

"Hope it's a hit. I want Sid Stradman's name to be synonymous with big wind."

Once the white security booth had allowed them off the lot, Rick said, "After you've visited the art store can you swing by Brentwood? I need to check in on my apartment."

At Caxton's, Alex got immense pleasure shopping art supplies without worrying about cash. He purchased experimental materials with no guilt. In fact, he went crazy stocking up on pigments and different boards and papers. He found a ready-made case perfect for wet works up to twelve by sixteen inches. After the art shop, Alex headed to Brentwood as requested. He turned off Barrington and onto San Vicente, a wide, tree lined road with a grassy median strip.

"There, it's the one on the right." Rick pointed to a spanking new four-story apartment building. "Parking entrance is off Gretna Green."

Alex pulled up before the ironwork gates to the underground lot. Rick told him the code, which he punched into the electronic key pad. The gate swung open. After parking up, Rick led the way past a gym, open-air swimming pool and foyer with mailboxes. Rick collected a wad of letters crammed into his box and went to the elevators. Apartment 110 was at the end of the beige shag pile carpeted hallway on the third floor.

"They only just finished the place," said Rick unlocking the door and sniffing disdainfully. "Everywhere smells of paint and plaster."

Rick's apartment wasn't the ritzy pad Alex had imagined. A taupe couch and glass coffee table were the only furnishings in the living room. Otherwise it was empty, except for several large packing cartons stacked in one corner. A small balcony overlooking the treetops on San Vicente led off this room. "Not exactly stamped your mark on it," Alex said, surveying the soulless room.

Rick sorted the mail into two piles on the kitchen counter. "Before this I'd a rental in West Hollywood. We had a couple of break-ins nearby and I stupidly told momma about them. Back when we were on speaking terms that was. Next thing I know she's commanded Sid to move me into a place with gates and security. This place has searchlights and armed guards on the roof I hear."

"Thanks for the tip, I'll shimmy under the razor wire on my way out." Alex wandered around opening doors. "Three bedrooms?"

"Sid thinks big." Rick tipped one pile of mail directly into the garbage bin, then began ripping open the other. "This place is the reason I was out at the beach that day." Rick stared absently into the distance. "I only spent one night here after Sid gave me the keys. Momma rang five minutes after I'd moved in and we had a terrible row. I woke up the next morning and needed to get out, so I just jumped into the car and drove. That's how I ended up at Sunset Cove," said Rick. He looked away like he was leaving something out of the story. After stacking the opened mail into a neat pile he approached the boxes in the corner. He carried one into the kitchen and ripped off the tape. "Want to give me a hand?"

"With what?"

"Unpacking. I need to make this place livable."

"I thought you didn't like it here?"

"I don't."

"It sounds like you're moving back from the beach house." A sick feeling washed over Alex. He'd blown over hundred bucks at the art store. Was Rick now planning to move out? The prospect of a return to poverty was not pleasant. A myriad of worries and contingencies flashed through his mind.

Rick delved into the box, pulling out sheets and towels still in their cellophane wrapping. "I can't commute from Sunset Cove to Universal. I'd be on the road more than at the studio. It's only for the shoot." Rick looked gloomily around the apartment again. "I still don't feel great about being here by myself. This place makes me feel lonely."

"Maybe that's because it's the size of a football field?" Relieved Rick wasn't planning on moving out completely, and the rent would keep coming in, Alex picked up another carton and carried it to him.

"This is a big favor to ask but would you stay here with me? You know, during the shoot."

That was a thinker for Alex. Their relationship at the beach house was one thing. He could still put it down to a summer fling, even though Rick had become a nightly fixture in his bedroom. But moving into town together, even temporarily, was something else altogether.

Rick sensed Alex's reticence. "You said you want to do more urban studies. We have some great intersections nearby. I'll let you go play in the traffic!"

Alex felt Rick made a good point. He could also catch up with the crowd at Barney's while in town. Touching base with old friends would be a good test of if he was still the man he thought he used to be. "What the heck. Okay," said Alex.

"Really?" Rick hurled himself at Alex and flung his arms around his neck. "You truly *are* a lifesaver!"

Alex pushed him away, saying very firmly, "But there will be conditions."

Rick twisted his mouth in concern.

"I shall decorate the place how I choose. You will have one room and use of the kitchen ..."

"Very funny." Rick shoved a carton towards Alex. "Hurry up and get this sorted and I'll make a list of what we need delivered."

Alex ripped the tape off the box and surveyed the apartment. His imminent new home. Could this summer throw any more curve balls his way? A short while later Rick was making up the king size bed while he was carrying bags of trash to the garbage chute.

Welcome to the Stradman-Morgan's of Brentwood.

FIRST IMPRESSIONS

Alex realized he had never owned a suitcase.

Preparing to decamp to Brentwood, even if only for a couple of weeks, involved more organization than he'd envisaged. His seemingly simple 'What the heck' to Rick's request not only required packing clothes (admittedly not a huge task as he didn't have many) but also the professional supplies he needed for his work; the opportunity to do some plein air work in the city was the main reason he'd agreed to accompany Rick, after all. Easels, palettes, paints, brushes, thinners, pencils, plus all the other odds and ends added up to a sizeable amount of kit. Having everything to hand in the studio made the infrastructure of his art invisible. Deciding what was vital and then stowing it into boxes and bags made it evident he was doing Rick a big favor – there were a lot of boxes and bags.

In between sorting out his own affairs, Alex also found himself supporting Rick's preparations for the T.V. shoot. The red Mercedes was built for zipping along cliff roads with minimal luggage not transporting equipment, that's why his poor old Chevy had become the packhorse. Rick's inability to drive a stick-shift meant his impromptu description of Alex as his chauffeur was close to reality. One day, frustrated by Rick needing yet another ride for yet another errand, Alex cajoled Rick into giving the stick a go by saying, "Come on, man. You can do anything if you put your mind to it." Nervously, Rick got into the Chevy's driving seat, Alex took up position on the passenger side. Alex tasked Rick to drive from the parking lot up to the highway. Within the first hundred yards Rick had failed to get into the correct gear once. The Chevy's poor old gearbox was screaming with pain. By the time they'd made it up to the highway, Alex was pulling his newly glossy hair out by its well-nourished roots. Arriving at the conclusion Rick was truly incapable of driving a stick, Alex surrendered all hope of being spared transportation duty and gave in.

A few days prior to the shoot Rick had managed to drive himself to Universal in the Merc for costume fittings and pre-production. On his return he told Alex about the clothes they'd had selected for his character. Rick had apparently expressed uncertainty about an orange and yellow flower-pattern shirt, but not wanting to be considered 'difficult' he'd gone along with the costume designer's choice. Together with packing, driving and assuaging Rick's insecurities, Alex had also assumed the role of script reader and prompter to help Rick learn his part. After over a week of repeatedly going over his lines, if Rick couldn't fulfil the role of Bradley, Alex felt he could easily stand in for him.

After the frenetic activity of preparing to decamp from the beach house, finally being installed at the Brentwood apartment was a major relief to Alex. They'd driven there in their respective cars so they could be free agents over the next couple of weeks. Now up to speed on his lines, his foot neatly re-dressed by a Beverly Hills doctor, and his nerves allayed, Alex was looking forward to getting Rick out of his hair at the studio and settle down to some work of his own. He'd reconnoitered an area near the 405 and planned to set up his painting equipment there first thing tomorrow morning.

Unpacking the soft furnishings and adding a few lamps had made the apartment more hospitable, but Alex acknowledged there was still something oppressive about the place. The bare walls in white builder's finish, however, made a perfect backdrop for several of Alex's works. They'd hung the two pieces he'd done on the highway side by side; they made a striking combination. Another barren expanse of white wall was broken up by a lesser work from the *Mendocino* series. With clothes in drawers, towels on rails and pictures on walls, it became clear there was only one thing they didn't have in the apartment ... food.

Rick suggested they go eat at The Daisy on Rodeo Drive. Alex guessed the place would be expensive, but since Rick would be picking up the check that wasn't his problem. Rodeo Drive was not his usual stomping ground but having been there a few times recently he knew the most convenient place to park. The crowd on The Daisy's red brick patio dining under fringed parasols was a swank affair. Alex couldn't have given a damn if the place was a two-bit burger joint with a clown outside; he was starving and needed to eat. A hostess seated them amidst the young starlets and aged producers. While they waited on menus, Rick filled Alex in on the place's history; it was one of the first 'Members Only' clubs in the early sixties. Its exclusivity making it a magnet for girls in skin tight pants who wanted to dance the frug while banging elbows with Robert Redford, Steve McQueen and the like.

Alex had emptied the bread basket and Rick was downing his second martini by the time their food arrived. The conversation dipped for ten minutes as Alex devoured his hamburger. The warm glow of a full stomach was lulling him into a sense of false security when Rick chugged his third martini and casually asked, "Would you drive me to Universal tomorrow?"

Alex nearly swallowed his last mouthful without chewing. "Are you serious?"

"Only tomorrow." Rick gave him a wide-eyed long lashed blink.

"If I drive you there it means I have to hang around all day to drive you back. Why can't you drive yourself in the Mercedes?" Alex pushed his plate away.

Rick toyed with his vegetable and chicken salad. "I don't want people's first impression of me to be getting out of some fancy car. I play a student on the show. When you gave me that ride to the reading I think their seeing me get out of your beat-up car swung it for me. It telegraphed my free spirit and rebellious nature."

"Isn't there a bus service over the hills? Free-spirited rebels always take the bus."

"I don't want people to think I got this part just because of who my dad is. Or god forbid, if anyone still remembers her, momma."

"And the car you turn up in makes a difference to that?"

"Showing up on the first day in a fancy sports car will make me look like a spoiled rich brat."

"And you intend to surprise them with that fact later?"

"Don't be a prick. It's just, well, it's just that your car's so, you know ... so real."

"Let's say I drive you there, and you get out my car and look *real*. How do *I* look ferrying you around? Jeez, Abbott and Costello were seen apart more often than we have been lately." Alex screwed up the linen napkin and tossed it on the table.

"I know it knocks a day out of your work. But you could bring your field easel and do some plein air studies on the backlot? Please, please ... please?" Rick turned on the full Bambi doe eyes.

Alex grumpily took out his cigarettes. "I suppose ..."

Rick heaved a sigh of relief and snapped his fingers to summon a server. "Dessert."

"But only tomorrow. I need to do *my* work after that."

"Of course. Thanks, Al." Rick rested his hand on Alex's.

Alex snatched his hand away to light his cigarette. Flicking his eyes left to right, Alex took a drag. "We ought to skip dessert. Your call's at seven."

Rick reluctantly nodded in agreement and asked for the check.

♦ ♦ ♦

Waking up at four thirty in the morning was brutal. After a bleary-eyed kitchen and bathroom shuffle in the unfamiliar apartment, Alex and Rick hit the road in the cold gray dawn. At least this time Alex was familiar with Rick's route of choice to Universal, which was a blessing as his brain was still fuzzy from the early start. Pulling up at Gate 2, Alex recognized the security guard was the same one as the day he'd brought Rick to the reading. As soon as the guard clapped his eyes on the battered Chevy he approached with his clipboard. Alex wound down his window. "Morning."

"Ah, the chauffer. Those dry cleaners sure are taking their time with your uniform." The guard bent forward to check on Rick in the passenger seat. "Morning, Mr. Stradman. You guys want Stage 44. Go straight ahead."

Rick cut him off tartly. "I know the way."

Alex smiled apologetically at the guard.

"Mr. Stradman, there's a parking space by the stage marked with your name. Give way to pedestrians, buggies ..."

"... and studio trams," added Alex pleasantly.

"You got it, bud." The guard backed off.

"Don't I need a pass?" Alex called after him.

The guard came back, running his pen down the clipboard. He let it rest. "This you?"

Alex saw his name. "Yep."

"No need. You're on the list." The guard went into his booth and lifted the barrier.

As Alex drove onto the lot he asked Rick, "How come I'm on the list? I only agreed to drive you here last night."

Rick hugged the script to his chest. "I told Mike to put you on the list, just in case."

"In case of what?"

"Just in case." Rick defensively checked his watch. "It's a quarter off seven. Take it slow to the stage."

Glancing over, Alex saw Rick mussing up his hair and loosening his collar. "What's that in aid of?"

"Getting into character," muttered Rick.

Alex crawled past the bulk of the soundstages, then he spotted a gaggle of people outside Stage 44's open elephant door. After pulling up in the space bearing Rick's name on the low blue railing, Rick didn't move. "Um, we've arrived," said Alex.

"I know, I know." Rick reached to the rear seat and hauled up a denim shoulder bag covered with PEACE buttons and C.N.D. badges. Still he didn't get out.

"What're you waiting for?" asked Alex.

"Preparing," answered Rick staring at the stage.

Irritation building, Alex snapped, "I'm getting out if you're not."

"Wait!" Rick restrained him.

Alex took a few deep breaths to temper his frustration then saw a couple of heads curiously turn their way.

Rick gave it a few more beats until more cast and crew were looking their way. "Here goes," said Rick as he slunk out of the car. He leaned casually on the door, dipped into his shoulder bag and took out a stick of gum. After taking time to unwrap it, crunch the wrapper and pop the gum in his mouth, he hissed back inside the car to Alex, "Give it a couple of minutes then follow." The entire crowd outside the stage was focused on Rick by the time he'd slammed the car door and swaggered to the stage.

Wondering what had ever possessed him to get caught up in this madness, Alex threw back his head and covered his tired eyes with his hands. Figuring he'd allowed Rick enough time to make his grand entrance, he got out. The throng outside the stage had dissipated, the elephant door was sliding shut and there was no sign of Rick. Alex lingered beside the Chevy, feeling like the biggest spare part on earth. A pale blue sports car drew up alongside. Two young women got out, one dark haired and the other blonde. Both very attractive in a fresh-faced way. Alex guessed one of these two was the show's star. A quick glance at the name plate on the blue rail in front of her parking space confirmed this.

The blonde woman carried a couple of bags to the stage, while the dark-haired one, who Alex now knew was Susan, locked the car. She dropped her keys into her patchwork slouch purse, then rummaged for something else. Looking up, Susan called over to him, "Good morning!"

"Hi," said Alex adding a casual wave.

Susan flicked her eyes from side to side and gave him a quizzical smile. "You okay? You look kinda lost."

"Yeah. No. I mean, I'm okay. Not lost. I'm waiting for someone … there he is." Rick appeared from beside the stage and beckoned impatiently. Alex pointed to Rick. "I'm with him."

"Cool." Susan pulled a pair of sunglasses out of her slouch purse. "See you around."

"Alex!" Rick shouted and beckoned him to come again, more urgently this time.

"Gotta run," said Alex feeling like a poodle in the park.

"You better had." Smiling, Susan watched Alex scurry to obey Rick's command and put on her glasses.

"Where'd you get to?" asked Alex tetchily after catching up with Rick.

"The unit manager collared me to install me in my trailer." Rick shuffled Alex around the stage. "Donny, this is Alex." A bespectacled young man in a knitted tank top, carrying a walkie talkie and a clipboard, smiled vaguely. "Donny's an assistant director on the show. Here, get in." Before having chance to acknowledge Donny, Rick had pushed Alex up the steps into his dressing room trailer. It was a Spartan affair. Couch, fridge, phone, and cellophane wrapped fruit basket. Rick was about to shut the door, when Donny tapped on it.

"Mr. Stradman, I need to run you through the day," Donny said apologetically.

"Oh, fine. And please call me Rick."

Alex plopped himself on the tan moquette bench seat while Donny hovered in the doorway and outlined the shoot. First up was the scene outside the movie theater on the backlot, the one leading into the car hitting the McMillan's maid, Mildred. After lunch they'd do the actual car stunt and then set up for Bradley running after the car to get a visual on the plates. They'd finish the day with several dialog scenes. The plan was to stage the action on set, then the stand-ins would take over for camera focus and lighting while the cast went into wardrobe and make-up.

Donny was about to leave when Rick called him back. "Alex gave me a ride because I had car trouble. Now I've screwed up his day by dragging him out here. He's an artist. Would it be a problem if he set up on the backlot and did some painting?"

"I guess if no-one's shooting it'll be okay. There's coffee and pastries outside. I'll call you when we're ready," said Donny closing the door.

Rick sat on a yellow plastic chair in front of the dressing table mirror. He flicked on a switch. Bulbs around the mirror flared into life. Taking a few deep breaths, Rick stared at his reflection. "This is ridiculous." He flicked off the lights. Scraping back the chair, he stood and declared flatly, "Can't do it."

"Can't do what?"

"This show. Act! I can't do any of it." Rick went to the dressing room door.

Alex dashed after him, braced the door with his foot and pushed Rick back. He gripped Rick's arms and found he was trembling violently. "They're about to shoot," hissed Alex not wanting anyone outside to overhear.

"I can't remember my lines. It's all a mistake. Why did I sign that dumb contract?" said Rick, practically hysterical.

A knock, then Donny's voice called, "Mr. Stradman. Sorry, Rick, we're ready for you."

"One moment!" answered Alex loudly. He dragged Rick deeper into the trailer. "You know the script backwards. Hell, *I* know the script backwards. You're a good actor. You're prepared." Alex stared him down. "You can do this. I believe in you."

Closing his eyes, Rick's breathing calmed. "Okay." He opened his eyes and clenched his fists determinedly. "I can do this."

"That's the spirit." Alex hugged him, it was either that or slap him.

Donny knocked insistently. "You're needed urgently on set, Rick."

"Now get out there and do some fucking acting." Alex swung open the door. An expectant Donny peered up from the foot of the steps.

"I'm ready. Where do you want me?" With a supreme display of confidence Rick rolled back his shoulders and walked down the trailer's steps. The cast and crew greeted him warmly. Laughter and happiness ensued. Coffee was put into hands, donuts and pastries passed around. Golf carts rolled up to transport everyone to the backlot.

Leaving them to get on with their work, Alex grabbed a coffee and mooched the craft service table. Result. One potential crisis averted today.

And it had only just gone seven a.m.

♦ ♦ ♦

Once the golf carts had whisked the cast and crew off to the backlot Alex was left alone at the stage. He used the time to gather his thoughts. Hauling his painting kit out of the car, he slung it over his shoulder, grabbed his broad brimmed hat and set off on foot in search of the unit.

Heading in the direction the carts had taken off in, he strolled between the beige soundstages. The technical work going on all around was fascinating. One giant stage had its elephant door rolled back. He paused to watch scenic painters at work inside. They were on cradles suspended from the roof creating a city scape cyclorama. Did anybody ever think that the skyline and cityscape backdrops of film sets were painted? He certainly hadn't until now. The door began to slide shut and Alex continued his journey.

After passing parked trailers loaded with bits of scenery and reels of cables, greenery up ahead indicated he was approaching the backlot. A few hundred yards farther on and a manicured city park appeared. After hitting the park, Alex came across a street of brownstone houses complete with walk-up stoops. Getting closer, he saw the McMillan crew set up beneath a movie theatre's canopy on the street corner.

Shouts and commands echoed between the lighting crew as they erected arc lamps. Black and gray cables snaked across the street, guys were hooking them up to a couple of humming power trucks. Five beige and white trailers were parked out of shot, costumes dangled in the one at the back with its side door open. A green smocked woman with a tape measure around her neck was helping a girl with a beehive hairdo into a red jacket with gold epaulets. About twenty-five assorted extras, all dressed in colorful city clothes, were clumped on the street corner. Another assistant director on a walkie-talkie was relaying instruction to them.

Alex picked out Rick. He was standing between Susan and a diminutive actress in a blue headscarf. They were lined up next to the theater kiosk in front of three sets of theater style double doors. The actors were listening intently to a man, who every so often took a couple of steps to point at various colored chalk marks on the ground. There was a lot of nodding and moving back and forth, peppered with occasional laughter from the women. Rick was taking it deadly seriously though, furrows of concentration on his forehead.

After ten minutes of rehearsal, they were ready to run the action. The main actors went through the fake doors into the fake movie theatre. Roughly half the extras followed them in. The beehive lady in the red jacket took up position inside the ticket kiosk. The remainder of the extras split themselves on the street either side of the doors. Donny scampered onto the set and passed a loudhailer to the director.

After a long pause, the director said through the megaphone, "Everyone in place?" Various crew members gave the thumbs up. Everyone stopped moving. Silence descended. "Rehearsal! Background action!" The extras on the street started walking. "Action!"

One set of movie theater doors flew open. Several extras burst out, laughing and chatting like they'd just seen a movie. Susan, Rick and the short woman then came out. Alex deduced the woman in the blue headscarf must be Nancy playing the role of Mildred. The actors paused on their chalk marks while more extras came out of the theater. Alex was too far away to hear the dialog, but he'd run through the script so many times he knew this was the scene where Sally berates Bradley for going to the movies rather than seeing the sights.

"Cut!" yelled the director.

Activity and hubbub resumed around the set. The director had a conflab with several crew then gave a nod to Donny. Three stand-ins took the places of Susan, Nancy and Rick, and Donny guided the leading actors off set to the parked trailers.

Alex hurried to catch up with Rick. "Hey!"

Rick broke away from Donny to greet Alex. "Great, you found us."

"Looks like you got everything under control. I'll take a hike and do some work."

"Fine. Come back at lunch. What time do we break?" Rick asked Donny.

"Should be around one. They really need you in make-up, Rick," said Donny with urgency, indicating the steps up to the trailer beside them.

"Gotta go. Have fun," said Rick.

Leaving the buzz of the set behind, Alex walked down the fake street. It continued through various styles of big city architecture. Jarringly, a green jungle appeared beyond a turn-off on the block resembling Wall Street. Going farther, Alex took a left down a road leading to tree-lined square surrounded by stores, a gas station and low houses. He'd left the big city behind and was now in a deserted small-town square complete with ornate bandstand. It was eerie, like being in one of those movies where the townsfolk have vanished and you're the last man on earth. An imposing civic building, a stone structure with four columns supporting a triangular roof, dominated one side of the square. Circling around, Alex discovered it was a yet another painted façade supported by rusty scaffolding and blackened struts.

Alex selected a vantage point where he could contrast the solidity of the building's frontage with the lattice of supports behind. The sparkling morning light created crisp black shadows and intensified the verdant shrubbery, making sharp pops of lime and emerald against the cool stone. He unfolded his field easel, opened his paint box, positioned the water bottle, stuffed rags into the cross section of the easel's legs, tipped his hat's brim to shield his eyes from the sun's glare, fixed a fresh board in place, and began to paint.

The only disturbance came from the occasional tram rattling by when the studio tours started up. Once the sun had moved around, and the shadows had changed too much to continue, he quickly finished this first study. Although practically dry, he nevertheless slipped it into his wet work case, the interior grooves preventing any smudging.

His next set up contrasted the set's rearview fakery with the realistic buildings on the other side of the square. With the sun behind him, he tipped his hat's brim to shield the back of his neck. He lost track of time and got deep into the work. The hat's brim not only shielded his neck from the sun but his ears from any sound behind him. The light crunch of gravel suddenly announced a presence. Knowing someone had sneaked up sent a shiver of unease down his spine. He glanced over his shoulder, half expecting to come face to face with Norman Bates.

Instead he found a middle-aged woman with short dark hair brushed forward in a pixie style was watching him work. She wore a white shirt, set off by a perky multicolor neckerchief, beige slacks and tennis shoes. She drew back like a deer caught feeding. "Sorry to startle you, I didn't want to interrupt your work. May I watch?"

"Be my guest." Alex resumed his painting. The heat was building up, he needed to finish the piece fast as his water bottle's level was low and the paint was drying quickly. The jasmine scent the woman wore wafted across him.

"I've worked here for many years, but I've never seen anyone do this before," the woman said softly.

"You surprise me. The studio's teeming with painters."

"I've seen people painting sets, but I've never seen anyone *paint* a set, if you see what I mean. You work here?"

"No. I'm with a friend who's got a part on a show." Alex rinsed his brush in the dirty water pot, snatched the rag and dried it off. After stowing the brush in the paint box, he picked up the board and blew on it.

"May I take a closer look?"

"Be my guest." Alex passed the board to the woman. "Be careful of your blouse."

The woman took the painting by the edges, holding it at arm's length from her pristine white shirt. She appraised it thoughtfully, then raised her gentle brown eyes. The sun twinkled in them as she said, "You're an excellent painter."

Alex shrugged modestly. "Thanks."

The woman switched her focus between the backlot building and Alex's painting. "I've passed by this set so many times I don't even notice it anymore. You've made me see it with fresh eyes. Could I buy this?"

The woman's request was flattering and yet massively awkward. Alex had never considered putting a price on his art. How could this nothing little study be worth anything? The woman wasn't carrying a purse. If he asked for money this could all get involved and awkward. "Take it. My gift to you."

"But I couldn't ..." The woman dropped her eyes to the painting and passed it back.

"I insist." Alex set about packing up his paints and folding the easel. He felt the woman's eyes remaining on him. Conversation was required to cover his departure. "You've worked here a long time, you say. What department?" he asked over his shoulder.

The woman smiled, a charming crooked smile. "Which do you think?"

Alex had asked a dumb question and she'd asked one back - one he now had to answer. He considered her simple but stylish outfit and comfortable shoes. She could be anything from a smart canteen lady to a dressed down designer. Best to aim high so as not to offend. "Producer?"

The woman laughed out loud. "Ha! I wish!" She carried on chuckling.

Her laughter was infectious, Alex smiled bashfully in response. "I don't know anything about the movie business. Sorry if I offended you."

The woman held up the painting. "Thanks for this. And you didn't offend me. In fact you flattered me by placing me well above my station. May I ask your name?"

"Morgan. Alex Morgan."

"I'll watch out for your name, Alex Morgan," she said.

Alex bent to gather his things. He slung the easel over his shoulder and grabbed the wet work case and paint box. When he turned to say goodbye to the woman, she'd gone. No sign of her anywhere. Like she'd vanished into thin air. Alex headed back to the unit and promptly forgot all about it. A couple of right turns took him from idealized American small-town square, via fake financial district New York, to pseudo downtown San Francisco. This land of movie magic had gelled into a roadmap in his head.

Getting back to the unit, Alex found work on set halted and the action moved to the catering truck. The cast and crew waited in line for lunch. Alex took a quick look around. Rick stood out from the crowd as he was wearing a loud orange and yellow flower-patterned shirt. Alex assumed this was the costume he'd had reservations about. It was *very* eye-catching. Rick stood beside the costume trunk while a mature female extra in a paisley pants suit and floppy hat chatted animatedly to him. He was twitching like an animal with its leg in a trap. As the woman paused to draw breath, Rick spotted Alex and relief flooded his face. Extricating himself from the woman, Rick made a bee line for Alex. "There you are!" Rick practically shoved him towards a beige and green motor home parked behind the costume truck. "I thought you'd got lost."

"No such luck. Here I am."

"Dump your things in my trailer." Rick quickly led him to a Winnebago with his name on the door, albeit written in marker pen on a sheet of paper.

Inside, Alex laid his painting gear on the brown moquette bench seat. "Looks like you've made a friend out there."

Letting out an exasperated sigh, Rick bent open a couple of slats of the venetian blind and squinted through the gap. "Just my luck. One of the extras actually worked on momma's one and only movie a hundred years ago. By the end of the day it'll be all over set who momma is." He let the blind snap shut and silently seethed. "I could kill her."

"But apart from that, anyone try to murder *you* yet?"

Rick cast a sidelong glance at Alex.

"In the show, I mean."

"They're getting everything in place for the stunt with the car now."

Alex could tell Rick was stewing about the extra. "There's nothing you can do about it. And people will find out about you sooner or later, if they don't already know. Let it go."

"I'll tell Donny to put that overly familiar extra in my eye line to help motivate my anger," said Rick darkly.

"There you go. When life throws lemons ..."

Rick let out a small laugh and relaxed. "You should see the stunt man they've got doubling for Nancy. He's the same height as her but built like a prize-fighter. They've dressed him in a copy of her blue suit and put him in high heels and a red wig. And for the finishing touch they've put red lipstick on him! We had to bite our cheeks to stop ourselves cracking up when he walked on set. Anyway, he marches up to Nancy to introduce himself. She takes a beat, looks him up and down, steps back and says, 'Uncanny. Like looking in a mirror'. Then she puts her hand on her hip, turns to the crew and says, 'A funhouse mirror'! You hungry?" asked Rick.

"I could eat."

Warily, Rick opened his trailer's door and peeked out checking for the pesky extra. "The coast's clear."

The line at the catering truck had thinned out, so they got quickly served. They selected a couple of plates of chicken salad and sat at one of the collapsible tables set up around the truck. "Nice shirt," said Alex slyly.

Rick tugged it down, as if removing the wrinkles would improve its appearance. "It's hideous, isn't it? Bradley must've been on mescaline when he bought this. I'd want to hit someone with a car if I saw them wearing it."

"This scene revolves around someone trying to run down Bradley. It's important you're the focal point, they put you in it to stand out." While chewing his salad, Alex saw Rick rolling this around in his mind. "How far have you got in the scene?"

"We're at the point when the car's going to mount the sidewalk. They broke Nancy before lunch. She's doing another show over at C.B.S."

A walkie-talkie's crackle alerted them to Donny's arrival. He hovered apologetically beside their table. "Rick, you're needed back on set."

"Thanks, Donny." Rick pushed his plate aside, then frowned. "Salad was a bad move. Have I got stuff in my teeth?" Rick smiled broadly at Alex.

"All clear, good to go."

"Are you going to paint on the backlot again this afternoon?"

"Nah, I'm beat. Can I hang out here?"

"Sure. Have a sleep in my trailer." And with that, Rick departed to the set.

Alex watched the crew get the scene ready while he finished his lunch. Then he hung out by the craft service table, availing himself of the endless coffee supply to keep his eyes open. How did these movie people cope with constantly waking up in the small hours? He guessed being in bed by ten every night might help. No wonder L.A. wasn't a late-night town.

The filming process seemed laborious and quite unsatisfying to Alex. Large amounts of time were spent setting up for small chunks of action, which from a distance looked like nothing. It was a jigsaw. The individual pieces only transmitting meaning when spliced together. The gaffer was finally satisfied the lighting was in place, the grips had secured the camera on a dolly for the tracking shot, and the boom operator had his position worked out for the dialog recording. Alex had absorbed a lot of information during today's crash course in film production.

The director decided they were good to go. Everyone around the set craned forward to watch the action.

Take 1 - As the sedan went to mount the sidewalk, the stunt driver realized that the 'Mildred' double wasn't in exactly the right spot and aborted the pass.

"Cut."

Take 2 - The sedan mounted the sidewalk, the 'Mildred' double took their tumble and Rick vigorously chased the black car while emoting shock, concern and anger.

"Cut! Print."

They didn't move on. Instead, a couple of bigwigs drew the director aside. A muttered conversation took place out front of the brownstone houses. Leaving the bigwigs behind, the director got back on the loudhailer and told the crew to reset for another take. While the offset pow-wow had been taking place, a make-up man had tucked tissue inside Rick's shirt collar and powdered down his face. The make-up guy backed off as the director had a private chat with Rick. Alex watched intently, wondering what it was all about. Rick nodded a few times then smiled in understanding. The director patted him on the shoulder and walked away.

"Quiet on set. Action!"

Take 3 - The sedan mounted the sidewalk. After being hit, the 'Mildred' stunt double did an extra roll as he hit the ground, making the extras scatter back farther. Due to this added drama, the extras reacted with more shock than the previous take. Rick used added vigor and pumped his arms higher when chasing the car, which made this section more dynamic too. Rick ended the scene with a very convincing look of distress, before punching his fist in frustration when the sedan sped off before he could see the plates.

"Cut! Print. Moving on!"

The crew applauded. The 'Mildred' stunt double extricated himself from the extras. He dusted himself off and took a bow, which he spontaneously adapted into a curtsy, holding out his blue skirt to reveal a pair of knee pads; this got a big laugh and another round of applause. Receiving a few pats on the back himself, Rick left the set, picking his way over the cables back to his motor home.

"Hey, nice work!" congratulated Alex trailing Rick up the steps into the Winnebago.

"Shut the door," said Rick curtly and flopped on the brown moquette bench seat. He undid the laces and took off his shoe. "I'd a feeling something was wrong." A band of red blood was oozing through his beige sock. "I've bust the stitches."

"Oh, no," said Alex sitting beside him to look.

"I felt something rip on that last take. Shit."

"Shall I ask someone to come take a look? They must have a nurse on set."

Rick pondered. "I don't want them to know I've got a problem. They'd probably be pissed I hadn't said I was injured before the shoot. I need to get this sorted tonight. The Berkeley scenes are up tomorrow with two sequences where I need to run. Hudson and Milland will be on set, I don't want to get on their wrong side by looking like an amateur." Alex scratched his head, not knowing what to suggest. "I know," said Rick suddenly. "Can you go back to the stage and call Sid? See if he can get me into his doctor tonight."

"Wouldn't it be better for you to call him?"

"They're moving onto the close angle for my end of scene and there aren't any phones out here. I don't have time to go back to the stage. Please?"

Jeez, Alex didn't want to have to speak to Sid again, but there didn't seem to be an alternative. "Give me his number."

Rick scribbled on a pad and tore off the page.

Alex stuffed it in his pocket and turned to go.

"And Alex ... "

Alex turned back to Rick.

"Can you swing by the costume truck and ask them for a fresh pair of socks? Don't tell them why."

Chauffeur and now personal assistant, Alex felt his list of duties for Rick growing. Knocking on the costume wagon's door, Alex passed on Rick's request to the woman in the green smock who was doing something drastic to a costume with a pair of shears.

"No worries, hon, I'll have someone run a pair to his trailer," replied the woman while slicing five inches off a pleated plaid skirt.

Alex began the trek back to the soundstage. He hadn't gone far when a member of the lighting crew, a guy in a baseball cap, aviator sunglasses and yellow polo shirt, drew up behind him in a buggy. "You headed back to the stage?"

For a moment Alex thought the guy was talking to someone else, then replied, "Yeah."

"Hop on, I'll give you a ride."

"Cool." Alex jumped on the buggy and they trundled back towards the stages.

"You're with the new kid on the show, right?" asked the lighting guy.

"He had car trouble so I gave him a ride today." An explanation hadn't been requested, but Alex felt it necessary.

"The kid did good. We could've gone on all day if he hadn't got the timing right. And that would have truly loused up tomorrow's schedule."

"Is that bad?"

"The folks in the Black Tower get mighty twitchy if we fall behind schedule. Do it fast, do it right, that's what keeps 'em happy." The lighting guy kept up the chat until they pulled up outside Stage 44.

"Thanks for the ride," said Alex patting the buggy.

"Anytime, bud," said the guy cheerfully before trundling off.

Back in Rick's dressing room, Alex dialed the number Rick gave him. It was Sid's production office at Fox. Shirley, Sid's assistant, asked tersely what his call related to. When he explained Rick's problem, her mood softened. She said Sid was on set, but she'd send a runner and have Sid call him back. After hanging up, Alex crashed on the couch and promptly fell asleep.

The ringing phone jarred him awake and he leapt to answer. It was Sid. Shirley had filled him in on the backstory, he was understanding although brusque. Shirley called twenty minutes later having set up an appointment at Dr. Rosen's on North Canon. With that sorted, Alex left the dressing room to return to the backlot. He was saved the journey as Rick was just getting out of a buggy and came limping towards him.

"They did my last scene and broke me for the day," said Rick. He was back in his street clothes. The sheen of T.V. make-up had worn off and he looked very pale. Sitting on the couch in the dressing room, Rick took off his shoe - the fresh sock was drenched with blood.

"Shirley's made an appointment for you," said Alex.

Rick gingerly put his shoe back on. "Let's get out of here fast. I don't want anyone to see there's something wrong."

"Darn!" said Alex. He thumped the steering wheel in frustration as he joined the Hollywood Freeway.

"What's wrong?"

"I've left my painting gear in your trailer on the backlot."

"It'll be safe there. I'll be in it again for tomorrow's scenes."

Rick was already upset so Alex stifled his irritated response. It wasn't the safety of his equipment that bothered him. He couldn't do any work without his gear, which meant tomorrow would be another wasted day for him.

Dr. Rosen's waiting room was a plush affair with gold chairs and green shag pile carpet. Since it was the sole reading matter on the glass coffee table, Alex absently flicked through a celebrity magazine. He was shocked to recognize some of the people in it - he was absorbing Rick's world by osmosis.

When Rick emerged from the surgery, he looked a heck of a lot better than when he'd gone in. Things were less dramatic than feared. One stitch had given way and part of the scab had rubbed off, resulting in the bleeding. Dr. Rosen's nurse had re-stitched and tightly re-dressed the wound and supplied some additional dressings. Just before they left, the nurse summoned Alex in to her. She studiously demonstrated how he should redress Rick's wound if the same thing happened again. As she was doing so, Alex had an out of body experience. Fucking Rick was one thing, but this was beginning to feel like he'd adopted him. Why was everyone suddenly acting like he was solely responsible for Rick's welfare?

Including Rick.

On the drive to Brentwood, Alex wanted to snap every time Rick opened his mouth. He was fuming that he'd allowed himself to become a cross between Rick's lapdog and his factotum.

Rick sensed his bad mood. "Have I done something to upset you?" called Rick heating up a pizza in the arid Brentwood kitchen.

"Nah," Alex replied gruffly finishing off his cigarette on the mean balcony overlooking the San Vicente traffic. He came in and slammed the sliding door shut. "I'm going to turn in."

"You're not hungry?"

"No." Going through to 'their' bedroom felt like entering a jail cell. Shit, why hadn't he taken his equipment back to the stage when he left the backlot? When Rick came to bed, he rolled away and hugged the edge of the mattress as Rick leaned over to kiss him goodnight. Lying awake with closed eyes, Alex tossed the day over in his mind. Were his heckles rising because people were treating them as a couple? Not necessarily a romantic couple but two people who had an overt bond. Even when he'd dated in the past, he'd always felt independent, single, in control. Today with Rick he'd felt none of those things. Everything between them suddenly felt like a huge mistake. Alex cursed himself for letting his body rule his mind and always playing the good guy. That would have to change.

Tomorrow, after reclaiming his equipment at the studio, he'd tell Rick it was over and return to Sunset Cove before he lost himself completely.

He needed to go back to being the 'old' Alex.

Whoever that was.

ASSEMBLAGE

The alarm's shrill ring went off just before sun up. Opening his bleary eyes, Alex was relieved he'd skipped dinner and gone to bed at nine. He flung one hand out to mute the annoying clock and used the other to shove Rick out of bed. Gripping the wheel for another unwanted dawn trip over the hills, it took all of Alex's strength to resist blurting out his misgivings about their relationship. He grimly negotiated Laurel's twists and turns as Rick nervously chattered random concerns about today's scenes on the backlot. "Thank God it's the last day of this action stuff. I can't wait to stand still on a set and talk," said Rick finally with a sigh.

Yet again the same guard was on Gate 2, Alex wondered if the poor guy ever went home. He didn't even approach their vehicle today, soon as he saw Alex behind the wheel he raised the barrier with a mock salute. Alex gave a cheery wave in return, he didn't have any beef with the guard. After parking in Rick's dedicated space, Alex escorted Rick to his dressing room trailer. Donny showed up with the day's schedule, casually acknowledging Alex. While Rick was engaged, Alex grabbed a coffee from craft services and picked one up for Rick too. He carried the coffees into the dressing room just as Rick was putting down the phone.

"That was Monica. They've finished the shoot with your painting," said Rick. The bulbs were illuminated around the mirror and he prodded his face with dissatisfaction. Making eye contact with Alex's reflection, he said, "You were bored out of your brain yesterday. That's why you were mad at me last night, isn't it?"

Was this the moment to break it to Rick the reason for his funk was that their relationship was kaput? Alex, however, had enough heart to know with an important working day ahead, this wasn't the time to lay such a hurtful truth on Rick, so he answered evasively, "Kind of."

"Look. Come out to the backlot with the unit, grab your painting equipment and go back into town. You can swing by Fox, pick up the *Cliffs* and go do some work."

"How'll you get back to Brentwood?"

"I'll ask the office to book me a cab home."

Alex wanted to snarl that if the office could arrange transport today why Rick hadn't requested it yesterday, but he let it ride. Despite that red flash of anger, it touched him that Rick had sensed a problem and was trying to stick a Band Aid on it. Although he didn't want to upset Rick, he still wanted to put an end to their dalliance as soon as possible. The journey home could be an ideal opportunity to break the news. "I'll swing by and pick you up tonight."

"Only if you're sure you're okay with that?"

"Yeah," said Alex formulating a plan. He could have the Chevy packed, drop Rick off at Brentwood and cleanly escape back to his life of single freedom.

"This is the production office's number, Candice can take a message." Rick handed him a number. "By the way, while you're at Fox picking up the painting dad asked you to go see him. He'll be on Stage 15 all morning."

Why on earth would Sid want to see *him*? Silently smoldering with rage, Alex noted that once again Rick had imparted information in the order needed to get the result he wanted. Sid may have requested a meeting, but there was no reason now to grant his request. Dark thoughts rumbled through Alex's mind as the golf buggies took them to the backlot.

Rick's mobile trailer had been moved to a new spot on the opposite side of the civic building he'd painted yesterday. He gathered from the crew this backlot set was known as

Mockingbird Square - toda doubling for Berkeley Law. The fresh batch of extras milling around were young and costumed in headbands, afghan jackets, plaid mini-skirts and knee socks. Two glossy black trailers were parked outside the fake gas station across the square. Rick told Alex these housed the big stars, Milland and Hudson, who'd be shooting today. Not in any mood to hang around, Alex reclaimed his stuff from Rick's trailer, declined offers of rides from various crew members, and hiked back to the stage under his own steam.

Alex drove off the lot, the guard on gate 2 giving a cheery wave and another mock salute as he left. Back on the freeway, Alex realized how much of L.A. life was spent behind the wheel, this being his second trip over the hills in less than an hour. When Alex checked in at Fox's security booth, he found Raphael had put him on 'the list' and he drove straight to Stage 8. After reclaiming *The Cliffs of Mendocino* and stowing it in the trunk, Alex pondered Sid's request to go see him. He wondered if Sid was still unhappy about Rick's 'hippie' phase of living on the beach. If that was the case, and Sid chewed his ear off about it as he had on their first meeting, this could lend weight to his break up speech to Rick tonight. Alex decided to go see Sid, practically hoping for him to be aggressive and unreasonable to aid his argument about feeling stifled and uncomfortable. He drove back to Stage 15 on the opposite side of the lot. The stage's red light was lit, so he hung around the parked trucks, trailers and garbage skips in the alley until the bell sounded and the light went off. Alex swung open the outer door and through the inner door onto the stage.

The main set, filling half the studio, was a full-scale deluxe high-rise office interior. A nicely painted skyline cyclorama surrounded a phalanx of bronze floor to ceiling windows, all shattered and with shards of glass hanging precariously in the frames. Two wind machines moaned ominously as their blades powered down. Crew scurried around clearing papers and office detritus off the set. A blonde actress was modestly tugging a ripped chiffon blouse around her shoulders while a make-up girl mopped a trickle of blood off her cheek. Alex searched the onset activity for Sid. Shirley's yellow notebook was visible before Shirley, she was hovering at Sid's side by the camera. Alex picked his way over the cables.

Sid was talking ten to the dozen while Shirley scribbled furiously on her pad. He clocked Alex from the corner of his eye, gave a hand signal indicating 'give me a moment', and then wound up his notes. As Shirley hurried off, Sid hauled Alex aside muttering seriously, "Need a word."

Trying to stop a smile of relief coming to his lips, Alex followed Sid off the stage and into a golf cart. This meeting promised to go exactly the way he'd hoped. Manny, the elderly buggy driver with liver spots as prominent as a Dalmatian's, shuttled them to Sid's production office near the commissary. Alex took a seat in the mustard chair opposite Sid's desk. Sid offered him coffee, water, or Scotch, but Alex declined all three. Sid went to sit behind his desk, but then his eyes flicked to the clock on the wall. After a moment's thought, Sid said, "I need air. Let's walk." Sid stuffed his hands in his pants pockets and led Alex outside. They walked in silence past parked cars and palm trees until they hit the New York street set.

Then, without looking at Alex, Sid said out of the blue, "I'm grateful."

Alex jerked his head up in surprise. "What for?"

"That Gina's out of his life. Something's off in that dame's head. Damaged goods if you ask me. Why his mother thought marrying her was the way ahead for Ricky beats me. I tell you, she'd have dragged the boy down with her."

Alex had no idea why Sid was mentioning Gina. They resumed walking in silence, Alex now unsure what Sid was going to say next.

Sid halted outside the Gothic church on the *Hello, Dolly* street. The weather-beaten elevated railroad station with its faded period billboards for Heinz ketchup loomed above. "When the hospital called me the other night my heart nearly stopped," said Sid.

"It must've been a shock. Sorry for that."

"You guys didn't have cash or I.D., the hospital didn't have a choice. That's not what worried me. You see, in the past Ricky's done things ..."

Alex struggled to understand what Sid was driving at. "I'm not following."

Sid shook his head and looked to the sky, unable to meet Alex's eyes. "Things to hurt himself. Attempts to take his own life. When they said he'd been cut, I was afraid he'd slashed his wrists." Sid toughened his chin and puffed out his chest. "Here." Sid dug in his pants pocket and gruffly shoved a piece of paper at Alex. "This is for you."

When Alex unfolded it, he saw it was a check for a thousand dollars. With his head reeling from a total loss of equilibrium, he asked, "Why?"

"You're an artist, right? You should be stippling a fresco or whatever you artist guys do instead of running around after Limping Lord Fauntleroy. Time's money. I appreciate you looking out for my Ricky."

Alex stepped back, slightly overcome. Of all the things he'd been expecting, this was not one of them. "I don't know how to respond."

"Terrific! Best goddamn news I've had all day. I can't deal with all the yakking that goes on around this place. Know what? You're an okay guy, Alex."

"Don't you mean, Dex?" asked Alex with a half-laugh, still unsure of Sid's intentions.

Sid set his feet in motion back towards his production office. "What do you think I am? A dummy. Do I look like a dummy?" asked Sid looking for an audience that wasn't there. He tossed off a self-deprecating laugh. "I'm not as dumb as I make out. If Ricky knows you think something's good for him, just stand back and watch him find an excuse to piss it away." Sid jabbed his finger in Alex's face. "And do *not* tell him what I just told you or about this money. Got it?"

They ended the walk as they'd begun, in silence. Alex's mind was in overdrive, trying to arrange all these random pieces of new information into a recognizable shape. Sid was about to peel away and return to his office when Alex held up the check and said, "Thanks."

Sid took a beat to gather his thoughts. Then, staring at the floor, he said solemnly, "What you two get up to in private's your business. Hell, it's nineteen seventy-four and you're both adults, but keep the gay thing under your hats. It's bad for business. It'll kill your careers." Sid momentarily locked eyes with Alex, nodded and walked away.

Alex lingered between the *Hello, Dolly* street and the soundstages. His hands and feet were numb. Alex watched Sid walking towards the production block and just when he didn't know what to feel anymore, he saw a blonde girl in hot pants and cowboy boots running up the palm lined walkway after Sid. Catching up with him, the girl tapped Sid on the shoulder. When Sid turned, the girl threw her arms around his neck and kissed him, joyously hugging him while lifting one cowboy booted foot behind her in the air. Alex squinted, wondering if his eyes were deceiving him.

They weren't ... it was Julie.

Alex drove back to Brentwood, finding it hard to keep his eyes on the road. His stomach was churning and his head swimming. He picked up the phone. "Hi ... Is that Candice? ... Yeah, let Rick Stradman know something came up and I can't give him a ride home ... Tell him Alex called ... He'll know who ..." Alex dropped the red Princess phone's handset onto the cradle. The apartment caged him. Like one of the lions in the L.A. zoo, he paced the room. He rolled Sid's check around in his hand. Sid had been perfectly nice to him, more than nice ... what troubled him most was Sid voicing what he'd hadn't voiced to himself - he was having an affair with a guy. And it wasn't a dalliance, or one night stand - it was something deeper. As if that hadn't rattled him enough, that shattering interchange was climaxed by catching Julie greet Sid so intimately. Thinking about it, Sid had glanced at the clock in his office before he suggested they take a walk. Was Sid expecting her? After all, he'd given Julie his card that day at the Beachcomber. She hadn't appeared interested and professed to have no desire to work in Hollywood, but then everyone says stuff they don't mean. The apartment was suffocating. Alex raced down to the parking garage, threw himself in the car and pointed it to where the highway meets the ocean ... Venice Beach.

Pulling into a parking spot a block off Mildred Avenue the sea air hit his face and he could breathe again. A peaceful sensation cooled his heart as he strolled around his old hood noting the changes. The murals on the walls of the vacant businesses had grown in size. The number of skateboarders had increased too. The chicks trying to attract their attention had grown in similar proportion. Three pimply teenage girls in knee socks chewed their mousy pigtails and giggled shyly while watching a bare-chested boy in tan shorts perform acrobatic moves on his board. The boy didn't notice the girls, lost in his own world.

Alex stepped over a stoned guy on the sidewalk and here he was, back at his old studio. A sign on the door read, 'Gallery Open - Come On In'. A shower of sparks flared in the depths. Alex pushed in through the door. The front gallery space was pretty much the same as when he'd lived there. The ceramics and assembly art on display were all rather dark. Over to one side stood an interesting piece; battered parts of an old car had been welded together in the shape of a standing human, two headlights sitting on top as eyes.

"They light up, man!" yelled a muffled voice out back. Another shower of sparks erupted in the darkness. After they'd died down, the figure in a welding mask came up to Alex and tipped back the visor. "Here, let me show you."

"Cool," murmured Alex.

An expression of disbelief crossed Hank's face when he realized the customer was Alex. "Shit, man! Long time." Hank enfolded Alex in a bear hug. "We thought you'd got lost at sea."

"I was out and about and thought I'd swing by. Nice piece of work."

"Like I said." Hank flipped a switch and the headlight eyes burst into life.

"Good to see you can still pay the electric bill."

Hank patted car man's arm which was made out of stripped tire rubber. "For now."

"You making any sales?" asked Alex glancing around the gallery.

"It's not about the money, man." Hank flicked off the lights. Taking off his helmet, he swept long thinning locks from his face. "I'm exploring our relationship with cars. The freeways aren't bringing people together, they're tearing neighborhoods apart. Roads are the new fences dividing a hostile landscape and enclosing the ghettoes. Corporate America's taken our country hostage. I'd like to make a wall out of abandoned cars, use them like bricks. That would be a great fuckin' piece, wouldn't it? The Great Wall of America!" Hank's eyes lit up as bright as the car man's. "Hey, come out back and see Kaori."

"Where's Scoop?" asked Alex following Hank into what used to be the storerooms and offices when the place used to be a store, now the living space in this re-imagined environment.

"Moved out. Just me and Kaori for the time being."

Sunlight flooded the store's rear. The doors onto the concrete yard housing the garbage bins were flung wide open. Kaori sat on the grubby tiled floor cutting out faces from a magazine. Bits of paper and tubes of glue lay scattered around her.

"Look what the cat dragged in!" Hank called.

Kaori tucked crimped dirty blonde hair behind her ear and looked up. "Al!" Heaving herself from the floor with her hands, her blue floral smock dress revealed a large bump. "What's been going down?"

"Not much. How about you?" Alex's eyes rested on Kaori's stomach.

Kaori sighed and rubbed the small of her back. "The same."

"You should sit at the table to work, babe." Hank took over massaging Kaori's back.

"The floor grounds me. Can you pick my stuff up?" Kaori asked Hank.

"Here, let me help," said Alex. Picking up Kaori's work, Alex saw she'd been cutting out movie stars' faces and sticking them onto paper dolls. "Getting into practice for the kid?" Alex asked with a smile.

"It's the new piece she's working on with Scoop." Hank took the papers from Alex and carefully laid them on the laminate bench.

"While the man of the house is welding with his boy's toys, I'm doing a girl's work and playing with paper dolls." Kaori showed one of the dolls to Alex, it had a movie star's face stuck to it. "These folks are going on a bus trip." Kaori led Alex over to what looked like a large cardboard box. When Kaori swung one side open, however, the box revealed itself to be a model bus. Inside were beautifully crafted cardboard seats, luggage racks and cut out windows. A cyclorama of trees and sky painted on a roll of paper ran around the outside of the windows. "Audiences know the movies are all special effects and stunt doubles. The actors are glorified paper dolls. I've written a script for my dolls. When we've established what each doll wants and what their journeys mean to them, we'll set the bus on fire."

"We're going to clear the junk out of the back yard," added Hank, helpfully jerking his head in that direction, "and burn it out there."

"Scoop's going to video it. Yeah, it's a cardboard box pretending to be a bus filled with paper dolls pretending to be characters, but the fire's going to be real." Kaori rubbed her belly with a sense of satisfaction and rested her tousled head on Hank's shoulder.

Alex could see a few paper dolls already placed in seats on the bus. A doll at the back had Kaori's face stuck to it.

Kaori saw Alex make the connection. "It would be a cop out not to include myself in the jeopardy I create," she said.

"Does anybody make it out alive?" asked Alex.

"Depends when we set fire to it. It's all down to chance. Hey, you want to be on the bus? I got a boy doll longing for a face."

"Pass. One bad bus trip in my lifetime was enough."

Kaori stared at him and rubbed her belly. "No problem."

"Hey man." Hank snapped his fingers. "Scoop left a couple of his suits and his board behind. Wanna hit some waves?"

Thank you, Hank! That was exactly what Alex wanted. Scoop was a slimmer build so tugging on his wetsuit was hard work. Once he'd wriggled in and zipped it up, however, it felt fine. Barefoot, Alex and Hank carried their boards the couple of blocks to the beach. Incense, patchouli and pot wafted from open apartment windows. They crossed the road in front of Zucky's deli. The weight pen on the edge of the beach was busy; seven tanned muscle hunks with sideburns and lush moustaches grunted and groaned while working out in tiny Spandex trunks. As soon as their bare feet hit the sand, Alex and Hank sprinted towards Ocean Park. Reaching the water's edge, they ran into the sea, jumped on their boards and paddled out. The salty surf and film of oil on the water comforted Alex.

They spent a couple of hours catching waves. After paddling out and sitting on their boards for the umpteenth time, Alex and Hank bobbed around. Flicking water off their hair and squinting at the hazy horizon, they saw a big one heading their way. Hank glanced at the derelict Pacific Ocean Park's pilings jutted darkly out of the aqua sea, still supporting the burned out pier's black carcass. "You up for it?" Hank called over to Alex.

"What?" Alex followed Hank's eyes. "Surf the Cove? You crazy?" The Cove was the nickname the locals gave the old pier's U-shaped wooden pilings. Surfing through the derelict supports was fraught with danger but also promised a thrill ride like no other. The wave was coming. They paddled away from it. Alex walloped the water faster and harder, picking up speed. The wave was nearly under them.

"You going for it?" yelled Hank over the tide.

Fuck it, thought Alex, if he died surfing the Cove at least he wouldn't have all this other shit filling his head. "Yeah!" Hank and Alex were paddling full out. The wave rolled beneath them. They both leapt to their feet. Alex braced as the wind whipped around him. The wave was solid. Alex rode it. He was hurtling to the shore ... hurtling towards the Cove. This was the moment he either had to ditch or make a perfect ride through the jagged pilings. He didn't ditch.

The wave broke against the rotten piles and his clean ride disintegrated into spray and foam. Using core strength, he bent his knees and flexed his hips to navigate between the posts.

What a ride!

Alex's board skidded onto the sand. He leapt off, using the wave's momentum to haul his board from the water. He turned, expecting to see Hank coming up behind. No sign of him. Pushing wet hair off his face, Alex blinked away salt water and scanned the piles, afraid Hank had hit one. Then he spotted Hank dragging his board out farther up the beach. "What happened, man?" asked Alex jogging up with his board under his arm.

"I blew the timing." Resting in the low surf, they both unzipped their suits. Hank grinned and said, "You were fucking awesome, man. Fearless as ever."

"Like the old days, huh?" laughed Alex. "Though back then you'd have risked it too."

Shaking water out of his ears, Hank's smile faltered. "There's more than me to think of these days." Walking up the beach, they found a quiet spot. After jamming their boards upright into the sand, they kicked back in their shade. "Still working the abstracts then, huh?" asked Hank.

"I've been experimenting with new things. Been doing some plein air of late."

"Plein air?" commented Hank with a guffaw. "You had a sex change or something?"

"Fuckwit." Alex untangled his salty hair with his fingers. "It's helped me get back in touch with myself. Anyway, I'm enjoying the work and people like it."

"You always were the classicist. And the best at drawing among us. Glad you're finding your truth."

Alex acknowledged Hank's compliment with a manful nod. "A baby. How'd you feel about that?"

Hank flopped on the sand. "I didn't intend on being a dad."

"Accident then?"

"Think I'd do something as dumb as that on purpose?"

"Did you consider abortion? "

"Kaori's dead against it, bad karma and that shit. Whatever, the kid's on its way and we'll deal with it." Changing the subject, Hank said, "I guess Scotty's told you about her show by now. She must be stoked."

"She is."

"You still got that thing for her?"

"I had a thing for her?" asked Alex running a hand through his matted chest hair.

"Sure did."

"Nah, not really. Anyway, she's with Bob for the long haul now."

"Lucky escape. No way was she right for you. Too precious." Hank choked back a chuckle. "I bet she needed defrosting before you could fuck her."

Alex flicked sand up at Hank. "Jeez man, what's your damage?"

"Shit." Hank sat up with a jerk and brushed sand off his arm. "You can't have a great fuck unless they surrender to it. They gotta really want it."

Visions of Rick flickered behind Alex's eyes. He bit his tongue, then said, "I'm wondering who is right for me. I've been seeing someone new ..."

"When do we get to meet her?" asked Hank with a wry smile.

Alex took a deep breath. A *very* deep breath. "It's a guy."

Hank watched the sea smash into the old pier's burnt-out piles.

Alex waited for Hank's reaction.

There was none.

Alex pulled Scoop's board out of the sand. "Good to catch up."

Hank grabbed Alex's wrist. "Where you going, man? Stay."

Alex stuck the board back into the sand and sat down. "I didn't go looking for it but this guy's really knocked me for a loop."

Zipping up his suit, Hank laughed ruefully. "Do our dicks get us balls deep into shit or what?" After a beat, he shook his head in embarrassment. "I didn't mean it like that."

"I know how you meant it." Alex picked up a handful of sand and let the grains trickle between his fingers.

After a pause, Hank asked nonchalantly, "Have you ... you know?"

"What? Played Mah Jong? If you mean have we fucked, then yes."

"Wow." Hank fell silent, then asked, "What was it like?"

How do you answer a question like that from your best friend? What the hell, Alex spoke honestly, "You know what you said about them wanting to be fucked? Well he wants it. And he's so uptight and proper all the time, but when you've loosened him up and you're shafting him, you know, balls deep in, and he falls apart and each thrust of your cock makes him moan and beg for more until you both can't hold it in any longer, well it's …" Alex checked himself, then let himself finish the thought, "it's like glimpsing eternity together."

Hank hugged his knees to his chest. "Graphic."

"You asked," said Alex. He stretched and yawned, feeling a release of tension in his chest. "And anyway, how'd Kaori get pregnant? I guess it wasn't from you two kneeling in silent prayer. Why's this so different?"

"Where'd you meet him? You live in the middle of nowhere for Christ's sake."

Alex leaned back on his elbows. "I was jogging on the beach and saw this guy climbing the cliffs. They're dangerous and I was afraid he'd get hurt so I went up after him."

"Have you got a Jesus complex or something?"

Alex let out an involuntary laugh. "Guess I've spent too long working as a lifeguard." A wave of guilt for getting so angry with Rick washed over him, he suddenly felt real mean to have just left an offhand message about not picking him up. The doubt he'd felt about their relationship had freaked him out, and he'd reacted badly. Being as frank with Hank as he just had, and Hank being cool with his honesty, had assuaged his insecurity about his manhood. In fact, revealing all that private stuff had given him a new-found strength. Maybe he didn't have to go back to being the 'old' Alex, he needed to find how to be the new one.

They pulled their boards out of the sand and wandered back towards Windward. In front of the shabby stores, a pair of blonde twins in red vests, white hot pants and roller skates were flirting with a shaggy dude lounging on a Corvette's hood. Up ahead, Kaori sat on the concrete wall by the weight pen, swinging her grubby bare feet and sucking on an orange ice pole.

"How're you guys going to manage for cash?" Alex asked Hank quietly.

"I'm making some dough spraying boards at the Zephyr. I'm getting interest in the car stuff too. Don't stress, man. We'll be fine. Hi, babe." Hank kissed Kaori and rubbed her neck. Turning to Alex, he asked, "What say I round up Scoop and Rod and we make a night of it at Barney's?"

"Cool. I'll call you."

Hank laughed. "How the fuck you gonna do that, man? You got the number of the payphone on the corner? I'll borrow a quarter and give you a bell."

"I'm not at the beach. I'm in Brentwood." Alex laughed awkwardly. "At Rick's place."

"Who's Rick?" asked Kaori.

"A friend," said Alex quickly.

"Brentwood," repeated Hank slowly.

"I'll give you my number," said Alex.

The three of them meandered through Venice Beach, barefoot amongst the skateboarders, the muscle men, the girls in hot pants, the flower power camper vans, and the smoky incensed early evening air.

♦ ♦ ♦

"Where you been?" Rick called from the living room when he heard Alex open the front door.

"Out and about." Alex tossed his keys onto the console table in the entrance hall. Having just revisited his old grungy place at Venice Beach, Alex saw this apartment with fresh eyes. He hadn't noticed before how dreamily creamy the rugs were, how lush the drapes and how turquoise the pool. Alex was tired and needed to sit. Rick was reclining on the lone taupe couch, his foot elevated on the back. "Budge up," he said and Rick moved enough for him to squeeze on. Rick looked up at him and smiled. Not just any smile, a real smile of pleasure to see someone.

"You've caught the sun, your nose is burned," said Rick. "You should always make sure to put sun block on."

"Yeah, I forgot."

"Puts lots of moisturizer on before bed, you don't want to peel."

Alex resisted a chuckle, never thinking he'd see the day when he'd be chided about skincare. It was novel to have anyone care about him in such a way. He smiled down at Rick. His eyes were puffy and the rims tinged with red. Alex figured he'd been crying. Just because he was having difficulty dealing with his own emotions was no reason to punish Rick, was it? "How'd filming go?" Alex gently asked. "Foot hold up okay?"

"Yeah, just about," sighed Rick.

"How was Mr. Milland?"

"Cool and distant. But Professor Miller and Bradley aren't meant to be best friends, so it helped with the scene."

"And Hudson?"

"Nice. Cordial. Our scenes went well. At least, I think they did. I spent the afternoon delivering lines like, 'There's one thing I don't understand, Mac,' and dodging bullets from Miller's corrupt cop. Pretty much your average Tuesday." Rick rested his head on Alex's thigh. "How was Fox? Get the *Cliffs* back? Everyone happy?"

"Yep, all smiles."

"You go see dad?"

Alex absently ran his hand through Rick's hair. "I did."

"What did he want?"

"Not much. Kind of wanted to apologize for being so brusque when we first met. Hey, guess what? He actually knows my name's Alex."

"Incredible! Go Sid." Rick patted Alex's thigh. "I'll miss Dex. He was much more fun than you."

"And you'll never guess who I spotted being very chummy with Sid on the lot?"

"Please, don't say momma. I sleep better with the Atlantic ocean between us."

"Apart from the fact I wouldn't recognize your mother if she fell on my head, no. It was Julie. You remember? That waitress from the Beachcomber. She ran up and kissed him."

"Dad's a dirty old man! Soon as I laid eyes on her I knew she was his type."

Alex thought Rick's judgement was harsh. Although it had been his first thought too. "We don't know what she was doing there. It could be something entirely innocent."

Rick struggled to keep the glee out of his eye. "Move over Letitia! This year's blonde's on the horizon. Imagine the bloodbath if it turns out to be serious? Letitia and the no-neck monsters will be homeless. I see it all now. Lawsuits, recriminations and an ex-waitress as my next step-mom."

"No-neck monsters?"

"My step-brother and sister. I named them after the kids in *Cat on a Hot Tin Roof.* You know, when Maggie says, 'Their fat little heads sit on their fat little bodies without a bit of connection'? That's Tiffany and Tyler. You eaten?" asked Rick.

"Nope." The gnawing ache in his stomach reminded Alex he hadn't had a bite all day.

"Let's go out."

"Don't you have to be up early?"

"I'm not called tomorrow. They're doing the McMillan and Professor Miller scenes."

"I don't know if I want to go out. I've been behind the wheel enough for one day."

"There's an Italian a couple of blocks down. We can walk."

"In Los Angeles? The police arrest you for that."

"Let's take a chance."

The night air was fresh as they walked down San Vicente to the trattoria. Alex noticed Rick limping. His foot obviously wasn't fine. The whiff of guilt returned.

"Where'd you go after Fox? Were you out painting?" asked Rick.

"I swung by Venice and caught up with Hank."

"And?"

"We shot some waves."

"Look, I know yesterday was a big dull dud. I ruined your day and then had you running around after me. No wonder you got mad with me."

"Nah, it was okay."

Rick stopped. "The real reason I wanted you to take me to the studio wasn't to do with the car."

"What was it then?"

The headlights of passing vehicles shone in Rick's eyes, reflecting off the retinas behind those big black pupils. "I was scared and didn't want to be on my own. You make me feel safe. It was selfish of me. Sorry."

And with that, any reservations Alex still had about being with Rick melted away. "C'mon, let's go eat, I'm hungry. And go easy on the martinis, buster. Remember we need to walk back," said Alex warmly.

The meal was good. The atmosphere relaxed. They strolled home with Rick still sober. After they'd made love, Alex couldn't sleep. He pulled on his boxers, lit a cigarette and took a smoke on the balcony. He watched the traffic on San Vicente for half an hour, wondering what he should do with Sid's money. A thousand bucks. And Rick's rent money on top of that. The fancy restaurants, the new clothes, being waved onto movie lots with no questions, having influential people in the art world ask to see his work and actually know his name. A multitude of new experiences of late.

Funny how quickly you got used to new things. Things you didn't think you wanted and now didn't want to lose.

THE MARKS WE LEAVE

Rick was catching up on his sleep the next morning. He was snoring lightly when Alex slipped out to make an early start on his work. In retrospect he'd really enjoyed the paintings he'd done on the backlot. Rather than being in a funk yesterday, he should have stayed at the studio with Rick and done more work there.

His idea for lyrical studies of cloverleaf interchanges was not engaging like it had last week. From seeing Hank's work, it was apparent other artists were already investigating our relationship with freeways and automobiles. What the mysterious woman on the backlot had said popped into Alex's head. The element of looking at something so often you stop seeing it. He thought of a place people headed to every day, and not with the intent of savoring its beauty. He headed downtown.

Alex parked up in a side street on the edge of Skid Row, slung his equipment over his shoulder, put on his hat and grabbed his wet work case. The business day was in full swing and the streets were busy. He wouldn't be showing his picture anonymously after the event, setting up his easel on a street corner would mean an audience watching him work. That was what stressed Rick out about performing in front of people, now he'd be in the same situation.

Alex swallowed his nerves. He'd done some pretty adventurous gay stuff with Rick in the bedroom, and elsewhere, so setting up an easel and painting in public should be a walk in the park in comparison. After scoping out locations, he picked a corner on 7th and Broadway out front of a parking garage. It wasn't attractive in the conventional sense, but its view of the run-down Loew's Theater and jewelry store windows crammed with age-curled handwritten signs exuded faded charm.

He unfolded his tripod, opened up his paint box and fastened a fresh board on the easel. Taking a deep breath, he went into his head, ignored any funny looks and began his composition. He smashed in the buildings, then detailed the curve of the stop light over the street, the blown-out bulbs on the State Theater's canopy, the Z shapes of fire escapes, red bricks, yellow light, purple shadows, a blast of green from a tree ...There was a vigor amidst the urban decay which excited him. The faded thirties architecture reeked of dashed hopes and lost dreams.

After five hours, Alex stood back to consider his work. A harassed woman in a mint green mini skirt, flat shoes and a bad perm brushed past. Shooting his painting a dirty look, she muttered, "My kid could do better." Great. Everyone's a critic. Alex was taking the board off the easel when a pair of down at heel brogues shuffled by. A homeless black guy stopped to stare at Alex's painting. "You shoulda seen it in the day." The guy smiled, although the poor old man only had eight teeth. He jabbed an arthritic finger at the Loew's. "That used to be one o' the biggest movie theaters in town. Mighty fine place. What do they show now? The Exorcist." The man shuffled his feet. "Folks pay to see the devil. The town's gone to hell." Alex smiled at the guy in return, fumbled in his pocket and slipped the guy a twenty. "Bless you, son." The old guy tipped his head in gratitude and shuffled off. Alex knew how tough life could be when you were alone with neither luck nor money.

On his way back to Brentwood, Alex stopped by the market to pick up supplies. He bustled into the apartment with his painting gear and a bag of groceries, quickly kicking off his paint spattered shoes to avoid schmutzing the rugs. Alex tugged his t-shirt's collar from his sweaty neck. "Jeez, it's like a furnace in here."

"Air con's on the fritz! Super's looking into it. Take a swim in the pool," said Rick grabbing the groceries.

"I didn't bring any trunks."

Rick dumped the sack on the counter and disappeared into their bedroom. A few moments later he returned twirling something around his finger. "Here." He tossed it to Alex.

The item in question was a pair of 'European' swim trunks. Most likely purchased from the same establishment as the miniscule turquoise ones Rick had a penchant for. Alex held them up aghast. "You cannot be serious."

"They're swimming trunks, aren't they? We're about the same size."

"When we were twelve maybe. I can't wear these in public."

"You used to be a lifeguard, didn't you? What did you wear then?"

"Shorts and a tank, not some go-go boy's G-string!"

"Nobody's ever around the pool. I'll come down with your lifeguard's whistle and blow it if anyone's in danger of seeing your body. We wouldn't want to psychologically scar anyone."

Alex examined the very, very small black trunks. They were tiny, but after a hot day on downtown streets the pool was too tempting a proposition. "If I look ridiculous or if everything," he patted his junk, "doesn't fit in then forget it."

"They're *very* stretchy," assured Rick.

Reluctantly Alex went into the bedroom, stripped off his stinky duds and wriggled into the trunks. They did contain everything ... just. He grabbed a towel from the bathroom then pulled on a pair of jeans and t-shirt to go down in. Rick was right, the pool was deserted. Alex glanced nervously at the blind windows and empty balconies surrounding the pool.

"What you waiting for? Drop a shoulder strap, Louise," said Rick dragging a lounger around to catch the last of the sun.

Taking a deep breath, Alex tugged off his t-shirt and the cord with the pendant and slung them to Rick. He folded his arms shyly over his hairy chest.

"Are you Amish or a Mormon or something? Take your pants off and get in the pool!"

One by one, Alex undid his fly buttons. He gradually slid down his pants. "Do they actually wear stuff like this in Europe?" Alex asked, nervously tugging the trunks' elastic around his butt.

Rick waved his hand around the courtyard. "Nobody's looking! No-one cares."

Moving to the edge of the pool Alex stretched one arm behind his back and then the other. He stretched his shoulders. The right one was still very painful from rescuing Gloria. Alex turned and paused mid-stretch to find Rick was staring at him.

"Bello," said Rick softly.

"What?"

"Italian. The male for beautiful. You're very nice to look at."

"That's me, a regular Charles Atlas." Alex popped a couple of physique magazine poses, juggling his pecs while gripping one hand with the other.

"Overcoming your shyness, I see?" Rick's powder blue eyes twinkled.

Alex locked eyes with Rick's big black pupils. "You're pretty bello yourself." Alex leaned down and quickly kissed Rick on the lips. He strode to the edge of the pool and made a perfectly angled dive, entering the water with an inaudible splash.

Their days at Brentwood fell into a rhythm.

Early each morning Alex would drive off to discover new subject matter, and Rick would drive over the hills to Universal. They'd reconvene early evening for a swim and a light dinner before turning in at a sensible hour ready to do it all again. After a day of doing some interesting pastel work around the La Brea tar pits, Alex arrived home to find Rick on the couch shuffling papers. He agitatedly waved a wad of pink script pages in Alex's face. "Rewrites for tomorrow. It's insane!"

"Why the new sides?" Alex opened the fridge and took out a beer. "Want one?"

"No, I gotta keep a clear head. They changed a plot point which means they've had to rewrite the scene where Professor Miller gives Sam and Bradley the assignment. They also thought the beginning of the episode was too dark so they've added more comedy."

"It'll be a laugh riot when Sam gets strangled," said Alex. Leaning on the counter, Alex picked up a couple of bills lying on it, both fifties. "These yours?"

"For you. For gas and other stuff. I don't want you out of pocket on my account."

"Thanks." Alex shoved them into his back pocket. "Everything okay at the studio today?" He sat next to Rick on the couch and read over the pink pages.

"We did the Berkeley and police H.Q. interiors and visited Mildred in hospital."

"How's she doing?"

"Terrific. Her comedy timing wasn't injured. We're on location tomorrow for the showdown scene with Professor Miller and then go into a night shoot for the bell tower finale."

"They found a bell tower in L.A.?"

"Yeah, Mudd Hall at Exposition Park. It's Milland's last day on set and we've a lot to get through. The guy playing Sam blew his lines twice today, and that was with the old script. The Black Tower won't be happy if we fall behind schedule. By the way, Hank called. Said he spoke to Scoop and Rod and they'll be at Barney's tomorrow night. Scoop? What kind of name's that?"

"He wanted to be a journalist then found he enjoyed the photography more than the writing. His real name's Allen Swaine."

They skipped the swim and dinner, and Rick disappeared to bed extra early to prepare for tomorrow. Buying art supplies and not worrying about every dollar meant Alex had been ploughing through his cash. He took out the bills Rick just gave him, a hundred bucks would definitely fill that hole. Hank and Kaori had been on his mind. He was worried about how they'd manage with a kid, being as dirt poor as they were. He remembered Sid's check in his drawer. Sid had given that money to him in good faith for looking after Rick. And boy, the kid did take some looking after. Rick didn't know about the money, and Sid didn't want him to know about it. Five hundred dollars could make a huge impact on Hank and Kaori right now. And keeping the remainder of the cash would allow him to pick up the check at Barney's tomorrow. He could do with buying some new clothes and getting his hair cut too, and he didn't want to ask Rick for a rent advance. He'd cash Sid's check in the morning. Decided.

♦ ♦ ♦

The following evening, Alex pulled off Santa Monica, parked in the lot at the side and strolled around the corner. The mustard and orange sign announcing Barney's Beanery in black text warmed his heart. He passed below the flapping green and white awnings which were showing signs of wear and tear, opened the door and went in. It smelled the same. Beer, bacon and sweat. A haze of cigarette smoke hung over the bar. Alex scanned faces through the fug.

Almost immediately a voice shouted, "Yo, Alex!" A scrawny ginger guy with wire rimmed glasses hopped down from his bar stool.

"Scoop!" Alex hustled through the punters and bumped shoulders with him.

"What you drinking, he says?" Scoop wriggled back to his stool and leaned across the bar.

"Same as you."

"Kayla!" Scoop waved his empty bottle at the girl behind the bar. "Hit me again. One for Alex too!"

"Howdy, stranger!" Kayla called to Alex with a grin. Kayla's white tank nicely displayed the fresh tattoo of a snake with a knife through its head on her left shoulder.

"Hey, you!" Alex greeted Kayla and turned back to Scoop, "Where you shacked up now you moved out of Venice?"

"I got a place in Granada Hills. Good space. Kind of a long way out, but I'm teaching a couple of days at Cal Arts so it's cool for that."

"Teaching?"

"One of their faculty got sick, and I was in the right place at the right time." Scoop laughed modestly. "To tell the truth, they were desperate."

"Teaching. That's great."

"Two beers." Kayla set the bottles on the bar in front of them.

"Can I run a tab?" asked Alex.

"Sure," replied Kayla.

"I'll split it." Scoop picked up his bottle. "I'm employed, after all. Don't you think taking a job's a kind of failure? We were meant to be living on our art by now. Have I copped out?"

"Money's money and we all gotta eat. Seriously, tonight's on me," said Alex. He grabbed his bottle and clinked it to Scoop's.

Scoop studied Alex. "You look different."

Alex swept his shiny hair off his moisturized face. "Older?"

"Apart from that. Kind of assured. Glossy. Like you've been laminated."

"Let's snag a table. Hank and Rod'll be rocking up any minute." Alex picked up Scoop's beer, as well as his own, and hustled through the bar to one of the multicolored booths in the rear. He liked this booth, it was Janis Joplin's favorite. She'd carved her name, Janis Lyn, in the table's edge with a penknife. Alex traced the indent with his finger - the marks we leave on the earth. "What you working on?" Alex asked Scoop.

"Reforming images. I've moved on from using movie stills as the source to print adverts. I block out the brands and the product's identifying parts to make generic images. The only recognizable part's usually the model's smile. Everyone's happy all the time in commercials. I'm experimenting with video too. Cal Arts just invested in new Sony Portapak equipment. I'm gonna use it to film Kaori's burning bus project."

"She showed that to me last week."

"People will be down on her work, but remember when we faked that shooting outside the gallery opening? People were outraged then too."

"I guess they weren't expecting to step over a blood-stained chalk outline to get into the exhibit."

"Exactamundo. Cops shoot bad guys every night on T.V. detective shows. And there's got to be some level of belief that people are getting killed, or what's the point of watching the drama? And now the studios offer up burning bodies falling from buildings as entertainment. All to satisfy the public's lust for death, it's bread and circuses. Paper dolls on a cardboard bus is a perfect analogy for today's entertainment. Has there ever been so shallow a time for art?"

Alex sipped his beer. "I dunno. I don't look at T.V. and movies how you do."

Scoop laughed and shook his head. "Yeah, you always were content with the waves and the beach. Why'd you think we called you *Nature Boy*? You know, the song, 'There was a boy, a very strange enchanted boy'?"

Alex shrugged. It was true, part of him was always happiest on a boat or walking on the cliffs; he wasn't aware they'd given him a nickname though. Where were Hank and Rod? Alex was getting antsy. "You hungry?"

"Yeah."

Alex hustled through to the bar, caught Kayla's eye and ordered a couple of bowls of chili and more beers. He slumped back into the booth and they shot the breeze. Part of Alex's mind wasn't listening to Scoop though, it was considering memories of this old place. What had made Hank, Scoop and him start coming here? Did they think sitting at the same bar that Altoon, Ruscha and Al Bengston once sat at would rub some of their stardust off on them? The beers and chili arrived. Digging into the food reminded Alex that one of the place's big draws was the food here was good and not crazily expensive.

"Hey!" Hank shouldered through the bar to their booth.

Alex looked behind Hank, expecting to see Rod following.

Hank pushed in, sat and bumped fists with Scoop. "Yo."

Alex looked at Hank quizzically.

"Rod can't make it. Copley Van Sant made him an offer to be in a group show. He needs to finish up some stuff," said Hank, slightly evasively.

"Cool," mumbled Scoop through a mouthful of chili. "That gallery's big. What's he putting in?"

"They want his collages of corporate logos." Hank went on to explain, "He uses the logos to build a picture of the product they embody. Like using Ford, Mercedes, and B.M.W. logos to make the image of a car. Like pointillism."

Scoop nodded enthusiastically. "Fuckin' ace. You don't have to see it to get it."

Alex felt in his pocket for the wad of fifties he'd put aside for Hank. As soon as Scoop went to the bar or men's room he'd give the cash to Hank. Alex pondered how to phrase it when he passed it over. Maybe best to say nothing. After all, Hank and Kaori were family to him.

Lovenia, one of the regular waitresses who'd just come on shift, approached their booth. She patted the back of her beehive and asked, "Can I get you boys something'?"

"I'll take a Reuben with a side of onion rings," Hank answered without looking.

"Drinks?" Lovenia peered at them, with attitude, through her cat's eye spectacles.

Alex and Scoop waved their bottles, "Same again."

"You?" Lovenia fixed her gaze on Hank.

"A TAB."

"Mmm, hmm." Lovenia scribbled on her pad.

"TAB?" asked Scoop incredulously.

Hank rubbed his beard then patted his belly. "When we hit the Cove the other day I could barely zip up my suit."

"You shot the waves at the Cove?" asked Scoop incredulously.

"I chickened out, but buster here went through with no issues. Pure gold," said Hank. "They had another fire on the pier last week. Sounds like they're going to clear out the winos and druggies and demolish it. The Cove will be history."

"It's the death of the fifties," said Scoop glumly.

"And once they've prettied up the neighborhood, watch gentrification take over and see rents rise. First Ocean Park and then Venice. The bigshots will move in, it won't be our territory anymore," said Hank bitterly.

"Tearing down Ocean Park ..." said Scoop thinking out loud. "I should get the cameras and go inside while it's still standing. There'll be some great visuals. Kaori will find some interesting take on this, you bet."

"She will," said Hank nodding in full agreement.

Due to Lovenia taking their order, Scoop hadn't needed to go to the bar. Alex was itching to hand the cash to Hank, but the moment still wasn't right. Hank and Scoop carried on riffing about performance art and conceptual takes on how to shoot the old pier before it got torn down. Alex finished his beer in silence. This wasn't the evening he'd been expecting. He leaned back in the booth, imagining he was Janis keeping an eye on the front door. That's why she liked this booth's position, or so legend had it, so she could check out new arrivals. Alex felt he'd rather be in the Brentwood apartment than here. At least he could slope off for a swim in the turquoise pool then slide between the cool cotton sheets. Or slide his cock between Rick's butt cheeks. Alex drifted, Hank and Scoop's conversation became noise. Barney's front door opened. A guy walked in, hovered on the threshold and scanned the place. What on earth was he doing here? Alex stood and waved to catch his attention.

"Is it Rod?" asked Hank. "He said he'd try to make it."

"It's Rick," said Alex guiding him in. Out the corner of his eye, he noted Hank and Scoop exchange glances. "How come you're here?" Alex asked as Rick came to their booth.

"They broke me early. I guessed you might still be here, so thought I'd take a chance and swing by," said Rick breathlessly.

Alex instinctively wanted to give Rick a welcome hug, but this wasn't the place. He looked down into the booth to find Hank and Scoop gawping up at Rick.

"Hi, I'm Rick," said Rick extending his hand to Hank.

"My roommate," Alex said to Scoop and Hank.

"Hi. You must be Scoop," Rick said to Hank.

"No, I'm Hank." Hank popped out the booth to shake hands with Rick.

Scoop leaned over and added, "I'm Scoop."

"Well, hi Scoop and Hank!" Rick smiled warmly and inclusively. "I need a drink, I've been running from a killer all evening."

Lovenia arrived at their table. "How you guys doing?"

"Hi!" said Rick smiling warmly at Lovenia.

Alex was captivated by Rick's face. Perhaps standing under arc lights with a camera pointed at you all day long does something to a person. Perhaps there was a sheen of make-up left on his skin, making it appear the spotlight was still on him ... whatever, Rick emitted a glamorous glow.

"Hi, honey." Lovenia immediately connected with Rick. "What may I get you?"

Rick checked with Alex, "You know the menu. Can you order for me?"

"Bowl of chili and a very dry martini," said Alex decisively to Lovenia.

"Perfect." Rick patted Alex's shoulder appreciatively.

Lovenia peered over the top of her cat's eyes frames and flicked a look at Hank and Scoop. "Mmm, hmm. A little class in the place at last." She nodded to Rick, touching up the back of her beehive she said, "Coming right up, honey."

"How come you've finished early?" asked Alex.

"I nailed my last scene. And as I'd been on the clock since eleven they were happy to break me," said Rick.

Alex noticed Scoop and Hank looking intrigued. "Rick's working on a T.V. show," he explained.

"It's called *McMillan and Wife*. You heard of it?" asked Rick.

Hank recoiled, "Heard of it? I've done more to it than that when wifey does a bedroom scene wearing that red football jersey. Boy, she's hot!"

"And pregnant," interjected Alex surprising himself with his sanctimonious tone. "In real life, the actress who plays the part, that is," Alex added knowingly.

Rick carried on telling Hank and Scoop about the shoot. Scoop was particularly interested because Rick had been filming a scene with gunfire. Scoop shared his views on violence and death as entertainment. While Rick and Scoop discussed this, very intelligently and referencing other performance art pieces, Alex was aware that Hank was studying Rick. After he'd finished eating, and Lovenia had delivered his second martini, Rick suggested a game of pool. This move on Rick's part took Alex completely by surprise. Scoop took Rick up on his offer. They shuffled out of the booth and commandeered a recently vacated pool table. Alone with Hank, Alex dug into his pocket and, keeping the bills covered by his palm, slid the cash across the table. "For you and Kaori. Don't let anyone see."

Hank surreptitiously glanced at the wad of bills under the table. "You serious, man?"

"I'd some luck and wanted to pass it on. You're a good friend, Hank."

Rick had his back to them, bent over the pool table.

"This luck got anything to do with him?" Hank jerked his head in Rick's direction.

"In a way," said Alex.

"I gotta admit when you told me about him last week, you kinda took me by surprise. I mean, have you always ... well, I never figured you for being ... like that."

"Like what?"

"Liking guys. When we hung out you were always on our wavelength. You digged the chicks back then. And man, you had an eye for them ... Didn't you?"

"I haven't changed. This is just another part of me. A part I hadn't truly acknowledged. Maybe repressing it's why I was blocked. I don't know if it's forever, but I need to feel how I feel for a while. And to tell the truth, I was lonely till Rick showed up."

Hank digested his words. "I'm not judging you, but it kinda makes me feel like I never really knew you."

"I never thought you'd be shacked up with Kaori and having a kid. I never thought Scoop would take a regular job or Rod would give up a night out with the guys to work. Life happens, things change. But that doesn't mean we're different at heart, does it?"

"This Rick guy, by the looks of things he's not short on dough," said Hank.

"He's paying me rent to stay at the house, that's all. The money I just gave you is from someplace else. Nothing to do with him."

"In that case, thanks. It'll help."

"Hank, are we still buds?" asked Alex nervously.

"Yeah, man. It's the seventies, this is what we protested and fought for. Everyone free to be what they want to be."

They didn't speak again until Scoop and Rick returned laughing from the pool table. "Who won?" asked Alex.

"Rick, but only because he kept distracting me with witty banter about minimalism." Scoop laughed, picking up his beer.

Wiping perspiration off his forehead, Rick chuckled. "It's true. The easiest way to organize your stuff is get rid of everything except the essentials! Same goes for art."

"Where'd you learn to play pool?" Alex asked Rick.

"I used to hang out at a place in Milan. Pretty much like here only they served pasta instead of chili," said Rick.

Scoop smiled warmly at Rick, although Hank still seemed to be weighing him up. Alex took a backseat and listened to them talk. Rick was on top form, engaged and interested in both guys. The more they talked, the more removed Alex felt from the past. If he had to choose right now where his happiness lay, it'd be hanging out with Rick rather than these guys.

The night had run its course. Alex cleared his tab with Kayla and left a more than decent tip. As Scoop bantered with Kayla and Irwin, Rick's eyes roved over the multitude of old license plates nailed above and behind the bar. "In the depression folks who couldn't pay their check left their car's plate as collateral. When their luck changed, they'd come back and pay off the debt to reclaim their car," explained Hank.

Rick carried on staring at all the battered plates. "That's a whole load of dreams that didn't come true." Then, between all the license plates, Rick's eyes rested on another sign behind the bar. This sign read boldly, 'Fagots – Stay Out!'

Hank noticed Rick linger on the sign. "That don't mean nothing. It's been there for years," said Hank dismissively.

Out in the parking lot, after waving off Scoop and Hank, Rick leaned on the Chevy while Alex unlocked the door.

"Aren't you taking your car?" asked Alex.

"Too many martinis and I'm not called till the afternoon. I'll get a cab and come pick it up in the morning," said Rick. On their way back to Brentwood, Rick mumbled, "It does mean something, that sign behind the bar, the one about faggots."

"Don't dwell on it, babe."

The streetlamps flashed by, shafts of light chasing across Rick's face. "It means us."

"It's a leftover from when the place kept getting raided for immorality. They put that sign up to throw off the cops," said Alex.

"But that's the past." Rick threw his head back on the rest.

Alex didn't speak for a few miles then blurted out, "Sid guessed we've got something going on. That day I saw him at Fox, he said we should keep the gay thing under our hats."

Rich sighed and knocked his head against the window. "Dear old dad. Never knowingly under dramatic. It's something I've been dealing with. Now I've dragged you into it too."

"You make it sound like being forced into joining the Book of the Month Club. Are you on commission? A hundred bucks for every guy you bring in?"

Rick let out a throaty chuckle.

"Must we define ourselves with labels? And if Sid's cool, isn't that a bonus?"

"Maybe I shouldn't have come to Barney's tonight," said Rick.

"Why did you?"

"I wanted to meet your friends. I want to get to know you better. But more than that, I wanted to be with you. Sorry if my turning up out of the blue put you in an awkward position with them, I didn't think it through."

"To tell the truth, I was happy you showed up." Alex took his hand off the wheel and patted Rick's hand. "And very impressed with your pool playing. Swap the martinis for beers, let your personal grooming go, stack on some weight and you can join our gang."

"I'll pass."

They were nearly back at Brentwood. Rick was dozing. Alex mulled over the money he'd given Hank. In retrospect, cashing Sid's check had been a dumb thing to do. Admittedly that money wasn't from Rick, but it wasn't exactly unrelated. If its source ever came to light it could be misinterpreted. Some things should remain a secret forever, and Alex knew Sid's giving him that thousand bucks was one of them.

MANIPULATED IMAGE

Gina's flight from New York was due in. A mass of people swarmed around Rick and Alex. Another 747 had just disembarked. Alex dodged out of the irritable passengers' way, but Rick didn't budge. A nasal twang over the public address intoned, "Pan Am Flight 817 from New York now arriving at gate 17." They made their way through the terminal, and Rick stood sentry by the gate. Although he didn't know her, Alex guessed Gina was the striking brunette wearing sunglasses so dark it was a miracle she didn't need a Seeing Eye dog. She walked slowly and lethargically amidst her fellow travelers as the jumbo jet disgorged its self-loading cargo.

When Gina finally noticed Rick through her tinted lenses, she waved feebly. Rick rushed up and hugged her warmly, but Gina visibly stiffened in his arms. "I could have got a cab," she said withdrawing her head.

"I couldn't let you do that. And I wanted to see you," said Rick.

Gina rested her bag on the floor. "At last we meet again. I almost forget your face."

"How was the flight?" asked Rick.

"We got here without crashing. Which as it is a Pan Am flight is good, no?"

"Both the Pan Am crashes this year were in the Pacific," said Rick.

"If an airline has two crashes in a few months is a sign. I did not know my agent had booked me on this flight till I arrive at J.F.K. By then is too late to change. Bad things happen in three," said Gina darkly.

"Well, you're here safe so everything's fine," said Rick trying to lighten the mood.

Gina put her hand to her brow. "The man in the next seat talked for three thousand miles. My head spins."

Alex sensed Gina radiating pure frost. He found it hard to believe she and Rick ever had a romantic thing going. Hard to believe on so many, many, many levels.

"Gina." Rick dragged Alex proudly in front of her. "This is Alex Morgan. He's an artist and I'm staying at his house on the beach."

Alex's jaw almost hit the floor at Rick's lack of tact.

"I see," was Gina's only response before turning back to Rick. "The beach? What happened to Brentwood?"

"That place creeps me out. We only stayed there during the shoot. Once the show wrapped we went home to the beach." Gina wobbled. Rick put his hand out to steady her and asked, "Are you okay?"

"The plane was hot. I feel faint."

"There's a coffee shop by baggage reclaim," said Rick. "You should sit for a moment." They took a corner table. Gina asked for an espresso, which the server said they didn't do. After emitting a discontented grunt, Gina settled for a strong black. The coffee bar's lighting was extremely subdued, practically stygian. The darkness compelled Gina to remove her shades. Her brown eyes were sunken with dark circles underneath. Rick stroked her hand. "You look beat."

"I am." Gina rifled through her purse, took out a brown bottle and tipped two blue tablets into her palm. She swilled them in one gulp. "Tylenol Extra," she explained in response to Rick's quizzical expression. Rick dragged out some painful conversation. Alex sipped his coffee. It was bitter, so was Gina. During one of her rambling, almost nonsensical monologues, Rick's eyes wandered. "Rick?" Gina said sharply. "Do I bore you so that you cannot bear to listen?" Gina put on her dark glasses, got up and strode out of the coffee shop. Rick scuttled after her.

Alex tossed some cash on the table, picked up Gina's bag and followed. Gina strode through the terminal with vigor. The coffee must have hit the spot, for her energy was back full strength.

"Why'd you take off like that?" Rick asked as he caught up with her.

Halting abruptly, Gina answered, "I feel like you do not wish to see me."

"Would we have driven all this way to pick you up if I didn't want to see you? Calm down," Rick said soothingly, "let's go find the car."

"You guys wait here. I'll pick you up outside." Alex handed Gina's bag back, overjoyed to extricate himself from this awkward reunion. He savored the reprieve while he retrieved the car and tootled to the pick-up lane.

When Gina laid eyes on Alex's beat-up Chevy her mouth bent into a shape of distaste. "They offered me a limo."

"Isn't this better? We can talk on the way to the hotel," said Rick.

Gina flung her bag into the rear seat and sullenly slunk in after. "I stay at the Beverly Hills Hotel. I don't suppose you know how to get there?" she said to Alex.

"Sure do," Alex replied blithely over his shoulder, "like a home from home." He pulled off with a needless jerk. Maneuvering out of the airport, Alex couldn't help glimpsing Gina glowering behind her sunglasses in the rear-view mirror. She slouched in the rear seat, stuffing her hands in the pockets of her eggplant leather bomber jacket like a kid being driven back to school after the holidays. On arrival at The Beverly Hills Hotel the parking valet took the car, thankfully with no quips about its age this time. "I'll wait out here," said Alex.

"Come in. I don't know how long this will take," said Rick insistently.

Resisting the impulse to sigh, Alex complied and trailed Rick and Gina up the red carpet surrounded by tropical foliage. While Gina was checking in at the front desk, a smartly dressed businessman came up to her. The man greeted her warmly, placing an overly familiar hand on the small of her back and saying something close to her ear. Gina pulled away slightly then whispered something back to him. The guy said, "Later, then," before moving on. He was the advertising executive of a company she'd recently worked for, she explained flatly. Then the hotel manager rocked up, exuding fulsome charm in welcoming Gina to the hotel. His efforts were wasted. Politely giving up, the manager summoned a bellman to guide them to her suite. On arrival in Bungalow 16, the bellman demonstrated the Air Con and T.V. controls. Gina ignored his spiel and closed the drapes, shutting off the banana leaves outside tapping on the window.

"Nice room," said Rick. His comment received a surly glare from Gina as she removed her dark glasses. Rick gestured to Alex as the bellman backed out of the room.

It took Alex a beat to realize Rick was indicating the bellman needed tipping. Alex fished in his pocket. A five-dollar bill came to hand, he slipped it to the bellman. The guy nodded appreciatively, although getting away from Gina's toxic aura was likely tip enough.

Gina flopped on the bed.

"Do you want to rest or shall I stay and talk?" Rick said conversationally.

"Talk if you like," Gina mumbled. "I go nowhere now."

If Rick was going to persevere with Gina, Alex needed a smoke. "I'll hang in the gardens," said Alex. He installed himself on a white bench with green and white striped cushions in the bungalow's porch. The door to the room remained ajar and he overheard snippets of Rick and Gina's conversation. Some of the intelligible moments included Rick asking gently, "Are you working too hard? ... I've heard good things about a spa in Santa Barbara ... Why not book yourself out for a few weeks to get on top of things?"

Gina's responses were forthright and easier to overhear, "I must work to live ... I cannot turn down jobs ... I have no-one to support me."

"If money's the problem ..."

"Money is neither the problem or the solution. I need other things. Am I meant to be relieved you are still alive? Is that your gift to me?"

Alex's back stiffened. What Gina had just said could be taken in many ways. He strained to hear Rick's response, but Rick lowered his voice. Full volume was suddenly restored and then, after a few minutes of escalating anger in fluent Italian, Rick said firmly in English, "You need sleep, Gina! You're not making any sense." Hearing Rick coming out of the room, Alex backed onto the pink paved path. "I'll phone you later," Rick said into the dark room from the stone porch. Gina suddenly appeared in the doorframe. She hung her head and glared from under her eyes at Alex. There were no more goodbyes, she just slammed the door. "That was painful," said Rick as they retraced their path from the bungalows through the tropical gardens to the main hotel. "Maybe it was a bad idea for you to come with me."

"I could have told you that," said Alex, mentally kicking himself for agreeing to the trip.

"I wanted to make clear we can't go back to how we were because I've moved on."

"I think she's got the message," said Alex. On the highway back to Sunset Cove, Alex sensed Rick's mind still churning.

"You know what really makes me mad about her?" blurted out Rick. "She makes me out to be the heavy. She lays all her unhappiness at my feet. And when I offer any help to make things better, she snaps my head off. I can't figure her out."

"Maybe it's to do with being left at the altar? Girls tend to be sensitive about that, I hear."

"Marrying her wasn't my idea. That whole situation was due to momma's meddling."

"But you must have gone along with it. To call off a wedding means it has to be on in the first place, doesn't it?"

Rick eye's blazed and he thumped the dash with both hands. "You've not met my mother. You've no idea, Alex! No fucking idea!"

"Cool down. Sorry. The situation between you, Gina and your mother must be very complex."

"Unlike the rest of my life," said Rick with a snort with laughter. He took a couple of minutes then said, "I promised to take Gina out for dinner tomorrow night. If I don't follow through, she'll be poisonous."

"As opposed to her usual cheery self?"

"It shouldn't just be the two of us, I mean just me and Gina."

"You definitely need witnesses."

"Do you think Scotty and Bob would be up for joining us?"

"Scotty and Bob? What, as some kind of retaliation for that awful evening at their place?"

"She and Bob love rubbing shoulders with the rich and famous. They'd get a kick out of dinner with a top model, don't you think? They'd pay her lots of attention. That'd keep her in check and take the heat off me. We could go to The Daisy."

"Wouldn't Barney's be better?" Alex asked deadpan. "We could invite Hank and Scoop too, you know, make a real party of it."

"I'm not sure if that's a great idea," said Rick chewing over Alex's suggestion.

"As if. I was kidding."

Rick allowed himself a relieved chuckle. "You've got a warped sense of humor. Anyone ever tell you that?"

"Only once." Dean had said exactly the same thing to him on that yacht delivery up to San Francisco from San Diego. The voyage wasn't going smoothly. While they were both up on deck battening down yet again, Dean yelled over the spray, "This guy's meant to be the best captain in California!" Alex responded as quick as a flash, "He probably is, but we're in Mexico now!" That had really cracked Dean up. Alex smiled at the bittersweet memory. Laughter was entirely off the menu back at the beach house.

Rick spent the remainder of the afternoon in a miserable fug to the accompaniment of gloomy music from the cassette player. Alex pottered in his studio, trying to tune out the doom-laden backing track. His mind wasn't in the mood for painting, he picked up his sketch pad and went outside. It had been so long since he'd drawn that it had taken Hank reminding him he was good at it to do it again. Barefoot and bare chested in denim cut offs, Alex lolled on the front steps sketching anything that came to eye. He heard Rick inside on the phone. The conversation was in Italian, he was obviously on to Gina, but the tone was calm. Another call, this one conducted in English, apparently garnered a positive response from Scotty about tomorrow night.

Rick came out and sank onto the sagging gray sofa. He was only wearing shorts too but with the addition of a thick white sock covering his injured foot. The wind tousled his increasingly sun-bleached hair. "Scotty and Bob are on for tomorrow night."

"I'm holding my breath in anticipation," said Alex glancing up from his sketch pad. He saw Rick scratch his foot through the sock. "Nursey nurse told you not to scratch it! Or, more precisely, she told me to tell you not to scratch it. Leave it alone or it'll never heal," said Alex sternly.

"The fricking scar's damn itchy." Rick stretched his arms behind his neck and tipped back his head.

Alex was struck by Rick's profile. The arch of his neck, the line of his chin and the tilt of his nose were exquisite. "Don't move," said Alex flipping over a new leaf.

"What?" said Rick immediately moving.

"Stay as you were."

"Why?"

"I need to draw you. Go back to how you were a moment ago."

Rick re-assumed the position.

"Don't pose," said Alex.

"Now I know you're looking at me I feel self-conscious."

"Don't you feel self-conscious with a movie camera trained on you?"

"I'm playing a part then."

"Close your eyes. Listen to the surf," said Alex. "Don't make yourself look how you think someone wants you to look. Just *be*." It took a few seconds but once Rick stopped trying to assume a pleasing shape the change was visible. His neck and chest relaxed, his chin dropped, the back of his neck lengthened and the tension in his jaw dissipated. Alex went to work, using his pencil to translate his vision to the page. He took sensual pleasure tracing the curve of Rick's upper lip, the arch of his brow and the sternocleidomastoid muscle with the perceptible pulse. "Finished."

Like waking from a dream, Rick opened his eyes. He heaved himself off the sagging sofa and came to sit beside Alex, their bare shoulders and biceps pressed together.

"How'd I do?" Alex offered up the sketch. He was his own worst critic but thought it was pretty good. Rick's face possessed a classic beauty but in repose his profile had an air of melancholy. Rick stared at the drawing then got up without speaking. "Don't you like it?" Alex scrambled to his feet and followed him into the house.

Rick was poised at the bottom of the stairs, biting his lip. He looked up and said, "You've made me look nice. And after what went down with Gina today, I don't feel nice. I did an ugly thing to her."

Alex put down the pad and wrapped his arms around Rick. Chest to chest, the eternity pendant got sandwiched between their sternums. "It would have been worse to go through with the marriage and condemn you both to lives of misery, wouldn't it?"

Rick locked his eyes onto Alex's. "I guess."

Alex held Rick tight, feeling his heart pumping close to his own.

The next morning, while Rick was in the shower with a plastic bag taped around the dressing on his foot, Alex dragged the phone onto the verandah. "Hey, Scotty," he said in a low voice.

"Hey, yourself. What's with this dinner date tonight?"

"How much did Rick tell you?"

"Only this model friend of his is in town. He said she was low, and it'd be good for her to spend time with fun people. I took it by that he meant me and Bob," said Scotty with a laugh.

"There's more to it than that. You see, he was getting married to her but backed out at the last minute. It's still raw. Just keep away from talking about marriage and stuff like that."

"How about the topic of his mother?" asked Scotty.

"Steer clear of that too. Seems she was involved in the situation."

"Could you write a checklist of suitable dinner table subjects and distribute it to the class beforehand?"

"And there's something else you should know. Rick and I are seeing each other. You know, like romantically."

"Is that meant to surprise me?"

"What do you mean?"

"It's pretty obvious."

"But it only just happened."

"I knew from the first moment I met him."

"I didn't know then. How could you?" asked Alex.

"I just did. It's great news."

"It is?"

"You two get on great, you're both crazily good-looking, why shouldn't you have some fun," said Scotty.

"You're cool with it?"

"I've known you for eons. I love you no matter what."

Alex swallowed hard to push down the lump in his throat. "Aw, thanks. But I think it'd be best if you ..."

"Don't bring the subject up at dinner. Got it. See you later."

Around seven p.m., Alex and Rick swung by the Beverly Hills Hotel to pick up Gina. As a gesture of consideration to Gina's style they were using Rick's Mercedes. As a gesture of consideration to Alex's nerves Rick was letting him drive it.

"I should take up yoga," muttered Rick crawling around the passenger seat to get into the sports car's cramped rear. Gina slunk out the hotel in a red midi dress and strappy platform heels. She shoved back the passenger seat to give herself more leg room. Rick yelped as Gina's seat crushed his knees.

"Sorry," said Gina over her shoulder, giving Alex a sly smile.

Alex decided this was a huge improvement on yesterday when she'd looked like she could have cheerfully garroted him. During the short journey, Gina was positively effusive. She said her agent had told her they'd be shooting in the Los Angeles River tomorrow. Calling it a river led her to imagine a lush waterway. With a good deal of amusement, Rick set her straight that the river was actually more like a concrete flood drain. She'd also just found out there was a problem with the other model, who'd been booked from a Paris agency. The girl had just flown in. On arrival, it became clear someone had converted from centimeters to inches incorrectly and she was two inches shorter than Gina. Gina suspected tomorrow would be spent devising tactics to make their height difference less noticeable. Rick's suggestion that Gina do the entire shoot on her knees was not greeted with the hilarity he'd expected. Gina's eyes shone unnaturally brightly under the street lamps of Brighton Way as they got out of the car.

"Now I know how a pretzel feels," said Rick with a groan, extricating himself from the rear seat.

Scotty and Bob were ensconced at The Daisy's bar making a head start on drinks when they entered. Scotty looked very elegant in a high-necked white blouse with navy pants. Bob was his usual formal self in navy pinstripe suit, pale blue shirt and red tie. Gina was lagging behind, Alex turned to check she was still with them. He looked around to see her enter the restaurant with a catwalk stalk. She paused, dipped her head and adjusted her gold button earring, attracting the dinner crowd's attention. Her poise and dark looks were a major draw, her plunge front scarlet jersey dress was another. After Rick had made the necessary introductions, the hostess led them to a booth. Bob broke away to briefly converse with a couple in the booth on their left. Bob beckoned Rick over to the table too. They all chatted for a few moments before Bob and Rick re-joined their party.

"When we go out to dinner it takes all night before we can eat," Scotty said to Gina with a long-suffering smile as Bob and Rick slid behind the booth's circular tables. "Bob knows *everybody* in this town and everybody knows him."

"That's Sherry Lansing," said Bob in a hushed tone. "I met her when she was doing some acting work a few years back. She's moved behind the scenes and just joined the company that produces Rick's show."

Rick shook his head at Bob. "*My* show? Please, I've done one segment."

Bob drew them forward conspiratorially. "The top brass was very pleased with your work."

"That's kind of you Bob, but no-one's said anything to me."

"Mark my words, this could be the start of something big."

Gina appeared relaxed. Although not forthcoming with conversation, she listened and responded appropriately as Rick filled them in on the *McMillan* shoot. He got a big laugh from relating the story of the burly stuntman doubling for Nancy

Walker. Scotty wheedled for behind the scenes gossip, but Rick responded with the 'everyone was lovely and professional' line. Which, from what he'd seen on set, Alex could only confirm was the truth. A server came to take their order and they stopped gossiping long enough to decide what to eat. The Daisy's menu was notable for naming dishes after their famous clientele. Currently the 'Sonny Bono' was liver and onions, the 'Natalie Wood' a vegetable salad with chicken, and the 'Ray Bradbury' was a hamburger, which struck them all as rather odd. More wine was ordered as the first bottle had disappeared. Alex stuck to Perrier, a gut instinct told him he needed his wits about him tonight.

"Anything new with you, Alex?" Scotty asked with an arched eyebrow as conversation resumed. "That you're willing to share with the table, that is."

Knowing she was subtly teasing him, Alex decided to tell them about his move into plein air painting. This segued into the work he'd done at Universal. "I was deep into a study of a set on the backlot, some façade that looked like a stone civic building, and the whole area's deserted when suddenly I get the feeling I'm not alone. I turn around to see this woman behind me, like she's just appeared from nowhere. She asks if she can watch me work, so I say sure. When I finish, and this is the crazy bit, she asks if she can buy the painting. I'd no idea what to say. Like, what if I said, 'Hey, how about a thousand bucks, lady?' It was all too complicated, so I gave it her as a gift. I turn away to pack up, only for a minute or so mind, and when I turn back she's gone. Vanished into thin air."

Bob beckoned them closer. "Clients who've worked on that backlot set have told of similar experiences. What did she look like?" asked Bob gravely. A stillness descended around the table.

"Mature lady, white shirt, chiffon scarf, dark hair," said Alex.

"Jesus Christ. That sounds like her." Bob picked up his glass and took a large drink. He leaned back in the booth.

"Who?" asked Scotty.

Bob shook his head. "I shouldn't have said anything. Forget it."

"Bob, you can't leave us hanging like this," said Scotty impatiently.

"Very well, if *you* insist." Bob reluctantly carried on the story. "The woman Alex saw was Rita Roman, a contract player from the fifties. Everyone thought she was going to be a huge star. Then a scandal broke in the press about her and an unsuitable lover. The studio got cold feet and terminated her contract. She couldn't face the fact she'd lost her shot at stardom just because of loving the wrong man. One hot October night, with the Santa Anas blowing fierce, Rita broke onto the backlot. A security patrol found her the next morning, dangling behind that courthouse set. She'd hung herself with a chiffon scarf ..."

Goosebumps upon goosebumps erupted down Alex's spine. "What are you saying?"

"You saw the Backlot Ghost." Bob lowered his voice, so much so everyone around the table had to lean forward to hear. "You know what happens to any poor bastard with the bad luck to encounter her?"

Alex's heart pounded. What was the terrible curse? What could be worse that all the crazy shit that had taken place lately?

"They say that any man who has the misfortune to see her ..." whispered Bob raising his hand to beckon Alex closer.

Alex craned his neck forward, desperate for Bob's revelation.

Bob lightly whacked the back of Alex's head with the flat of his hand. "Gets slapped for being a dumb sucker to swallow that bullshit story!"

"You just made that up?" asked Scotty incredulously.

"The Rita Roman thing was inspired, don't you think?" said Bob with a broad grin. The dissipation of tension had them all collapsing into laughter. Even Gina.

"You rat! You seriously had me thinking I'd seen a ghost." Alex chuckled in spite of himself. "You're on the wrong side of the camera, Bob."

In the lull after Bob's ghost story, Scotty turned to Gina, "How'd you get into the modeling business? Apart from being stunningly gorgeous of course!"

Gina pursed her lips. A protracted wait for her response built tension, she then said, "In Milan, I was a girl. I love the fashion. I love the colors. My mamma sew clothes in a factory and she teach me how to put fabric together. I make decision to be designer." Gina sipped her wine. "I start to make fashion. Our little town has a show for new talent and they ask my designs to take part. I am very happy. Is the day of the show and I see the girl they choose to model my design. She wears it on passarella and I get angry!" Gina's eyes widened, her hands began to fly. "She ruin my outfit! I run up and push her out the way. I shout, 'This is how you wear my dress' and I show her. But she does not listen to me. I demand, 'Dismiss this girl'. They do as I ask, then we are left without model! Is my fault, no? My temper spoil their show. I have no choice but to take her place."

Rick interjected, "And with your style and looks you had it made."

"And this is how I meet *him*." Gina glared at Rick. "I like the designing. I grow to like the modeling. Rick and I, we have simpatico, you know how I say?" Everyone around the table nodded as if they did. "But Rick has this vision. He see me as more than designer and model in Milan. He see me as great model of the world. He spin his magic. He and his mother introduce me to designers and agents. I am no longer face in the crowd, I am girl photographers want. I am face of nineteen seventy-two." Gina drained her wine and held out the glass. The server immediately appeared and refilled it. Gina took a large gulp.

"Quite some success story ..." Rick glanced around the table for reinforcement.

"But I gain my success alone." Gina put down her glass, loudly. Everyone around the table shifted uncomfortably. Mercifully, the food arrived and the need to remember who'd ordered what changed the subject. While the rest of them attacked their main courses with gusto, Gina merely toyed with her salad. Between forkfuls, Scotty filled Rick in with the latest gallery news.

Rick noticed Gina wasn't eating and asked, "Something wrong? You haven't touched your 'Katherine Ross'."

Gina ignored Rick's question and turned to Scotty. "Your work has interest to me. When I design I too think of flowers. Their colors are the only true colors in this world." Gina drained her fourth glass of wine and tossed another dark glare at Rick.

Sensing a storm brewing, Scotty changed the subject and enquired about Gloria Waverley. Bob hadn't heard the blow by blow account of Alex saving her life. Rick filled him in on the story, sparing no sentiment or the story's happy ending. "Move over Superman!" Bob declared when Rick had finished.

"In such story I see the Superman as Harry," said Gina abruptly. "In Gloria's crisis the man she love return. Is unusual to have someone care so much." Gina held out her glass and Bob topped it up.

"Go steady on that," Rick said softly to Gina.

Gina glowered back at him and took another mouthful of wine.

Rick's jaw muscles rippled. "I hear Jerry Lindquist's new movie's doing boffo box office," said Rick to the table. "Jerry knows how to pick a winner."

"And that is why he's the hottest producer in town," agreed Bob.

"The big question is who he'll cast as the lead in his new picture," said Scotty.

"Dunaway's a front runner," responded Bob with authority.

Rick shook his head. "He's more likely to go for someone totally against the part ..."

Gina tilted her chin aggressively and shouted at Rick, "You are so clever, analyzing the lives of people! To make or break is all you understand!"

Heads turned in the restaurant. "Don't make a scene," Rick hissed sidelong to Gina. "Not here."

"That is all you want of me, my silence! We must not dirty your public face. It would be terrible if the world should see the real Rick Stradman!" Gina reached for her glass, but she missed and knocked it over. The glass hit the table, shattered and the wine splashed out. Scotty recoiled in surprise, but not fast enough to avoid the red wine drenching her white blouse. Gina stared at it, aghast.

"Here, honey," Bob casually passed Scotty a napkin.

"It's not too bad," said Scotty dabbing at the dark stain.

Bob couldn't restrain chuckling at Scotty's understatement. Two servers rushed up to clear the broken glass. Gina glared at Bob then leaped up and stumbled out of the restaurant, knocking into tables as she went.

"Scotty, I most sincerely apologize," said Rick. He extricated himself from the table, tossed down his napkin and took off after Gina.

"It was an accident," said Scotty getting up from the table too. "I'll sponge it off in the restroom."

"Nothing like a quiet dinner out," Alex muttered once Scotty had gone.

"True," said Bob, "and this is nothing like a quiet dinner out."

"Excuse me." Scuffing back his chair, Alex got up too. He caught up with Rick in the street outside. Rick was chasing after

Gina, who was striding unsteadily along Rodeo Drive waving her purse to attract a cab. The wind was whipping her hair around her face and her red dress around her calves.

"Where are you going?" yelled Rick to Gina.

"Back to the hotel. I make fool of myself in front of your friends," said Gina.

"They're cool, Gina. Please, come back." Rick's words were lost in the wind.

A vacant cab pulled in to the curb. Gina clambered in, slammed the door and the cab took off with a screech. Alex stood beside Rick, watching the red tail lights weave into the traffic. "Nice move inviting Scotty and Bob. I see how this evening could've been awkward with just the two of you."

"Don't make me feel worse than I already do. I didn't want it to turn out this way," said Rick. Back inside the restaurant, various eyes flicked in Rick and Alex's direction as they returned to their booth.

Scotty had returned to the table. "Is Gina okay?" she asked with concern.

"She's tired," said Rick draining his glass. "She's been working too hard. Send me the bill for the dry cleaning, Scotty."

Bob caught the server's eye and raised the empty wine bottle. "Another." He saw Scotty looking askance and said, "This isn't the night to quit drinking."

"The modeling world sounds very high pressured," said Scotty artfully arranging a napkin to disguise the stain on her blouse.

A woman brushed past their table. What Scotty was doing with the napkin caught her attention. The woman glanced around the table, then said, "Rick?"

Rick looked up. Recognizing the woman, he smiled broadly and exclaimed, "Danielle!"

"My lord. How good to see you!" The woman had a southern lilt to her voice, her below shoulder length auburn hair curled softly around her face.

Rick stood. "Everyone, this is Danielle Brown. We worked together on *Eddie's Girls.*" Introductions were unnecessary for Bob, as they already knew each other. "Won't you join us?"

"That's mighty kind, but I'm with people." Danielle gestured to a corner table, where an elegant black man and a blonde woman with a bouffant hair-do were engaged in deep conversation. Danielle chatted with them around the table for a few more moments. Rick got her up to speed on his *McMillan* guest spot and Danielle showed genuine interest in Scotty and Alex's art work. "I'm somewhat of a collector myself," Danielle confided modestly to Alex. After promises between Rick and Danielle to catch up in more detail and exchanges of current numbers, Danielle re-joined her party.

"She's very beautiful," said Scotty after Danielle had gone. "Shame her marriage crashed so spectacularly."

"Are there any secrets in this town?" asked Bob.

"Secrets don't sell papers if they stay secret," said Scotty knowingly.

The server arrived with a fresh bottle and poured for all except Alex. Rick glanced at Danielle's table. "Her marriage was on the way-out last year. The press was following her everywhere looking for dirt. Turns out the husband had been having affairs all over town."

"I should invite Danielle to my opening," said Scotty, almost to herself. "Wouldn't it be great publicity if she came?"

"My dear, your craving for attention's showing," Bob pointed out. "It's unseemly when you're wearing a half bottle of red wine."

Alex stifled a yawn listening to Bob and Scotty banter. He noticed Rick was a million miles away, tapping him on the shoulder he asked, "You ready to make a move?"

"Yeah, I'll get the check," said Rick distractedly.

"Still thinking about Gina?"

"More about Monica's charity auction. I'd thought about inviting Gina, but after tonight there's no way."

"Why on earth would you even consider inviting Gina to something like that?" asked Alex.

"Monica's auction is a high society event. Photographers will be there. The press leap on famous faces and Gina fits that bill." Rick snapped his fingers. "I'll invite Danielle! The press can't leave her alone. A photo of you and her would make the society pages without doubt! That'd get your name known."

Alex felt this was getting into weird territory. "Don't try to manipulate everything Rick, let fate take its turn."

"Here, here," said Scotty raising her glass.

"To fate." A *chink* as Bob touched his glass to Scotty's then winked at Alex. "Because everything happens by chance in Hollywood."

Alex allowed himself a small laugh. "You guys are beyond cynical."

"The business is all about perception. How you're perceived is more important in getting work than talent sometimes," said Bob.

Rick leaned forward. "Five years ago, Gina was a skinny teenager living with her mother in a tiny apartment on a Milan backstreet. Today she's one of the highest paid models in the world. All because of the image she projects."

Before any more discussion ensued, the hostess appeared with the check, which Rick insisted on picking up. In the process of settling the bill and them all saying goodbye, the previous conversation was forgotten. Alex thought that was lucky because it avoided him asking Rick the big question - Gina may be one of the highest paid models in the world, but was she happy?

♦ ♦ ♦

"Phone!" yelled Rick.

Rick was doing his usual trick of shouting that the phone was ringing rather than answering it. Alex came out of his studio wiping paint off his hands. He made a face at Rick so much as to say, 'Why don't you pick it up?' This question had been asked before, and out loud. Rick settled on the standard response that he suffered from 'phonophobia'. "Y'ello. Say again, only slower please. Who you looking for?" Alex struggled to identify the caller. When she spoke again, however, he detected her accent was Japanese. It dawned on him it must be Yumi Mihara; it had been weeks since Koenig said she'd call.

Working hard to make sense of Yumi's speech, he learned she'd called the house many times. Apparently, if he hadn't been at home this time she was going to give up. Getting attuned to her broken English, Alex discovered Yumi liked the works he'd left with Koenig and was considering taking him for her gallery. He mentioned he was going to be in town for a charity auction and could meet with her before that. Yumi casually asked if the event was the one for the Los Angeles Arts and Crafts Association. He said it was and that he had a piece in it. Yumi agreed to the meeting and they set a time.

The phone conversation with Yumi carried on running through Alex's head after he'd hung up. The stitches were out of Rick's foot and it had healed enough for him to walk barefoot on the beach. They celebrated this news with an evening stroll in the surf.

"Hey, I got an advice note in the mail this morning. My fee for the show came in. While we're in town for the auction we can pick out a new couch," said Rick

"I don't need a new couch."

"Your old one's got a massive bloodstain on it. Do you want people thinking your interior designer was Lizzie Bordern?"

"Seriously, it doesn't matter."

"I want to buy you a new one, so I'll just choose it. Oh, and I left you a check on the counter. I made it out to cash for two thousand dollars."

Alex stopped walking. He screwed up his face at Rick. "Why'd you do that?"

"To cover the rent to summer's end. And to say thank you."

Three months ago, Alex had been flat broke and on the verge of selling his wheels to make ends meet. Thanks to Rick and Sid, today he had more cash on hand than he knew what to do with. "Seeing the way things have changed between us, it feels wrong you giving me money to live here. By that logic, I should have paid you for staying at Brentwood."

"All I gave you to swim in there is that small pool. You've given me the ocean."

"I've given you nothing compared to what you've given me."

Rick bumped his head against Alex's. "Like turn you gay?"

Alex jokingly wagged his finger at him. "You can't take all the credit for that. There might have been some other help in the past." He stuffed his hands in his pockets and they carried on walking in the surf.

"So there have been others before me then?" asked Rick.

"Not exactly."

"But you've felt something for another man before?"

Alex's hand went to the eternity pendant around his neck. He fiddled with it as he said, "There was this guy, Dean. We worked together on the yachts one summer. He was, well, he was more than my best friend. You know that feeling when you see someone in the morning and they make your day better without them having to do anything?"

Rick's eyes drifted to the horizon. "He feel the same way about you?"

"I thought so." Alex couldn't help but cough as a repressed sadness burst from his chest. "We were running a yacht up to San Francisco. We'd hit heavy weather and had to put into Morro Bay overnight. There weren't enough rooms and we had to bunk up. We'd had a few drinks and, well, something happened. It was pretty intense. It blew my mind."

"And he gave you that pendant?"

"No. I bought this at the surf shop first thing next morning. I was going to give it to him in San Francisco after we'd handed over the yacht. I had it all planned, this dream of some kind of relationship together."

"And?"

"When I got back to the room, Dean was dressed with his bag packed. He apologized for being drunk and didn't remember anything about the night before. He hightailed it to Portland with another crew. That was the last of Dean. I vowed to never let myself get into a situation like that again. You see, I'm not one of those guys that tends to separate sex and love. For me, falling for someone is what leads to the passion. The way Dean left hurt so deep because he made me feel like nothing, like a shameful convenience. I'd have preferred if he'd punched me. At least I'd have had another bruise on my jaw rather than my heart." They walked in silence for a couple of hundred yards. "How about you? Have you had other guys like me in the past?"

"There was somebody last summer."

"Did it last long?"

Rick laughed. "Not until fall obviously. That was back in Italy."

"You end it or him?"

"A mix of mutually declining interest. But it made me realize I couldn't go through with marrying Gina. I didn't want a big scene with momma, so I told her I was coming back to America to get into acting. She never knew the full story, thank god. But I didn't understand how deeply in love with me Gina was. It's a big responsibility having someone fall in love with you, isn't it?" Rick kicked through the water "Is there always the one who loves and the one who is loved? Do you think there's ever an equal balance, a perfect love?"

"Maybe, but perhaps we just don't recognize perfect love until we lose it, perhaps full emotions can only exist in memory because the present is liquid. We may not even know we had true love until years later when the past has solidified."

"I hope we have a future together, Al. I hope we'll be in a place twenty or thirty years from now when we can look back and know what this moment really means."

The sun was sinking, casting a fiery glow over the beach.

"Don't waste time on the future. We have one perfect summer evening right here and now. Isn't that enough?" said Alex staring out to sea.

Rick followed Alex's gaze, then took his hand.

They stood side by side in the surf with the wind blowing their hair, just two guys on Sunset Cove feeling the sand slip away under their feet, watching the sun fall from the sky.

♦ ♦ ♦

"It's too much." Alex twisted from side to side in front of the mirror.

"It's fabulous." Rick brushed an imaginary speck off the tuxedo's shoulder.

Alex raked his fingers through his pliant hair. "My art's up for auction, not me."

"Take it off." Rick held out his hand for the jacket. "Shirt too."

Alex unbuttoned the white dress shirt and handed it to Rick. He waited bare-chested, flexing his muscles as Rick foraged in the chest of drawers. He rubbed his bicep and elbow. "Don't know what I've done to my arms, but this ache will not go away."

"Pants off too, mister."

Alex undid his belt and peeled down the dark gray formal trousers. Adjusting himself in his boxers, he stood while Rick looked him up and down. After a minute he asked, "What you waiting for?"

"Nothing, just savoring the view. Put these on." Rick tossed him a pair of dark indigo jeans and a black tee. "Now try the jacket."

Alex put on the tux. The dark jeans and tee killed its drama. He considered his reflection. "I can go for that."

They carried the paintings Alex wanted to show Yumi Mihara out to the car and placed them carefully in the trunk. "You got Danielle's address and number?" asked Rick.

Alex patted his pocket. "Yep."

"I've arranged for the limo to pick us up from her place at six-thirty."

"Monica didn't mind you adding Danielle to the guest list?"

"She was thrilled. Her charity auctions need to make the society pages. The bigger the names the better."

"See you later." Alex nodded towards the Mercedes. "Drive safe."

Rick rolled his eyes. "I'll be fine. Now go, and good you know what." He casually kissed Alex on the mouth.

"Thanks." Unsure how he felt about this open display of affection, Alex jumped in the car and took off. Traffic was light on the 405 but the smog was heavy; the fumes stung his eyes. He wound up the window and turned on the fan. Finding a parking spot directly outside the Mihara Gallery, he gave the two-story double fronted on La Cienega a quick once over. The building's stucco had been freshly decorated in a pale taupe. Sloping bronze canopies over the windows either side of the entrance gave the exterior the look of a benign face. Leaving his tux neatly folded on the rear seat, Alex checked his appearance in the wing mirror. Feeling more confident then when he'd visited Koenig, he took his work out of the trunk and went in.

The gallery's interior had dark walls and a black lacquer floor. The subfusc styling made a neat change from the relentless white boxes of other galleries. A perfectly formed Japanese man dressed entirely in black greeted him. Alex introduced himself. The man bowed slightly and saying, "This way, please," led Alex to the office at the rear. Together with Rick, he'd selected the beach painting with the blood, the two plein airs of the highway at dusk, a couple of urban studies and the first backlot painting he'd done at Universal to show Yumi.

Yumi was on the phone by her desk. She waved Alex to come in and her assistant departed. While talking in her indecipherable accent, she pointed a red talon at a chair, indicating that Alex should put the pictures down and wait. Alex studied Yumi as she finished her conversation. She was tiny, but her height was increased by piling her black hair into a topknot and a vertiginous pair of platform heels. Crimson lipstick dominated her pale face. Her outfit consisted of a ferociously pared down ivory linen shirt and pants.

Yumi put down the phone, nodded at Alex without any expression, then uttered something unintelligible. He kept his cool. Rather than asking her to repeat herself, he told her how happy he was to be meeting her and how beautiful her gallery was. She stared at him inscrutably, then smiled. Whatever vestige of a smile she'd arranged her crimson lips into vanished when she placed his first piece on the rosewood easel under an intense spotlight. She gazed at his work with steely eyes, then asked him something which he really didn't understand at all. Summoning all his charm and concentration, he played a question and answer game to guide her through his background, his work and his aspirations. The aggressive air conditioning in Yumi's office was a godsend, without it he'd have dissolved into a sweaty pool on the lacquer floor. This was either going to be a very long meeting, or a very short one …

♦ ♦ ♦

Monica Aigner's house occupied a prime spot in the treelined foothills north of Sunset. The manicured grass verges were like emerald velvet. Alex sat between Danielle and Rick in the limo's rear. The car turned off North Roxbury, passed through a pair of wrought iron gates and pulled up beside a marble fountain which dominated the driveway. Bushes, trimmed so perfectly they looked like plastic, curved towards the arched reception. The limo driver got out and opened the rear door. Danielle, Rick and Alex emerged and walked towards waiters in white mess jackets. Gloved hands proffered silver trays laden with champagne flutes.

"I'd heard Monica was wealthy," said Danielle discretely to Rick while taking a glass, "but I'd no idea she was *this* wealthy."

Rick took one too and gave the glass a knowing look. "Who doesn't have a hundred matching Baccarat champagne flutes on hand for entertaining?"

"She could have hired them," pointed out Alex, also availing himself of a glass.

"Maybe she keeps them locked in the basement for her functions," said Rick, "along with the waiters."

Danielle gasped with laughter, nearly choking on her champagne. They mingled with other guests passing through the vaulted entrance hall, the marble clad foyer with galleried upper floors, the formal living room, the formal dining room, until finally exiting onto the glittering terrace. White marquees with dining tables spilling out surrounded an under lit Tiffany Blue swimming pool. A five-piece band played on a raised dais.

Alex realized his worries about being overdressed were unfounded. It wasn't a black-tie event, but everyone had come formal; the women all plumping for long gowns accessorized with diamonds and face lifts.

A vision in electric blue taffeta rustled up to them. Monica's dress featured a large bow tugging its asymmetric neckline to one side. The bow rose up to her right ear making her look like she'd been gift wrapped. Sapphire pendants dangled from her lobes, the one on her right ear kept catching awkwardly on the dress's bow. "Darlings!" Monica bussed Rick on the cheek. "You're such a sweetheart. Thank you for that autographed photo of Rock Hudson."

"Treasure it. He doesn't care for signing things," said Rick.

"I'll keep it on my bedside table and kiss it every night." Monica greeted Alex, who in turn introduced her to Danielle. Monica took a step back to take in all of Danielle's dark emerald gown. "My dear, your photographs don't do you justice. Isn't she truly lovely? Alex, if you're in need of a beautiful subject I don't think you need to look far!"

"That's mighty kind. But I do believe Alex can find more interesting subjects than li'l ole me," drawled Danielle with self-deprecating charm.

"Each to his own." Monica brushed the bow on her dress from her earring. "Anyway, dinner will be served at seven-thirty. The auction begins at eight-fifteen sharp! It's a Monday and I know you T.V. people like to be in bed by ten. This is wonderful, so many gifted people here tonight I almost feel inferior. Please, enjoy. Alphonse is on hand if you need anything." Monica gestured at an elderly man in a Nehru jacket, then left to greet new arrivals.

Alex, Danielle and Rick sipped their champagne and wandered across the perfect lawn. "Don't look. On your left. Leather jacket and bolo tie," hissed Rick.

Danielle surreptitiously looked around. "Jerry Lindquist?"

Rick nodded. "We should go over and bump into him."

"Why?" asked Alex.

"He's casting a new movie which doesn't have a leading lady attached," said Rick, as if Alex was totally dense for not immediately thinking the same thing.

Danielle rested her hand on Rick's shoulder. "Sugar, you and I are T.V. actors. There is no sane producer in this sweet world who'd cast either of us in a movie."

"Never say never," said Rick huffily. "What harm can trying do?"

Danielle shot a long-suffering look at Alex.

"Surrender to him," said Alex. "It's easier. Believe me."

"If you insist, sugar," said Danielle to Rick.

Rick casually chatted with Danielle while propelling her in Jerry's direction. As they passed through the crowd, a barrage of flashes went off from the press photographers for the society pages. Alex drifted to the fringe to observe the greeting rituals of the rich and famous. He took a seat at a table laden with silverware, wine glasses and an abundant centerpiece of white lilies and lilacs.

"Very decorative," said Scotty coming up from behind.

"Oh, hi." Alex smiled at the table, "Yeah, lavish."

"I was talking about you," said Scotty running her finger along his tuxedo's satin lapel. "Sweet little jacket you have on."

"I see you've made no effort either." Alex noted her black velvet sheath dress. It was high in front, but the back dropped to a low cowl revealing her perfect back. Diamond stud earrings were all she wore as jewelry.

"Here we are, madam." Bob came up carrying two glasses of champagne. "Hey Alex, where's young Rick?"

"He's dangling Danielle in front of a movie producer in the hope of getting her a job."

"That's not gonna fly," winced Bob. "She's a T.V. name. Still, have to hand it to the kid. He's got the chops to try." Bob took a sip of champagne and made an appreciative face. "Not bad."

"Dom Perignon Brut, vintage '69," said Alex raising his Baccarat crystal glass.

"When did you become a wine connoisseur?" asked Scotty seemingly impressed.

"I read the label as they poured," said Alex.

"I figure each mouthful runs at ten bucks. Monica's gone to town tonight." Bob took a sip. "I'm not sure which town, but she's definitely gone."

They raised their heads in response to Monica clapping her hands up on the terrace. Once everyone hushed, Monica announced, "Dear friends, dinner is served. There are name cards on the tables. No cheating. I've put you all in your places!" She waved her hands, shooing them all to sit. The guests drifted to the tables by the marquees. With great relief, Alex found Monica had put him on a table with Rick, Danielle, Bob and Scotty. Rick and Danielle joined as they sat down.

"Hi, how are you?" Rick greeted Bob and Scotty.

"Good, good. Hey, Danielle," Bob kissed Danielle on the cheek. "Any luck with Jerry?"

Danielle stroked Rick's shoulder. "He made a valiant effort of parading me in front of Jerry, but I warned him it was in vain. The only role Jerry would consider me for is *The Invisible Woman* because that's what I am to him!"

"Can but try," laughed Rick.

"Rick, how's Gina?" asked Scotty.

"More importantly, is the Beverly Hills Hotel still standing?" Bob asked.

"Bob!" Scotty reprimanded him.

"That's okay," Rick said understandingly. "She was a disaster area the other night. Sorry about your blouse. Honestly, I'll buy you another."

"I dyed it pink and it looks terrific. It made me look like a secretary in white. Gina's subconscious was designing for me."

Alex marveled at Scotty's social skills, turning an embarrassing situation into a joke.

"So, Danielle," said Bob across the table, "you started shooting on the new season yet?"

"Next week. I just got the first script." Danielle made an expression of distaste.

"What, it's no good?" asked Rick.

"The script's fine, but they've introduced a new character. During hiatus I've gotten myself a younger sister. A *much* younger sister. And she has gotten herself a mighty big slice of the action," Danielle sighed. "Guess I'll have to watch my back. And my face. One more wrinkle and li'l sis will be taking over my part."

"Who's playing her?" asked Bob.

Danielle shrugged. "A new face. Or should I say a young face. Her name's Jill, or Janet, or some such. The only thing Aaron let slip was she was a waitress until last month. Hell, I shouldn't judge, five years ago I was one too."

Rick caught Alex's eye and whispered, "Do you think it could be Julie?"

"That'd be one hell of a big coincidence," muttered Alex.

"You saw Julie at Fox. That's where *Eddie's Girls* shoots." Rick's speculation was halted when Monica swept up to their table.

"Scotty and Bob, my darlings." Monica bussed Scotty on both cheeks. "Sorry I missed you on arrival." Monica opened her attention to include the whole table. "I shall cross my fingers for the auction. Alex, you're an unknown so don't hope for the moon. Rest assured every dollar your painting raises, however few, will benefit the Los Angeles Arts and Crafts Association. Please acknowledge our gratitude for your kind donation. Bon Appetit." Monica fluttered her hands over them in some kind of Beverly Hills benediction.

"L.A.A.C.A.?" Bob chuckled as a white jacketed waiter served the appetizer from the left. "Heck, I can't keep up with all these acronyms."

"I wonder if the Chicago Arts and Crafts Association is C.A.C.A.?" mused Rick.

Hilarity ensued as the acronyms grew longer and more salacious. Other guests looked around to see where the raucous laughter was coming from. Dinner over, attention turned to the large marquee by the pool. Everyone took their places on golden chairs with red velvet seats. Alphonse passed out auction catalogs and the white jacketed waiters offered more drinks. The Dom Perignon had been replaced with a choice of a '67 Sauternes or a 1970 Bordeaux. Hard liquor was available on request, also Perrier.

Alex tried the Sauternes. It had the ring of apricot and honey. Altogether too sweet for his taste. He swapped it for a Bordeaux when a waiter passed. The lighting dimmed. The M.C. took his place on stage. There was a round of applause as a man wearing a powder blue velvet jacket picked up the microphone.

"Who's he?" whispered Alex to Rick.

"Ted Burns, game show host."

Ted opened with some patter and a couple of dud jokes, which apparently the lavish quantities of alcohol rendered funny. Pleasantries out of the way, Ted kicked off the auction. The first few lots were unremarkable and achieved unremarkable prices. The waiters kept coming around with drinks. This must have loosened up someone's check book, for the third lot picked up a decent price.

"Just for the record, does anyone know what L.A.A.C.A. does with the money raised?" Bob whispered to Rick and Alex.

Rick shrugged. "No idea. But if Monica simply gave them the money she spent putting on the fundraiser we'd all be at home in bed by now and it'd probably work out even."

Bob chuckled, "It wouldn't be as much fun though, would it?"

"Depends on who you're in bed with," shot back Rick. He giggled and covered his mouth in embarrassment.

"Shh, you two." Scotty glared at Rick and Bob. "Don't make any random hand gestures or you may find you've bid on a ceramic reproduction of Tina Seattle's left breast."

"Odd she doesn't do them in pairs," Bob commented drily.

"That'd be too obvious." Scotty stiffened her bare back.

The lots were coming thick and fast. The sold prices were rising, most items hitting the five-hundred-dollar mark. Alex checked the catalog. His painting was next. Up with him on the dais, Ted Burns had a young woman with flicked blonde hair dressed in a silver-gray jumpsuit and white platforms showing the pieces. Ted indicated that she should place the next lot on the stand. Suddenly Alex's painting, *The Cliffs of Mendocino,* was under the spotlight. "Lot 18. Oil on canvas. This is a piece by a new artist by the name of Alex Morgan. Monica informs me this young man happens to be with us tonight." Ted shielded his eyes and peered into the crowd. "Where is he? Alex Morgan, come on, stand up and take a bow!"

Although wishing to remain anonymous, there was no way Alex could avoid acknowledging Ted's request. Apologetically raising his hand, he got to his feet. The follow spot swung off Ted. Momentarily dazzled when the light found him, Alex was relieved it made everyone disappear into darkness. He dipped his head in acknowledgement of the moderate applause. Mercifully, the light quickly swung back to Ted.

Ted continued, "To add some spice to the mix, this piece recently took its place alongside paintings by some guys called Picasso, Renoir and Munch in the upcoming Warner Brothers and Twentieth Century Fox co-production *The Towering Inferno*. I assure you the fire crew got this one out before the blaze took hold and it suffered no smoke damage." A ripple of knowing laughter ran through the crowd. "This could be the best investment you've made since your B.P. stock. We're going to start the bidding at fifty dollars. Do I hear fifty?"

Alex covered his eyes. This was as humiliating as being up for sale himself.

"What's wrong?" asked Rick.

"I shouldn't have let it go, I love that painting. Bid on it. Get it back."

Rick leaned close and whispered, "Are you nuts? Listen, it's at three hundred."

Indeed, after a slow start the bids were escalating rapidly.

"I have one thousand. Any advance on one thousand?"

There was.

Scotty craned her neck to discover who was driving the bidding war. A flurry of bids and counter bids flooded in. As this wasn't going to be the humiliation he'd envisaged, Alex removed his hands from his face. His piece's popularity was a pleasant surprise. Maybe Monica was right, having it featured in a movie had added to its appeal.

"You are loving these cliffs, ladies and gentlemen. We stand at an impressive two thousand and seventy-five dollars. Alex Morgan already has some aficionados in this audience. It certainly is a stunning piece of work. Who of you out there's going to add it to their collection? Do I see any advance on two thousand and seventy-five?"

"Three thousand!" called a woman's voice from the back.

A collective gasp met this leap in bidding.

"We stand at three thousand! Any advance on three thousand dollars?" Ted Burns scanned the audience.

"Still want me to bid on it?" Rick muttered to Alex.

"Shh." Alex cut Rick off. He was on the edge of his seat along with everbody else. Monica's lavish garden fell silent, apart from the high-class chirruping of the Beverly Hills' crickets.

"Alrighty, for the last time at three thousand dollars, we are going, going, gone!" The rap of Ted's gavel on the block signified the close of this lot.

Alex received a generous round of applause and bobbed his head in acknowledgement. Inquisitive faces focused on him, curious about the provenance of the handsome surfer dude in the Giorgio tuxedo. Growing accustomed to having eyes on him, Alex allowed himself to take a good look at the crowd. Faces came into focus, all of them smiling, but then he spotted Monica on the periphery. Although she was applauding along with everyone else, her face wore a disgruntled expression. What was that about? Surely, she'd be happy his piece had raised a good price for her cause.

"Congratulations to the lady in the back." Ted Burns squinted at the follow spot operator. "Hey, can we throw some light on the little lady with the big wallet?"

The follow spot panned across expectant faces to find the winning bidder. Once it illuminated its target, a second wave of applause began. Everyone was getting to their feet, peering over each other's heads and clapping. The applause grew, including cheers and shouts. Rick, Bob, Scotty and Danielle strained to see whom the ovation was for. Alex stood too now, curious about the mystery buyer who was the cause of so much fuss.

The spotlight fell on a mature woman standing behind the gold chairs. She had dark hair and a stunningly made up face. The light bounced off her white dress and chiffon scarf, giving the illusion of an aura radiating from her. She waved graciously and modestly in acknowledgment of the ovation. The chill that had run down Alex's spine at The Daisy rippled down it once more. The woman who'd just paid three thousand dollars for *The Cliffs of Mendocino* was the same woman from the backlot to whom he'd given the painting.

Bob may have been kidding with his bullshit story, but Alex couldn't have felt any more unsettled if this woman really had been a ghost.

A WOMAN OUT OF THE SUN

The price *The Cliffs of Mendocino* achieved had galvanized the crowd. Each successive piece triggered a bidding war ending in stratospheric final prices. The humid night air was dense with excitement.

"Ladies and gentlemen, you've been incredibly generous tonight. Let's see exactly how generous," said Ted Burns extending his hand. Monica teetered up onto the stage and passed him a slip of paper. Ted read the paper then looked to Monica for confirmation. She nodded with a proud smile and teetered off the stage, Alphonse lending her a steadying hand down the steps. Ted ran a finger around his collar. "We've some high rollers in the room! If my producer's out there," Ted squinted into the crowd, "I'll be asking for a raise. Anyhoo, the sum our auction has raised, and our benevolent hostess will be donating to the Los Angeles Arts and Crafts Association, is the staggering total of forty-one thousand, two hundred and fifty dollars!" A resounding wave of applause capped off the evening. Monica bowed in gracious acceptance. The waiters resumed their rounds, this time offering coffee and dessert wine.

"Who is she?" Alex jerked his head at the gaggle of folks milling around the woman in white.

"Rosemarie Rodgers," said Bob. "Morton Harrington's wife. Daughter committed suicide, son died of cancer. She's been a recluse for years but now she's making a comeback in a new sitcom at Universal. Morton and Rosemarie are very generous in their support of the arts."

Flash bulbs popped around the knot of guests paying homage to Rosemarie. Alex couldn't stop himself staring at her in disbelief.

"What's up?" asked Rick. "You look like you've seen a ghost."

"According to Bob's little story at The Daisy, I have. That's the woman I gave the picture to on the backlot."

"For real?" Bob shook his head in disbelief. "You met Rosemarie Rodgers in the flesh, I'll be darned. That's some fan to have."

Rick beamed at Alex with unalloyed pride. "Quite a feather in your cap."

Alex held up his hands, just in time to take a glass of dessert wine from a passing waiter. "I take no credit for doing anything other than painting a picture."

"Congratulations, Alex," murmured Danielle. "I hope you give me first pick of your work."

"Too late," butted in Rick. "Yumi Mihara's got that honor."

"How come?" asked Scotty in surprise.

"We haven't had chance to tell you," Rick said to Scotty, "but Alex had a meeting with Yumi Mihara this afternoon. She's taken several of his pieces for her new gallery."

Scotty tipped her head at Alex. "Yumi has impeccable timing."

"You must go over and say hello to Rosemarie," Rick urged Alex.

"Must I?" asked Alex.

"She just splashed a wad of cash on your work. And there are photographers swarming around her." Rick dragged Alex through the throng. Monica had gravitated to Rosemarie's side. Flashbulbs were popping left, right and center as they spoke. Rosemarie appeared relaxed, but Monica seemed ill at ease.

Despite the flashes, Rosemarie spotted Alex as Rick propelled him towards her. Monica was mid-sentence as Rosemarie raised her hands warmly to Alex. "There you are! I was hoping you'd be here tonight."

Monica's lips formed a tight smile, but her eyes were cool. "Alex dear, here was silly me under the impression you were a total unknown."

Considering his words wisely, Alex replied, "That's the truth."

"Then how does Rosemarie know of you?" Monica asked with a flash of big teeth.

Alex hesitated, that was a thinker.

Thankfully, Rosemarie answered on his behalf. "It's been many years since I've set foot on a set and I was terribly nervous that day. We were on a break from camera blocking and I took a stroll on the studio backlot. Revisiting the scene of my former glories, if you will. That's when I stumbled across this man. He was painting with such concentration and artistry, I was simply entranced. And when he tried to guess what job I did, it dawned on me that he had not an inkling of who I am. Or rather was." Rosemarie let out a tinkling laugh and smiled at Alex. "I was touched when you gifted me that painting. I returned to the set refreshed, my nerves allayed by an act of kindness from a stranger. As soon as I saw your name in Monica's catalog I had to come tonight." Rosemarie eyes glistened, and she kissed Alex's cheek. Photographers jostled to capture this photo opportunity of an emotional Rosemarie Rodgers and the handsome young artist. In the melee, Monica got shuffled off to the sidelines.

Rick sidled up and introductions were made between him and Rosemarie. Then Scotty, Bob and Danielle were joining in their conversation too. The waiters served more syrupy dessert wine. After witnessing Rosemarie greet him so warmly, people gravitated to Alex. Having received her seal of approval, folks were keen to shake his hand and enquire about his paintings. He found it empowering being able to tell them they could visit the Mihara Gallery to see his work ... and buy it if so desired. Relaxing into the party mood, Alex chatted and laughed with Rosemarie and Danielle. There was one downer, Alex noticed Monica Aigner on the periphery with a displeased expression. Her bulbous nose was severely out of joint. It was clear Rosemarie Rodgers had stolen her thunder, and she was not happy about it.

Not happy at all.

♦ ♦ ♦

After every high comes a low. That low was Alex's pounding headache courtesy of the dessert wine. Its silky sweetness must have disguised the fact it was twenty per cent proof. After the auction, the limo had driven them back to Danielle's house to pick up their cars. But on arrival it was clear neither Alex nor Rick was in a fit state to drive home. Without hesitation, Danielle offered them her guest room for the night.

"It's that obvious, huh?" asked Alex the following morning, lounging with Danielle beside her lap pool.

She poured him a cup of strong black coffee from a silver pot. "What?" Danielle stretched her long, tanned legs and adjusted her orange pareo over her one-piece swimsuit.

"That Rick and I are a couple." Alex plopped a couple of sugar cubes in the coffee, hoping the mix of caffeine and sugar would revive him.

"Why'd you ask?" Danielle fixed him with her deep brown eyes.

Alex wrapped the white terrycloth robe a little tighter over his chest. It was rather small, and he felt shy in front of Danielle. "Last night you gave us the guest room."

"Honey, I couldn't let either of you get behind the wheel with the amount you'd had to drink."

"I mean one room with one bed." Alex relaxed back, carefully crossing his legs - very aware he was naked under the robe.

"I didn't think you'd care about the arrangements. Me and my girlfriends often share a room when we travel. It saves time running between each other's rooms to borrow heated rollers and gossip all night."

Alex let out a small laugh. "I guess a couple of male friends sharing a room might do different things, but I get the picture." Momentarily, he wished he hadn't brought up the subject as now he couldn't shy away from the subsequent conversation. "I just wondered if, when people meet me for the first time with Rick, they immediately assume I'm gay."

Danielle picked up her cup. "Would it matter if they did?"

"I don't know. This is kind of new to me."

"Honey, if you hadn't mentioned this it wouldn't have crossed my mind. Putting you both in that room was purely out of convenience, but I'm glad it worked out well." Danielle poured herself more coffee. "One more cup, then I'll haul these weary bones into that pool. I need to get in shape before we start shooting."

Alex studied Danielle. She was just over five foot four, but her fine bones and taut body gave her the impression of being taller. "You look in pretty good shape to me already."

"That's mighty nice of you to say, but the naked eye's more forgiving than the camera." Danielle picked up a hair elastic off the frosted glass cane table and slipped it onto her wrist. She twisted her hair into a rope and restrained it with the elastic. "When you said this was new to you, what did you mean?" Danielle stretched the turquoise swim cap between her hands and pulled it over her hair.

"I've had girlfriends, serious relationships with women and the rest. But I've always been attracted to men too. I guess I'd blinded myself to it, just didn't see how a relationship with a guy could work long term."

"Until Rick?" asked Danielle tucking stray hairs under the cap.

"Pretty much."

"Are you in love?" Danielle unknotted her pareo. Stepping to the pool, she began to stretch in preparation for her swim.

Not wanting to raise his voice, Alex came closer. Taking care to keep his robe fastened, he sat on the pool's edge and dangled his feet in the water. He considered his feelings towards Rick. The guy could be totally irritating but also endearing. He enjoyed being with him, and physically their relationship was on another level to anything he'd had in the past with anyone. The feeling for him was strong, but was it love? "Maybe ..."

"Jesus Christ!" uttered Rick bursting through the double doors onto the patio. He was wearing nothing except a white towel slung around his hips, and sunglasses.

"Glad to see you're making yourself at home," laughed Danielle.

Dropping to the lounger, Rick cradled his head in his hands. "What the fuck did Monica put in those drinks?"

"I guess the sheer quantity of hooch is what makes Monica's charity auctions so fruitful. By the end of the night the whole crowd's smashed and would buy anything," said Danielle with a laugh.

"Coffee's still hot," Alex told Rick, sensing he needed it.

"Great." Rick sloshed some in the cup Alex had been using.

Danielle flicked her attention between Rick and Alex. "I sincerely hope there's not a photographer from *Confidential* magazine lurking in those bushes. This would make a great cover story, 'T.V.'s recently divorced golden girl frolics around pool with two naked men'."

Rick swilled back the coffee. "Put the frolicking on hold. It's a miracle I'm even walking."

"Rosemarie *was* sober when she bid on my painting, wasn't she?" mused Alex.

"She doesn't strike me as a drinker," said Danielle. "To lose both children in such awful ways is tragic. If she was going to hit the bottle she'd have done it bigtime by now."

"Talking of hitting things, I need to hit the road." Rick stifled a yawn. "Gina's expecting me to pick her up."

"Are you sure it's a good idea for her to stay at the beach house?" asked Alex.

"That night at The Daisy was a disaster. I can't let her leave town on that note. I need to finally put the past to rest and move on."

Danielle dipped her hands in the water and wetted her legs. "Excuse me, I have to get to work." Danielle stepped onto the board, took two steps and elegantly dived in.

Alex reached to Rick and waggled his fingers. "Hey, come here."

Getting to his feet, Rick's towel dipped tantalizingly low over his abdomen, displaying the light trail of sandy hair down the middle of his chest and flat stomach. Alex gazed up. The sun's glare behind Rick's head blessed him with the glow of a Greek god. "Sexy look you got going on with the towel and sunglasses," said Alex.

"I'll recreate it when we're back home. I may even remove the sunglasses if you're a good boy."

"Nice idea, but you're forgetting one thing."

Rick's shoulders sagged, and he sighed, "Gina."

"But we still have the guest room here ..." said Alex standing up.

"I'm sure Danielle won't mind a late checkout," said Rick with a lustful glint in his eye. He grabbed the belt of Alex's robe and dragged him inside the house while Danielle, with her head down, cut through the silky blue pool with a speedy front crawl.

♦ ♦ ♦

Cleaning his brushes and sorting them into sizes and grades was a useful distraction. Alex was pleased Rick had taken Gina out for lunch. It gave him time to air the house and his mind. A car door's slam and voices coming towards the house alerted him that Gina and Rick had arrived. Girding his loins, he opened the back door. "Need a hand with the bags?"

"No, we got it," said Rick ushering Gina inside

"You perhaps think it impossible for a woman, but as you see I am able to travel light." Gina held up a small shoulder bag and grinned.

"Come in. Welcome to ..." Alex was on the verge of saying 'Our home' then realized that may sound like he was rubbing their relationship in her face. What should he say? To *my* home. That could upset Rick, making him feel like he didn't have a place here. After a split-second's indecision, Alex said, "... the place."

Gina looked around warily, like a cat entering new territory.

"This is where you'll be staying" Rick led Gina to Dora's old room. He'd made it up with the white bed linens and bought new aqua throw pillows. It looked stylish, welcoming and with a definite sense of the beach.

The dark bags under Gina's eyes had disappeared and her skin was luminous. She must have been resting by the hotel's pool as her tan was up and her tangerine silk jumpsuit, worn unbuttoned with sleeves rolled up and a chunky gold bangle, set it off tremendously. "You have lovely home." Gina said to Alex.

"Thanks. It was my grandmother's."

Gina raised her hand and made a fist. "It has good heart. Rick, the drive here was very long. I make rest for hour or two."

"Go for it," said Rick.

About to close the door to her room, a thought struck Gina. "I need water."

"Fine, I'll get you some," said Rick.

"Her head's in a better place," said Alex quietly in the kitchen.

Rick filled a tumbler from the faucet. "We had a pleasant lunch at the Marina. She's getting it together." About to leave the kitchen, Rick changed his mind. He emptied the water into the sink, took a bottle of Perrier out of the refrigerator and refilled the tumbler. "Madam will only send it back if it's not chilled to her liking."

After Alex heard Gina's door open and close, Rick returned to the kitchen. "You two talked everything over then?" asked Alex.

"More or less." Rick began taking onions, garlic and tomatoes out of the refrigerator and lining them up by the chopping board. "Not sure how many times I have to say I'm sorry before it counts though." Rick took a knife out the block and passed it to Alex. "Here, chop the onions."

"Pretty clear she still loves you," said Alex taking the knife.

Rick fished out a cast iron pan. "And I still love her. Just not the way she wants. Not anymore, anyway."

"You did once?" Alex cut the top and bottom off an onion and peeled away the outer skin.

Rick poured oil into the pan, lit the gas and swirled the oil. "I thought I did. Perhaps I convinced myself I did. Whatever, it made momma happy for a while." With a couple of deft movements, he skinned the garlic, separated the cloves and pushed the biggest into the garlic press. He squeezed the press, letting the garlic drop into the pan. A moment later there was a gentle sizzle. Rick deftly lifted the pan off the range, reduced the heat and tilted the pan to cover the crushed garlic with the oil.

Alex sliced the onion in two. "Am I doing this right?" Preparing food with the master in the kitchen was moderately nerve racking.

Rick glanced over. "Once you've cut it in half, lay the onion's flat surface on the board. Then use the point of the knife like a hinge, rock the knife up and down to chop. Make the first cuts in the direction of the rings then go against them to dice it."

Following Rick's instructions, Alex did his best to achieve the desired result. Rick rested the pan on the low heat and tore the cellophane off a pack of ground beef. Having finished cutting the first onion, Alex checked with head office. "This okay?"

Rick glanced at the chopping board. "Excellent. But you could go less fine. Do two more."

Alex repeated the process with onion number two. "Did you ever worry you were leading Gina on just to please your mother?"

Rick grunted defensively. "It wasn't like that. And I was confused about myself too, remember. And life in Italy's different. I was different."

"Shit," muttered Alex.

"You haven't cut yourself, have you?"

Squinting, while pulling his head away from the chopping board, Alex tried to blink back tears from his stinging eyes. He lifted the back of his hand to wipe his cheek.

"Wait!" barked Rick. "Don't put your hand near your face."

Unable to see through streaming eyes, Alex heard a paper bag rustle.

"Open your mouth," commanded Rick.

With his eyes watering to the extent they made his ears ring, Alex obeyed orders. A moment later Rick popped something soft and spongy into his mouth.

"Give it a moment." Rick went back to the pan.

As his eyes cleared, Alex realized Rick had put a chunk of bread in his mouth.

"Hurry up with those onions," said Rick.

Alex went to take the bread out of his mouth.

"Leave it," commanded Rick. "The bread absorbs the gas from the onions."

It sounded kooky, but what the heck it worked, and Alex's tears stopped. Chewing the bread slightly, while leaving a bit sticking out of his mouth, Alex finished chopping the onions and passed the board to Rick.

"Great." Rick tipped the diced onion into the pan, added salt and tossed it in the oil.

Alex lingered by his shoulder. "Good tip about the onions," he mumbled while chewing the last of the bread.

"Thanks, nonna!" Rick blew a kiss to heaven.

The mellow scent of frying onion and garlic in the dying daylight lent the kitchen a homey feel. "Need me to do anything else?" asked Alex.

"Go relax. I'll finish up here."

Alex patted Rick's ass and kissed him lightly on the cheek. "Cool." Alex turned to go and saw Gina standing motionless in the half light of the hallway. She'd changed into a pair of denim shorts, a baggy cream sweater and removed all her make-up. Standing there, barefoot and bare faced, she resembled a nervous young girl. "Everything okay?" Alex asked her.

"Have you water that is non frizzante?" asked Gina holding out the tumbler of Perrier.

"Only from the faucet," said Alex.

"Va bene. Is okay," said Gina. Alex filled a fresh tumbler and exchanged it for the one she was holding. "Grazie." Gina watched Rick stirring the meat in the pan. "Smells good."

"He's quite something in the kitchen," said Alex.

Gina looked like she was going to respond but thought better of it and went back to her room. A moment later her door clicked shut.

"Hey, before you go there is something you can do." Rick said to Alex over the hiss of the onion and meat frying.

"What?"

"The onions are making me cry too. Rip off a chunk of that bread, I can't leave this."

"Open wide," said Alex. He popped the bread in Rick's mouth. Rick mumbled something. Taking it as a thank you, Alex grabbed his cigarettes, headed off to the deck and let Rick get on with dinner.

An hour and a half passed ... Gina was still asleep.

At a loose end while waiting to serve dinner, Rick ran upstairs and came down with something wrapped in black silk and tied with a cord. Undoing the cord, Rick unfurled the silk to reveal a deck of fancy looking cards.

"Tarot?" asked Alex.

Rick cocked an eyebrow. "If I could read the future do you think I'd have made the dumb choices I have? This isn't divination, it's a game. I'll teach you Briscola. We play it in the bars and cafes back home." Rick expertly shuffled the cards. Dealing them out, he ran through the cards and the rules. Unlike an ordinary deck, this one had only forty cards, their suits being coins, swords, cups and clubs. It was a trump game, so gave power to one suit and then used the highest value card in that suit to win the trick.

Although some strategy was involved, it appeared to Alex that chance and card counting ultimately determined the winner. And luck was on the newcomer's side when Alex got dealt the seven of coins. The seven of the trump suit takes the Briscola if a player's already won a hand, therefore Alex took the first game. The cards distracted them until Gina woke up an hour later. Soon as he heard movement in her room, Rick put the pasta on to boil, warmed the bread and shaved the parmesan. By the time Gina had fully roused herself and spent a further ten minutes in the bathroom, Alex had lit candles around the kitchen and Rick had plated up the food. They all gathered around the glowing table.

Gina must have built up an appetite for she hoovered down the spaghetti. "Deliziosissima!" she exclaimed, grabbing the last piece of bread to mop up the sauce. "This man, he know how to cook." After they'd eaten, Gina sat reflectively at the table as Rick gathered up the plates. The candle light danced in her limpid eyes. "I'm a very sorry I upset your friends last week. I was a little crazy. These days I get, how do I say … crazy nervous before I do job."

"What do you have to be nervous about? You're an incredibly successful model," said Rick with surprise. "Coffee?"

"Is late. If I have coffee, I no sleep," said Gina.

"How about a brandy?" asked Alex, getting up from the table.

"I stick with water."

"You?" Alex asked Rick.

"What the hell." Rick rinsed the plates and stacked them on the drainer.

Alex opened the bottle. "On the rocks?"

"Yeah," said Rick.

They decamped onto the deck with their drinks and Alex lit the candles in the glass bowls. Rick and Gina flopped side by side on the old gray couch. Instinctively Rick shuffled the cards. "You want to play?" he asked Alex.

"I'm off to bed as soon as I finish this." Swirling his brandy over the ice, Alex watched Rick deftly deal. This was obviously a game he and Gina played regularly, she needed no explanation of the rules. By the time they'd finished a couple of hands, they'd both stopped speaking English and switched to full on Italian. Having zero understanding of the language, Alex's only clue to the nature of their conversation was the timbre of their voices. Their tone was mellow, and they were laughing merrily. "Okay, kiddies, I'll leave you to it. Goodnight." Alex downed the last of his brandy.

Gina stood. "Thank you to invite me into your home, Alex. Buona notte."

Unsure what she was going to do next, Alex was taken aback when she reached out and hugged him. Gee, she was a tiny little waif without her heels and bravura. He felt like a giant enfolding her in his arms to return her hug. "Sleep well." Alex said to Gina. "And you," he ruffled Rick's hair, "don't stay up too late."

Up in bed, Alex listened to Rick and Gina giggling and chattering away in Italian, getting all het up about the turn of the cards or some such. He fell asleep wondering why life had to be so complicated, when at heart you didn't need much more than a roof over your head, a couple of bucks and a few good friends to be happy.

♦ ♦ ♦

"I never have a sleep like that before." The next morning Gina sat at the kitchen table watching Rick scramble some eggs. "When I wake, I feel reborn. I understand why you find this house so special. Is like being on another planet."

"The drive into town makes it feel that way at times." Rick scraped the eggs onto Gina's plate.

Alex poured a coffee and took it into his studio. He thought this would be a good day to head up the coast and scope out some new views, so he began to get his portable equipment ready. The phone rang and for once Rick actually answered it. A few minutes later, Rick tapped on the studio door and pushed it open. "That was Mike."

"Everything okay?"

"He needs me to come into the office."

"This minute?"

"Apparently."

"Why the urgency?"

"He wouldn't say, but it sounds important. I hope I'm not in trouble." Rick glanced over his shoulder at Gina still eating in the kitchen. Rick stepped inside the studio and closed the door softly. "I'd planned to spend the day with Gina," he said quietly.

"Can't you take her with you?"

"Things have been okay between us but I daren't risk a breakdown in détente in the vicinity of William Morris. Can you keep an eye on her while I'm out? Maybe take her up to the

Beachcomber for lunch or a walk on the beach? We can all go into Laguna for dinner tonight, then she leaves in the morning."

Spending the day with his lover's ex-fiancée hadn't been top of Alex's 'to do' list but felt it would be churlish not to help Rick out. Gina's moods had stabilized, and she'd been perfectly pleasant last night. "Sure."

Rick went and had a gentle conversation with Gina in the kitchen. No screaming and shouting ensued. After a quick spruce up in the bathroom, Rick fluffed his damp hair and snatched his car keys. "Sure you'll be okay?" Rick asked Gina on his way out. She'd taken it upon herself to clean up the kitchen and stood at the sink, her hands deep in soapy water.

Alex brought in his empty cup. "Here." Gina extended a sudsy hand to take it off him. "I be fine," she said to Rick. "You say I need rest. That is what I do today. Rest. Go!" Gina waved Rick away with one soapy hand and slushed Alex's dirty cup into the water with the other. A couple of minutes later, Rick's red Mercedes crunched past the kitchen window on its way up to the highway. There was a gurgle as the water drained from the sink and Gina picked up a towel to dry her hands. She said to Alex, "I should use the rubber gloves. Still I do not expect I am reduced to hand jobs just yet."

Alex's indecision over what facial expression he should use to greet her statement must have been evident.

Gina saw him looking confused. She waved her hand. "The photos when the only part of the model you see is the hand. You know? Hand jobs."

Alex smiled with relief. That made sense now.

"While my face and figure exist, I still get covers and fashion spreads. Or so I hope. Every morning without fail I must ring in to my agency to see if I have work. Always I fear a day with no bookings, but today I hope for none. I would like to spend more time with Rick." Gina draped the towel over the dish drainer, adjusting the ends to hang evenly.

"I'm going to work in my studio. You okay by yourself?" asked Alex.

"Do not worry about me," Gina said with a smile and went to her room.

Going into his space, Alex left the door slightly ajar to hear if anything untoward occurred. Sifting through his pieces leaning around the walls, he picked a couple that vibed with him. If he couldn't go out and work from life, working with memories would have to suffice again for today. A beach study he'd done with a storm heading inland possessed a bleak beauty. Where was that pencil sketch of Rick on the porch? Finding it, Alex placed it next to the painting. Juxtaposing the sketched figure with the beach painting was a nice fit. Working in the studio from references meant he could do something on a larger scale than en plein air. Beginning to sketch out the composition on a fresh canvas, he heard Gina come out of her room and make a phone call. He figured it was the daily one to her agent. She spoke quietly, and he didn't even notice her hang up and go back to her room. He was so lost in his head, it was hard to tell if it was minutes or hours later when the phone rang. "Gina, can you grab the phone!" he yelled from the studio. She mustn't have heard, as it kept on ringing. He came out and Gina's door was still closed. He picked up the phone and muttered, "Y'ello."

"Ricky!" exclaimed the voice on the other end.

"No, it's Alex."

"Oh hey, you sounded like him. Sid here. Is boy wonder around?"

"Er, no, he had to go into town to see his agent," explained Alex immediately regretting passing on uncalled-for information.

"His agent? What's that about?"

"Not sure," said Alex vaguely.

"Okay, he can tell me all about it on Sunday. We're barbecuing at the house. Nothing fancy, just friends and family. I want him there. You too."

"Oh, er, I'm not sure if ..."

"Actually, it's great you picked up. Left to his own devices he'd find some bullshit reason not to show. Ten four sixty-three Bellagio Road. One o'clock. Got it?

"Really, I don't know if ..."

"Tell him you're taking him to the zoo, or *Bob's Big Boy*. Tell him anything but get him here. I'm relying on you. We got an understanding you and me, don't we?"

Alex knew cashing that thousand-buck check of Sid's had been a dumb thing to do. "I guess, I'll see what I can do."

"Great. See you Sunday. Ciao."

Alex figured that was one call he should have let ring out. While chewing over how to break Sid's invitation, or rather ultimatum, to Rick, an ominous mood descended on the house. Maybe it was the bleak beach scene, maybe it was Sid's call, or maybe it was Gina's silent presence hanging over Alex's head like a dark cloud. In the studio, he was back to the old days of being blocked. His eyes couldn't engage his mind to control his hands and apply paint in a coherent manner. He wondered what Gina was doing. Sleeping this long in the daytime wasn't natural. Going to her room, he tapped on the door. "Gina?"

No answer.

Could she have gone out without him hearing? Maybe that was why she was so quiet? Alex jumped off the deck to look in through her window, but the drapes were closed. Coming back inside, he knocked harder on her door. "Gina, you in there?" Still nothing. He figured if she'd gone out there was no harm in going into her room. And if there was something up with her at least he'd know. Slowly, he opened the door. Gina lay sprawled on the bed, her head twisted at an awkward angle away from the door. Standing very still, he listened.

Phew.

She was breathing. Alex thought it was an odd way to fall asleep, looking more like she'd passed out. Cursing himself for panicking, he was about to leave when a cause for concern caught his eye. On the nightstand, beside her tumbler of water, he saw red torpedo pills spilling from a jar lying on its side. He then noticed Gina's overnight bag down by the closet, its zip partially open. More pill bottles were visible inside. Kneeling, Alex tentatively unzipped the bag a little more. Gina may have been travelling light in regard to clothes and make-up, but she hadn't stinted on packing pills. Taking out a bottle, Alex examined the contents. Green torpedoes. He rifled through the other jars and bottles. All the colors of the pharmaceutical rainbow were here. White tablets with crosses, yellow torpedoes, blue capsules. Silently, he put the bottles back, zipped the bag and went to leave. Alex put his hand on the doorknob.

Shit.

Gina's head had turned towards him and her eyes were open. "I knocked. When you didn't answer I got worried," stammered Alex, "just wanted to check you were okay." Gina stared blankly, like she wasn't back in her body. After making a hasty exit, Alex took a smoke out on the deck. The pills certainly explained Gina's erratic behavior. She was either on downers or hyped on bennies. Maybe last night was the only time he'd seen her sober. The sound of high heels on the boards inside jolted him out of his reverie. Gina stomped onto the verandah, fully made up, dressed in her tangerine silk jumpsuit and fixing a couple of large gold hoops to her ears. "Sorry, I didn't mean to ..."

"Look in my bag? Open my bottles? Find your ammunition?" Gina's eyes blazed.

"I don't know much about drugs, but I suspect you have a problem," said Alex calmly.

Gina faced him defiantly. "We all need ways to get through the day." She pointed at his cigarette. "What are those and your brandies? Are they not drugs too?"

"A couple of smokes and a drink is different to ..."

"Is all different to you. You have nice house, big talent, handsome face, and you get Rick too. You win."

"It's not a game."

"Is all a game. Like the stupid cards. When I met Rick the trump was tits and cunt and I win the trick. The trump is now cock and balls so you take the Briscola. Congratulations, conquistatore."

"Rick didn't want to hurt you. He cares about you ..."

"Rick care for nothing but himself! I have many fears. I fear I lose my looks. I fear I put on weight. I fear I forget my session. I fear I am alone. I take pill and the fear go away."

"You need help, Gina."

Gina tossed back her hair and pushed the sleeves of her silk suit further up her arms. "Only one thing I need. But is no more."

"You mean Rick?"

"He will use you as he used me. You wait to see what Signor Rick Stradman will do for you. He may take you to the top but then he leave you there, alone. One day he turns his spotlight away from you and you are left in dark. Something will happen, something he cannot cope with, and he will run out on you as he ran out on me. Rick knows only one thing about love, running out on it."

"I don't think so."

Gina tipped her head and snorted. "We shall see what time has to say."

Above the sound of the blood pumping in Alex's ears, he heard a car horn from the back of the house.

"Is for me," said Gina matter-of-factly. "I call in to agency. They book me for sudden job in New York. They arrange cab." Gina ducked into her room. A moment later she came out with her bag. "Is why I took pill. I get no sleep now for twenty-four hours. I go New York. I go studio." Gina shrugged. "Is my life."

Alex followed Gina out of the back door and she slung her shoulder bag into the green taxi's rear seat. "Take care, Gina," said Alex reaching out to her. Gina recoiled, put on her dark glasses and got into the car. The green taxi reversed to the

Beachcomber, turned and then climbed to the highway. Alex wondered which piece of news he should give Rick first? That Gina caught him going through her pills, making it clear she was an addict caught up in a spiral of self-destruction. Or that Sid had forced him into delivering Rick to the family barbecue on Sunday. Jeez, Alex thought it might be worth checking to see if Gina had left any of her red pills behind. Feeling as lousy as he did right now he'd be tempted to try one. He relied, however, on a few more smokes and a couple of beers to settle his nerves.

"Hi, hi!" called Rick merrily on arrival home a couple of hours later.

Looking up from not really looking at the canvas on the easel, Alex saw only one way to break one piece of news to Rick ... quickly. "Gina's left," he called from the studio.

"What you talking about?" Rick frowned as he tossed his car keys on to the counter and began unbuttoning his shirt.

Walking into the kitchen, Alex said, "She has to ring in to her agency every morning to see if she has work. A job came up suddenly in New York, and they got a cab to pick her up."

"That's a shame, we didn't get to say goodbye. At least we had a good time last night. I think it'll be okay between us from now on."

Alex found it impossible to hide his dubious expression.

"Did something happen between you two?" asked Rick in concern.

"Kind of." Alex shook his head and stroked his stubble. "She'd been in her room so long I got spooked. Anyway, I knocked on her door to see if she was okay, but there was no answer. I tried to look in from outside, but she'd closed the drapes. That's why I went into her room. I found her crashed out on the bed, completely passed out."

Rick stretched his neck. "God, I'm so tense from the drive. Can you rub my shoulders?"

"Okay." After checking his hands were free of paint, he placed them on Rick's neck and began to knead his trapezius.

"She did say she needed to rest," said Rick rationally.

"She'd passed out because she'd taken pills." As Alex spoke he felt Rick's neck tense. Taking a firmer grip, he swirled his thumbs into the discernable knots in Rick's muscles. "Big red ones from a bottle on the nightstand. She had more pills in her bag. Different colored ones. Lots of different colors."

"Ah," gasped Rick as Alex's fingers probed his neck. "That hit the spot."

"Take that off so I can work properly on your shoulders," said Alex roughly stripping off Rick's shirt. "Come here." Alex pushed his butt deep into the couch, spread his legs and pulled Rick to him. Rick nestled into the crook of Alex's legs with his back to him. "Let that tension go." Alex worked his fingers into Rick's knotted muscles. After about five minutes of kneading he felt Rick's shoulders drop. Alex massaged his thumbs into the valleys either side of Rick's vertebrae. "I'm sorry to tell you this, but Gina has a drug problem."

Rick sighed. "I'll call Maurice at her agency. I'll suggest he gets her to see someone."

"Will she?"

"I hope so." Rick hung his head.

"Why'd Mike want to see you so urgently?" asked Alex. The warm vanilla scent of Rick's skin and the vestige of almond shampoo on his hair drifted over Alex's face. Rick's shoulders may be softening, but Alex's dick was growing hard.

"It seems the powers that be liked the Bradley character and his set-up in the *McMillan* episode. They're spinning his character off into a *Mystery Movie* slot and calling the show *Legal Eagles*. They want me to be in it."

"That's great news!"

"I guess. The lead characters are law students who turn detective. Professor Miller will be replaced by a new positive mentor. They're envisaging this character as a brilliant female lawyer who's turned to teaching. She'll have the bright ideas while us kids do the running around. They mentioned Katherine

Hepburn or Bette Davis, but I can't see Hepburn doing episodic T.V."

"They must have really liked your work on the show," Alex said as he clenched his knuckles and rolled his fists along Rick's spine. "Sounds like a great meeting."

"That bit was. They're announcing the pilot in the trades tomorrow. But then Mike started chatting about contracts and stuff. He mentioned morality clauses. Like I can't do anything in my personal life to bring the show into disrepute, dunno what brought that up. That feels good." Rick rolled his neck around then reached behind and took Alex's wrists. "My chest's tense too. Can you work on that?" Lifting Alex's hands over his shoulders, Rick placed them on his pecs.

"I'll try." Alex traced around Rick's nipples, then lightly pinched them. He gently nibbled and sucked the back of Rick's neck. "Hey, you got anything planned this Sunday?"

"Mmm," Rick moaned gently as Alex's hands slid down, undid his belt buckle and the top button of his jeans. "Don't think so. Why?"

With Rick's waistband loosened, Alex swirled his fingers around his belly button, then paused a moment before plunging his palm deep into Rick's pants. "I thought we could do something."

"Like what?"

"Go to the zoo, perhaps." Grasping what he was looking for in Rick's pants, Alex bit deeper into Rick's neck. He lifted Rick's hips, then pushed his pants and shorts down to his knees. Alex ran his hands down the outside of Rick's thighs and then slid them inside and up to his balls. As he began to roll Rick's balls around in his hand, making him moan gently, Alex wondered when to break the news about Sid's lunch. Come to think of it, maybe telling Rick about it after they'd done what they were about to do would be better timing.

Alex's blood was up, and he didn't want to spoil the moment.

A SUNDAY AFTERNOON IN THE HOUSE AT BEL AIR

If looks could kill, he should be lying on a slab in the L.A. Morgue by now. However, Alex manfully continued to ignore the shade being thrown his way from the passenger seat as he swung off Sunset onto Copa De Oro Road. He'd wrestled to find exactly the right moment to tell Rick he'd been ordered to deliver him up to Sid's Sunday barbecue. Although tempting to invent some fake outing, it'd only end in an ugly scene upon arrival. Once the ripples of Gina's premature departure had dissipated, Alex had hemmed and hawed for a couple of days but still couldn't find the right moment to break the news to Rick. Sunday was getting closer, and so early Friday evening, while Rick was making an appetizingly smelling lasagna, he casually said, "It slipped my mind, Sid phoned."

Spooning in another ladle of white sauce, or béchamel as Rick accurately described it, he responded cryptically, "He's heard about it then."

"About what?"

"The *Legal Eagles* show."

"He didn't mention that. He just wants us to come to lunch on Sunday. He's having a friends and family barbecue."

"When did he call?" asked Rick.

Alex scratched his head nonchalantly. "Dunno. Yesterday? Maybe the day before?"

"And you only remembered to tell me about this now?"

"I don't know. I guess I forgot. I ..." It was no good, the witness broke down under questioning. "I took his call when all that drama was going down with Gina and the pills. I knew that business had upset you and I didn't want to upset you more. Sid literally ordered me to take you there. He was very insistent."

"Dad's always very insistent. I find ignoring him helps tremendously."

"I took his call. He'll hold me personally responsible if you don't show up."

"And that'd be my problem, why?"

"You can't force me to talk to Sid when you don't feel like it and then expect me to treat him like a stranger when it suits you. Now he's asked me to do something for him and I'm stuck in the middle. Can't you meet him halfway?"

Rick turned on the oven and ignited the gas. "Sounds like Sunday at Sid's is a fait accompli then."

"'I guess it is."

With unnecessary vigor, Rick noisily ripped off a length of foil to cover the lasagna dish. "I'll need to go shopping tomorrow."

"He didn't say to bring anything."

"I'll be expected to bring gifts for the no-neck monsters. Maybe I can buy them some necks? And maybe I'll get something for Letitia. Wonder if Tiffany's do diamond encrusted muzzles?"

"She has a dog?"

"For her."

That was so spectacularly nasty Alex found it impossible not to laugh. "She can't be all that bad."

"Let's see how you feel about that on Sunday evening."

And that's how they came to be pulling off Copa De Oro onto Bellagio Road. The clipped box hedges grew high around these parts, masking the lavish mansions of Lower Bel Air. The gray gates to Sid's house were set into the greenery. Once the gates had automatically opened, Alex rolled along the driveway towards a two-story mock Georgian. It was just a quarter off one o'clock. Cars were already parked in front of the house; a rust Bentley, a maroon Rolls Royce, a couple of dark Bimmers and a white V.W. Beetle.

"Here goes. Don't say I didn't warn you," Rick said grimly pulling the shopper filled with gifts out of the trunk. "Take the booze," said Rick passing Alex the tote containing two bottles of Pol Roger and a six pack of beer. Walking beneath a porch supported by four Doric columns, Rick pressed the bell beside the six-paneled navy gloss front door. After the chimes rung out, they heard pattering footsteps and children's voices.

"Wait a minute, wait a minute," said a woman's voice inside the house. The heavy door swung open. A young woman in white lace pants and a midriff baring top greeted them. Her gold chain earrings jangled against her sleeked back bleach blonde hair as she flung open her arms. "Ricky, honey. It's so good to see you," she said with a genuinely warm smile.

"Ricky, Ricky!" Two little kids were jumping up and down behind her.

"Let Ricky get inside before you jump all over him. You must be Alex. Lovely to meet you. I'm Letitia, Sid's wife. Pipe down you two, please!" Letitia shooed the children back as she ushered in Rick and Alex.

"Hi. Where should I put these?" Alex lifted the tote with the drinks.

"We're out by the pool. We got ice buckets there." Letitia led them through the black and white checkerboard lobby with sweeping staircase.

"Hey, you two," said Rick coolly to the kids fussing around his legs. "you've grown since I last saw you. How old are you now anyway? Twenty?"

"Noooo! We're three," said the boy.

"And a half," added the girl. She looked up at Alex and said proudly, "I'm three and half *and* fifteen minutes."

"Twins," explained Letitia leading Alex onto the patio. "Tiffany was born first and never lets Tyler forget it. She calls herself his older sister. Come, meet everyone."

Across the lawn, people were mingling with drinks around the rectangular pool surrounded by tables shaded with yellow umbrellas. Vases of golden marigolds and yellow chrysanthemums punctuated the terraces. Verdant trees swayed above the tennis court at the rear. Tiffany had grabbed Rick's hand and was dragging him towards Sid, who was at the barbecue wearing khaki shorts, a red neckerchief and an apron.

"Brother Ricky's here, big brother Ricky!" yelled Tiffany.

Tyler trailed along, tugging at the Rick's bag. "What's in the bag, Ricky? Is it something for us?"

"Give me a minute, it's a surprise," said Rick.

An expression of intense happiness lit up Sid's face when he laid eyes on Rick. Putting down the barbecue tongs, Sid held out his arms and announced to the crowd, "The prodigal returns!" Rick rolled his eyes and gave his infuriated fourteen-year-old expression as Sid wrapped him in a bear hug then patted him on the back. "Blake, give the kid a drink!" Sid barked at a gray-haired guy in a lime polo shirt and black and white dogtooth flares who just happened to be standing beside the chillers. Sid beckoned to Alex, still lingering with Letitia on the patio outside the house. "What you doing there standing like a bump on a log? What you want from me, an engraved invitation?" Sid turned to his guests, "Is that what he wants? An engraved invitation? Get your ass over here and join the party!" Sid shouted to Alex then went back to his barbecuing.

Letitia took Alex by the arm and walked him to the pool. She leaned close and whispered, "That's Sid for you. Love him or leave him." Letitia took the bottles off Alex and put them in the chillers. A champagne cork popped. Blake handed Rick a generous glass of fizz.

"Presents! We want our presents from Ricky!" shouted Tyler.

"Hey, everybody!" Letitia called out. "This is Alex. He's Rick's roommate."

The guests around the pool acknowledged Alex with polite smiles. Alex knew there wasn't a hope in hell he'd remember any names as Letitia introduced them all. The guests were uniformly late to middle aged, the women dressed in primary colored two-pieces worn with gold jewelry and mules, the men in vivid short sleeved shirts with garishly patterned leisure pants.

"Glad you guys made it," said Sid. He gave Alex a knowing smile as he passed by the barbecue, then asked gruffly, "What you drinking?"

"A cold beer would hit the spot," said Alex.

"Blake! Get this man a beer!" Sid bellowed at the guy in the lime shirt. Judging by Blake's strained expression as he opened a beer and passed it to Alex, his duty as barman was not of his choosing.

"Presents!" The kids kept pestering Rick.

Rick swiftly drained half a glass of champagne. "Okay, okay." With ceremony, he took out two large gift-wrapped boxes. "This one's for Tyler. And this one's for Tiffany."

"What is it? What is it?" The kids cried, taking their presents away to open them.

"It's some plutonium and a Build-It-Yourself nuclear reactor kit," said Rick sweetly.

A nearby female guest tittered nervously, unsure of how to take Rick.

"The kid's a joker," laughed Sid shooting Rick a 'be careful' look before turning back to his chicken breasts and thighs.

Everyone watched the kids rip off the wrappings. Tiffany and Tyler appeared a trifle bemused when they found two wooden boxes with hinged lids inside. Tyler worked out how to open the gold latch and lifted the top. The guests gathered around. As the kids investigated the contents farther, they discovered the boxes contained paints and colored pencils. Alex mooched over to where everyone had grouped around the kids. Rick had gone into Laguna by himself to buy the gifts, so they were as much of a surprise to him as to Tyler and Tiffany. The art boxes were beautifully crafted with hinged lids that lifted and pivoted to become easels.

Rick noticed Alex looking approvingly as he swigged his beer, then said to the kids, "You're very lucky, you see uncle Alex is an artist and he's going to teach you how to paint a picture." Rick retrieved his champagne and drained the glass.

"What now?" asked Tyler in amazement.

"Yes, right this very minute! Let's take these to the pool house and get this art lesson under way." Rick closed up the paint boxes. He picked one up and roughly shoved the other at Alex.

"Cute gifts," smiled Letitia. "What do you say to Ricky?"

"Thank you, Ricky," murmured the kids.

A ripple of interest ran around the pool as the guests watched Rick, Alex and the kids trail off to the pool house. "I'm expecting masterpieces from both of you by the time we eat," Rick said to the kids. The kids skittered across the pool house's terrace and Tyler flung open the double doors.

"Thanks for this," muttered Alex to Rick.

"You're welcome," said Rick sweetly, then out of the corner of his mouth hissed, "You got me into this, only fair I should spread the suffering." Once inside the pool house, Rick opened up the art boxes, fixed the easel tops in place and put the sketch pads on them.

Letitia appeared in the doorway. "Maybe you shouldn't use paints?" she said, nervously glancing at the pure white furnishings.

"Don't worry," Alex called to her. "We'll do some drawing."

Letitia relaxed.

"What shall we draw?" asked Tiffany.

"Come and sit here, either side of me," said Alex. He selected the right pencils and made sure the kids were settled. "First, I'll show you how to draw a face."

"Have fun!" Rick called merrily and departed with Letitia to rejoin the party.

Actually, Alex thought being holed up with the kids in the pool house was infinitely preferable to being stuck outside with Sid's contemporaries. Tiffany and Tyler watched attentively as he demonstrated how to draw a face, starting with a ball for the back of the head, then adding an oval with a mid-line for the face. He got them to really look at each other, taking note of where their eyes were in relation to their nose and mouth and to notice how far back on their heads their ears were. After a couple of failed attempts, the kids got the hang of it and seriously got on with their portraits of each other. Uncle Alex took this respite to kick back with his beer. Watching them work, their little pink tongues sticking out the sides of their mouths in concentration, he felt it unjust of Rick to call them no-neck monsters. They did have necks, admittedly not a lot of them, and were nowhere near monsters.

Three quarters of an hour later, Sid yelled, "Tyler, Tiffany, food!" The kids were engrossed in drawing and didn't immediately respond.

"May I see?" asked Alex. The kids dutifully presented their work and cuddled either side of him on the wicker couch. "Hey, well done! These are pretty good." While naive in style, natural for their age, they'd got the features in the correct places. Tiffany's drawing actually looked like Tyler. Tyler seemed to think Tiffany had a great deal more hair than she did, and one eye lower than the other, but otherwise not bad. "You guys got talent. Now, go get some food!" The kids scurried off and Alex tidied up.

"Have we a pair of budding Da Vincis in our midst?" Letitia asked when Alex rejoined the party.

Alex took a seat next to her by the pool and passed her the kids' pictures. "More along the lines of Modigliani."

"I'll have to take your word on that." Letitia looked at the pictures. "Oh my, they've done well. You're a good teacher, Alex. Go and relax. You've done enough babysitting for one day."

Being served burgers by Sid while surrounded by Hollywood producers, directors and their wives was a bizarre experience. Alex grabbed a fresh beer from the ice bucket. Blake had obviously had a basinful of Sid bellowing at him and excused himself from bar duty, so everyone was serving themselves. Alex took his food over to a table where Rick was sitting with a well-tanned, but jaded looking, couple.

"Mind if I join you?" asked Alex pulling out a chair. As he sat down, the glasses on the table rattled against each other with a tinkle.

"Be my guest," said Rick with a slight slur. He'd obviously been knocking back the champagnes. "Betty was just telling us a fascinating story about how she got mugged in Miracle Mile."

Alex thought joining Rick in this mood maybe wasn't the greatest idea. However, it would look rude to run off now, so he sat down.

"As I was saying," drawled Betty, "there I was, walking from the museum to my optometrist appointment, minding my own business, when this, well out the corner of my eye he looked like a black vagrant, pushes me over. I fell to the sidewalk, very painfully I might add, and then this lowlife yanks my purse out of my hand and runs off with it. In broad daylight with people around, can you believe it?" Betty, who appeared to be in her late fifties with suspiciously jet-black hair, picked a tiny piece of meat off her burger and placed it on her tongue like a pill.

The man sitting next to Betty, who must have been her husband as he appeared to share the same hair dye, patted her hand sympathetically. "Imagine if that was an old lady the guy had attacked? The bastard could have broken her hip. Nobody's safe in this town. We got so many intruder alarms on the house it takes an extra twenty minutes to lock up of a morning."

Betty had swallowed the morsel of burger. Vigorously nodding her agreement, she said, “Leo used to keep our gun in the safe, but after this he keeps it in the nightstand.”

“I tell you, in ten years' time we’ll all be carrying guns. It’ll be the only way for upright citizens to protect themselves from the scum. It’s the Wild West all over again,” muttered Leo darkly.

“I must admit, keeping a gun in the nightstand’s convenient,” said Rick conversationally. “I mean, if you get the urge to blow your brains out in the middle of the night you don’t even have to get out of bed.”

Betty was taken by surprise by Rick’s comment, she laughed awkwardly unable to tell if he was joking. Leo pretended he hadn’t heard what Rick said. Having successfully ratcheted up the level of social awkwardness, Rick sat back and carried on drinking.

“What do you do in the industry?” Alex asked Leo. Moving the topic away from gun crime didn’t lead to scintillating conversation. Leo turned out to be Sid’s accountant. Neither he nor Betty were balls of fire, but thankfully Leo’s stories were dull and didn’t provoke further acidic comments from Rick.

During the afternoon, several guests left and a few more arrived. With no-one on bar duty Rick’s drip feed of champagne dried up, so he wasn’t so spiky. Letitia gently, but firmly, encouraged Rick to spend some time with the twins, so he took them into the den to watch cartoons. With Rick out of the way, Alex sloped off to a corner with a couple of other smokers. He found Sid’s acquaintances perfectly pleasant, showing no particular interest in him or his work. Their comfort topics were the movie industry, the dire state of the U.S. economy and lamenting how the country wasn’t the one they remembered. It was clear he was in Republican territory.

The party began breaking up around five and the housekeeper came out to help Letitia clear away. Sid had hung up his apron, downed several neat whiskies and was lolling by the pool with Blake when Rick came out of the house. "Thanks, dad. It's been a blast."

"You off already?" asked Sid with disappointment.

"I'm beat," said Rick adding a yawn for emphasis.

Sid got unsteadily to his feet and dug his hands into his pockets. "I read in the trades about your *Mystery Movie* spin off."

Rick sighed towards Alex with an 'I told you so' expression.

"Why'd you look like that? What's with all the sighing and the looks?" asked Sid. "I'm one hundred and ten per cent in your corner. This is terrific news! You did good, kid. All on your own."

Rick grinned warily. "I took on board everything you and momma taught me about acting. Anyway, I did my best and it must have worked out this time."

"I'm proud of you, son! Both of us are, me and Letitia. I prayed you'd turn the corner and finally it looks like you have."

"When did you start praying, dad?"

"I've taken it up on a regular basis. Usually when the box office figures are about to be released." Sid laughed, looking to anyone nearby for a response to his joke. "Let me walk you to the car."

After saying goodbye to people they hadn't really said hello to, Rick and Alex followed Sid inside. Rick was about to go into the den and say goodbye to the kids, still watching loud cartoons, when Sid draped a fatherly arm around him. "You got a lead in a big new show. Your name's gonna get known. People are gonna get interested in you."

"You think so, dad? They're talking about a really, really big name for the show. And I mean a real star like Davis or Stanwyck or Crawford. I don't think anyone's going to be that bothered about me."

Sid shook his head. "The networks all want younger viewers. Mark my words, they'll do features on you and interviews to promote the show. You're going to have to be careful."

"About what?" asked Rick askance.

Sid shifted his attention between Rick and Alex. "Things."

Rick wriggled free from Sid's arm. "This is why you wanted me here today, isn't it? The pep talk."

"Don't be that way. I wanted you here to spend time with your family, which you haven't done much of lately. We love you, Ricky. All I'm saying is, I know what this business can be like. When things are on your side, it's great. But when they're not, it's not so good. Especially if you're not mentally strong."

Rick clenched his fists. "Don't do this now."

"Keep your voice down," urged Sid nodding at the den. "I'm not criticizing you. I'm telling you to be careful. Contracts have clauses. Morality clauses."

"I'm not doing anything immoral," said Rick vehemently.

"Not everybody's as modern as you'd like to think." Sid gently stoked Rick's arm.

Hearing raised voices, Letitia poked her nose from behind the kitchen door.

"Tell me dad, do you have a morality clause in your contract? Or are you above all that when you're giving out your phone number to waitresses? Some people have a different word for what you call 'talent spotting'."

Letitia shot out from the kitchen. "Tiffany, Tyler, time to go upstairs. Say goodbye to Ricky!" Shushing Tiffany and Tyler's protestations, Letitia switched off the T.V. and hustled the kids past Sid and Rick and upstairs at the speed of light.

"Don't do this here. Not now, please," hissed Sid looking around.

"Why not here, dad? Because you don't want me to embarrass you? Well, how about you embarrassing me and Alex? How do you think this makes us feel?" The sun, booze and anger flushed Rick's face, the vein on his neck throbbing visibly.

"Cool it, Rick. Let's just go," said Alex urging him towards the front door.

"I've never done anything untoward to any of the girls I've helped get a foot on the ladder," said Sid.

"Get both feet on your casting couch, more like! You're a dirty old man, dad!"

"That's a low blow, Ricky. I've made mistakes, I admit. But I always try to do right and make good."

"Really? I know all about you and Julie, that blonde waitress from the Beachcomber," blurted Rick angrily.

"Why the hell are you bringing her into this?" Sid gasped, dumbfounded.

"Alex saw you with her on the Fox lot. He told me she threw her arms around you and kissed you," said Rick with a glint of triumph in his eye.

Having installed the kids safely upstairs, Letitia came back down.

Rick carried on, unable to stop his vitriol. "Danielle told us there's a new character coming into *Eddie's Girls*. She's being played by a newcomer who was a waitress last month. Some coincidence, huh? It's Julie, isn't it? You said she should be in T.V. Did you pull some strings for her to get a part? Did you, dad? And what did she have to do in return for you, huh?"

Letitia paused at the bottom of the stairs.

Alex stared at Sid, unable to say anything to make this hideous scene any better.

Sid took a deep breath and looked at Letitia. Letitia nodded knowingly and said calmly, "There's nothing to hide, Ricky. Sid's told me about her."

"He has?" Rick stepped back, deflated.

"You're right," said Sid resignedly. "I did give that girl my number at the beach. And yeah, she called me, and yeah, I got her a job. But not on *Eddie's Girls*. How the hell could I get her a part on a show I got nothing to do with? I helped her get a waitress job in the commissary. Her mom lives in Van Nuys and she's real sick. Julie needed to find a job closer to town cause the drive back and forth to your godforsaken beach was killing her. Julie came to my office that day to thank me for helping her. Julie's a nice girl with a good heart. You could learn a thing or two from her about gratitude." Sid grimly turned away from Rick, stomped down the corridor, went into his study and slammed the door.

Letitia shook her head at Rick. "Nice going. Just for once I wish it didn't have to end up like this. Goodbye Alex, it was nice meeting you. If you'll excuse me, I still have guests to attend to." Letitia looked at Rick with disappointment, went to the kitchen and shut the door.

"It always ends like this because dad always pulls some shit like this!" Rick shouted at the closed door. "Let's get the hell out of here," said Rick to Alex.

"I need to apologize to Sid. Thanks for dropping me into this."

"Whatever," snarled Rick and he left the house.

Alex tapped on the study door, "Sid, you got a second?" Pushing the door open, he found Sid leaning on the desk.

"What now?" barked Sid keeping his back to Alex.

"I'd no idea Rick was going to go off like that. I said I saw Julie with you, but I told him not to jump to conclusions. I wish I'd never mentioned it. You're right, she is a big-hearted girl. I'm glad you were able to help her."

Sid turned, his usually robust face was haggard. "I don't know what it is with Ricky. There's something between that kid and me. Whatever I do is wrong. I guess we're oil and water and we ain't never gonna mix."

"I'm truly sorry today ended like this." Alex backed out the room.

"Don't you be sorry. What you got to be sorry for?" Sid took himself around his desk and opened the drawer. "Here. Buy yourself a decent car. I can't have you driving the kid around in that pile of junk." He wrote a check, ripped it out and handed it to Alex.

"Seriously, I cannot take this," said Alex when he saw the check was made to cash for two thousand dollars.

Sid slammed his fist on the desk. "Take it while I still got it. The kid won't listen to me. I'll have to rely on you to keep an eye on him if things go wrong. I've seen those dark moods that come over him. Just don't let him do anything stupid. I'd much rather have a gay son than a dead son." Sid crumpled in the chair behind his desk and put his hand to his head.

Alex was letting himself out of the front door when Letitia's mules came clattering across the tiled floor. "We wanted to give this to Ricky before he made that little scene. Would you give it to him?" Letitia passed Alex a gift wrapped in *Happy Birthday* paper and tied with a huge red bow. "His birthday's next Saturday."

"I'll be sure he gets it," said Alex.

"And Alex, you're always welcome in this house. No matter what." Letitia smiled and watched him go to the car and get in.

Most of the other vehicles had left, so Alex found pulling out of the drive was easy. As he drove past the front door, Letitia was still standing there. She gave a small wave, but Rick turned his face away. After Sid's electric gates had opened and closed, Alex had to take deep breaths to control the roiling anger in the pit of his stomach. They drove in stony silence. When he finally could speak, all Alex could blurt out was, "That was pretty fucking embarrassing!"

"Don't go there," said Rick curtly.

"How'd you think that made me feel? I've jumped through hoops for you and you can't control your filthy temper for one afternoon. I could've been doing a million things other than having you put me through that excruciating experience."

"A million other things? Like what? Sitting on the deck and smoking?"

Alex took his hands off the wheel and slammed them back on it. "Your dad's right, when you get nasty you hit low and mean."

"When you've been raised in a snake pit you learn to bite first."

"You were unfair to him."

"Me? Unfair to *him*? How about him being unfair to me? When he said he was proud of me and I'd done good on my own account, for one second, for one split second, I felt good about myself. Like I was actually something in his eyes. Then he starts in with all the morality shit."

"He wants to protect you ..."

"Don't believe that for one second! Dad's only worried about how anything I do may affect him and his reputation. This job's the first thing I got on my own account because of my talent. *My* talent! Not because of people making nice to me because of who my parents are, or because they want something from them, or dad asking someone for a favor. I actually felt good about myself. Then he has to start on with this talk like we're criminals or something. I'm acting in a show for fuck's sake, not being made Pope. What business is it of anyone's what I do in my private life? And why does dad have to harp on about it like he agrees with them?"

"You're thinking the worst of him. Sid cares about you. Letitia does too."

"Yeah, and before Letitia there was Helen and before Helen there was Deanna. And all their respective spawn."

"There are more kids?"

"Yeah, I got five more half whatevers. And that's only the ones we know about. That's why it bugs me his morality never comes into question. Dad only needs to brush past a secretary or make-up girl and she gets pregnant. Then he does the so-called 'right' thing and marries them. Like that makes everything all right. The newest wife always thinks she's the one where it'll be different and won't end up in divorce. But then a new blonde comes along and bang goes the happy family. The ex-wife gets shunted off with her kids and I get thrown out on my ear. Have you any idea what it's like to be shuffled from one side of the Atlantic to the other, never feeling there's anyone totally there for you? One day I'm in a house with a family and kids and the next they're gone and I'm back in midair to an empty villa filled with momma. I'm not getting suckered in again. I don't want to argue with you Alex, never with you. You've been good to me. The only one in the whole stinking mess of my life who has." Rick's voice trembled.

Taking his eyes off the road for a moment, Alex glanced across. It was clear Rick was struggling to hold it together. "I can see your point of view, but you're wrong about Sid. I wish you hadn't said I'd seen Julie kissing him. It made me feel like a spy. And although you're mad at Sid, I don't have a beef with him."

"How come you're Sid's number one fan all of a sudden?"

"I just don't see the point in making a war where there isn't one."

"This is priceless, so you're on his side now?" Rick raised his voice.

"This isn't about sides, Rick! Let it go, I can't ... shit, something's wrong."

"You're ..."

Alex struggled to control the steering wheel, it was moving of its own volition.

The car shook violently. Rick steadied himself on the grab handle above the door.

Alex fought to maintain control and stay in lane.

An orange car streaked past them, it was veering wildly, almost clipping their wing as it swerved along the highway.

"Is something up with the car?" Rick asked nervously.

The traffic slowed. Drivers started indicating and pulling over. The elevated section of the highway they were on shook violently. "It's an earthquake," said Alex.

"Shouldn't we stop?"

"I will, soon as I get off this section. I don't want us up here if it collapses." Keeping watch for errant drivers, Alex motored on for another two hundred yards with the car swaying from side to side. As soon as the highway descended to solid ground, Alex pulled onto the shoulder. Traffic had come to a halt as far as the eye could see. After killing their motors, shocked drivers started getting out of their vehicles. An eerie stillness descended, not even a bird was singing. "That was some jolt," said Alex as they got out and stood either side of the car.

"Is it over?" asked Rick, a tremor in his voice.

As if to answer his question, a deep undulating ripple juddered under their feet, shaking the highway and the parked cars. Alex and Rick steadied themselves either side of the hood. Car alarms went off. A woman screamed. Everyone stood frozen, wondering if something bigger was on its way. But after a minute, when no other tremors occurred, people returned to life and cautiously began getting back into their vehicles. Distant sirens cut through the air.

"It's passed," said Alex. Getting back into the car, they heard one siren grew louder. As Alex started the motor, a police car flashed by at high speed. One by one vehicles got back on the road to resume their journey. Alex had only just built up speed when a knot of traffic formed ahead, forcing him to slow. An officer was waving a baton to direct traffic into the inside lane. Crawling past, they saw the police were attending a collision. An orange Mustang, the one which passed them at high speed, had smashed into a truck. An officer was helping the hysterical woman driver out of her car. She was sobbing and holding her hand to a massive gash on her forehead. Blood streamed down her face, dripping on to her lilac jacket.

"Jesus, that was the car that nearly hit us." Rick spun around in his seat. "She must have lost control."

"That was a close call," said Alex somberly.

Chastened by the quake and the road accident, their moods calmed on the rest of the drive as dusk turned to darkness.

"Letitia asked me to give you this." Alex passed the gift to Rick as they walked to the house from the dunes. "Seems it's your birthday next week."

"Roll on twenty-six," said Rick grimly.

They heard the phone ringing inside the house. Unlocking the door and going in, Alex dashed to answer it. "Y'ello." He held out the phone to Rick. "For you."

Rick took the phone suspiciously. After listening for a moment, he relaxed and said, "Don't worry, dad. We're both fine ... Yeah, it happened as we were coming off the interchange. Alex got us onto solid ground before stopping the car ... Yeah, that was a wise move. Everything okay with you and the kids? ... Good ... And dad ..." Rick paused, swallowed hard and then said, "I'm sorry I went off at you like that. It was wrong of me ... You too, dad. I'll tell him ... Bye." Rick put down the phone. "That was dad checking we're okay. They'd been ringing for over an hour and were getting worried. If we hadn't got home by now Sid would have been sending out a search party."

Hearing Rick apologize to Sid, with no prompting, softened Alex's heart. "Did they feel the quake too?"

"It cracked that big mirror in the upstairs powder room and rattled the chandeliers but otherwise no damage. He and Letitia thanked you for coming." Rick's chin wobbled slightly. "I was mean to you today too. I behaved like a brat. Sorry."

Rick may be approaching twenty-six, but at this moment he looked all of fifteen with his sophisticated bravura and arrogant bluster stripped away. Driving back before the quake hit, all the reasons to end this crazy relationship had buzzed through Alex's head again. He'd even rehearsed the words to say when they got back to the house, the, "It's not you, it's me, it's over," speech. But at moments like these, like hearing Rick say sorry to his dad and to him without prompting, these moments when Rick was genuine and vulnerable and sweet, Alex couldn't deny the tug in his heart that he'd never felt so strongly for anyone before. He wrapped his arms around Rick and patted his back. "Gee, thanks for a swell Sunday."

"Wanna do it again next week?" asked Rick leaning back with a quizzical smile.

"Maybe we should leave it till Christmas. Come on, time for bed."

"Yeah, and one bright spark came out the whole day."

"What?"

"It you don't make it as an artist, you can always teach art to three and half year olds."

"Tiffany will kill you for forgetting her extra fifteen minutes," said Alex with a grin dragging Rick upstairs.

SAILBOAT IN YELLOW

"I'm desperately in need of two strong men," said Scotty breathlessly over the phone.

"What you calling here for, then?" retorted Alex.

"I've no time for jokes," she said tartly. "I need to deliver the gardenia piece today and the contractor I booked to install it just let me down."

"Why'd they do that?"

"Family emergency."

"Bummer. Why the panic? Can't you just book another contractor?"

"Why didn't I think of that? Oh, apart from the fact that I did. And I just wasted twenty precious minutes ringing around to find no-one can take the job at short notice. R.J.'s given me a window between one and three to get into their house and hang it *today*. He insists it's done while she's out. Bob's got meetings he can't cancel and I've no-one else to turn to. I could lose this commission and piss off a very famous client if I don't deliver on schedule. I got the drill and the fixings, but I can't even lift the piece by myself let alone hang it. Can you and Rick come to my rescue? Please. Please. Pleeeease?"

The angle of the sun out back told Alex it was just before ten. "Hang on." Covering the mouthpiece, he hollered upstairs, "Rick!"

It took a few moments before a sleepy voice muttered down. "Yeah?"

"Got anything planned today?"

Another pause. "Why?"

"Scotty needs us to help her hang something."

A longer pause. "What?"

"It doesn't matter what! I need a quick answer. Can you help, yes or no!"

"I suppose," uttered the sleepy voice from on high.

"Then we need to leave now! And when I say now, I mean five minutes ago!" Alex got back to Scotty on the phone. "We'll be there fast as we can."

"I love you, love you, love you! Bye!"

"Move your ass, boy!" yelled Alex. Shrugging on a denim jacket, he grabbed his billfold and car keys. Slipping the billfold in his pocket, he felt something. It took him a moment to recall it was the check Sid had given him at the barbecue. He stuffed it back into his pocket.

Rick shambled down to the kitchen, pulling a ratty purple tee shirt down over some scuzzy jeans. "What's the drama?"

"The guys Scotty booked to hang a commission bailed on her at the last minute. She needs us to help her."

Rick yawned. "Holy hang-ups, Batman."

"Robin needs to use the john, brush his teeth and jump in the Batmobile within sixty seconds if we're gonna save the day." Alex scooted out. A minute later he was revving the Chevy outside the back door. Perfunctorily abluted, Rick got in the car.

As Alex drove up to the highway, Rick pulled down the sun visor to check himself in the mirror. He licked his hand and tried to tame his bed hair. "Where is this art crisis precisely? LaFonte's exhibition's not till September, is it?"

Looking for a break in the traffic, Alex replied, "It's her big-name commission. Remember?"

Rick squinted in the yellow morning glare as he thought. After some protracted fumbling in the glove, he extracted a random pair of sunglasses that he must have left in there at some point. "You don't mean the one for Robert Wagner, do you?"

"Got it in one."

Rick grumpily pushed the sun visor back up. He donned the dark glasses as Alex swung onto the highway. "Forget it. No way am I meeting the Wagner-Woods looking like this!"

"You won't have to. Everybody's going to be out. They're having a birthday party for her on Saturday and this is the only time to get in the house with no-one around."

"My birthday's on Saturday too."

"As I'm aware. You haven't opened Letitia and Sid's gift yet, have you?"

"I'm saving the thrill. It'll be a check in a box. Sid expresses love through money."

"There are worse ways of expressing love." Talk of the ways fathers express love was reviving repressed memories, memories Alex preferred to keep repressed. Not wishing to continue this conversation he flicked on the radio. The smog lent the coastal scenery a washed-out look, even the blue sky had a greenish tint. Alex twizzled the dial. After static and indistinct signals, the radio locked on and the mellow sound of the Carpenters filled the car. *We've only just begun ...* Alex let the pop rock station play in the background as they drove along the hazy Pacific coast.

"When's your birthday?" asked Rick.

"November twentieth."

"How old you going to be?"

"Take a guess?" asked Alex.

"That game can go horribly wrong. Under fifty?"

"Thanks. Twenty-nine."

"Good job I started you on the moisturizer before your face flew south for the winter," said Rick.

"Moisturizer and hair conditioner. Boy, have you turned me to the dark side."

They rocked up at the Los Feliz house just before noon. Scotty stood poised anxiously beside her front door. "Thank God you're here! How's the traffic?"

"Not bad. Where do we have to get to?" asked Alex.

"Flats of Beverly Hills," said Scotty, "North Canon. Oh, hi Rick."

"That won't fit in my car." Alex scratched his head as he looked at Scotty's huge artwork leaning in the vestibule just inside the front door.

Scotty took a deep breath. "Give me a minute. I'll have to get Bob's station wagon out of the garage. We can drop the back seat." Scotty hustled out of the house.

"This thing's frickin' enormous," said Rick, examining the piece which was carefully entombed in layers of plastic. The protruding wire work gave it a solidity akin to a sculpture rather than a painting.

"Okay, Robin, let's get this thing on its side so we don't bash the door frame." After some heavy grunting and shunting they got it into a position to carry it.

"Holy hernias, Batman," moaned Rick, "it weighs a ton."

With perspiration dripping off both their foreheads, Alex and Rick maneuvered the artwork out of the house. On the street, Scotty was raising the rear door of a pale blue Rambler. "Did they ever find out who burglarized the house across the way?" asked Alex. Taking deep breaths, he and Rick heaved Scotty's artwork into the station wagon.

"Not a clue. And we had another break-in down the hill last week. Bob's taken to keeping a gun on every level of the house."

"And that makes you feel safer?" asked Alex skeptically.

"Honestly, it does. And there she goes." Scotty slammed down the rear door.

"You got the drill and fixings?" asked Alex.

"Yeah."

"Spirit level?"

"Dust sheets. Band Aids. Flasks of whiskey. There's nothing I've overlooked. You guys go on ahead, and I'll see you there," said Scotty. She gave them the house number and they jumped in the Chevy and set off whilst she locked up the house and set the alarm.

The drive to North Canon was quick. On arrival, Rick and Alex sat in the car, gazing up at the high-top palms lining the street while waiting for Scotty to show.

"Cute house," said Rick surveying the two story with gabled windows set behind a white picket fence they were parked out front of.

"Looks homey," said Alex. "She's here."

Scotty's Rambler pulled up behind them. "We're kind of early," said Scotty checking her watch as she approached their car. "I'll see if it's okay for us to get in." Scotty swung open the white gate and ran up the pathway to the house.

"Don't you think this is a weird," muttered Rick, getting out of the car.

"How'd you mean?"

"Us going into Robert Wagner and Natalie Wood's house like this."

"If we weren't doing it then a professional hanging company would be. I'm sure they must have plumbers and electricians go in and do work," said Alex.

"I guess. Just feels weird *us* doing it. Look, somebody's home."

Scotty was exchanging words with the woman who'd answered the door. The woman went back into the house, leaving the front door open. Scotty dashed back to them. "Coast's clear. The housekeeper says we can do it now." Alex and Rick stood behind Scotty as she clunked open the Rambler's back door. A wave of hot air gushed out. Getting the painting out was harder than getting it in. Within moments, Rick and Alex were drenched with sweat. "Be real careful getting it into the house. The housekeeper says they only just decorated and don't want the paintwork damaged," said Scotty.

"Terrific. No pressure then," said Rick with a grunt. The plastic wrapping grew slippery in Alex and Rick's sweaty hands. On the crazy paving path up to the house, Rick nearly lost his grip.

"Careful!" snapped Scotty seeing her painting about to tumble.

Rick's eyes widened as he struggled to prevent the painting crashing. Sensing a snappy retort from Rick, Alex cut in fast. "Rest your end on the ground a moment, Rick. We'll be able to get it inside in one when you've got a firmer grip." After wiping his brow with the back of his hand, Rick dried his palms on his purple tee shirt, leaving behind dark trails of moisture. "Alley oop," said Alex. He and Rick managed to heave the painting up the front steps and inside the house without incident. With the dust sheets and tools in her arms, Scotty followed them in.

"Mind the paintwork!" warned the lady who'd answered the door. "You're not going to make a lot of noise, are you? The baby's down for her nap."

"We'll be as quiet as we can," said Scotty with conviction.

The housekeeper regarded her with suspicion. Then, for added measure, threw a questioning look at Rick and Alex.

"And we'll be as quick as we can," added Alex politely. Rick didn't say anything as he stood holding the other end of the painting. Alex sensed he was getting one of 'those' looks on his face.

"You'd best come this way, then." The housekeeper led them along the entry hall to the main staircase.

The décor in the house consisted of floral wallpapers, Mexican tiles, soft drapes and comfortable furnishings dotted with needlepoint throw pillows. The place felt warm and welcoming and, although newly decorated, had a lived-in look. Anywhere the eye fell saw flowers, white flowers. The heady scents of gardenia and jasmine floated in their wake. Alex hoped the floral fragrance would compensate for the man sweat radiating off him and Rick as they humped the gigantic piece up the stairs.

On the upper story, the housekeeper showed them into the dressing room of the master suite. "That's where he wants it." Sure enough, before them stood the expanse of blank dove gray wall Scotty's work was destined for. "I'll leave you to it," said the housekeeper. She quickly slid shut the door to the bedroom, hiding the matrimonial bed and personal items from view. Rick and Alex set the painting down on the floor. Rick wafted his t-shirt to dry the sweat. In the confines of the dressing area, Alex's dripping perspiration became a tidal wave. He swept a sweaty hand through his damp hair and fluffed it from the back of his neck.

"This may help," said Scotty handing him a rubber band.

Alex pulled back his hair, twisted it a little and slipped the band around to restrain it. With his hair out of the way, the back of his neck cooled somewhat.

"I feel nauseous," moaned Scotty. "Did you get a look at the other art they have here? That looked like a Bonnard casually hanging over the mantle. What if she doesn't like my painting in real life?"

"R.J. commissioned it for her and you're delivering," said Alex bluntly. "They can always sell it if she doesn't like it."

"You've not read the script," said Scotty. "Here's where you say Natalie will love it without question and prevent me having a nervous breakdown."

"She'll love it without question. Better?"

"Better." Scotty flapped open the dustsheets. "Can you guys take off the wrappings?" She threw out the dustsheet and set about taping one edge over the baseboard. Rick and Alex set about peeling off the plastic. "It has four fixing points because we need to spread the weight. You have to get the points on the wall positioned exactly right," said Scotty bossily.

"Thanks for the tip, but I have hung art before," said Alex beginning to get tetchy himself. "Here, take over the unwrapping," he said to Scotty and she moved back. He picked up the yard stick and a pencil. "What do you want as the mid height? Standard sixty-two inches?" That was the common height for modern art, Old Masters usually being hung higher.

Scotty considered it as she balled up the discarded plastic, then said, "Make it fifty-eight. She's not tall, I don't want the piece to dominate her."

"Fifty-eight it is. Put it on its side." Alex checked the back of the painting, measuring the fixing points in relation to the piece's mid-line. Back on his feet, it only took a few moments for him to pencil mark the crosses on the wall for the drilling points. "Feels solid enough," he said after some exploratory tapping.

"Let's do this, then," said Scotty clapping her hands together. She then held the drill in one hand and had its power plug dangling from her other. After looking around, she muttered, "Shit."

"What?" chorused Alex and Rick.

"The only power point in here's by the credenza. The flex isn't long enough to reach!"

"Don't you have an extension reel?"

"I've everything else except that! Dear god, this project's a disaster! Alex, I can't afford to screw this up."

Alex placed a reassuring hand on her shoulder. "They've had building work going on. There must be an extension reel knocking around." Scotty was ultra-tense, and Rick's mood was rapidly deteriorating too. That was all Alex needed, two high maintenance personalities to contend with. "I'll go find the housekeeper." Alex went downstairs. Rick was correct, it was totally peculiar to be walking around inside someone else's home. Hearing activity in the kitchen, Alex tapped lightly on the door and said softly, "Hi. Excuse me ..." then swung the door open.

The housekeeper shot her head out from behind the refrigerator door.

"The cord on our drill won't reach across the room. Do you have an extension reel we could borrow?"

The woman took a moment to finish what she was doing. After shutting the refrigerator, she put her hand to her chin and thought. Then she raised a finger. "Aha, I recall seeing one out back. Let me go look." She moved away, then came back, pointed at the floor and said firmly, "Don't move."

After the housekeeper had left, Alex shifted from foot to foot. To one side of the refrigerator he saw a bunch of kids' paintings thumbtacked to a cork board. Suns, bunnies and big yellow flowers. Happy pictures. Then he spotted a photo of a boat stuck to the refrigerator's door with a magnet. Disobeying orders not to move, he took a step closer. The boat was sleek thirty-two-footer, moored in the waters off Catalina by the look of it. The sea dog in Alex's heart emitted a howl, pining to be back on the ocean. He was lost in a reverie when he heard the scrape of a key turning in the front door.

Leaning back to peek around the half-open kitchen door, Alex saw a woman enter the house. His heart sank. It was Natalie. She wore a denim bomber jacket with applique patches, her hair was shorter than he recalled from seeing her in pictures. Taking off her sunglasses, she tossed them into a bowl beside the front door. Tucking her dark hair behind her ear, she came towards the kitchen carrying a parcel. "I know I should stop buying things, but this lamp in that antique store on Robertson spoke to me and I could not ..." Her voice trailed off as she came through the kitchen door. She stopped dead in her tracks on seeing Alex.

If ever there was an opportune moment for the San Andreas Fault to open and swallow you, this was it. Monstrously aware of his ratty hair, rancid man sweat and the fact he was in a stranger's kitchen, Alex wondered if he should make a run for it.

Natalie frowned. Shaking her head, she rested the parcel on the counter. "Who the hell are you?" she asked bluntly.

Alex knew he had to say something but what? He settled on a cheery, "Oh, hi. I'm here with ... um, we're doing ..." and pointed upstairs. Scotty said this painting installation was a surprise so he didn't want to blow it. But how on earth could he explain his presence in Natalie's house if not with the truth? Any second now he expected she'd call the cops to arrest the crazy hippy who'd invaded her home. Where the fuck was that housekeeper? Had she gone to the next zip code to look for that reel? As Alex fidgeted uncomfortably, he saw the penny drop behind Natalie's velvet brown eyes.

"Is this to do with the artwork?" she asked.

Alex let out an audible sigh of relief. "It's meant to be a surprise. I didn't want to blow it. You know about it then?"

"I'd the suspicion something was afoot when my husband began taking such a keen interest in my schedule." She visibly relaxed. "My appointment ran shorter than expected. Sorry. I've ruined his plans by coming home early." She glanced at the wrapped lamp base and gave a small laugh, "Guess I should have carried on shopping. Hi, I'm Natalie."

"Hey, I'm Alex. Sorry I startled you. The guys Scotty hired to deliver the piece bailed on her at the last minute and she drafted us in to help. We hit a glitch when the cord for the drill wouldn't reach the socket. Your housekeeper's out back looking for an extension."

They both raised their heads on hearing Rick's footsteps coming down the stairs, "What's the fuckin' hold up?" said Rick grumpily at the foot of the stairs. "Scotty's about to have kittens. Do they have an extension reel or not?" Walking into the kitchen, Rick came face to face with Natalie.

Alex waved his hand vaguely in Rick's direction. "That's Rick. He's helping Scotty too."

Natalie stared at Rick and her eyes narrowed.

"I knew I'd seen one. It was out by the pool house. Here ..." The housekeeper came in triumphantly holding out the extension reel.

Natalie waved her finger at Rick. "Don't I know you from someplace?"

Rick tried to flatten his hair a bit more. "I doubt it." He half laughed, shielding his face.

"You want it or not?" asked the housekeeper proffering the extension reel to Alex.

"Yes. Yes, thank you." Alex took it off her.

"My appointment finished early. I'll take the baby outside and let these guys finish up," Natalie said to the housekeeper.

"She's down for her nap. Let me go see if she's waking up," said the housekeeper. She went up to Natalie and, after glancing at Alex, exchanged a few confidential words. Then the housekeeper brushed past Rick to go check on the baby.

"I'll run this up to Scotty." Rick snatched the extension reel off Alex and went to go back upstairs.

As Rick passed to leave, Natalie exclaimed, "You're Sid Stradman's son, aren't you?"

With his back to them, Rick stopped. Turning slowly, he nodded bashfully and said, "Yeah."

"I knew I recognized you. It must have been about eight years back, you were at one of Sid's parties. I remember feeling so bad for you. He was proudly introducing you to everybody, but you just sat on the sidelines looking miserable."

Rick gave a small sigh and a self-deprecating smile. "That wasn't a great time for me. I'd been sent here to study against my will and ended up caught in the crossfire of Deanna and Sid's divorce."

Natalie nodded understandingly. "You had a guest role on a T.V. show we watched last year. It made me so happy to see you all grown up and working. It was funny because the next day Sid called my agent to check on my availability for his new movie."

"It wasn't *Tornado* was it?" asked Rick darkly.

"Don't forget the exclamation point," added Alex.

Natalie smiled wryly at Alex, "You know Sid?"

"Oh, yeah," said Alex.

"I had to turn it down because I was having the baby," said Natalie.

"Not because of the crummy script?" asked Rick with a knowing laugh.

"No," said Natalie meeting Rick's eyes. "The timing couldn't work."

"Lucky escape," said Rick, "dad's movies are uniformly lousy. Still, I guess no-one ever went broke underestimating the public's intelligence."

Natalie's back stiffened. "Most people consider any movie that makes money is a success. And Sid's produced plenty of those, so he must be doing something right. Anyway, it was nice of him to think of me. Please remember me to your father and wish him well with his movie," said Natalie coolly.

"Sure, if I see him" said Rick averting his eyes. "I'll take this up to Scotty before we need paramedics to resuscitate her. Nice meeting you again." Rick gave an embarrassed smile to Natalie and scooted off up the stairs.

After Rick had gone, Alex hung around for a moment. "Sorry about that. He has a stormy relationship with his father," Alex said apologetically.

Natalie smiled ruefully and toyed thoughtfully with her butterfly pendant. "It happens. Families, huh?"

"Yeah, families," said Alex giving an empathetic nod in agreement. He glanced at a framed photo of Natalie and R.J. on a boat. "Looks like you guys sail a lot." As soon as he'd spoken, Alex hoped he hadn't intruded. "I couldn't help noticing the photos. It's just that I really miss being out on the ocean. You see, I crewed on yachts for several years after I'd left Dayton."

Natalie took off her denim jacket, hung it on the back of a chair and began taking the brown paper off the lamp base she'd brought in. "Really? Whereabouts?"

"Mostly up and down the Pacific coast. That's why I recognised Catalina. I've been through the Panama Canal a couple of times too when we were delivering a yacht to Florida and bringing another back."

"Gets in your blood," said Natalie, "being on the water away from everything. It's seductive, isn't it? My husband's currently looking to buy a boat rather than charter."

The photos of the Wagner's having happy times on boats made an idea pop into Alex's head. He'd been wondering what to give Rick for his birthday. This could a part of his life experience he could share. "You say you charter. You wouldn't know of anyone who does bareboat charters, would you? I've been out the loop so long I've lost my contacts in the sailing world."

"What kind of boat have you got in mind?"

"Something like a twenty-two-foot sloop?"

"A sailboat?"

"I like sails. The wind's either for you or against you and it's up to the sailor to deal with the challenge."

"And what do you do when there's no wind at all?" asked Natalie with a twinkle in her eye.

"Drop anchor, stare at the horizon and drink beer," replied Alex with a chuckle.

Natalie laughed in response. Her eyes locked with Alex's and a moment of understanding and warmth passed between them. "Here, I'll give you Ken's number. He's bound to know someone at the Marina or Newport who can point you in the right direction." Natalie scribbled a number on a pad and tore off the page. "Hope it works out. Must say I was a pretty good first mate when it was just the two of us out at sea."

"I don't think I'll get so lucky on that front. I'm planning on taking Rick."

"Oh!" Natalie laughed. "Oh?" She thought for a moment. "Oh ..." She smiled knowingly, and their gaze connected again.

"His birthday's coming up. Just struck me, as we were talking, that I could take him sailing as a surprise."

"I hope Ken can help. Now I should let you get back to work." Natalie screwed up the wrapping and considered the ornate ceramic lamp base.

"Thanks for this." Alex waved the phone number. "And sorry to spoil your surprise."

"I'll act surprised. I'm good at it, it's what I do for a living." Natalie smiled kindly, saw Alex out of the kitchen and firmly closed the door behind him once he'd gone.

Climbing the stairs to the master suite, the whirring of the drill told him Scotty was up and running on the install. In the dressing room, Alex found Rick with the hammer in his hand, ready to knock another drywall anchor into place. Two anchors were already in situ.

"How's it going?" Alex asked peering over Scotty's shoulder.

"On a one to ten scale of nightmares, about an eleven," muttered Scotty. "Where've you been?"

"Chatting with Natalie."

Scotty released the power button and the drill fell silent. "She's not coming up, is she? This was all meant to happen out of her sight."

"She's taking the baby into the garden. She's cool."

"How will it sound when she tells R.J. I had to rope in two friends to help? The guy that let me down will have another family emergency if I get my hands on him. His!" Rick swiftly slammed the anchor into the hole as Scotty moved on to the final one. The drill kicked back into action. Scotty spoke over her shoulder, "Al, can you screw the wall fixings into the anchors? Screwdriver's down there." Once she'd drilled the final hole, Scotty swept flecks of plaster off the baseboard onto the dustsheet. Rick hammered the last anchor home while Alex put in the screws. Scotty carefully folded the dustsheet to contain any mess.

Alex made the last turn of the final screw. "Job done." Together they lifted the picture flat to the wall, gave it a gentle push, then slowly released their grip and let the painting drop onto the screws in the wall. Scotty's artwork was installed in its new home. Alex had to admit her piece was stunning. The translucent wire hovering over the huge gardenia painting gave the giant flower an ethereal yet intensely dramatic quality. When you moved, it moved too. It had a relationship with the viewer.

The viewer gave life to the art.

Rick placed his hand on Scotty's shoulder and gently squeezed. "Good job."

"Impressive." A woman's voice from behind made them all jump.

They turned to find the housekeeper coming into the room.

"We'll get out of your way," said Scotty to her. "I need to add the finishing touch." Alex and Rick gathered the dust sheet and tools while Scotty draped a pelican blue silk sheet over the painting. She then added a faux white ribbon bow with a gift card dangling from it. "All ready for the unveiling on Saturday." Scotty assured the housekeeper.

"Thanks for finding this," said Alex returning the extension reel.

As they backed out of the room, the housekeeper quickly cast her eyes over the rugs and paintwork. Their cleanliness must have passed muster, for she said, "I'll see you out." Following them down the stairs, she scooted around to open the front door.

Alex noticed Scotty take one last look into the house. He guessed she was wondering if Natalie was going to show. But the open front door and the housekeeper on the threshold, practically booting them out, signaled no further engagement with the lady of the house.

"Thanks, guys. Couldn't have done it without you. I owe you big time," said Scotty and hugged each of them when they got back to the cars.

"No worries," said Rick dryly, "it's not every day I hammer anchors into a movie star's drywall."

They said their goodbyes and headed off in separate directions. Alex could hardly wait to get home and call the guy at the marina. As soon as they arrived back in Sunset Cove, Rick dashed into the shower to wash off the multiple layers of sweat. While the water was running, Alex dialed Ken's number. Not unexpectedly, seeing how he was a boat captain, the guy didn't pick up on the first attempt. Alex spent the next couple of hours on tenterhooks, waiting for any opportune moment for Rick to be out the way long enough to try the number again. Just when he was at the point of going up to the Beachcomber to use their pay phone, Rick decided to take a walk on the beach. No sooner was Rick out of the door than he picked up the phone. After five rings, Ken picked up.

Turned out Ken knew someone at Newport with a Catalina 22 whom he thought would be amenable to a day rental. Ken was in touch with a couple of captains that Alex had crewed under, including the one on the bash up to San Francisco. Ken said he'd call back in the morning to pass on the Cat's owner's details once he was satisfied with Alex's references.

Friday was a great time for the call to come as this was Rick's errand day. Ken called around ten, while Rick was doing whatever he did for in Laguna for three hours every week. As expected, Alex had been given a glowing report and within ten minutes he'd made contact for the rental. The boat's owner wanted two hundred bucks. It sounded steep but as it was a bareboat charter, with no captain or crew, an element of risk was involved - which kind of justified the fee. Alex still had cash left from the thousand bucks Sid had given him at Fox and he'd stashed Sid's most recent check for two thousand in the back of his underwear drawer. He didn't plan on cashing it, but it was there as a back-up in case of emergency. Bearing that in mind, Alex accepted the offer. For an extra forty bucks the boat's owner would throw in a picnic basket of cold cuts, beers and a bottle of champagne. What the hell, Alex bit the bullet and agreed to the whole deal. His next step was how to get Rick on board.

Literally.

Just before dinner, Alex casually threw into the conversation, "With helping Scotty, I haven't done any work for a couple of days. I'd like to try some hard-edged stuff. I was thinking of setting up outside Newport tomorrow. I'll need someone to keep an eye out for the cops, would you play lookout?"

Rick took less than a moment to reply brightly, "Sure, anything to help."

"I want to get to work before the day's too hot so we'll set off around seven. And seeing as we'll be out in the sun, make sure to pack sunscreen and a hat and stuff."

"Pack?"

"Bring with ... you know." Alex's plan, if the wind favored him, was to take the boat south. It would be fun to hoist the sails and make a run, then drop anchor in a cove for lunch. Then they could spend the afternoon relaxing in the sun or swimming off the deck.

Due to past experience Alex never prayed. He couldn't get on board with the whole God thing. However, going to bed that Friday night he did the closest thing to it, sending a heartfelt wish to a higher power for fine weather and fair winds to celebrate Rick's birthday.

♦ ♦ ♦

It was hard to tell if Rick knew something was afoot when they set off in the morning. Alex had snuck up to the car to tune into the mariner's forecast prior to the crack of dawn. Rick had woken up early and got ready very quickly (for him). He was actually waiting by the Chevy when Alex came out with his field easel and paint box.

"Hey, happy birthday," said Alex, pulling onto the highway and heading north.

"Just another day. And probably a black one for momma. If only Sid had used birth control when passion overtook so many problems would have been avoided."

"But then you wouldn't exist."

"Exactly," said Rick with a snort.

Alex knew the jig was up as soon as they turned into Bayside Drive and approached the yacht basin.

Rick stirred restively in the passenger seat. "Not exactly what I'd describe as hard edged," he muttered running his eyes along the rows of yachts bobbing on the water.

"Change of plan. Sit tight, I'll be right back." Alex quickly found Sam, the boat's owner. He was the guy in the gray sweats and baseball cap with his arm in a sling. He stood waiting by the slip of a great looking twenty-two-foot sloop with a yellow hull. Turned out Sam had broken his wrist, hence couldn't skipper his boat which was why he'd been doing bareboat charters. They did a walk around. When both were satisfied with each other's part of the deal, Alex passed Sam the two hundred and forty bucks. Alex filed a route plan and estimated time of return. Once the business was done, Alex left Sam and collected his cargo. The cargo, namely Rick, was pacing beside the Chevy.

"What's going on?" asked Rick suspiciously.

"Take this." Alex handed him the field easel and took the rest of his equipment out of the car. "Hope you got your sea legs."

"Me too," said Rick, with a dubious expression.

Alex hopped on board and stowed the equipment. "Pass me that." Steadying himself with one hand, he reached for the field easel and took it off Rick. "Careful, hold onto me." Extending his right hand, he took Rick's left, gripping his forearm to secure him as he stepped onto the boat. Once onboard, Rick took a quick look around the vessel and appeared a little apprehensive. "Ever been on a boat before?" asked Alex.

The boat rocked, and Rick braced himself on the cockpit's coaming. "We crossed the Atlantic on the Queen Mary in fifty-eight."

"You're an old hand then. Now before we get underway here's the safety briefing. Full attention please." The captain in Alex took control. However much fun he wanted the day to be, safety on board was prime. He pointed out the lifejackets, fire extinguishers, hand holds, emergency flares, and life raft. He outlined basic engine operation (just in case the captain became incapacitated), explained the dangers of the boom, warned of the perils of slipping and tripping, and closed with the sailor's mantra, 'One hand for you, the other for the boat'. This was a hangover from when mariners clung to the rigging with one hand while working the sails with the other. In other words, whatever you're doing make sure you keep hold of something solid. "Most importantly, when I tell you to do something you obey. No questions, no hesitations. I need to know you've heard and understood. When I give an order I need a loud 'Aye, aye captain' from you. Got that?"

"Masterful, or what?"

"I'm serious. What do you say?"

Rick knuckled his brow. "Aye, aye captain!"

"Very good, matey," said Alex. Then he slipped on his shades and a peaked cap, rolled up his sleeves to cast off and fired up the outboard. It felt great to be back on the water. Being in charge of the sloop, with one hand on the tiller and the other around Rick's shoulder gave Alex a sense of control. It was refreshing to be back in an environment that was his forte. He motored out of Newport, passing Lookout Point and Corona del Mar Beach, then headed out to sea. As he steered, he gave Rick a rudimentary education about the names of parts of the boat and the sails. But however seriously he explained 'cleats', 'topping lift' and 'boom vang', Rick found every technical term a cue for juvenile giggling and ribald comments.

"I'll never remember any of this shit! You know what you're doing," said Rick.

The shoreline receded. Once in open water, Alex turned off the outboard. He lifted his head to the sky, sensing the wind. After checking the Windex on the top of the mast for good measure too, he said, "Here goes. Remember, keep your head down!"

"Aye, aye captain." A faint expression of trepidation crossed Rick's face.

"I've done this a million times. You're in safe hands."

Rick smiled into the sun, the wind tousling his sandy hair.

Alex briefly wondered if he should have picked something more to Rick's taste for his birthday, like a chichi dinner at a swank hotel rather than roughing it out on the ocean. What the fuck, too late now. Alex hoisted the mainsail. The wind was coming across from behind. He went up to the bow to unfurl and raise the jib. The wind's velocity picked up. Alex couldn't help the broad smile of delight crossing his face as the force of nature began to power their journey. The swoosh of the ocean and flap of the mainsail was music to his ears. An air current caught them, its propulsion carried a mighty heft. "Ready to gybe! Boom coming across. Duck!" Alex pulled Rick under the boom as it moved across so that their combined weight would balance the boat as the wind tipped it. The boat leaned harshly, instinctively Alex held Rick securely until it settled.

Taken by surprise from the wind's sudden movement of the boat, Rick clung to Alex. "Aye, aye, captain," he murmured. The exhilaration of sailing on the ocean soon took the place of Rick's nervousness. He clutched the rail and squinted into the wind as Alex handled the sails.

"This is a broad reach!" Alex yelled loudly above the air rushing past as they skimmed the sea. "The wind's coming obliquely from behind. If the wind was with us, it could take us right around the world! There's no gas crisis for sail boats!"

"Alex, look. Over there!" Rick pointed off the starboard stern out to sea.

Alex spotted three or four fins swooping in and out of the ocean. "Dolphins! And, see, more of them coming to join!"

An expression of pure delight lit up Rick's face as the fins came closer. "This is amazing!" he shouted.

The dolphins swished alongside, slightly below the surface. Further off the bow, Alex spotted a couple of sea lions breaking the water.

"They're so beautiful …" exclaimed Rick breathlessly. He peered over the boat's edge, watching the quicksilver flashes of the dolphins. Every so often, a fin broke the surface with a fizz of whitewater. "They're so close I could touch them!" In response to Rick's voice, a couple of the dolphins cried out with their distinctive chirrups as they crested the waves.

"The sound of the boat cutting the water attracts them!" Alex shouted above the wind flapping the sails. "They always come to see what's going on."

Rick held on tight and leaned over the side, entranced by their travelling companions. "I see fish down there too!"

"The wind's changing!" Alex felt it going around directly behind them. He needed to drop the jib and angle the mainsail. "Hold on!"

"Aye, aye, captain!"

A few minutes later, Alex had the jib down. The wind slapped into the mainsail, blowing them south. Half an hour later, a familiar sight appeared on their port side, it was the headland of Sunset Cove. From many years' experience Alex tightened the sail and brought it into line with the wind, reducing the propulsion to nil. He furled the mainsail and then fired up the outboard. They went a bit farther south before he angled around to bring them back up the coast. Turning to Rick, he asked, "How'd you like that then?"

"Sensational. We saw dolphins! Impressive boat handling, captain."

"The crew aims to please." Alex pointed at the shore. "Look, you can see the Beachcomber."

Rick shielded his eyes and followed his gaze. "How small everything seems."

"We can drop anchor in Oyster Bay."

A short while later the yellow sailboat was bobbing in the secluded cove's turquoise waters. Alex had raised the cabin's top, opened the chiller and laid out lunch. He poured the champagne. "Sorry, I didn't pack the Baccarat crystal," he said passing Rick a plastic beaker.

"Shocking, but I'll manage."

Alex tapped his plastic tumbler against Rick's. "Happy Birthday." Alex bent forward and kissed him, savoring the salt spray on Rick's lips. "Hey, I put this on board." Alex took out Sid and Letitia's gift which he'd hidden in his equipment bag. "They took the trouble to make sure you had this for your birthday," said Alex.

"It's more than momma did, not even a card from her. Not that I give a damn."

"You ought to open it." Alex pushed the gift to Rick.

Rick put the plastic beaker on the dinette table. Pulling the ends of the red bow, he said, "It'll be a check." Letting the ribbon flutter to the deck, Rick opened the box. Removing a wad of Tiffany blue tissue, he lifted out a silver photo frame. After studying the photo in it, he turned away and blinked several times.

"May I?" asked Alex. Rick passed the frame to him. The photo was of a young Sid, with dark hair and Hollywood smile, protectively holding a white blonde child of about two years. By their side stood a woman wearing dark glasses and two-piece tailored suit. She gripped the boy's leg with one hand, as if she didn't trust Sid to hold the child safely. "I take it the kid in the picture's you?"

"Sid's special effects department could never fake something as convincingly as that. This was taken when we came back to America and they were on speaking terms again." Rick took a small envelope out of the box and read the gift card. "To my wonderful darling son, Happy Birthday! Although you may not believe it, the only thing I ever want is for you to be well and happy. Love from Sid, Letitia and the twins." Rick put the card back into the box and took the frame. "I was being a brat again when I spoke to Natalie about him, wasn't I?"

"A little." Alex topped up their beakers with champagne. "Actually, a lot."

"I made her uncomfortable in her own home. I'll have to send her flowers and a note to apologize. But I still think she dodged a bullet not being in his movie."

"I can't figure out why you're so hostile to him."

Rick put the frame back in the box and placed the tissue over it. "I always feel like I disappoint him. Well both of them, momma too. I haven't pushed myself into a great career or carved out a big niche in the world, and I won't be giving them grandchildren. Although that'll be more momma's disappointment than his. That's only because she'll worry about where the family fortune will end up. Sid's produced enough spawn to populate Nevada, missing out on one or two from me won't make any difference to him."

"You're being too hard on yourself. You've got the new T.V. show coming up. If that's a hit it'll be looking good for you on the career front. And getting over all those other issues in your head's part of growing up. I can vouch for that from personal experience."

Rick put the lid back on the box, retrieved the ribbon and re-tied it. "You seem pretty together. Your lack of neuroses is one of the things I find so comforting about you."

Alex drained his beaker. He reached into the cooler and pulled out a beer, Rick could finish the champagne, it was too acidic for his taste. "I've had issues, believe me. Things were bearable back in Dayton until mom died." He paused, this was an area he hadn't delved into for some time. "It was very sudden you see, a massive hemorrhagic stroke. She'd been the peacemaker between dad and me, but without her in the house I couldn't do anything right by him. Those were a real bad five years for me. I tried so hard not to anger him, I walked on eggshells every day. Then one Friday night he came home late from the bar. I hadn't taken out the trash or put away the dishes or something else to rile him. He lost it and whipped off his belt. Feel this." Alex took Rick's hand, spread his fingers and touched one to his brow. "Feel this dent?" Rick nodded. "See the scar under my eyebrow?" Rick looked closely and nodded again. "That's where the buckle hit me. I was crying so hard and had so much blood in my eyes I couldn't see a thing. He cried about it too afterwards. Said he didn't want to hurt me, but it was for my own good. At that moment I promised myself that nothing and no-one would ever make me cry again. I'd always forgiven him in the past, but that beating was the last one I was willing to take. Soon as I'd saved the bus fare I headed west. No goodbyes. No explanations. Just left and never looked back." Alex fought to stop his chin quivering at the memory. He closed his eyes and felt Rick's arms wrap around him and his lips gently kiss the dent on his brow. It was a nice feeling, a safe feeling, a loving feeling. Alex patted Rick's hand and gently pushed him away. "Enough of my sad stories, this is your day." Alex stood and the boat rocked gently. "We got a cove, the sun, and I bought along this excuse of a swimsuit for you." He tossed the tiny blue trunks to Rick.

"Good thinking, captain. But unnecessary." Rick steadied himself, then stripped off his t-shirt, kicked off his sneakers and pulled down his board shorts and undershorts. "That's the beauty of secluded coves. Swimsuits not required."

"Good point. And why I chose this spot to drop anchor." Alex unbuttoned his shirt and pants. "Cause I forgot to bring mine." He wriggled out of his deck shoes and jeans. He pulled Rick's naked body to his and kissed him passionately.

"They say after eating you should leave half an hour before swimming."

"We've only just eaten. What can we do to pass half an hour?"

"We'll think of something." Rick pushed Alex backwards. He fell down onto the v-berth in the prow and let Rick crawl on top of him ...

♦ ♦ ♦

The afternoon's languorous haze lingered on their journey home as the sun was going down. Rick rested his head on Alex's shoulder as he turned off the highway down to Sunset Cove. The last embers of the day cast a rosy glow over the sea. "Thank you. This was the best birthday I've ever had," said Rick.

"You still up for driving into Laguna for dinner?"

"You bet."

"Wonder whose car that is?" mused Alex glancing at the white Mercedes in the dunes.

"Rental plates. Lost tourist, I'd say." Rick picked up the field easel and helped Alex unpack the rest of his stuff.

They strolled down to the house. "Quick shower and then we'll head back out," said Alex.

"Aye, aye, captain!"

"You may have the makings of a good first mate yet." Alex unlocked the back door and flicked on the kitchen light. "Although what you did sexually to the captain this afternoon might be classed as mutiny."

Rick walked in the house and put his hand on Alex's arm in fright. "Al, someone's out on the deck." Through the living room windows they could make out a figure silhouetted against the crimson sunset.

"Wait here." Alex strode through the house. He wasn't normally nervous, but the recent talk of burglaries, muggings and intruders had got him rattled. It crossed his mind that if one kept a gun in the house, when was the point you'd arm yourself to confront a trespasser? Alex flicked on the verandah light, unlocked and rattled open the front door. "Hey lady, you're on private property," he said fiercely.

The woman didn't look like your average itinerant, she was dressed in a cream jacket and turban and smoking a cigarette. Gold button earrings glinted on her ears. She dropped her cigarette and stubbed it out with a taupe suede platform sole. "Forgive me. I'm looking for someone."

"Who?" asked Alex sensing Rick's breath on the back of his neck.

The woman walked right up to the front door. "Rick Stradman. I trust I have the right address?"

Alex recognized the high cheekbones and full lips from the photograph in Sid's frame.

"It's okay," said Rick pushing past Alex.

The woman clasped her hand to her mouth. She then flung her red nails out to Rick. "You can't think I'd have forgotten? Buon compleanno, mio bello!" She placed her hands on either side of Rick's face, pulled him to her and smothered him with kisses.

Rick extricated himself from her grip, wiping maroon lipstick off his cheek.

"I've waited so long and travelled so far. Aren't you going to invite me in?" The woman's bottom lip quivered, her eyes glazed with tears.

"The cherry on the icing of my day." Rick turned and gave a half smile to Alex. "Meet Luisa D'Onofrio ... my mother."

PORTRAIT OF A MOTHER

If Saturday had dawned perfectly in every way, Sunday made up for it with torrential downpours and thunder. Alex lay beside Rick in bed, listening to rain rattle on the roof. Although it was getting light, Rick had only just fallen asleep after tossing and turning all night. If one were prone to seasickness it would have struck in this bed rather than the open sea. Although Rick had portrayed Luisa to be a monster, the Luisa Alex met last night could not have been further from that image. The remainder of last night, after Rick had introduced her and grudgingly invited her into the beach house, played out in Alex's mind ...

"Ah, so this is where you are living now," said Luisa stepping over the threshold and looking around. She had that same x-ray attention as Rick, her eyes roved over everything. The moment they rested, you wondered why the copper jello mold hanging on the kitchen wall or the lime green surf board leaning on the deck were worthy of her interest, and why, in the moment her vision lingered, you felt your taste being judged. "Thank you for taking in my son." Luisa graciously extended her cream gloved right hand.

Assuming she was going to shake his hand, Alex reached out. But before their hands connected, her left hand came around to take off her glove. In the mistiming his hand hit her wrist. "Sorry," said Alex.

Luisa slipped off her glove, then shook his hand. "My fault, Mr. Morgan."

"Call me Alex."

"Alex," she repeated in her husky voice. Her amber eyes glinted as brightly as her filigree gold earrings. "Let me take a good look at my little boy." Luisa tossed her cream gloves onto the couch, then held Rick at arm's length to drink in his face.

Rick squirmed. "Oh, momma."

"I've not seen you for over a year and I want to look at you! Do you not at least owe your momma that?" Luisa grabbed Rick's chin and tilted his face to hers. "You have lost weight. Very handsome, no?" Luisa glanced to Alex for verification.

"Have you lost weight?" asked Alex.

"Not that I'm aware of. Momma let go, you're embarrassing me." Rick wriggled out of Luisa's grip. "What are you doing here?"

"It's your birthday," said Luisa petulantly.

"You could have sent a card. This isn't a good time, we're about to go out for dinner."

"Forgive me, I did not know." Luisa shrugged. "Not hearing from you for so long upset me. I could not allow this bad blood to go on any longer."

"So you just hopped on a jet?"

"I had to know if you have forgiven me for whatever it was you thought I'd done to upset you." Luisa dropped her eyes. "And other business brings me here too."

"Great, I forgive you, you got good value from the plane fare. Look momma, we were about to leave."

"Fine. Do not let me interrupt your plans. I had to let you know your momma loves you now and always will. I shall give you your gift and let you get on with your evening." Luisa picked up her glossy crocodile purse, flicked open the gold clasp and withdrew a slim brown envelope. "Happy birthday, darling."

Gingerly, Rick took the envelope.

"Open it and I shall leave you in peace."

"Sounds like a deal." Rick slipped his finger into the envelope.

"This is to show you how happy you have made me. Your father told me you were seeing someone new."

"He did?"

"He said they were good for you and I shouldn't judge. Then, when I saw those photos of you at the charity auction, I put two and two together." Luisa tapped her nose.

"What pictures?" Rick's finger was still poised in the envelope.

"The society pages, darling. The photos of the charity auction given by that ghastly Beverly Hills woman. She was wearing the most grotesque dress. As Dorothy Parker said, if you want to know what God thinks of money look who he gave it to." Luisa laughed gaily, glancing to Alex for confirmation.

Alex wrinkled his nose. It seemed a neutral reaction to let someone know you'd heard what they said without making a value judgement on their statement.

"You two made a lovely couple in the photos. I'm so happy, darling. And with your new T.V. show you'll be bright stars together."

"I've zero idea what you're babbling on about, momma." Rick tore open the envelope.

"You and Danielle Brown. Arm in arm and clearly with eyes only for each other. Your father did mean her when he spoke about this new relationship, didn't he?"

Rick slipped a parchment document out of the envelope. "What's this?"

"For your future."

Rick put the piece of paper back in the envelope and shoved it back to Luisa. "The commute from Venice to L.A. takes too long."

"The Ca' dei Venti's your legacy. When the gallery opens it will be around for many, many years and will need your care once I am gone. The palazzo has been in our family for generations and I want you to have your share now."

"I've told you before, momma, I won't ever take anything from you again because it all comes with a price tag. This is another ploy to tangle me back up in your orbit." Rick's blue eyes were pure ice. "And I am in a new relationship, but it's not with Danielle."

Luisa's smile faltered. "Your father assured me you were going to be all right now. He said I should come here to see how happy you are for myself."

Rick plopped the envelope into the open gold jaws of Luisa's crocodile purse. "I ought to have been more honest with you in the past, momma. I should have told you the real reason I couldn't marry Gina. Well, now you know. This is who I'm in the relationship with." Rick took Alex's hand in his and stared defiantly at her.

The colors in Luisa's amber eyes changed as her synapses made connections. She stood like an animal frozen in the headlights of a vehicle about to run it down. Luisa looked from Rick to Alex, and then back to Rick. She raised her hands.

Alex flinched, afraid she was going to strike Rick.

Luisa balled her hands into fists and clapped them to her forehead. "Your poor stupido momma!" She opened her hands and extended them to Alex. "Forgive me. I am from another time. This is not the first thought that came to mind, but now I see. You say you have dinner plans? We shall eat dinner together. Family, no?"

Rick squinted suspiciously at Luisa. "You're okay with this?"

"Your father should have been more specific, but that is your father. If he answered more questions than he asked we would all be better informed. I can't say I am not a little shocked and somewhat hurt, but this is not a time for anything but happiness. Today celebrates the day I gave birth to you, no? I am staying at a hotel in Laguna. Come, let us all take dinner there. It is a perfect opportunity for me to find out more about you, Mr. Morgan, sorry Alex. This is a name I shall have to grow used to saying. It appears you've tamed this wild boy of mine. Bravo." Luisa firmly grasped Alex's shoulders with both hands.

Alex felt Luisa's breath ruffle his stubble as she kissed him on the left and then the right cheek, her depth of emotion digging her maroon nails into his flesh. He pulled away and said, "Rick, you and your mother go on ahead in her rental. I'll follow in the Chevy so I can drive us back. Which hotel are you at, Luisa?"

"The Sands." Luisa snapped her crocodile purse shut then looped it over her arm. "This is a good idea of Alex. While I drive, you can tell me all about your wonderful new T.V. show. Andiamo, Ricardo." Luisa forcefully hustled Rick out of the house. Once they'd departed, Alex savored a few moments alone to compose himself. After allowing ten minutes for them to get going, Alex picked up his keys and meandered to the car.

The Sands had rustled up their finest table. It was an impressive feat, for the restaurant was full and Luisa hadn't made reservations. A lithe waiter guided them through the pastel shaded dining room. He graciously pulled back a chair for Luisa at a perfectly situated table for three; one positioned by a doorway onto the terrace with an uninterrupted view of the glittering ocean.

Luisa had removed her turban and fluffed out her caramel hair, it softly curled around her face and shoulders. "I forbid you to look at prices!" Luisa waved her hand in front of the menus. "Take whatever you want." She handed the wine list back to the sommelier without looking and said, "A bottle of the Perrier-Jouët." The sommelier was about to fulfill her order when her maroon talons fastened on his arm. "Make that two. Is my son's birthday."

While Luisa engaged in full blown Italian conversation with Rick, Alex took the time to observe how meticulously the sommelier opened the champagne. After he'd brought it to the table and showed the label to Luisa, the wine waiter cut the foil, removed the wire cradle, then restrained the cork with one hand while gently twisting the bottle with the other. Alex guessed the trick to avoid exploding fizz was restraining the cork at the moment the gaseous contents were desperate to escape. An anti-orgasm, if you will. Alex sat back and sipped his freshly poured champagne. Luisa was overflowing with love for her son, although in a foreign tongue. Every other second she trailed her hand over Rick's shoulder or his hand. A couple of times she even included Alex in the love fest, which pleasantly surprised him considering how Rick had thrown their relationship in her face without warning.

The food arrived. All very high class. The salmon starters being so minimally presented as to be almost unnoticeable. After only two mouthfuls it seemed the sword fish main courses were in front of them. Alex didn't know much about Italy, but Luisa's conversation, when conducted in English for his benefit, peppered in every city from Milan to Palermo - with the added spice of an anecdote about a different artist to flavor each location.

"Alex is an artist too," said Rick resting his knife and fork on the plate once they'd finished eating.

"How nice." Luisa clicked her fingers at the sommelier and tapped the upturned bottle in the ice bucket, then she took a compact out of her purse. Touching up her lipstick in the mirror, she looked beyond her reflection to Alex. "Do you sell anything? The L.A. market is very competitive, no?"

"One of my paintings just sold at a charity auction. Yumi Mihara's taken several of my pieces for her gallery too."

"Mihara? I think I have heard the name. Did she discover you?"

Rick cut in. "Koenig introduced them. He'd seen some of Alex's work and thought Yumi would be a good fit for him."

"Koenig? You know my dear Walter!" Luisa smiled warmly at Alex.

"Yes. Through Rick, of course."

"Ah." Luisa wound down her lipstick, snapped her compact shut and dropped them both into her purse as the busboy came to clear the fish detritus. "Now it is time to reveal *my* big surprise. Your momma may be making a return to the silver screen." Luisa rested her hand on Rick's arm and stroked his wrist.

"But you hate Hollywood," said Rick frowning.

"Pah." Luisa puffed out air between her moist lips. "One should never let the past rule the future. It is the other reason I am in California." Tracing a pattern on the tablecloth with her red nail, Luisa said self-effacingly, "The producers of your show have been in touch."

"What?" Rick's eyes narrowed.

"Si, si!" Luisa laughed gaily as the waiter refilled Luisa and Rick's glasses from the fresh bottle, Alex declined. "Once they found out I was your momma it seems they remembered me from my Hollywood days! They know of me from my Italian movies too. They have already written a script for me to guest star in to tempt me back! The part is an Italian movie actress who wants to buy the McMillan's house." Luisa fixed her eyes on Alex's. "Being wanted is a good feeling, no?"

"I guess," said Alex in reply. He drained his water glass, then said to Rick, "Been a long day, bud. Maybe we should head back to the Cove?"

"I've more to tell!" Luisa was practically jumping up and down in her seat. "They also think I would be perfect to play the lead in your new show!"

"*Legal Eagles*?" asked Rick in astonishment.

"They were considering Stanwyck or Davis and then thought of me! They still think of me as a big star! Imagine if I got the part, we would be working together every day! Don't go, don't go yet. Let me get you rooms here so we can talk more."

Rick finished his champagne and put the glass down with a sense of finality. "As much as I could discuss this all night long, I'm tired and would like to sleep in tomorrow."

"Of course," said Luisa, a little deflated. "You must live your life." She waved her hand in a fluttery manner at the waiter. He immediately understood the universal language of a mimed signature on the check. "Buona notte, Alex." Luisa brushed her lips against Alex's cheek. "Happy birthday, darling." Luisa hugged Rick.

Driving back to Sunset Cove, Alex kept his eyes on the road. He feared the rage simmering in Rick's chest. After parking in the dunes, Rick jumped out and slammed the door. He leaned on the car, trying to calm his breathing. "See what it's like? What she's like. And do you know what the kicker is?"

"What?" Alex draped his arm around Rick in an effort to calm him as they walked to the house.

"This news of hers has me wondering if that's why the producers are so keen to have me in their new show. Maybe they never wanted *me* at all but just as a lure to reel her in."

"Don't think of that way."

"I bet that big mouthed extra shooting off her yap was how the producers found out who momma is."

"It's not exactly classified information, is it? There's still a bit of your birthday left. You may get one more present tonight." Trying to make the evening end well, Alex dragged Rick into the house and up to bed.

Halfway up the stairs, Rick withdrew. "Do you think you can use sex to distract me from my anger?"

"Worth trying."

"The way I'm feeling right now you may have to try very hard."

Alex smiled and reached out to Rick's crotch "I'll work on it ..."

A clap of thunder jerked Alex back into the present. He saw Rick turn in bed and his eyes flicker open. "Some night, huh?" he asked Rick.

Rick blinked sleep from his eyes and half-laughed, half-coughed. "Yeah, happy fucking birthday to me."

"Coffee?"

Yawning, Rick rubbed his face awake. "Wait a minute, I'll go down and put it on."

"Stay. Take it easy, you only went to sleep a couple of hours ago." Alex pulled on his boxers. Padding downstairs, he reached the bottom just as the phone rang.

"If that's momma, tell her I'm dead!" Rick yelled down.

"What shall I say was the cause?" Alex yelled back up.

"Suffocating love!"

Picking up the phone, Alex answered, "Y'ello?" A moment of high pitched indecipherable speech on the other end afforded him the time to work out who was calling. "Yumi, good morning." Through the half fug of sleep, last night's champagne and the ache in his shoulder from handling the sails, he deciphered enough of Yumi's speech to fill in the parts he couldn't understand. She'd sold two of his paintings to people who'd been at Monica's auction. Even better was the amount of the check she was mailing him. "Twelve hundred and fifty dollars?" he repeatedly incredulously.

"Whaaat? I gotta make commission!" Yumi screeched down the phone. "You not one of them greedy bastards, is you?"

"I didn't mean it that way, Yumi. I was surprised that you got so much."

Yumi relaxed and chuckled. "When you get bigger name, you get bigger price. Then I sell you to the name fuckers. What else you got? I can take more of your work."

Alex scratched his head. "I'll have a look."

"Next week, come see me."

"Well okay, but I don't know what I'd bring to show you, all my work's here. Say, why don't you come to Sunset Cove so you can see everything? If you don't want to drive here, I can pick you up?"

"I come to you. But I take cab. I seen your car. I be there Saturday. Noon." With no further pleasantries, Yumi hung up.

Slightly stunned by the bizarre interaction and abrupt end to the call, Alex was still holding the phone in midair when a creak on the stairs alerted him to Rick coming down. "I told you to stay in bed!" barked Alex putting the phone down on the cradle.

"I couldn't get back to sleep." Rick went into the kitchen, huddled the beige cotton robe around himself and sat at the kitchen table. Alex lit the gas. Rick crossed his hands on the table, laid his head on them and muttered, "I'm not going to do it."

"Create nuclear fission? Cross the Arctic? Clue would be helpful," said Alex adjusting the flame under the pot.

"The T.V. show. I mean, do you think they want to make me and momma into some kind of macabre double act? You know, like teaming up Cheryl Crane with Lana Turner."

"Who the fuck's Cheryl Crane? Listen, Luisa only said they were interested in her for the part. Interested isn't an offer, is it?" The pot whistled, and Alex took it off the heat.

"I guess."

"Hey, that was Yumi on the horn. She's sold two of my paintings." Alex poured two cups of steaming coffee. "She's coming here to see if there's anything else she's interested in."

"Terrific. I'll give up work and you can be the breadwinner."

Alex's hand hovered over the pot. "Say what?"

"Kidding."

They carried on talking, but Alex's head wasn't present. Rick's off the cuff comment had set his mind whirring. Was that what they were now, a couple discussing who makes the money? Honestly, money wasn't a big issue for him - enough to get by was all that mattered - but that was for himself. Rick was accustomed to a lavish lifestyle. However vigorously he professed he could be happy with nothing, in reality would Rick be able to live from hand to mouth like Hank and Kaori?

"So, do you think I should?"

Alex became aware Rick was hanging on an answer to an unknown question. He screwed up his eyes, "Um ..."

"You're weren't listening, were you?"

"Honestly babe, no."

"Should I go see momma and tell her how I feel? That I'd rather rip off my right arm and hit myself over the head with it than have to act with her every day."

"You're overreacting."

"Overreacting?" Rick snorted. "Notice how she took back the deeds after I said I wasn't seeing Danielle. Guess this means I don't get the palazzo."

"Do you need the palazzo? Do you want the palazzo?"

"That's not the point."

"You're totally fucked up." Alex kissed the top of Rick's head.

"You're fucked up too." Rick grabbed his hand and gently squeezed it.

"See? We got stuff in common. Now, I'm going to do some work. Me man. Me make art." Alex thumped his chest caveman style, went into his studio and lost himself in the memory painting of Rick on the beach.

♦ ♦ ♦

Holding a brush and trailing it across the canvas had filled Alex's last few days. Rick had grown as silent as the boy in the painting he was working on. A phone call from Rick's agent asking for a meeting had triggered an even deeper depression in him. Rick had brooded for a full twenty-four hours before announcing over breakfast, "I'll break the news to Mike today that I'm turning down the show. It all feels wrong."

"But you don't know even they've offered Luisa the part?" reasoned Alex.

"She's taken a suite at the Beverly Wilshire for a couple of months, she obviously plans on sticking around. If she hasn't already got the part, she must have a pretty strong suspicion she will."

"You'll be turning down a featured role that could make your career. Don't make any rash decisions." Alex picked up the mail off the counter.

"I'm willing to pay the price. All those pep talks about 'lifestyle' and morality clauses combined with the thought of spending every day on set with momma's a total downer. If they offered me the part because they think I'm a good actor then something else will come up. And if they only want me as a sideshow attraction alongside momma then its better I should turn it down."

"Up to you. You're a big boy." Alex ripped open an envelope. He read the enclosed card, flipped it over, turned it back and read it again. "We've been invited to an exhibit of performance art." He skimmed the card to Rick.

Rick caught the card and read it out loud. "*The Interrupted Journey – An evening where fate intervenes.*"

"Kaori's performance art piece. It appears they've thrown open the taping." Alex took the card back. "Nice artwork on the invite." Indeed, the invitation was very professional and felt expensive. Perhaps some of the five hundred bucks he'd given them had gone on it. "You up for it?"

"When is it?"

"Saturday night."

"Sure." Rick picked up his car keys and left to see his agent.

If Rick's mood had been dark when he left for the meeting, it was pure black when he arrived home. He slammed his car keys on the kitchen table.

"Guess Mike didn't take your decision well?" asked Alex.

"I can't turn it down!"

"What do you mean?"

"The option on the contract wasn't for more segments on just the one show, it includes any other show they produce. I can't turn down *Legal Eagles*. If I do I'll be in breach of contract and they can sue me."

"Call Bob, he can look at it."

"There's no point. It's a watertight contract and I signed it. I've been summoned to Universal tomorrow to read with the potential female lead for the law professor role. Guess who my scene partner is?"

"I'd love to say I've no idea."

"Watching Kaori's cardboard bus catch fire will be this week's highlight." Rick swept his hand through his hair with frustration.

"Look on the bright side, maybe Luisa will choke in front of the cameras? She's gone on record to say she's renounced acting."

"Life doesn't dole our favors like that."

"We can live in hope." Alex rubbed his shoulder which was aching badly again.

"You okay?" Rick asked with concern.

"I can't shake off this pain. I had to quit painting this afternoon because it was bugging me so bad."

"Here, let me help. Sit down."

Alex complied with Rick's request.

Rick knelt on the couch next to him and began to knead his trapezius and deltoids.

Alex flinched.

"Is it that painful?"

"If you were trying to get state secrets out of me I'd crack after ten minutes."

"You've mentioned pain in your arms and shoulders for as long as I've known you. You need to get it checked out."

"X-rays and tests are expensive. It's nothing."

"If I'm going to be condemned to the treadmill of episodic T.V. and bowing to my family's will, we should at least get something out of it. I'll call dad and ask him to get you into that doctor who fixed me up."

"I hate doctors."

"Shut up. You've got something wrong with you. Let's find out what it is while we have the means."

Rick's hands on his muscles kept sending shock waves of pain through his joints. What the hell, although a trip to the see the doctor was the last thing Alex wanted, maybe it was time to face facts and try to put things right.

♦ ♦ ♦

"My God, where are the violets? Where the hell are my goddamn violets?" Scotty's voice was seized with panic. Frantically she bustled around, dipping into the already packed crates.

Calmly, Alex consulted the list on the clipboard. "Crate twenty, in with the orchids. Stop worrying! Everything's accounted for."

Scotty hustled over to crate twenty, gasping with relief when she discovered the violet painting safely packed away. "I'm so nervous it's unreal. I know my exhibition isn't for another three weeks, but only when my work's arrived at LaFonte's can I relax. That guy letting me down with the Wagner's delivery freaked me out. I need to double check the people who packed these for me have done it correctly and everything's secure. Thanks for offering to help."

"Happy to."

"What time's your appointment?"

"In an hour."

Scotty put the lid on the crate and picked up the hammer.

"I'll do that. You finish checking." Alex took the hammer from her.

Scotty resisted giving it to him. "You're not doing anything until we hear what the doctor says about your shoulders."

"That's why I hate doctors. You only have to mention you're seeing a physician and everyone's got you pegged as on the way out. It'll be nothing. Give me that." Alex grabbed the hammer in a manner that brooked no resistance. "Put a lid on it."

Scotty shuffled the lid onto the crate, then handed him the nails. She double checked the packing list while he hammered down the lid. "By the way, I got an invitation to Kaori's performance piece in the mail."

"You going?" Alex resumed nailing the lid to the crate.

"Performance art's not my bag. But I don't think many people will show up and she's gone to a lot of trouble with the invites. It's only loyal I make the effort. You and Rick are going, right?"

"Unless the tension around the T.V. show and his mother push him over the edge."

"I still can't believe she's here *and* you've met her. What I wouldn't give to spend a couple of hours with her. I could soak in all her knowledge of the European art scene. Does an aura of gravitas and power radiate from her?"

Whack!

Alex hammered in the final nail and laid down the hammer. "She radiates something, but I couldn't confirm it as that."

"But she was okay with you? You know, after Rick told her about you two?"

"Okay ... ish. I don't think the news made her summer complete, but her head didn't spin around and spit fire. Don't know why Rick's quite so angry with her."

"Most people paint their parents as monsters. Then when you meet them, adult to adult, they're usually okay. I think kids overdo how badly their parents treat them." Alex dropped his head. Almost immediately Scotty put her hand to her mouth. "Oh Alex, I know what your father put you through. I didn't mean that about you."

"You're probably right. Dad had his pals, co-workers, people he must have been able to interact with decently. Even my older sister was spared that side of him, she never believed what he put me through. Guess it was my bad luck to become the focus of his rage after mom died." He shrugged. "Or maybe he just instinctively hated me for something about myself. There's no law that says a parent has to like their child, is there?"

"There's no law forcing kids to love their parents either. But my god, Rick has a movie producer multi-millionaire father, an ex-movie star fabulously wealthy mother and he's still not happy. And here's little old me, the progeny of Mick and Niamh Scott, a Chicago stock man and a schoolteacher who couldn't afford to buy me a bed until I was four."

"What'd they do? Hang you in the closet like a salami?"

"A bed of my own, dum dum. Once I was out of the crib I had to share a bed with my older sister. Ma and pa struggle to get by even today. I'm glad I can send them money every now and then. My dream, if the exhibition goes well, would be to pay off their house so they don't have to worry for the rest of their lives." Scotty smiled, thinking about it. "Maybe even buy them a place on the lake one day."

"Hey, gotta run." Alex picked up the hammer. "Finish checking the inventory and I'll close the rest of these babies."

Scotty nodded. "Yeah, then I'll cross my fingers LaFonte makes a decent job of hanging them. I need to make sales. Ma and pa's retirement depends on it."

♦ ♦ ♦

The doctor's office was plush and calm. Sid, or more likely Shirley, had done their research and booked him in with a Doctor Svenson who specialized in connective tissue injuries.

With Alex's shirt off, Svenson probed his chest and prodded and manipulated his arms. Alex expected the next step to be an x-ray or some such, but instead the doctor told him to put his shirt back on and ordered a range of blood tests. Once the samples had been taken, he was back on the road to Sunset Cove with no answers, only a bruised left arm from the ham-fisted nurse who drew the blood. The anti-climax of no diagnosis was a downer. Driving past the back of the house, he figured his mood was unlikely to lift. Luisa's rental was parked alongside Rick's car up in the dunes. Alex steeled himself to face news of their meeting at Universal and the family situation in the house. Pots and pans were being rattled in the kitchen. That was a good sign, they obviously hadn't killed each other yet. Alex pondered what expression to wear on his face as he walked in the door.

"... darling, nonna never used as much garlic as you do. And this is how you should stir, otherwise you bruise the tomatoes." Luisa was bent over the range, stirring the pot.

Rick sat at the table drumming his fingers. As Alex walked in, Rick rolled his eyes and tossed his head in Luisa's direction, blinking slowly in frustration.

"Watch how momma does it, darling. You need simpatico. You cannot bully the meal into existence ..." Luisa glanced behind her and saw Alex closing the door. "The man of the house returns!" Luisa tossed him a brief but winsome smile before carrying on cooking.

"You okay?" Alex asked Rick quietly.

"You've been doing it all wrong," said Luisa while tossing salt into the pot. "Come watch, see how momma does it."

"In a minute. I need to talk to Alex," said Rick getting up.

Luisa rested the wooden spoon on a dish. Stepping back, she wiped her hands on a towel then fiercely slapped her palms on the table. "The kitchen table is the place for *family* talk." Luisa fixed Alex with a piercing stare. "Alex, sit here. You and Rick talk while momma cooks. No secrets."

Expecting Alex to bow to Luisa's command, Rick resignedly sat back down at the table.

"You're right." Alex nodded at Luisa. "And we will do just as you say. We'll talk round the table like family."

A flash of triumph crossed Luisa's face. "Bene."

"Over dinner. Because right now I desperately need a cigarette and I never smoke in the house. We'll pick this up in a minute," said Alex decisively. "And by the way, dinner smells great. I can tell where Rick gets his talent." Picking up his lighter and cigarettes, Alex went out to the verandah. He heard Rick's chair scrape back from the table and his feet chase after him. On the deck, Alex lit up and inhaled.

Rick came out. He let the front door swing shut and bang into the frame. "What did the doctor say?" asked Rick with concern.

Peeling off the small round Band Aid, Alex showed Rick the massive bruise on his inner elbow. "Apart from a nurse who took the bloods with a fork and spoon, it was fine. The doctor couldn't detect anything immediately wrong with the joints or muscles. It's likely to be rheumatological. We'll have to see what the results come back with. Talking of blood and pain, how'd your day go?"

"It was fine. Actually, the reading went great. I must admit, momma's a terrific actress. Once we'd got into the scene and were playing it as our characters, for one moment there I forgot she was my mother. It was quite therapeutic. She certainly brought power to the role. She played it as a cross between Sophia Loren and Mussolini."

Alex chuckled. "Maybe everything will work out all right?"

"Perhaps. And the funniest thing happened. Coming out of the Black Tower, we ran into Rosemarie Rodgers going into the commissary. Apparently they know each other from the way back when."

"Small world." Alex picked a stray piece of tobacco off his tongue and flicked it away.

"Rosemarie was very effusive in your praise to momma. She told Luisa she thinks you're quite the artist."

"How'd Luisa react?"

"She said she didn't have an opinion as she hadn't really looked at your work. Momma's taken the news about us better than I could have hoped. She must have mellowed in her old age.

Maybe the thought of being back in front of the camera's softened her."

"Perhaps."

The clump of platform shoes inside alerted them that Luisa was on her way out. The front door creaked open a little. "Darling, help momma." Rick leapt to open the door fully. Luisa edged her way out, the stems of three glasses in one hand and a bottle of champagne in her other. She handed the bottle to Alex. "Is the custom, the man of the house opens the wine."

Alex stubbed out his cigarette in the tin can lid and took the bottle. He read the label, Piper Heidsieck - and chilled to perfection. He glanced at Rick. "Did we have this in the refrigerator?"

Luisa set down the glasses. "Stupido! I bring this with me to celebrate. Open it now. Hurry, before the sun sets!"

Alex complied. He removed the foil, untwisted the wire cradle and set it aside. Then, recalling the wine waiter's technique at The Sands, gripped the cork in one hand while carefully, almost sensually, twisting the bottle with his other. When he felt the pressure start to escape he controlled the cork, easing it out gently. A small *pop* ensued. Pausing a second, to let the contents settle, he twisted the cork and removed it. He extended a hand to Luisa. "Glass?" Luisa nodded in admiration and handed him one. Alex poured with confidence. Slowly. Gently. He offered the glass to Luisa.

Luisa kept him under her watchful eye as he poured two more perfect glasses. "You know your way around champagne, Alex."

"One turns one's hand," he said with a confident smile.

"I propose a toast." Luisa raised her glass. "To the industry that brought my son back to me. To Hollywood."

"To Hollywood." Rick and Alex repeated as they clinked glasses with her.

"And to a man I need to get better acquainted with, but who I already see has made my son happier than I could have imagined. Dear Alex, I salute you." Luisa raised her glass again. Rick warily chinked his glass with hers.

Alex ran his tongue around his teeth wondering if Luisa's positivity carried a codicil, but she remained all smiles. The sunset was stunning. Luisa and Rick continued their superficial cocktail party chatter. Their rapprochement made Alex uneasy. There was too much champagne around of late for his taste. Once the sun had dropped below the horizon, Luisa returned to the kitchen. Half an hour later she summoned them to the table. Luisa's food was impeccable, maybe Rick did overdo the garlic and bruise the tomatoes. Even more admirable was the fact she'd prepared, cooked and served dinner whilst dressed in cream cashmere without an apron. The dinner conversation was relaxed, although Luisa dominated it with her machinations to sway the Venice Biennale committee from its current Communist leanings and ways to acquire funds to renovate its dilapidated pavilions. She asked Alex for his views on certain artists and delved into the ethos behind his own work. Luisa listened intently to his answers, making no arch comments or skeptical facial expressions, which pleasantly surprised him again.

Luisa stifled a yawn. "Is very late. I must make the drive back to the city. The hotel is adequate, but I should find an apartment of my own." Luisa patted Rick's hand. "If they offer me the part on the show, that is. And there is much happening in the art world here. Perhaps I did not take Los Angeles as seriously as I should." She flicked her eyes at Alex then shook her head. "I sense there are Americans who appreciate art on almost as high a level as we do in Europe. Maybe I should open a gallery of my own here to help educate them even more?"

"Like you said momma, it's late. We need to get you on the road," said Rick.

Luisa stood up. She wavered slightly.

"You should stay here tonight," said Alex impulsively.

Rick shot him a sidelong glare.

"But I've nothing with me," said Luisa.

"That's right," cut in Rick. "You can't sleep without your nightly ritual, can you?"

"That is true. But I am tired." Luisa touched her hand to her head. "And maybe a little too much of the champagne."

"Correct," confirmed Alex. "And we wouldn't want you to have an accident."

Rick pursed his lips with that 'speak for yourself' look on his face.

"As long as you're sure it is no inconvenience?" Luisa fluttered her hand around her throat, checking with Rick for his approval, which consisted of a reluctant grunt. "The couch will be fine, you do not need to give up your room."

"I sleep upstairs." Rick stared at Luisa. "With Alex."

"That's what I mean! I wouldn't want you both to be uncomfortable."

"Here." Alex beckoned Luisa. "This used to be my grandmother's room. The sheets are fresh."

Luisa scanned the room. "Most pleasant. Oh yes, it will do."

"Great." Rick scooted behind Alex on his way to the stairs, discretely squeezing his butt as he went. "Buona notte, momma."

"A domani, darling," Luisa called out as Rick went upstairs.

Alex jabbed his thumb over his shoulder at the bathroom. "There are fresh towels on the rack behind the tub." Leaving Luisa to settle herself in the guest room, he followed Rick up the stairs.

"What the fuck were you thinking of?" hissed Rick upstairs, pulling off his shirt, undoing his belt and kicking off his shoes.

"She's been drinking and it's late. We can't let her drive at this time of night," whispered Alex rummaging in one of the chifforobe's bottom drawers.

"I could," muttered Rick shucking off his pants and underwear. He jumped into bed and pulled the sheets up to his chin. "It's downright creepy having *her* downstairs."

Alex stepped back, a floral nightgown and robe in his hands. "Dora's," he explained on seeing Rick's quizzical glance. They were pale pink with little rosebuds and an apricot ribbon trim.

"Nice thought." Rick snuggled down into the bed. "Toss them into her room with some raw meat, lock the door and come to bed."

Alex sighed at Rick's juvenile protestations about his mother. He carried the nightclothes downstairs and tapped on her door. "Luisa, you okay?"

Luisa opened the door a wedge and peered around the crack. "Si, si."

"Thought these may help, seeing as you don't have anything with you." Alex offered the nightie and robe. "They're far from your style, but they're flannel and warm. This room gets kinda chilly in the middle of the night."

Luisa accepted them. She placed the robe on the bed and fluffed out the nightgown. "Very pretty."

"My grandmother's. This was her house."

"Thank you for these. And for inviting me to stay. You are most kind," said Luisa.

"Fine, I'll leave you to it. Goodnight."

Luisa nodded and shut the door.

Alex couldn't quite face going up to bed. This would be a good night for a joint but not a great idea with Luisa in the house, he didn't want her to suspect he was a dope fiend leading her son astray. Alex picked up the whiskey bottle and a glass and took them onto the verandah. He undid his shirt and let it flap open. The nighttime sea breeze fanned his sweaty chest. He unbuttoned the waistband of his pants, flopped on the sagging gray couch and poured a glass. Savoring the whiskey on his tongue, he heard Luisa's door click open and her bare feet pad across the living room. Alex got up, swung open the front door and leaned inside. "Need something?"

Luisa was at the foot of the stairs, staring up inquisitively. She jumped upon seeing him in the doorway. "See, a perfect fit." Luisa extended her arms for approval like a small child at a dance class.

Alex found it very odd seeing Luisa dressed in Dora's floral robe and nightgown. She'd belted the robe tightly, flipped up the nightgown's collar and rolled up the sleeves on both. No-one could accuse Luisa D'Onofrio of not having style.

"I didn't mean to disturb you. I was getting water." Luisa's eyes fell on the whiskey glass in his hand.

"Nightcap?"

"Why not? I have nowhere to go thanks to you."

Alex grabbed another tumbler from the kitchen. Luisa went into her room and came out onto the deck carrying a blanket.

Alex poured the whiskey and passed Luisa a glass as she settled beside him. "Cheers."

Luisa sipped her whiskey. Tucking up her ankles onto the couch, she covered her legs and bare feet with the blanket. "Forgive me."

"What for?"

"I confess I was shocked by this revelation of my son's lifestyle." Luisa glanced upstairs. "No, shocked is not the right word. Disappointed is more accurate."

Alex instinctively recoiled.

Luisa noticed. She quickly added, "Not disappointed in his choice of you. I do not mean that at all. I mean disappointed how this path will deny him certain things. For example, marriage and children. I worry it will bring a lonely life to him."

Alex sipped his whiskey and leaned back, it was too late at night to get into this. "Who knows what life will bring to any of us?"

"Si, si, very true. At any moment an earthquake could wipe California off the map. Then where would we be?"

"In the ocean?" said Alex laughing with a black humor.

Following his lead, Luisa laughed too. Seemingly his comment had genuinely amused her.

Alex became aware that his shirt had fallen open and Luisa's amber eyes were on his bare chest. He shifted on the couch as if to get more comfortable, in the process tugging his shirt fronts together.

Luisa giggled coquettishly as he fastened a button. "I apologize if I embarrass you. I find it hard to look away from beauty. The world's greatest art celebrates the male form, no?"

"I guess."

"Have you always been ... I hope you do not mind my asking ... have you always been a homosexual?"

Alex took a deep breath, he really regretted offering her this late night drink. "I wouldn't use that as the primary word to describe myself."

Luisa wriggled closer on the couch, snaked out her arm and rested her hand on his shoulder. "You have experience of women?"

"Yeah." Alex picked up the bottle and topped up his glass. "You?"

Luisa was momentarily confused, then realized he meant another drink. "As you say in the U.S.A., hit me!"

Alex filled her glass ... generously filled it, hoping if she drank enough she'd pass out.

"I often wonder about men." Luisa swirled the whiskey. "A woman grows older and finds herself less appealing to them. Young men that is. Nothing compares to the hard muscle and sexual stamina of the young man. But I accept young men no longer find me attractive. If I ever wish to feel a young man's touch again I may need to pay for it. Is easy for a woman to make love for payment, she only needs to be receptive. But as for a man, a man has to perform, he has to be active, no? Back in Italy, I sometimes see them on the beach ..."

Alex shook his head in befuddlement, the whiskey and the conversation were making him nauseous. "Who?"

"Gigolos. Men with handsome faces and bulging muscles. They spend their days in search of lonely women. Apparently a gigolo spots the single women on the beach by a patch of red sunburn in the middle of their back. You see, the center of the back is the one part of the body where a woman finds it hard to apply sun cream when alone. Clever, don't you think?"

"Learn something new every day." Alex drained his glass.

"But after a man of this type finds his client, I ask myself, how does he make love to a woman he does not find attractive? Or a man, for that matter. These boys are versatile, they turn their hand to anyone for the right payment. Does the money alone stoke their desire? Is that what, forgive my crudity, gets their cocks hard?" Luisa stroked his arm. "You're very handsome, Alex. I can see why my son would fall for you. But I could give you so much more than him. I could grant you access to the most powerful people in the art world. I could make your career. I could make you a star. I've money too, more money than you could imagine." Luisa traced her maroon nail along his forearm.

Alex gently took his arm away. "I'll leave this here if you want more." Alex put the bottle down next to her. "Sleep well."

Luisa parted her lips and ran the tip of her tongue around them. "Think about it."

Looking at Rick's mother dressed in Dora's nightgown and robe while accusing and seducing him in the same breath turned his stomach. He walked calmly into the house. But once safely inside, he dove into the bathroom and vomited. He dragged himself upstairs to bed, hoping Luisa remained outside and he wouldn't have to encounter her again.

THE INTERRUPTED JOURNEY

She'd left her cab with its meter running up in the dunes, obviously wanting to be in and out of this alien territory as fast as possible. She'd teetered over the uneven track down to the beach house on her five-inch platform heels like the first woman to step on the moon. "Is too quiet here!" screeched Yumi coming into his studio. "Is good preparation for death."

"Many people come to Sunset Cove in search of peace," Alex had replied with a smile as he showed her his work. Yumi regarded him like he was insane. It was clear she was a city girl. Alex positioned the last of the cliff studies on the easel in his studio and said, "Anyway, these are the rest of the *Cliffs of Mendocino* series."

"Nice. Commercial. You capture nature good." Yumi leaned into the canvas. "Is like you smell the sea spray off the canvas."

Alex resisted saying this was more likely due to actually being beside the sea rather than his artwork's finesse and graciously accepted her compliment.

"I take these. What else, what else?" Yumi checked her starkly utilitarian red plastic watch. "What those?" Yumi pointed at the downtown paintings leaning against the wall.

"Just some experimental work. They're not good enough to sell."

"Show me, show me. I decide. Quick!"

Obeying orders Alex removed the cliffs. Rapidly, he placed one after the other of the downtown plein airs on the easel. He genuinely had been doing these as an exercise. He was astounded when Yumi got progressively more excited as each new piece went up. "I never seen work like it. This town ugly but you make it artistic ugly. I take all these. How you feel if I can get you a commission along this line?"

Alex's head was spinning, he'd never dreamed Yumi would be so enthusiastic. "It would be great."

"I got client opening new hotel. He looking to put art in foyer. He ask for abstract, but these give me idea to sell him this look. Inner city. Gritty. Real, but with glamor. They gotta be big paintings, though. You can do big?"

"Sure can."

"I get these paintings pick up later in week. I take my cab fare out your fee." Yumi cackled, "Ha, a hundred bucks you can afford. I get you good deal on hotel job." Yumi prepared her hasty escape. She grabbed her bag, her dark glasses and her sun parasol to protect her face on the short walk to the dunes. Stepping out of the back door, she put up her sunshade and asked as an afterthought, "How come you know this Luisa woman?"

Her question caught Alex off guard. "She's my roommate's mother. Why?"

"She come in my gallery. Want me to show her your work and ask all kind of personal question how I know you and what I think of you."

Alex's esophagus cramped. "What kind of questions?"

"All kind. Bossy lady. She may be big noise in Italy but she nobody to me. No-one tell me who I can and cannot sell."

"She told you not to sell my work?"

"Not in so many word, but that what she mean."

"I don't know why she'd do that."

"Fuck her. She got strong feeling about you. Strong feeling about artist is good."

"Even if it's negative?"

"Even better! It mean you get reaction. Only bad thing in art is when no-one notice it."

Watching Yumi, with her clumpy shoes and dainty parasol, teetering to her cab, Alex was relieved this tiny spitfire of a woman hadn't let Luisa rattle her. In fact, Luisa's visit seemed only to have fired Yumi's enthusiasm for his work. In his wildest dreams of becoming a successful artist it had never occurred to him someone may ever want to sabotage his career.

♦ ♦ ♦

"Thank you, sir. You're in seat twenty-three E over the wing. Please stand on the line while I take your photo for the passenger manifest." A blue flash of light was followed by the Polaroid camera's whirr spitting out the print. "Please proceed to the departure lounge." The young woman dressed as a stewardess tweaked her purple chiffon neckerchief. She extended her hand, indicating Alex, Rick and Scotty should go to the rear of Hank's studio.

"I thought Kaori was setting a bus on fire, not a plane," said Scotty as they walked through.

"Seems we've been upgraded," muttered Rick.

"I can't believe how many people turned up," whispered Scotty taking in the buzzing gallery. "There's LaFonte with Monica Aigner." She jerked her head towards a tall man sipping white wine from a plastic cup. He had a sandy bouffant hairdo, very coiffured, and was wearing a red velvet jacket and flared pants with a frilly white jabot shirt. Monica, in a Pepto-Bismol pink tweed two-piece, was nodding vigorously at everything he said.

"So that's LaFonte? Did he join The Partridge Family?" said Rick with a snicker.

Scotty stifled a laugh. Alex didn't get the joke. While she and Rick continued to titter about LaFonte's outfit, Alex scanned the faces in the crowd. Scotty was correct, it was an incredible turnout. He spied Hank dodging through people towards them. He'd tied his long hair back and slicked down the sides. Dressed in a smart open necked black shirt and fitted black pants, it was the most pulled together Alex had ever seen him.

"Taking a walk on the wild side, huh?" Hank greeted Scotty. "You packing heat?"

"I leave that to Bob," laughed Scotty.

"Where is the man?" asked Hank.

"Had a meeting he couldn't cancel," explained Scotty nonchalantly flicking back her hair.

"That's rough on a Saturday night. Anyway, great to see you. And you guys too," said Hank to Rick and Alex.

"It's not every day you get invited to a plane crash," Rick replied pleasantly.

"Yeah, what's gone down with that? Kaori was setting a bus on fire when we last met," said Alex.

Hank and Kaori had cleared the living space in the studio's rear and opened up the concertina doors that usually shut it off. Through the open windows, the large cardboard recreation of a plane's fuselage was visible in the concrete courtyard. "Come, take a closer look," said Hank guiding them through the crowd. The model plane was raised off the ground on metal trestles. The fuselage's top was open revealing the different class compartments with rows of cardboard seats inside. A cockpit with wraparound Perspex windows sat at the front. "Kaori suspected people wouldn't vibe with a bus, too low key. These guys," said Hank giving a fleeting look to the wine sipping art lovers, "travel by plane all the time. She wanted this piece to be relatable. A bus wouldn't cut it."

"This shebang's taken some organization and money," said Alex.

Hank huffed gazing skyward. "You know how much Polaroid film and flash bulbs cost? We got eighty seats on the plane plus seven crew. So that's eighty-seven photos if everyone who got sent an invitation shows."

As Hank spoke a flash from the front of the studio caught Scotty's attention. "You mean you're photographing everyone who turns up?"

"Correct, and all the crew helping on the show. Kaori wants everyone to have an investment in the piece's outcome. Here's how it works ... when you arrive one of the crew takes your photo. Then they cut out the face, stick it on a paper doll and write your name on the back. Then we put the dolls in your allocated seats on the plane. Scoop and two of his students are filming the boarding."

Looking outside they observed Scoop, also dressed entirely in black, craning his video camera into the plane's interior. One of his students was settling the dolls in their numbered seats and checking their names on a list.

"Isn't setting that thing on fire in a confined space dangerous?" Scotty asked furrowing her brow.

"We got fire extinguishers on standby. But we won't use them unless we really have to. The storyline is that after an in-flight emergency the plane makes a crash landing. Everyone thinks they're safe, but there's a fuel leak. A random spark leads to the fire. Kaori wants the piece to function on several levels. It's a comment on capitalism, how profit's more important than human life. It's also about our codependency on oil, she sees our country as fuel addicted and likely to kill itself from an overdose. But more than anything else, she wants it to be about fate. On the stroke of eight, Kaori sets the plane alight. Then it's all down to chance. The wind could blow the fire out instantly, or maybe it'll rain and douse it, or the plane may not catch fire at all. Whatever, we let the fire run its course. When it's damped down we'll do a tally of any dolls that aren't burned. We consider them the survivors. On the way out a list will tell people if they're a survivor or a fatality."

"That's something to look forward to. Anyone else for a drink?" asked Rick merrily.

"Help yourselves. We've set up a bar over there," said Hank.

"Where's Kaori?" Alex asked Hank as Scotty and Rick scuttled to the bar. "She okay?"

"She's real nervous. She's taking a rest before coming out front."

"I meant about the baby."

"Nearly baked, ready to pop in a couple of months." They stood silently for a minute watching people gather to look at the plane outside.

"Last call for boarding, the gate will close in five minutes," came the stewardess's voice over the loudspeaker system.

"If anyone hasn't arrived by then, they don't get in," said Hank. "Once the plane's doors are shut there's no going back. Looks like Koenig's a no show. Still, it's great LaFonte came."

"You went to town with the invitations," said Alex.

"Took a leaf out of your book. We want the right people to know our name. Having a kid to raise means we need to make some serious moolah." Hank dropped his head and scuffed the grubby concrete floor with his boot. "Look man, about that cash you laid on us. We kind of used it for this. An investment in the kid's future, you know?"

"It was a gift to help you in any way."

"We're grateful, man." Hank bumped his fist to Alex's.

"Kaori's desire to raise involvement certainly worked," said Scotty arriving back with wine in hand. "There's definitely an air of expectation in the room."

"And fear," added Rick with a grin.

"I said hi to LaFonte," said Scotty in between sips of wine. "He's completely bummed they seated him in economy."

Rick smirked. "He ought to be more concerned about his hairspray's flammability."

Hank laughed along with Rick. As the four of them chatted, Alex became aware of Monica looking in his direction. He smiled at her, but she must not have seen for she turned her attention back to LaFonte without reciprocating.

"Last call, last call for boarding," announced the voice over the tannoy.

Hank glanced at the gallery's street doors, two people were hustling in at the last moment. One of the girls playing a stewardess shut the front doors, then rushed to help the other stewardess finish check-in. The two latecomers lingered in the gloomy frontage for a moment to look at Hank's car man sculptures. A couple of flashes followed as the final Polaroids were taken. "Cool, he did show. And he brought a guest," said Hank. The rest of the group followed Hank's eye-line.

"Ugh," uttered Rick throwing his head back in frustration.

"That's Koenig," said Scotty recognizing the man as he came closer. "Who's the woman?"

"None other than my dear old momma," said Rick draining his glass in one.

Alex hadn't seen Luisa since that weird night on the verandah. The next morning, she'd thankfully left before they came down. The only evidence she'd stayed was the neatly folded nightgown and robe on the bed. And, oddly, a crumpled twenty-dollar bill on the nightstand. Alex had kept the conversation with Luisa to himself, hoping he'd misinterpreted her drunken attempt to seduce him.

"Shit, she's seen us. Too late to make a run for it," muttered Rick.

"Darling, what a surprise to see you here." Luisa bent forward and greeted Rick with a double kiss. She was wearing a tailored black jacket and pants. Her caramel hair was scraped back into a chic pleat, maroon lipstick and ruby earrings completing her sophisticated look. It was blatantly obvious nothing was worn under her jacket, giving the room a display of her tanned cleavage every time she leaned forward.

"I could say the same thing," said Rick tartly.

"Walter took me to lunch and then invited me here. We were having such a delightful day we didn't want it to end." Luisa snuck a kittenish eye dip to Koenig, then said to Rick, "I know so little about performance art. I'm broadening my horizons. Aren't you proud of your momma? Isn't that what you want of me, to be open to new experiences?"

Noticing Rick's increasingly truculent expression, Koenig stepped in. "Ricardo, good to see you. It's wonderful Luisa finally graces us with her presence." Koenig warmly shook Rick's hand. He acknowledged Scotty with a curt smile, then turned to Alex. "I hear you found a champion in Yumi. I suspected your work may appeal to her."

"Yeah, she's already sold a couple of pieces. Thanks for the introduction," said Alex.

"It was naughty of you to confuse Walter in such a manner," Luisa said to Rick with a pout. "You made it sound like I was in town for the Weir opening. Imagine how disappointed he was to find that wasn't the case."

"Maybe someone passed the message on wrong?" said Rick coolly.

"Perhaps. Is so hot in here." Luisa ran her finger along the inside of her jacket's lapel. Possibly to let in air, possibly to show off more skin to anyone interested. "Darling, fetch momma a drink. And one for Walter too."

"I was off to the bar anyway. You want to give me a hand?" asked Rick turning to Alex.

"You don't need Alex's help, dear. As if you can't carry a few drinks on your own." Luisa pushed Rick away with such force he had no choice but to comply. Once he'd gone, Luisa turned to Alex. "It was rude of me to run off so suddenly after spending the night with you. I didn't get to say goodbye. Forgive me?"

"Don't mention it," said Alex really meaning it. "It was late when we'd finished dinner, so we asked Luisa to stay at the beach house rather than drive back to L.A.," Alex explained to Scotty and Koenig. Then he said to Luisa, "By the way, you left twenty dollars on the nightstand. I got it with me." He reached into his pocket and handed her a bill.

"That was no accident. It was for you, for services rendered," said Luisa coyly pushing his hand away. "I hear twenty dollars is the going rate."

Alex hardened his face as Scotty switched her attention between him and Luisa. Aware of the game Luisa was trying to play, he asked, "The going rate for what?"

Luisa laughed. "For the dry cleaning of the nightgown and robe you loaned me, of course. Such fine fabrics need tender care. Especially family heirlooms."

Koenig smiled warmly at her. "That's my Luisa, so considerate."

Alex tucked the twenty-dollar bill into Luisa's jacket pocket. "On the house. After all you did bring the champagne and cook for us. I had heartburn for a couple of days afterwards. Rich food obviously doesn't agree with me."

"And here was me thinking you were getting a taste for it," said Luisa with a hint of venom.

Alex didn't look away from her and maintained his smile.

"Sounds like you all had a cozy evening," commented Scotty to break the awkward silence.

Luisa tilted her head at Scotty, as if just noticing her.

"This is my friend Scotty," Alex said. For a moment he thought Scotty was going to curtsy to Luisa, thankfully she resisted the impulse.

"Luisa D'Onofrio, pleasure to meet you." Luisa smiled slyly at Alex. "A close friend?"

"A good friend. We went to art school together, along with Hank and Kaori. This is their studio, it's Kaori's piece we're seeing tonight," said Alex almost starting to enjoy this battle of wills with Luisa.

"You mean all the work on display in here is theirs?" Luisa pursed her lips.

"Hank does the stuff with the car parts and metal," explained Alex.

Luisa raised a hand to her sculpted clavicle. "They are superb! I am curating an exhibit in Florence about American influence on culture. His work would sit well in it. Solid. Dense. Simplistic, yet complex and brutally masculine."

"I'll make sure you meet him before you go." Alex wondered if introducing Hank to Luisa would be like introducing a bug to a praying mantis, but what the hell, anything to get himself out of her sightlines.

"Drink." Rick gracelessly shoved a plastic tumbler of wine under Luisa's nose. Utilizing a tad more civility Rick offered one to Koenig.

"Thank you, darling. Isn't this delicious? All meeting up out of the blue." Luisa took the wine from Rick. She sipped it, only making the slightest of grimaces on the first taste.

"Shh," hissed Rick to Luisa, "the plane crash is about to begin," then he firmly turned his back on her.

The lights dimmed; a few moments of darkness allowed the chatter to damp down.

"At seven p.m. Eastern Standard Time, flight one six five departs Boston Logan Airport," said Kaori's voice over the loudspeaker. A rustle of activity alerted the onlookers that something was moving in the room. A spotlight fell on a model plane above the heads of people at the back. As the crowd parted, everyone saw Kaori holding the model. She weaved through the crowd, the plane held high in one hand and a microphone in her other. "For the passengers and crew it's a routine flight, another ordinary day." Kaori paused in the center of the crowd, using the moment of silence to assert her authority; her crystal eyes connecting with as many people as possible. "You've all been given a seat number and your details put on boarding passes. Tonight, we are this flight's passengers and crew." An uncomfortable murmur passed through the room. Kaori, like Hank and Scoop, had dressed entirely in black, her kaftan dress not concealing her discernable baby bump. "We wake up every morning with expectations." Kaori tilted her head to the plane. "We expect to arrive at our destination. We expect to see the night. We expect to carry on living." Kaori lowered the model towards her pregnant belly. "But sometimes things happen we don't expect. Fate has something else in store. The pilots notice a vibration in the port wing. They shut down an engine. Ladies and gentlemen, we apologize for the inconvenience, we are turning back to Boston." Kaori lifted the plane again and walked through the audience. Scoop moved in to train his camera on the plane. "Cabin crew prepare for an emergency landing."

The two stewardesses stepped out of the crowd. They ceremoniously crossed their arms over their chests and began to chant, "Brace, brace, brace ..."

Kaori weaved through the onlookers, circling the model plane in the air, underscored by the rhythmic, "Brace, brace, brace," chanted by the stewardesses. Kaori gradually lowered the plane. Hank took the model off her and continued the plane's descent outside to the courtyard. Finally, Hank wheeled the model plane along the ground, bringing it to a halt before the model fuselage.

"All is well. Our plane has landed. We are safe." Kaori smiled as she stretched the microphone's lead out into the courtyard. "Or are we? Is there a plan to our lives, or is it all chance? We have cheated disaster, we are on the ground, but unknown to all fuel is leaking from the port wing." Like a witch stirring a cauldron, Kaori passed her hand over the fuselage loaded with paper dolls bearing their faces and identities.

"This is sick," someone blurted out with a half whisper.

"Shh." Several people quieted the dissenting voice.

"Has God smiled on us? Is fate on our side?" Kaori asked with a glint in her eye. Hank lit the taper with a cigarette lighter, the flame illuminating his face. Kaori stood beside Hank and ran a hand over her belly. "Do we spend sleepless nights worrying about those yet to be born? Do we worry about those who have passed? Is our only concern with ourselves, our own lives, our own desires, our own mortality. When you walk down the street, when you get in your automobile, when you get on a plane or lie in your bed, do you ever wonder if this could be the day that you die?"

The room grew uncannily still. All eyes riveted on the cardboard plane and its cargo of dolls.

Kaori's words had cast a dark spell. She continued, "A single spark then sets off an unstoppable chain of events. We are all together on this flight of life, bound together by invisible chains. Now we let fate take its course on this interrupted journey." Kaori took the flaming taper from Hank and held it above the cardboard fuselage. "Godspeed!" Kaori theatrically opened her hand, dropped the burning taper and lifted her palm. Taking a step back, Hank protectively wrapped her in his arms and moved her back from the plane.

Scoop and his two students hovered on the perimeter with their video cameras. The stewardesses continued to chant, "Brace, brace, brace," and picked up the fire extinguishers. The flame on the plane died almost instantly. A ripple of relief passed through the crowd, followed by a sigh of disappointment. This was a squib. A rumble of conversation began but was silenced when the flame caught hold. The fire surged with a *whoosh*! Within minutes, the flames had grown from inches to feet. Everyone craned forward, immediately invested in where their doll was seated on the plane.

The flames spread through the cardboard cabin, their red glow reflecting off the art lovers' faces inside. Alex blinked and shielded his face as a wave of heat stung his eyes. Rick turned to him, concern visible on his face. "They've got extinguishers," said Alex reassuringly.

"This whole night's weirding me out," whispered Rick.

Flakes of soot and charcoal whirled into the smoky air above the model plane. Scoop's students moved in for close-ups on the paper dolls being consumed by fire, their cut-out Polaroid faces curling and distorting in the heat. The rapidly growing blaze forced the cameramen to retreat.

"Oh god, it's out of control!" someone shouted, palpable fear in their voice.

A frisson of panic broke out in the rear of the studio.

Alex's focus moved to Kaori. There was an expression of fear on her face too. Kaori sought direction from Hank, he responded with a subtle nod, so much as to say, 'Let it go a bit longer'. The stewardesses had stopped chanting and flicked their eyes between Hank and Kaori, wondering what to do. When neither Hank nor Kaori gave the signal to put out the fire, the girls wavered, unsure whether they should break out the extinguishers without instruction. A couple of people hurried to the street doors and rattled them, trying to escape. Murmurs of disquiet turned to screams.

"Unlock the doors!" yelled a woman. "The doors are locked, we're trapped!"

"Call 911," screamed a man with a strangulated cry. "For God's sake let us out! We're all gonna die!"

"Stop! Stop this now!" Koenig broke free from the crowd.

With the subtlest of gestures, Hank tipped his head to the stewardesses. The girls immediately unleashed the fire extinguishers, directing the foam onto the cardboard plane. Within a few seconds the conflagration was under control. Dirty smoke replaced livid flames. Scoop and his students closed in with their video cameras to capture the fire's dying embers around the charred dolls. The flames had destroyed the plane's middle, but the front and rear were relatively unscathed.

A cool wave of night wind wafted through the gallery, heads turned to discover its source. People were confused, the front doors were now wide open. A murmur of disquiet passed from lips as everyone realized that the two people who'd screamed the doors were locked were the same two who'd just flung them open.

"Stooges," said Rick looking at the man and woman beside the front doors.

"Thank you for flying with us," said Kaori over the loudspeaker system. "We hope you continue your onward journey in safety. We apologize to anyone who misses their connection. But do not worry, fate will deliver you to your final destination in the end." Hank and the stewardesses surrounded Kaori in a flurry of activity, and in moments she'd been whisked out of sight.

A moment of stunned silence, then a single handclap started the applause.

The initial clap was nearby. Alex turned and saw Luisa had started the applause. Taking their cue from Luisa, the crowd followed her enthusiasm. The applause grew into an ovation. Koenig was truly rattled, his usually pristine white shirt rumpled and his tie pulled askew. Alex wondered if Kaori and Hank had designed this, to elicit such a reaction from a major player. It seemed the people who'd shouted that the doors were locked had been directed to ramp up the drama and generate fear. They'd had more than the desired effect on Rick, he was pale and trembling.

The stewardesses started passing through the gallery serving drinks from beverage carts. Hank was out the yard, sifting through the charred remains with a pair of barbecue tongs, extracting any dolls not totally incinerated.

"Can we leave?" asked Rick, his lips brushing Alex's ear. "I'm suffocating." He flicked his eyes at Luisa, whom Scotty was trying to engage in conversation.

"Rick, Alex, what an evening!" Monica's horse like teeth parted in a whinny.

"Yes, very ... dramatic." Alex struggled to find the right word to describe the event.

"And so relevant, don't you think?" Monica checked for agreement from Guy LaFonte, his white jabot dangling flaccidly behind her left shoulder.

"Certainly dramatic," said LaFonte with a slight lisp and Texan accent. "My little gallery openings will seem decidedly tame after this. And I thank the dear Lord for that!" He clapped a manicured hand to his chest.

Hearing LaFonte's distinctive voice, Scotty turned away from Luisa. "Guy, there you are. I saw you across the room earlier. Do you know Luisa D'Onofrio?"

"Only by reputation. I've not had the pleasure." Guy extended his hand to Luisa. "The Los Angeles art world is positively abuzz having you here. We are buzzing, are we not Monica?"

"Buzz, buzz, buzz!" brayed Monica with a flash of teeth and gums.

With a blank expression, Luisa considered Monica and Guy.

"This is Guy LaFonte. Owner of the LaFonte Gallery, my show's opening there next month. And Monica Aigner. One of our city's most knowledgeable and generous art patrons," Scotty said to Luisa. "And a very important collector."

"I gotta get out of here." Rick moved to go.

"We can't leave without congratulating Kaori," said Alex in a low voice. He grabbed a drink off a passing cart and handed it to Rick. "Here."

"Will you be gracing us with your presence in L.A. for long?" LaFonte asked Luisa, toying with his jabot.

"Highly likely." Luisa smiled mysteriously. "I cannot disclose details. The contracts are not quite signed, but my return to the screen is imminent."

"How delightful!" whinnied Monica. "I'm having a fundraiser next month, I'd adore for you to be my guest of honor."

"If my schedule allows, I would be most happy to assist this city deepen its appreciation and knowledge of art." Luisa bowed her head demurely.

"And you must come to the opening of this young lady's exhibit at my gallery." LaFonte rubbed his clear nail lacquered fingers along Scotty's arm while simpering to Luisa.

Rick finished his drink and said to Alex. "Kaori's on her way over. Can we just say 'well done' and leave?"

Smatters of applause announced Kaori's passage through the room. Her face was flushed. She brushed a corkscrew of blonde hair off her face. "Hi, Al, thanks for coming."

"It was terrific. You've really developed it from when I was last here," Alex said, genuinely impressed by her work.

"We couldn't have done it without your ..."

Alex cut Kaori off. "All your work, all your idea, all down to you."

"It wasn't too dark, was it?" Kaori asked nervously. "Oh, hi Scotty," she said as Scotty turned from Luisa and LaFonte.

"A plane crash isn't ever a light-hearted affair," reasoned Alex.

"I mean, putting everyone's likenesses on the dolls." Kaori twisted her hair around her finger. "My original idea was to put movie star's faces on the dolls. You know, because they're making all these disaster movies about burning skyscrapers, sinking boats, tornadoes, earthquakes and the like."

"Those movies are morbid curiosity," interjected Rick. "People just go to see death. They're like the Roman circus."

"Exactly!" Kaori nodded vigorously at Rick. "That's why I put everyone who attended on the plane as the dolls. I didn't want them to be an audience looking at a story, I wanted them to be the story."

"You call this art?" lisped LaFonte. "Is setting fire to a cardboard box filled with our images and scaring the bejesus out of folks art? I don't know about everybody else, but this had the ring of voodoo to me." LaFonte's diamond pinkie ring glittered as he fluttered his jabot.

Luisa nodded fiercely in LaFonte's direction. "This is most definitely art! Could you not feel how everyone invested in the piece?"

"But Luisa seriously, what about the theatrics? Were they necessary?" cut in Koenig, a note of anger in his voice. "People were genuinely frightened."

"The theatrics, if you can call them that, were most definitely needed," said Luisa decisively. "One puts a suitable frame around a painting, the theatrical elements were the frame around this event. The doors were not really locked, we were never in real danger."

"No more than living on a fault line or being shot in the street," laughed Scotty.

"Exactly," Kaori said wide-eyed to Luisa. "We face danger every day, but people don't relate to events unless they have a personal stake in them. I mean, it's like when the T.V. news shows film of people dying in wars or accidents. Those are real people we're watching suffering and dying, not actors. It's not fake but does it truly affect us? I feel we respond in a purely intellectual manner to such images. It's like hearing about somebody dying of a horrible disease. We empathize but don't *really* feel it. We talk about experiencing pain or joy through art, but it's a conscious reaction. I wanted to take the feeling deeper, to make an audience feel something genuine from art."

"To make them feel they were in mortal danger?" barked Koenig angrily.

Kaori's pale eyes met Koenig's dark ones. "If you see a plane crash on the news tomorrow it won't be just an intellectual response. After this, you'll have a different perspective don't you think? More empathetic?"

"I don't think so," muttered Koenig.

"It's fabulous work, Kaori. Exciting, vibrant, modern," declared Luisa. "Thrilling!" She kissed Kaori on both cheeks. "Come, tell me more about yourself." Luisa linked her arm in Kaori's and led her off to a quiet corner.

"Let's roll." Alex tapped Rick on the shoulder.

"Already?" Scotty asked. "Don't you want to find out if you're dead?"

Outside, Hank was placing what was left of the paper dolls onto white sheets.

"All too morbid for my taste," said Koenig. He checked his watch, then fastened his tie back into a central position and tugged his collar into shape. "I'm your mother's ride. I'll see if she's ready to leave. Excuse me." Koenig headed over to the Luisa-Kaori tête-à-tête which now had Monica and LaFonte in tow.

"I'm through with this shit. I'll wait by the car. Night, Scotty." Rick slunk out.

Art lovers drifted onto the sidewalk, cigarettes and plastic cups in hands. The two stewardesses had given up serving drinks and were now imbibing. They'd loosened their chiffon neckerchiefs, undone their blouses and removed the bobby pins from their up-does. The darker of the two girls was showing inordinate interest in Scoop's equipment, giggling provocatively as he guided her finger on his zoom control.

"What did you really make of it?" Scotty asked Alex in a whisper.

"I've hung around the studios with Rick and they are making movies about disasters. What Kaori did tonight isn't vastly different to what Sid Stradman's doing on a soundstage at Fox. Putting our faces on the dolls was genius. Look around, people really want to know what happened to their doll." A knot had formed of folks checking to see on which side of Hank's sheets their doll had ended up on.

"I suppose," said Scotty. "Luisa liked it. Look how deep she's in with Kaori. It appears LaFonte and Monica have joined the Luisa fan club too."

Alex sensed Scotty's disappointment that she hadn't become immediate gal pals with Rick's mother. He also noticed

Luisa and Monica glancing in his direction as they talked with LaFonte.

"How intense was that?" Hank came up to Alex and Scotty, wiping smoky smudges off his sweaty forehead with a Kleenex.

"Yeah, intense," agreed Alex. "Look man, I'm gonna shoot. Good show."

"Kaori's got a twisted but creative mind. God knows what kind of mom she'll make," said Hank with a grin. "Good news, guys. Your dolls were unscathed, you're both survivors."

"How about Luisa and Koenig?" asked Alex wondering why he was even interested.

"They made it too."

"And Rick?"

Hank stuffed the blackened Kleenex into his pocket. "Nah. Could only identify that one by the seat number."

Making his way out of the studio, Alex noticed Scotty pick up another drink. He suspected she was going in for another attempt to make nice with Luisa. It crossed his mind he should Luisa know that Rick had left, but he decided it best they go gently into the night. He scuffed along Windward to where he'd parked the car. Rick was leaning on the hood with his head bowed. Patchouli and pot suffused the humid air to the point it caught in your throat. The bass thump of a distant disco blended with the traffic's roar, car horns and drunken laughter. "Feeling better?" asked Alex unlocking the car.

Rick rubbed his eyes. "Why did she have to come?"

"Koenig invited her." Alex slipped into the driver's seat, leaned over and opened the passenger door.

"I mean to L.A. She claimed she never wanted anything to do with Hollywood ever again. Then, at the first sign of interest, she's headed west like Norma Desmond on Benzedrine."

"She wanted to see you too." Alex started the car.

"She didn't want to see me, she wants to be me. My mother's jealous of me. She's a fucking vampire." As they pulled out, Rick wound down the window. "What was the death toll from the plane? Tell me momma was fried to a crisp. I need something to make me smile tonight."

"She survived. Koenig and Scotty too."

"Whoopee fucking do. How about you and me, did we make it?"

Alex checked the rear-view mirror, indicated and merged onto the freeway. "Yeah. We made it." Alex felt it was better to lie, Rick couldn't take another downer tonight, even if it did only relate to the death of a paper doll on a cardboard plane.

COMPOSITION XIX – CONTROL AND CHAOS

A horizontal line of blue.

Alex's challenge was to keep it consistent across the canvas. He'd taken time to mix exactly the right consistency of paint, load the right amount of paint on the brush and then keep the motion of the brush smooth to create an even line of color. This had started off as a technical exercise, specifically designed to keep his mind off the doctor's report. But now, like carrying on a game of catch for as long as possible without dropping the ball, the technical challenge of painting horizontal lines of color had become something he didn't want to stop. He'd begun at the bottom with ochre tones growing paler as he moved up the board. This embryonic study put him in mind of the beach, so he carried on in that vein. After a couple of hours he had moved into gradations of blue as the sea morphed into sky. A moment of weakness struck his shoulder. The brush threatened to tremor. He summoned his mental power to steady his hand. He finished the line, keeping it smooth and even.

Rheumatoid arthritis.

Alex put down the brush and shook out his hand. The doctor had attempted to paint a rosy picture while delivering the bad news. The stylish medic, with his terracotta consulting room and blow-dried hair, had used warm words and upbeat terms to take the edge off telling an artist that he won't be able to hold a brush at some point in the future. At least the diagnosis explained the persistent aches in his shoulders and arms. This was not a typical symptom, so the fancy Beverly Hills doctor had been worth the dough, well Sid's dough, to determine the pain's root cause. A less thorough, and less likely to be sued, consultant may have written it off as muscle strain. The enemy had been identified, treatments and strategies could be devised to slow the disease's progress and alleviate its symptoms.

There was no cure.

And long-term medical treatments cost money. This diagnosis meant selling his work had moved up from being a personal goal to a vital necessity. Yumi's hotel commission would hopefully come through, he could really use the big bucks she'd promised.

Rick's pre-occupied mood had intensified after Luisa had been offered the professor's role on *Legal Eagles*. She'd reactivated her old agent to negotiate her deal, although he called himself a 'dealmaker'. From a one-sided phone conversation between Rick and Luisa, Alex gleaned she was confident the guy was going to get her the megabucks she felt she deserved for her stellar return. Rick hung up with an eye roll and a muttered, "Oh, brother ..." after that call.

Alex hadn't had any contact with Luisa since Kaori's show and was more than happy to keep it that way. Rick drip fed snippets of information, laced with invective, about what she was up to in the Beverly Wilshire Hotel's Presidential Suite, or 'Mission Control' as he'd dubbed it. Her 'dealmaker' also negotiated literary estates. Luisa thus concluded a book deal was a certainty too. Rumors of seven figure publishing deals were flying, according to her, for her life story, which she promised would set the record straight about her truncated Hollywood career.

Although he'd rested it, Alex's hand still felt unsteady. Not wanting to risk an unclean line on the new work, he ducked out of the studio and grabbed a drink. Taking his glass of water out onto the deck, he passed by the new decorative additions to the living room. The bloodstained old couch had been removed. Rick had replaced it with a brand-new one. Alex would frankly have rather kept the old one, bloodstain and all. The new couch's mustard color, spindly legs and angular lincs were too *Maison Moderne* for his taste. It wasn't a comfortable piece of furniture to sit on either. This piece's acquisition had kick-started Rick's rabid foray into interior styling, which at least distracted him from the boiling rage triggered by each new piece of information out of Mission Control.

The loft at the back of the house had been emptied of Alex's old pieces, now stacked against the walls of his studio or in Yumi's storeroom. In place of his art, the loft was gradually being filled with Dora's old things. Her homely Tiffany lamps and crocheted throws were being systematically replaced by chrome pedestal lights and op-art scatter cushions. Alex knew it was only a matter of time before the bedroom came into Rick's sights for a makeover. Alex hoped the T.V. show would start shooting before Rick had him trailing down to Laguna to pick out matrimonial beds and bedroom sets. He'd taken many things in his stride this summer, but that was something he wasn't quite ready for.

Alex lit up a cigarette. They weren't good for his health, but his health wasn't great due to something unrelated to nicotine and tar - so what the fuck. Mrs. Piper's white curls fluttering in the breeze caught his attention. She was sittting on her deck with a watercolor palette, concentrating on a study. "Hi!" Alex called over, expecting a comment about how 'rare' a day it was in response.

Mrs. Piper lifted her eyes from her work, sadly shook her head and called back, "Isn't it awful?"

Since Mrs. Piper was generally so upbeat, Alex was concerned. He hopped down onto the beach and walked over to her deck. He looked down at the small painting she was doing. "Very pretty," he said. Indeed, it was a charming watercolor of the view to the cliffs, it had warm tones and fine detail.

Mrs. Piper nodded her thanks. She swished her brush in the water jar. "You haven't heard the news?"

"I've been in the studio all morning."

"A bomb's gone off at the airport. It was on the wireless. Sounds bad. People killed and injured. You don't have anyone travelling today, do you?"

"Not that I know of."

"That's a blessing. Dear me." She began to mix yellow with blue in her palette. "Bad news always makes me want to create something lovely in its wake. This is a powerful weapon to fight the darkness." Mrs. Piper waved her paintbrush like a sword.

Alex smiled in response.

She let out a small wistful laugh. "Goodness knows, we had problems in the past too. But I suppose when you're young and in love the outside world doesn't matter that much, does it?" Mrs. Piper bumped her shoulder against his.

Alex sat beside her in silence, watching her finish the painting. Her technique, her simplicity and her spirit warmed his heart. After they'd had a little chat about Mr. Piper's health, Alex went back home. Going inside, he heard a vehicle crunch along the track behind the house. He guessed it must be Rick coming home, which was odd as he'd said he'd be gone for the whole day. Expecting to see Rick coming in through the back door, he was surprised there was no sign of him. Alex opened the back door to investigate the cause of the delay.

But up in the dunes, it wasn't Rick getting out of his car. Instead there was a woman locking the door to a slick black rental vehicle, flicking back her hair and positioning her oversized sunglasses over her eyes.

Luisa.

Although her dark glasses obscured her eyes Alex knew she'd seen him, which eliminated pretending to be out from the equation. Luisa rolled her shoulders back inside her cream jacket and strode towards the house. "You've had a wasted journey, Rick's not home," he called out as she neared the back door.

"I know. I came to speak to you."

Putting on an imaginary suit of armor, he swung open the door. "Come on in then. Coffee?" he asked once she'd walked into the kitchen.

Luisa took off her glasses and dumped her large crocodile purse on the kitchen table. "Let's not pretend to make this a social visit." She delved into her purse, pulled out her check book and brandished a tortoiseshell pen. "How much?" she asked repeatedly clicking the pen's gold button with her thumb.

"What do you mean, Luisa?"

"How much to end this travesty of a relationship and get out of Rick's life?"

"Is this some kind of joke?" asked Alex, unable to comprehend her motivation.

"There's nothing remotely humorous about this situation. I've been asking questions about Alex Morgan. And the answers have drawn a vivid picture of the type of man you are."

"Peachy. Please share with the class." Alex leaned on the counter, wondering what she was going to throw at him.

"I believe you targeted Rick in order to get your name known in the art world. I've no idea how you manipulated meeting him, but once you had him in your clutches you formulated a plan to exploit him."

"And how exactly did I do that?"

"You began by luring him to live in this ridiculous shack. And when you had him vulnerable and isolated, you seduced and overpowered him with those cartoonish masculine muscles of yours. And then, with him completely under your spell, you blatantly used his connections, or more precisely *my* connections, to meet influential people and inveigle yourself into their circle. Monica Aigner told me you presented yourself to her as a total unknown on first meeting. Out of the goodness of her heart she invited you to put a piece into her auction."

"I never asked Monica for anything ..."

"Exactly what a gigolo would say! They use their charm to entice the susceptible into offering them things. It was clever of you to tag along with Rick to the movie studios. Did you have to wait around long to *accidentally* bump into Rosemarie Rodgers? How cynical to target her fatal weakness for young men who remind her of her dead son and her fondness for low rent art. I suspect her walls are filled with weeping kittens painted on velvet. Monica believed she was giving a helping hand to a struggling unknown. Imagine her humiliation when Rosemarie stole her evening with a ridiculous show of overbidding. You must have been congratulating yourself immensely when that got your name known to Monica's wealthy friends. What a coincidence that you'd talked Yumi Mihara into taking your work earlier that very same day? From what I've seen and heard of Yumi, it appears the woman has an eye only for money. I suppose that's what attracted her to you, two of a kind."

Rage filled Alex's chest. If he had a gun in his hand, he could easily have put a bullet in this woman's brain. "You're wrong on every count! Look, if you took the time to really know me ..."

"I don't need time, I instinctively know you. You're a predatory homosexual with an eye on the main chance!"

Blood rushed to Alex's face. "Let's get one thing straight, if any predatory homosexuals are involved then it's your precious son! Rick came on to me!"

Luisa lips drew back in a sneer. "Is there no lie you wouldn't stoop to?"

"*He* practically forced his way into moving in here."

"You're dangerous!"

"And for your information, I didn't ask Rick for any invitations or introductions. Everything that happened to get my name known was entirely of your son's doing."

"How soon after you met him did you realize I was his mother? You must have thought you'd hit the jackpot when you got a direct line to the most influential woman in European art!"

"I'd no idea Rick was connected to the art world in any way, shape, or form when I met him. Oh, and there's a very good reason I couldn't have had any intention of wanting to meet his mother."

"Why was that?"

"Because he told me his mother was dead! He said she'd died from a shriveled heart." Alex suddenly realized those words had had a more devastating impact than a bullet to her brain. Luisa crumpled, her mouth drooped open. He'd struck bullseye. Deep down he knew he should stop, but his rage wouldn't let him. He was seeing red and wanted to hurt her as much as she'd hurt him. "Yeah, he told me his mother was dead. And you know why Rick came to Sunset Cove in the first place? He came here because you'd made his life so intolerable that he wanted to end his life. He came here to kill himself because of you!"

Luisa tossed her head back in denial. "Rick threatens to do drastic things, but he never follows through. His threats of suicide are manipulations, nothing more."

"Well, I found him on the edge of the cliff and he looked pretty damn close to jumping to me. If I hadn't gone up after him we wouldn't be having this conversation. You know why? Because he'd be dead! Yes, your son would be dead because you'd rather have married him off to Gina, who I must inform you's a psychotic junkie, rather than letting him live the life he wants to live. So before your start hurling wild accusations about me manipulating him, you ought to take a good look in the mirror, lady!" Alex swallowed hard, there was no way any of that could be unsaid.

Luisa fought to control her emotion. "You'd seriously have me believe that you're not using Rick to further your career? How do I know once he's served your base desires you won't discard him like yesterday's garbage? I love my son and don't want to see him hurt. How do I know that once you've got what you want, you won't throw him away and break his heart?"

"I've no intention of doing either of those things," said Alex firmly.

Luisa was momentarily baffled. "Then for what possible reason do you spend your time trailing around after him like a member of his court? Why do you abase yourself looking after him the way you do?"

Alex was as surprised as Luisa to suddenly hear himself declare, "Because I love him."

Luisa stood for a moment, uncertain how to proceed. She coughed, then folded up her check book and tossed it with her tortoiseshell pen into her crocodile purse. When she spoke again, her tone had softened. "This could be the beginning of a wonderful career for Rick. He's a good actor. If his T.V. show becomes a hit everyone will want a piece of him. You profess to love him, if you really do, if you really do love him, you should let him go. Let him live his life untarnished by scandal." Luisa's eyes disappeared behind her dark glasses. She picked up her purse and left without a further word.

After she'd gone, a toxic blend of outrage, anger and, oddly enough, empathy, hung like cigarette smoke in an unvented room. His hand was shaking too badly to paint. It wasn't shaking from the arthritis but from the resentment of the terrible things Rick's mother had said about him. And how, if being totally objective, what she'd accused him of could easily be construed as true. Alex maundered out onto the deck and sat ruminating, smelling the afternoon turn to evening.

"Hi, hi!" Rick's voice rang out cheerily when he finally bustled in just before six.

Alex went through to the kitchen and found Rick busily unpacking a couple of brown bags. There was a strong odor of fish. "You been hanging out down at the docks?"

"On the way home I stopped by the library to research how diet can help rheumatoid arthritis. Fish oil eases the inflammation, so they say." Rick pulled out a plastic bag which contained something gray slopping about in wet paper.

"Ye gods!" Alex waved his hand in front of his face.

"Bit strong, isn't it?" said Rick wrinkling his nose and looking dubiously at the bag.

"I'd rather have the arthritis than a fish diet, thank you very much," said Alex, unable to stop himself smiling about the awful fish smell and Rick's kindness in wanting to make him better. "You're very chipper. Good meeting?"

Clang. Clang. Clang!

"Pretty good," said Rick. "Hey, it's martini o'clock! I'll tell you all about it down at the Beachcomber. Oh, maybe we shouldn't drink? Alcohol isn't good for rheumatoid arthritis."

"I'd rather be dead than turn dry and eat sardines for the rest of my life, but thanks for the concern. Let's go drink." Alex slung his arm around Rick's shoulder.

Once installed in a corner table on the Beachcomber's deck, and drinks had been delivered by the brunette server whose name they'd never taken the time to learn, Rick told him about the meeting. Alex listened but his attention was distracted by the part of his mind still whirring on Luisa's visit.

"...they changed the title. Isn't that incredible?" Rick sat back waiting for Alex's reaction.

"Sorry, say again?"

"Keep up, babe, this is big stuff. My show isn't called *Legal Eagles* anymore, which was a sucky title in my opinion anyhow. It's now *The Brad and Carol Mysteries*. Insane, right?"

"How so?"

"My character name's in the title! *Legal Eagles* shared the plot between the four law students. The new script's downgraded the other students to minor roles. Bradley's now got a quirky girlfriend called Carol who works on the college paper. Her father's a San Francisco police detective. There's tension between the police detective and our new law professor. Carol's father thinks the attorney helps the guilty get away with murder and the attorney thinks the detective bends the evidence to get a conviction. Brad and Carol hear both sides of a case then investigate without prejudice. It's like one Hardy boy and Nancy Drew solving mysteries together. There's snappy dialog between the two kids. And the college paper has a wisecracking editor to supply the laughs and point Brad and Carol in the right direction when the case goes cold. Neat show, huh?"

Rick's genuine happiness was infectious. Alex raised his glass. "Here's to you. Well done, kiddo."

"When they offered momma the professor role, I thought they wanted us as some kind of freaky double act. But having my character's name in the title puts me in the driving seat. It makes hers a minor role. They can replace the professor any old time, but they can't get rid of Brad if he's in the title! They want me to go in later this week and read with the girls up for Carol. They want us to have sexual chemistry."

"Is Gina working?"

"Very funny. It's a pity Danielle's show hasn't been cancelled. She'd be perfect."

"Babe, exactly how old are these college kids meant to be?"

"It's not a documentary, Al. This is night time T.V. drama. With the right lighting and a kind director of photography you can play a student until your mid-thirties." Rick successfully caught Whatsername's attention and hustled up more drinks.

Alex could tell Rick was giddy with alcohol and excitement, it was a relief to see him so happy. "If your character's in the title, I guess that makes you the star of the show."

"And whoever ends up playing Carol, of course," said Rick.

"*One* of the stars of the show then. That's gonna put you in the public eye."

"They're floating a couple of other *Mystery Movie* pilots this season. We'll be lucky to get three or four episodes at most."

"On the other hand, you could be playing this part for years. Or at least until Brad and Carol finish college in their mid-forties," said Alex. Luisa's parting shot now resonated with what was happening to Rick.

"I guess. But if it goes on for that long there could be big money in this. I mean, we could be financially independent. We could do whatever we like without dancing to momma and dad's tune," said Rick with a thoughtful expression. Whatsername set the fresh drinks on the table and cleared their empties. Rick's hand leapt to his glass.

"We could be?" queried Alex.

"What?"

"You said, *we*. *We* could be financially independent. You see us as a *we*?"

"Don't you?" asked Rick.

Alex took a drink, put his glass down and ran his hands through his hair.

"Did I say something wrong?"

"No, no." Alex put his hands back on the table.

Rick rested his hand on Alex's and gently stroked the hairs on the back of his wrist.

Alex checked around the deck. "Careful, we're not alone."

"So what? Nobody cares," said Rick with annoyance.

"People may not appear to care now, not here. But what happens if you become a big star? Not everyone's cool with two men holding hands. Let alone doing anything else."

Rick's mouth hardened, he snatched his hand away. "Are you worried about people thinking you're gay?"

"This isn't about me. What if some negative story about you gets out? You heard from Danielle how the press twist things to dial up the dirt."

"What are you trying to say?"

"I know what it's like to be broke. You don't. You may have been unhappy, but you've never been broke. What happens if it all goes wrong?"

"You've got the beach house. It's not like I wouldn't have a roof over my head. That's if you wanted me to live with you."

"Could you really be happy living your whole life out here on the beach?"

"We could always get a boat. You could hoist the main sail and let the wind blow us where it wants. Remember you said the wind is free." Rick squinted towards the lowering sun. "You keep talking about if everything goes wrong. But what if it goes right? Just because I might be an actor on a hit show doesn't mean I don't have the right to love who I want, does it?"

"Are you saying what I think you're saying?" Alex put his hand back on Rick's.

Rick looked away from the sun and back at Alex. "I've been unhappy most of my life, rolling around the globe in search of the missing part of me. But since I found you this summer, everything feels right. For the first time people think I've got talent and want me for myself. For the first time in my life I feel like a man, a real grown up man! Can't I just enjoy the ride and put the what-ifs on hold until tomorrow?"

"I suppose. After all I'm in kind of the same boat as you." Alex lifted his hand, it tremored slightly. "Although if we end up in the same boat and my arms don't work anymore, you'll need to learn how to handle the sails."

"Aye, aye, captain." Rick knuckled his brow.

"Stop giving me money for living in the beach house."

"That was the deal. I don't want you worrying about money so you can work without distraction."

"You've provided other distractions than worrying about bills." Alex winked knowingly.

"I'm happy to pay for the rest of the summer?"

"We're beyond that. I'll give you the money back."

Looking around for Whatsername to order another round of distraction, Alex formulated a new plan. He knew what he had to do, and he'd make a phone call in the morning to set this new phase of his life into motion.

INTERIOR WITH MIRRORED CLOSET

"I've an appointment with Sid Stradman."

The gatekeeper at Fox consulted the list. "Alex Morgan?"

"Guilty as charged," said Alex.

Waving his pen towards the end of the *Hello, Dolly* street, the guard began to give directions to the production offices.

"Thanks, I know my way," Alex said winding up his window. The guard lifted the barrier and Alex's old Chevy rolled on to the lot.

Shirley glanced up as Alex walked into Sid's office. She was frantically hammering on the typewriter, her desk piled high with papers. Four orange buttons were lit on the switchboard, three more were blinking.

"Hi, Shirley," said Alex.

Shirley didn't break her typing's staccato clatter, she acknowledged him and said, "Go through." Glancing at the blinking lights on the switchboard, she added, "He's got calls backed up to last week. He won't have long."

"No problem." Alex was happy for this meeting to be as short as possible. As his hand went to the door handle of Sid's office, Shirley made one last interjection as the phone began to ring.

"He's like a bear with a sore head. Don't take it bad if he yells at you. He's yelling at everybody," said Shirley resignedly. She pulled out the pencil stuffed in her hair bun, jabbed its eraser tip on a newly blinking orange button on the switchboard. "Sid Stradman's office ... I'm sorry he's in a meeting. Can you hold?"

Alex entered Sid's office and shut the door behind him.

Sid was pacing behind his desk with the phone cradled in the crook of his neck, its curly cord straining as far as it could before pulling him back. Sid motioned for Alex to sit in the mustard bucket chair. Alex remained standing. Sid resumed barking over the phone, "Like I said, Albie, the model shots are no good. Heck, they're worse than no good. They're lousy! For Christ's sake, Tyler and Tiffany could do better with some cereal cartons and building blocks. People gotta believe they're seeing a city destroyed, they're not paying two bucks a ticket to see a school project! How much do you need to fix this holy mess? For Pete's sake, Albie, I'm already way over budget. You're killing me. Is that what you want, to see me dead? Is that what he wants?" Sid looked to Alex for confirmation. As usual, Alex could do no more than shrug in response to a typical Sid Stradman rhetorical question. Sid got back on the horn. "You got me by the balls, Albie. You better deliver those new shots by the end of the month. If they're up to standard, you get the dough. But if they're the same crapola I had the misfortune to witness in the screening room last night then I'll see you in court. Capiche? Yeah, whatever." Sid slammed down the phone and flicked a switch. "Hold all calls, Shirley ... For how long? ... Until nineteen ninety-one, that's how long!" Sid flopped in the leather chair behind his desk. His face was unnaturally red. He gripped the chair's arms and let out a sigh of resignation as he looked at Alex. "What fresh hell is this?"

Alex took out the check he'd written on his personal account and handed it over the desk.

Sid unfolded the check and sighed again. "Appreciate the sentiment, kid, but it's gonna take a helluva lot more dough than this to sort out the holy shitstorm of this movie. Why are you giving me money?"

"I'm paying back that thousand dollars you gave me. I don't feel right taking it."

"But you're okay with the other two grand I laid on you?"

"I never cashed that check. And let me know how much I owe you for the doctor."

Sid snorted. "What did that quack tell ya, anyhow? Tennis elbow?"

"Rheumatoid arthritis."

Sid got up and came around the desk to Alex. "They can fix it, right?"

"They can treat the symptoms, but there's no cure. Whatever, I wanted to pay back everything you've given me, so tell me how much."

Sid ripped up Alex's check and let the pieces flutter to the floor. "Banking this would be like replacing a grain of sand if someone stole the Sahara. I don't need any payback. You know why I was so keen to get that doc to fix you up?"

Alex shook his head.

"I need you fit so you can keep an eye on that crazy kid of mine. I can't shake off the fear he'll do something dumb, or just waste his life. Now, for the first time in whenever, he's making something of himself and has somebody other than me watching his back. And you coming here, offering to pay back what I willingly gave you, only confirms I was right to trust you, even if you do look like a hoodlum. It's not often in this goddamn lousy world you come across someone who wants to give rather than take."

"Thanks, Sid." Alex felt his throat tighten. "Rick doesn't know how lucky he is to have a father like you." Alex fought back the tears that threatened to come.

"Hey, we ain't got time for hearts and flowers, I got a movie to deliver! Get your ass out of here and don't come bothering me with anymore of your crap!" Despite yelling, Sid gave a half smile and warmly squeezed Alex's shoulder as he shoved him out of the door.

Shirley raised her eyes at the brusqueness of Sid's tone. She gave Alex an apologetic smile and said gently, "He's under a lot of pressure." Shirley jabbed a blinking orange button on the switchboard. "Sol Whitmore on line one, Mr. Stradman," she said into the phone. One blinking light turned solid and two more began to flash.

"Never lets up, does it?" said Alex sympathetically.

"That's showbiz," said Shirley with a sigh. She threaded a fresh sheet of paper into the typewriter and jammed the pencil back into her hair bun. Her typewriter's clatter underscored Alex as he left the production office and went back onto the lot. He had the key in the car's lock ready to head back to Sunset Cove, when a thought struck him. Putting the keys back into his pocket, he turned from the beige rectangle of the studio offices and followed the palm lined walkway to the commissary.

He mingled with the actors and technicians heading up the crazy paving steps for lunch. Hanging at the entrance, he cast his eyes around the large dining room. The gilded art deco ceiling and fancy murals on the walls were at odds with the utilitarian fluorescent lights and brown wood chairs. Faded glory mingled with the smell of hot food as he watched costumed cowboys, nurses and technical crew in overalls giving lunch orders to waiters and waitresses.

"May I show you to a table, sir?" asked a harassed waiter.

"It's okay. I was just looking for someone."

"Very well, sir," said the waiter, ready to move on.

"Hey, it's someone who works here," said Alex stopping the waiter running off. "You know someone here called Julie?"

"Julie?" The waiter looked blank, then after a moment's thought said, "Oh, the new girl. It's her day off. She should be in again tomorrow."

A tension released in Alex's chest. After feeling so warm about Sid just now, he couldn't quell the niggle that he did have ulterior motives with Julie. This answer confirmed Sid was on the level, he'd simply helped Julie get a job in the commissary. "I'll swing by and catch up with her later," Alex said to the waiter. Relieved, he made his way through the incoming lunch crowd.

"Do I spy Alex Morgan the renowned artist in our midst?" A woman's voice called from behind.

Alex paused on the steps, wondering who the heck the nurse in the white dress and hat was and why she was chasing after him. "Danielle?"

Danielle smoothed down her white uniform. "Your eyes do not deceive you," she said self-deprecatingly.

"I didn't know you played a nurse on your show? I thought you were a private detective."

"I'm undercover, sugar! The girls are trying to stop a corrupt doctor performing plastic surgery on a criminal before he can escape the country." Danielle laughed apologetically, moving aside to let people pass. She checked no-one nearby was listening, and added confidentially, "Sounds real dumb when you say it out loud."

"No, not at all," Alex said despite wanting vigorously to agree.

"I was about to head back to set. We could catch up if you'd care to come visit? You got time for coffee?"

"Yeah, why not?"

"Great. I'll let the girls know I'm going."

Alex lingered on the path and a few moments later Danielle came back outside and joined him. "Sorry. I didn't mean to interrupt your lunch," said Alex.

"We call it lunch, but it's really just pushing lettuce around the plate. We girls are afraid that even air has calories," Danielle laughed.

"Doesn't sound like much fun," said Alex sympathetically.

"It isn't. I've been hungry since nineteen seventy-one," replied Danielle, and Alex laughed in response. They carried on chatting as they walked down the pedestrian walkway and crossed a road lined with palm trees and parked cars. "Why are you on the lot? Is Rick shooting here?" asked Danielle. "I didn't think his new show had started rolling."

"It hasn't, and when it does they shoot at Universal. I came to see Sid. I'd some business with him."

"Here we are, home sweet home. Well from August to April, anyway." Danielle opened the door to her trailer parked outside Stage 4. "How'd you take it?"

Alex looked puzzled.

"Your coffee, honey."

"Black, no sugar."

"I'll be back in two shakes of a lamb's tail."

Alex took a seat on the green moquette bench. He thought it was odd how moquette had been deemed the covering of choice for all trailer interior furnishings.

Danielle returned with a couple of plastic cups of steaming coffee. She sat down and stretched out her slim legs, the clumpy white nurse's shoes accentuating the slimness of her ankles. She noticed Alex looking at her feet. "The one benefit of this costume is comfortable shoes. The episodes where we stand around all day in high heels are agony. We wear sneakers with our evening gowns if we can get away with it."

Alex blew on his coffee. "How's little sis working out?"

"In this episode I'm the one in the nurse's uniform investigating the corrupt doctor. She's the one in a tube top and hot pants playing a go-go dancer infiltrating the nightclub's criminal ring. By season finale they'll probably have me in a gray wig and orthopedic Oxfords."

"I'm sorry."

"Don't be. I got the score long ago."

"If it's any consolation, Rick thought you'd be perfect to play against him in his new show."

"What's the part?"

"A student reporter on a college newspaper."

Danielle's sudden laughter made her splutter her coffee. She put down the cup and grabbed a Kleenex, dabbing her white uniform. "You nearly got me into big trouble with wardrobe!" She continued to chuckle while checking no coffee had spilled on her dress. "Sweet boy but he needs an optometrist if he thinks I can still pass for a student."

"That's Rick. When he's for you he's all for you and totally blind to reality. But when he's against you ... well, that's a position I wouldn't like to be in."

"Everything okay between you two?"

"Yeah, for now. But there's a chance he could be a big T.V. star like you. I remember you saying how the press hounds you looking for dirt. I had a big showdown with Rick's mother. She came and told me to get out of his life or risk ruining it."

"What a bitch."

"My reaction too, at first. But the more I think about it the more I think she has a point."

"But honey, what does she want Rick to do? Go through his life denying his true self just to work on T.V.? You two are in a relationship. This isn't some sordid back street hook up. Though Lord knows I sympathize with guys who are put into that position because they can't be open about who they are."

"I don't want to be the one who jeopardizes his big chance. Rick's very sophisticated in many ways, but totally naive in others."

"I wish I had someone in my life as thoughtful and considerate as you. You're an easy man to love, Alex Morgan."

Alex drained his cup, scrunched it up and tossed it into the bin. "Luisa D'Onofrio may disagree with you on that."

A knock on the door.

"Come in!" called out Danielle.

A pudgy faced blonde girl in a headset poked her head around the door. "They're ready for you on set, Danny."

"Be right with you, sugar." The girl closed the door. Danielle picked up her script. "Hey, you got time to hang around? You can watch me in action. This afternoon I have to apprehend a bad guy outside the operating theater. It's going to be a challenge, as my hair's usually down which makes it easier."

"What?"

"I forgot you don't watch the show. This is how we do a stick up." Danielle put down her script to demonstrate. "Whilst holding the gun in one's right hand, one uses the left hand to flick back the hair on your left side, then flick back the hair on one's right side, then you place both hands on the gun, aim at the bad guy and shout, "Freeze! This is a bust, sucker!'"

Alex clapped his hands. "Impressive, I've simply no choice but to witness this."

"Wise move. It's an education in law enforcement. When the show ends they may employ me to teach at the Police Academy." Danielle picked up her script. They headed out of her trailer, squinting briefly as the harsh afternoon sun hit their eyes. Laughing together, they approached the open elephant door revealing the darkness inside Stage 4.

♦ ♦ ♦

"Anyone home?"

"In here?" Rick's voice came from the bathroom.

Alex picked up the mail. Nestled amidst the bills was an envelope addressed in Yumi's idiosyncratic handwriting. Ten out of ten to the mail system that got her letters to their correct destination.

Rick emerged from the bathroom scrubbing his hand with a nailbrush. "Where you been?"

"Something came up." Yet again an economy with the truth was needed. He couldn't tell Rick he ran into Danielle on the Fox lot. He couldn't mention that Sid had been telling the truth about getting Julie a job in the commissary. All because he couldn't think of a good reason to say he went to see Sid without telling Rick about the money. What he found in Yumi's envelope, however, proved to be a pleasant surprise and a conversational distraction. "Wow, lookee here!"

"Just tell me. I've been over half an hour trying to get this paint off my hands. If it lasts as well on LaFonte's walls as it does on my skin, Scotty's makeover on his gallery will be around in fifty years' time."

"It's a check for fourteen hundred dollars and seventy-eight cents! Yumi's sold two more of my paintings."

"Glad she included the seventy-eight cents. Good work, hon." Still scrubbing his hand, Rick kissed Alex on the cheek.

Alex licked his thumb. "You got some on your face too." Rick recoiled slightly as Alex attempted to rub the paint spackle off his forehead. "Jeez, what were you guys doing?"

"We had a paint fight, you know how wild Scotty gets."

Alex leaned back skeptically.

"As if. The woman's a slave driver. You know when you offer to do a friend a favor and then immediately regret it? Have you any idea how much wall area there is to cover in the LaFonte Gallery? I've done my bit for the past two days to help her paint the place, and we've still covered less than a third."

"It wasn't just you and her though, was it?"

"She's roped in Susie and a few of her other helpers, but I think she's gonna have to hire some professionals because I'm booked for the rest of the week with readings at Universal. Painting an entire gallery's way more work than calling in favors from friends."

"At least there's no rush, her show doesn't open for another few weeks."

"Lucky LaFonte was shutting down for August. Kind of lucky he's gone to Palm Springs too. He'd be having kittens if he was around. I'm amazed he agreed to let her paint the whole place dark green in the first place."

"That's Scotty, she thinks big and can be very persuasive when needed. You think it's gonna be worth the effort?"

"I do. The dark green makes the walls recede and lends the place a sense of luxury, which that downtown location sorely needs. You feel like going into Laguna for dinner?"

Alex kept turning Yumi's check around in his hand as Rick went back to the bathroom. Alex listened to the water running and Rick's gentle cursing as he tried to eradicate the last of the paint. "Sure," he answered.

Later that evening, expecting Rick to park in front of one of the restaurants on the beach, Alex was surprised when they pulled up outside The Cottage, an establishment on the highway known for its homely fare. The Cottage's down to earth menu, however, was exactly what he needed and made a welcome change from Rick's penchant for fine dining and champagne. "Unusual choice of venue," said Alex munching his last mouthful of meatloaf.

Rick considered the craftsman style building's rustic interior. Additions over the years to turn it into an eatery had bestowed the former home with a higgledy-piggledy charm. Its ramshackle décor sat well with its buttermilk pancake and hamburger menu. "Belt tightening's in order," said Rick with a sense of gravitas.

"How so?"

"To be truly independent means I need to cut the purse strings from dad. I'm going to give him back the keys to the Brentwood apartment."

"Won't giving up the apartment be a problem when you're shooting? Can you drive to and from the studio every day at those crazy hours?"

"Bette Davis lived in Laguna Beach in the forties and she managed."

"Why not phone Bette and ask what time she had to set her alarm clock to make a six-a.m. call?"

Rick nodded in grudging agreement. "I might be able to get Mike to negotiate a car service for early calls. And Scotty said I could stay with her and Bob if I need. That actually could work out great. Los Feliz is just the over the hill to Universal, more convenient than Brentwood really."

Alex settled the check in cash. This meal was a lot cheaper than his usual outings with Rick.

Rick continued to mull things over as they took a post dinner stroll past hippy stores filled with incense burners, macramé pot holders and hummingbird feeders. The night air was warm, the vibe chilled. Girls in off the shoulder peasant blouses hung out with long haired bearded guys in cheesecloth tops and headbands. Everyone was smoking something or other. A shaven headed monk in orange robes beat a drum while kneeling out front of a health food store.

"It's your decision," advised Alex sagely.

They walked on and passed a furniture showroom. "We need to buy new bedroom stuff," said Rick. "I'll have to move my clothes out of Brentwood. We could do with better storage at the house anyway."

There it was again ... *we*. Alex stared blankly in the showroom's window.

"Hello? Why so quiet?"

"It's a big change to process. You know, living with someone. It hadn't been on my radar."

A glimmer of the wounded puppy expression crossed Rick's face. "I thought you wanted this? To be together?"

"I'm not saying that I don't want it. It's just I hadn't ever considered being part of a couple, you know, a full time one."

Rick continued to peer into the store. His eyes roved across the displays of queen size beds, double nightstands and mirrored closets.

"And especially when the couple in question is two guys," said Alex. "I've no frame of reference for this. It isn't like a standard courtship with dating, engagement and marriage. Those options aren't open to us. And we've gone from naught to sixty in such a short space of time. One moment we're engaged in illicit sexual activity and the next we're laundering His and His towels. Jeez, in two years' time will we be sitting around in velour lounging robes and walking a couple of Pomeranians?" Alex ran his hand through his hair in frustration.

"I hear you," said Rick disconsolately. "I won't say anything to dad about giving up Brentwood. We'll keep things as they are. It's easier all around."

"Yeah, sorry. It isn't that I don't want to be with you, I'm just not ready for this."

"I get it. I was moving too fast." Rick reached out to take Alex's hand.

Alex took a step back and checked the street. "It's laid back in Laguna, but we should still be careful."

"Can't a guy hold another guy's hand?"

"The police have charged men with lewd conduct for less. Let's get this off the street and go back home," said Alex firmly.

"But it's still early. How about we check out the South Seas Bar at The Coast Inn. Maybe get a drink and hang for a while?"

Feeling bad about stifling Rick's attempt to consolidate their relationship, Alex felt it only fair to give him his head on this. As they drove down the highway, Alex mused out loud, "The Coast Inn? That used to be a Marine hangout."

"I heard on the grapevine it's attracting a new mixed crowd. Heard it's getting real popular."

"Mixed?" Alex felt his brow furrow against his will.

"Let's just go see," said Rick driving on.

'Popular' was an understatement. Alex could hear the pounding disco beat before the old Coast Inn came into sight. People spilled out of the bar's front door and were milling around on the sidewalk. "Looks lively," said Alex drily after they'd parked the car and walked to the bar. Young fit guys in shorts, sneakers and tanks hustled around them. Laughter, the sharp tang of cologne and an air of celebration filled the air. Rick and Alex jostled through the crowd. A mass of hot male bodies packed the faded Polynesian bar. The disco beat pounded in their ears. "What do you want to drink?" yelled Rick above the thumping bass.

It looked to Alex like everyone was drinking rum cocktails. "Beer," he yelled back gruffly. A tall woman in a pink sequin off the shoulder top got wedged up against him in the crush at the bar. "Sorry," said Alex realizing he was pressed up against her in a compromising manner.

"Don't be, honey. You're new around here, aren't you?" the woman drawled, looking down at him and fluttering her false lashes.

"Ah, yeah." Alex's vision adjusted to the light and the proximity of the woman's face. Through the fug of humidity and cigarette smoke it became apparent that 'she' was a 'he'.

Rick pushed the beer towards Alex. "Let's go over there." Rick indicated a corner near the postage stamp space filled with pulsing bodies which was acting as the dance floor.

"Catch you later," said Alex with a shy smile to the gal/guy at the bar.

"I hope so," winked the guy/gal with a twinkle.

Alex trailed Rick through the sea of men's bodies, and whilst they moved aside to let them pass, they didn't move aside that much. Alex felt firm thighs and bubble butts rubbing up against him as he moved through the room. Guys checked him out with appreciative nods and eyes whitened with Murine. "When you said a mixed crowd, I guess you meant gay," muttered Alex swigging his beer.

"Yeah. I wanted to come to a place where we can hang out and actually touch each without you tensing up for fear of being arrested. And a place which doesn't have signs behind the bar saying who is and isn't welcome."

Alex let Rick's dig about Barney's go. They lounged against the window with their drinks. After a while Alex relaxed and gave in to Rick's hip pressing against his. Rick's body began to undulate, following the beat of George McCrea's *Rock Your Baby*. Alex detected a stiffening in his pants. The proximity of Rick's hot body enveloped him in his familiar and comforting scent. Alex swept his hair off his face, rivulets of sweat dripping down the back of his neck. It was clear why most guys in here only wore tanks. In fact, some guys on the dance floor had stripped them off and tucked them into their pants. Perspiration trickled down toned naked male torsos as they ground and swayed in couples. *Take me in your arms, and rock me baby ...* The bass line pounded in Alex's ears and gut.

"The guys have a nick name for this place," shouted Rick. "They call it The Boom Boom Room."

"Very appropriate!" yelled Alex back with a grin. The heat, beer, Rick and proliferation of bare male flesh was unsettling and arousing in equal measure. He'd never considered how he'd feel in this situation. It was one thing having sex alone with Rick or socializing with him in polite company under the guise of roommates, but this was being 'out' - really *out*.

"Let's dance," said Rick taking Alex's bottle.

Alex grimly hung on to his bottle and didn't move. "I don't think so."

"Hold mine then!" Rick handed him his glass and hustled onto the floor as the record changed. The swirling strings from the intro to *Love's Theme* swept over the floor. Swelling horns and the gently pulsing beat turned the mood to sultry sensuality. The Love Unlimited Orchestra and Barry White's grunting vocals wrapped around the dancers.

Alex hung by the window and watched Rick gyrating with closed eyes on the dance floor. As Rick danced he unbuttoned his shirt, revealing the defined cleft between his pecs and the gleaming gold skin of his chest. Rick swayed alone amongst the dancers, his arms above his head. Alex spotted a bare-chested bald guy wearing a red neckerchief zero in on Rick. The bald guy rested his hands on Rick's waist and ground his groin into Rick's butt, pumping his hips to the beat. Rick followed the bald guy's rhythm without looking around. Setting his beer and Rick's drink down on a table, Alex moved in. Still with Rick's back to him, Alex cut in between the bald guy and Rick. "He's with me." Alex didn't shout but said it forcefully enough for the bald guy to get the message.

Baldy slung an appreciative nod at Rick's butt and said with a leer to Alex, "Sweet." Backing off, the guy went to try his luck with another lone dancer.

Moving in and swaying, Alex slipped his hands around Rick's waist and hooked his thumbs through his belt loops. Barry White's gasping vocals topped the wah wah guitars. Alex wondered if Rick had assumed Baldy was him when he came up behind him. Whatever, Rick hadn't turned around to find out exactly who was pressing their dick into his butt. Perhaps it was seeing another man desire Rick that made Alex want him even more. Baldy was correct, Rick did have a sweet ass. And Alex suspected that if he didn't step up his game, he could easily lose Rick to someone else. There were plenty of guys here hot to trot with him. Alex nuzzled his stubbly chin into the back of Rick's neck and bit him gently.

Rick dreamily turned around. He smiled in Alex's face and draped his arms around his neck. "I thought you weren't in the mood."

"It came over me," murmured Alex, then he pulled his head to him and swirled his tongue in Rick's ear. Bodies pressed together, they swayed to the sensual beat. Alex grabbed Rick's butt and pulled his hips into him. "Give up Brentwood," Alex grunted, grinding his hips into Rick's. "Move in with me."

"For real?" gasped Rick. "You really want it, you really want it?"

"Yeah. I really want it," said Alex locking his open mouth onto Rick's. The disco beat pounded the dance floor with its insistent rhythmic boom, boom, boom as their tongues probed each other's mouths. Alex felt his solid erection pressing against Rick's, both straining inside their pants. Alex knew that he really, really, really did want it.

And he wanted it now.

NUDE LOOKING OVER HIS RIGHT SHOULDER

"Yes, yes, yes, yes ... yes!" gasped Rick, breathless with ecstasy, "there is a God!"

Alex couldn't get on board with the God thing however good the news. He continued painting, working on his twentieth composition using the horizontal lines technique he'd taken to of late. "Your lottery numbers come up?"

"As good as, if not better." Rick clapped his hands in delight, "Momma's off the show!"

Picking up a rag, Alex cleaned his brush. "Say what?"

"She overestimated how much they wanted her and forced Swifty to overplay her hand. She forced him to give the producers an ultimatum, this is how much she wants and if you don't agree to it, she walks. They didn't, she did. Bingo!"

"She tell you this?"

"No, just heard it from Mike. Can you believe it? The producers couldn't come up with what Mike negotiated for me and her fee on top, so they dumped her! I suspect they thought she'd be so grateful for a comeback she'd take the role for peanuts." Rick rubbed his hands with glee. "I'm phoning Mission Control to twist the knife."

"You think that's wise? Luisa might not know she hasn't got the role yet."

"I hadn't thought of that. Even better! I can break the bad news. Ha!" Rick scooted off to the phone.

Alex still hadn't spilled to Rick about Luisa's attempt to buy him off and the horrible things she'd accused him of. Their very public display of affection at The Boom and having Rick move in full time with him at the beach house could be construed by Luisa as an act of defiance on his part. With a photo shoot and early publicity interviews scheduled, everything was going full steam ahead for the launch of *The Brad and Carol Mysteries*. Alex sensed a potentially explosive mix brewing. A humiliated and angry Luisa D'Onofrio could be the match that lit the fuse. He'd been the target of Luisa's malice and knew her history of uncontrolled outbursts to the press, under duress he considered her capable of anything. "Cool it, hot pants!" Placing his hand over Rick's, he pressed the phone back on the cradle. "You heard of the saying 'humble in victory and gracious in defeat'?"

"Fuck that," said Rick attempting to lift the handset. "You haven't been on the receiving end of momma's machinations."

Alex held firm, not allowing Rick to lift the phone.

"You suddenly gone to her side or something?" asked Rick grumpily.

"This isn't about taking sides, it's about acting like adults. You told me you'd put your big boy pants on when you made your declaration of independence from Sid, now give your mother a break."

"Spoil sport." Rick flopped on the ugly modernistic mustard sofa, picked up a throw pillow and punched it in frustration. "You're so sensible."

"One of us has to be," chided Alex preparing to go back to work. Rick threw down the pillow and trailed him to the studio. Alex picked up his palette and brush and began darkening a red and orange mix to make burnt umber. After dragging a stool across the floor, Rick perched behind him. "And this is a comment free zone, remember," warned Alex over his shoulder. "I'm finding my style and don't need additional guidance, thank you very much."

"Yeah, yeah." Rick held his tongue for a few more moments, then couldn't help letting slip, "That's if you think abstracts are really worth persevering with."

"That sounded like a comment. One more and the door gets locked," snapped Alex, "with you on the other side." Alex heard Rick tut behind him.

After a few minutes of silence, Rick said as if thinking out loud, "Momma's off the show … I wonder who'll replace her? Any of the big names they initially considered won't even think about taking the role once they learn they weren't first choice."

"You'll have to go in and read with the replacement, won't you?"

"Who knows? If time's running out the Black Tower may make a battlefield promotion." After a prolonged pause, Rick said, "You're going to see Rosemarie later this week, aren't you?"

"Correct. She's invited me to Malibu to show her my new work. Which is why I'm doing some new work as Yumi has the bulk of my old stuff." Alex then said archly over his shoulder, "That's when I actually can do some work without interruption."

Rick sighed, "Okay, I'll get out of your hair."

But the next thing Alex knew was Rick pressing up behind him and raking his fingers through his hair. Alex pulled his head away. "I need to work. You don't see me coming onto movie sets and molesting you."

"You could try but Carol might not be happy." Rick toyed with a curl of Alex's hair. "Rosemarie would be ideal to take over momma's role, don't you think?"

"Quit that! First you see Danielle playing Carol, although she's ten years too old, and now you see Rosemarie as the law professor. Are you turning into a casting agent? Nepotism incorporated."

"If Rosemarie's got a get-out clause her agent could ring my producers and tell them she'd be interested in something better. But if no-one tells her the part on my show's available nothing will happen."

"You want me to call Rosemarie and get her agent on to this. That's what you want, isn't it?" Rick's hands came over

Alex's shoulders, slid inside his shirt and began tweaking his nipples.

"If I didn't have paint on my hands, I'd slap you!" Alex wriggled away from Rick in annoyance. But Rick didn't quit, he began running his tongue around Alex's ear lobe and tracing his fingers down his stomach towards his pants. Alex's animal instincts were stirring, if he allowed Rick to actually get his hands inside his pants no work would be done today. "Okay! If it makes you happy, I'll call Rosemarie and tell her the part's free. Now lay off!"

Rick instantly withdrew his hands. Leaning over Alex's shoulder and studying the canvas, Rick muttered, "Don't you think burnt sienna would contrast better with the ultramarine?"

"Fuck off!" Alex waved his brush threateningly but couldn't help laughing as Rick scooted out of the room. He had to hand it to Rick, he was very skilled at getting his own way. But after experiencing Luisa, Alex knew that when it came to manipulation Rick had been taught by masters.

♦ ♦ ♦

A few days later, Rick was standing in front of the sink drying a plate when he suddenly said, "Did you notice a light on last night?"

In typical Rick fashion his comment came out of the blue with no idea as to what it referred, so Alex asked distractedly, "What light?"

"Next door."

"At the Pipers?"

Rick turned and rolled his eyes in exasperation. "No. The Waverleys."

"Was their Cadillac out back?"

"I didn't see it. That's why I thought it was odd."

"Maybe one of the kids is using the beach house? Hey, Brad and Carol are the mystery solvers. Now they've signed Tina

Mason as Carol maybe you should call her? She can scoot over with her magnifying glass and you two can do a group improv."

"You're getting very au fait with these acting terms," said Rick huffily.

"That's because I've got ears. This could be the first case for Hardy Drew and the Nancy Boy," said Alex picking up the last of the canvases he was taking to Rosemarie's.

"You're getting pretty au fait with the bitchy gay lingo too."

"Like I always say, I'm a fast learner."

Rick chewed his lip as Alex lugged the last of his canvases out of the house. "Give my love to Rosemarie. Don't forget to ask if she's heard anything about the show."

As he was going out of the back door, Alex said, "I told her about the role and her agent's looking into it. Quit bugging me! Bye." Alex was looking forward to when shooting started and Rick settled down to his work. At least organizing the house and making room for whatever he'd brought over from Brentwood that hadn't gone into storage had diverted his tension from the build up to the new T.V. show. Declaring his financial independence from Sid meant Rick was carefully monitoring his cash flow until his fee came in. This had deterred Rick from rushing out to buy beds and bedroom sets, which was a relief. Instead, Rick was rearranging the current furniture with a few thrift shop additions in his redecoration of the upper level. Alex wished Rick's funds had been so constrained before he'd bought the ugly mustard sofa which had taken up residence in the living room.

The drive to Malibu was a much-needed breath of different air. The couple of weeks after that night they'd gone dancing at the Boom had been a head trip. The two of them had talked about a lot of things since Rick moved in but not the L word. They still hadn't really said that to each other. Love. Alex wondered if it was real until they did.

With the mountains rising on his right and the ocean glittering between houses on his left, Alex was approaching Rosemarie's place. He spotted her street number pass by. Carrying on, he found a suitable place to U-turn and pulled up outside Rosemarie's Malibu home. Its rough concrete frontage, practically on the highway with no windows and a solid metal entrance door, lent the house all the allure of a military bunker. Getting out of the car, Alex buzzed the intercom. The voice that answered sounded like a houseboy. Whatever, a moment later the metal garage door automatically rose up. Once Alex had got back in the car and driven into the dark garage, the door lowered behind him. He was about to start hauling his paintings out of the car when he heard Rosemarie's tinkling voice call from the corridor, "Raul and Esteban will bring in your work. Please come through, Alex!"

If the house's exterior was inauspicious, its interior was spectacular. Fabulous art adorned every wall, even in the corridor from the garage to the house. Luisa had it dead wrong about Rosemarie's taste, there were no weeping kittens here. If fact, if his eyes didn't deceive him, that was an actual Titian hung in a spot well out of the sunlight. Rosemarie greeted him in her glass walled living room. The sparkling ocean rolled practically up to the windows. A huge white bowl filled with lemons adorned the Plexiglas coffee table, lush white orchids were dotted around the room, cerulean blue scatter cushions and terracotta throws accessorized the ecru couches.

"Nice place," said Alex, almost blushing at the extent of his understatement.

"Thank you. Morton and I have another home in the hills, but we love the ocean so much we spend most of our time here. It's kind of you to come to me, it's quite some drive from Laguna to Malibu."

Before Alex could respond, his *Cliffs of Mendocino* painting appeared in his peripheral vision. Turning to look at it, he noticed it had been reframed in a mount which appeared to be made of bone. It was hung dead center on the wall opposite the ocean view windows.

Rosemarie noticed him staring at his work. "I had it reframed. I hope you approve?" she asked nervously.

"It's perfect," he said, wondering why he hadn't had the idea of framing it in such a sensitive manner. Maybe a serious collector understood an artist's work better than the artist themself?

"I'm so glad." Rosemarie smiled with relief.

Pulling his eyes from his work, Alex was startled to find his paintings from the car were now leaning against the far wall as if by magic. With no fuss and no noise Raul and Esteban had brought them in while he was distracted. "Do you want to see them now?" asked Alex.

"Are you in a hurry?" asked Rosemarie, her voice tinged with disappointment.

"Not at all, but I don't want to hog your time."

"I've a few days break in shooting, so there's no hurry on my part. And Morton's in Argentina this week. I miss him dreadfully when he's away on business, so to tell the truth I'd be glad of the company. I just made myself a coffee, may I get you one too?"

"That'd be great," said Alex. Following Rosemarie into her sleek modern kitchen, Alex felt awkward having a movie star, wife of one of the wealthiest men in America, pour his coffee and fuss over whether it was too hot, too cold or needed more sugar.

Only when Rosemarie was satisfied that she'd made his coffee exactly right did she pass the white china cup and saucer to him. "By the way, thank you for the heads up about the part on Rick's new show."

"Rick was *very* insistent I tell you about it. He's real keen on working with you."

Thoughtfully, Rosemarie stirred cream into her coffee. "I'm contracted to the comedy, but I dread to think what the ratings will be like. It's not very good, you see." Rosemarie relaxed into one of her tinkling laughs. "I'd only tell you that because I know it won't go any farther. The show's so bad I suspect the network may cancel their order for the second six episodes before it even goes to air. A new job at this moment would be ideal. It's very kind of Rick to champion me, although my playing a law professor is almost as amusing as when you thought I was a producer. I can't think why he's so taken with me, but an actress always appreciates being wanted."

Alex smiled and took a sip of coffee. "Once Rick gets an idea in his head, he does all he can to browbeat it into existence."

"Don't be so hard on him." Rosemarie patted Alex's hand. "Isn't that what all we artists do, begin with a vision and work hard to turn it into a reality?"

"I guess." Alex had to hand that one to Rosemarie.

"Let's take our coffees outside." Rosemarie slid back the glass door that opened straight onto a glass walled deck. The surf crashed onto the jagged gray rocks only yards below. Raising her voice slightly to be heard over the waves, Rosemarie asked, "You and Rick, are you … I don't know the right term to use these days … are you two an item now?"

Alex felt ocean spray on his cheek as a roller crashed onto the rocks. He took a seat on a spiffy rattan set with lime cushions. "You could say," he said into the wind, brushing his hair out of his eyes.

Rosemarie took a seat too and cradled her coffee cup as if she needed the warmth. "Please don't feel any need to be reticent. You see, my son was gay. My daughter too. People asked me what I did wrong to have two gay children. People, sometimes even very intelligent ones, can be very narrow minded. My son died of cancer." Rosemarie averted her eyes to the rolling ocean. "And my daughter committed suicide. She struggled with mental issues. But they both had people in their lives who loved them until the end. It was a great blessing to me, knowing that they'd loved and been loved."

"That must have been tough for you," said Alex.

"I fell into a terrible depression for many years. To some degree I thought my life was over too. Hell, to some degree I *wanted* it to be over. But that's when I met Morton, at my lowest ebb. He came into my life and was like that big wind that blows in off the ocean. At first I felt like he'd put me in the middle of a hurricane, but if he hadn't come into my life I'd probably still be locked in my sadness, or be dead too. It's astounding how meeting someone new changes your life, it's as if they open a door into a whole new world. Quite miraculous when you think about it, isn't it?"

"Sure is."

Rosemarie put down her cup and asked seriously, "How's Luisa dealing with all of this? I mean, losing the part and your being with Rick?"

"I can't say how she feels about losing the part, but she's made it abundantly clear she hates me. She's convinced I manipulated Rick to get my name known in the art world. She also threatened that if I didn't break up with Rick, she'd do everything in her power to end my career. She actually visited Yumi Mihara to try and talk her out of exhibiting my work."

Rosemarie smiled graciously and stared sympathetically at him. "You know why Luisa acts that way, don't you, dear?"

Alex shook his head, baffled.

"It's because she's a cunt."

Alex nearly dropped his cup and saucer but controlled himself enough to put them gently on the table.

"Enough of this," said Rosemarie matter-of-factly, "let's go inside and look at art!" Rosemarie picked up their empty cups and led Alex inside.

Still reeling from the shock of hearing such a statement about Rick's mother from Rosemarie's fair lips, Alex struggled to concentrate as he began to show her his work. Raul and Esteban, whose snake hips and limpid eyes seemed more suited to world of modelling than domestic help, had unwrapped his pieces and propped them up around the room. As silently as the men had brought in the art, they'd slipped away to another wing of the house like two elegant ghosts.

Rosemarie was effusive and appreciative of all the pieces. She very much liked his new works with the horizontal lines. These beach abstracts attracted her. She studied them seriously, commenting on technique and tones. But she didn't get the glow in her eyes that the prospective buyer needs to make a sale. Alex began to wonder if he'd lost direction and gone off track. Then Rosemarie gasped and asked, "This can't be yours too?"

Alex saw that she was looking at the red abstract, the one he'd titled *Marooned on Red* that he'd been struggling with the day Rick turned up on the beach. A leaden pang of doom dropped in his stomach. She was obviously appalled. What had possessed him to bring it? In fact, he'd kept all of his red paintings out of Yumi's sight the day she'd visited. "Yeah, it's nothing. Just something I was toying with a while back. I'd been going through a tough time and I never could tell how I felt about this series. It was crazy of me to bring it, sorry you had to see it." Alex reached out to take the painting away.

Rosemarie pushed him back and rested her hand on her heart as she stared at the red abstract. "It has extraordinary power."

"It has? You mean you like it?"

"Very much. Very, very much." Rosemarie called out, "Raul!" A few seconds later Raul materialized. "Would you be so kind to hang this? I need to consider it in situ. Please, take down the Modigliani and put it there," said Rosemarie firmly.

Raul took a pair of white cotton gloves from the pocket of his black pants. After donning the gloves, and with great reverence, he took down the painting of a woman with an elongated face in a black top and maroon skirt and hung Alex's work in its place.

"Thank you, thank you. That's all." Rosemarie stared at Alex's painting as Raul blended back into the house. Rosemarie continued to gaze at his painting, seemingly losing herself in it while toying with her chiffon neckerchief. “This speaks to me. It’s full of rage and chaos yet such warmth. The tones of red are exquisite, and the way they drain to that pool at the bottom moves me.” She looked over her shoulder at Alex, “I’d no idea you were such a skilled abstract artist.”

Alex’s first thought was to contradict her, but after taking a moment to process Rosemarie’s compliment he smiled graciously in acceptance.

“I know this feeling. This pain in the heart. I know this red.” Rosemarie nodded at Alex. “I want it. I’ll have our attorney draw up the check.”

Yet again Alex was dumbfounded by how events could turn on a dime. His red paintings weren’t his favorites. He’d created them but couldn’t see in them what Rosemarie did. In fact, they disturbed him. Perhaps he should have burned them all and destroyed his unease along with them? What, on the spur of the moment, had impelled him to bring this picture today? Maybe there really was something to intuition and trusting your sixth sense, although he’d always written it off as mumbo jumbo. Or maybe life was simply what Kaori had been trying to convey in her performance piece, a series of random events on which our brains impose meaning.

On Alex’s return to the Cove, he stopped the Chevy outside the back door and started unloading the paintings. Something must be going on at the Waverleys, for he noticed their rear window blinds were raised. Glancing up at the dunes, their bronze Cadillac was parked there. Labor Day was nearly here, he concluded Gloria and Harry were back from vacation and had come to close up the house for fall. Alex kicked open the back door. “Hi, hi,” he called out as he carried the first couple of paintings into his studio. “Anyone home?”

An eerie silence filled the house. Going through to check if Rick was on the deck, Alex found the living room in disarray with half-empty packing boxes stacked around the place. He guessed Rick was upstairs trying to find space for his stuff from Brentwood. A creak on the floorboards overhead told him this was correct. "Hey, bud! Wanna give me a hand getting the rest of the paintings out of the car? Looks like the Waverleys are at the house and I don't want to block them in!" Getting no answer, Alex went back to the car to finish unloading by himself. Coming back inside, Rick appeared at the bottom of the stairs. His face was screwed up in rage, his top lip retracted in a snarl, his normally perfect skin mottled red. "What's up?" asked Alex putting down the last painting. Rick didn't speak, simply stood there fuming. "Bud, you're scaring me. Has something happened?" Alex's mind raced to deduce the cause of Rick's anger. Had Luisa paid a visit? He was just about to moot this, when he realized Rick had something in his hand. Shit … He'd meant to take that out from the back of his underwear drawer and destroy it weeks ago. Rick must have come across it when he was moving the bedroom around to put his clothes away. Yep, that's what Rick was holding - Sid's check for two thousand dollars.

"Sid's been giving you money?" spat Rick. He flicked the check with his finger. "Look at the date! That was the Sunday you forced me to go to Bel Air. You went back to talk to Sid after I'd gone to the car. Was this your fee for delivering me up to him?"

"I went back to apologize for your shitty behavior. He gave me this as thanks for looking after you."

"What the fuck? You're in Sid's employ! God, I was dumb to trust you."

Alex snatched the check and waved it in Rick's face. "I didn't cash it, see! I even went back and told him I couldn't take any more money from him."

"Any *more* money? You mean he'd given you money before?"

"No … Well, yes. He gave me a thousand dollars after the Beverly Hills doc fixed you up. He wanted to repay me for any expenses I'd incurred running around after you."

"Expenses incurred running around after me?" Rick's voice rose an octave, the veins on his neck bulged. "You're fucking joking! Was that why he wanted to see you at Fox while I was shooting *McMillan*?"

Alex held out his hands in surrender, there was no denying it was true. "Yes, but calm down and let me explain ..."

On the verge of exploding, Rick took a step back. "This is un-fucking-believable. Oh God, how could you do this to me?"

"Look, I went to see Sid at the studios because I regretted cashing that first check. I went to pay him back."

"Why'd you need money from him anyway? Wasn't I giving you enough in the rent?"

"I've never had money and I got carried away. I admit it was a mistake taking money from Sid, but I wanted to give Hank and Kaori something for the baby."

"You gave dead end Hank and fruitcake Kaori a thousand dollars?"

"I gave them five hundred. I used the rest to hire the boat for your birthday ..." As soon as his lips had moved, Alex regretted blurting that out.

Rick let out a hollow laugh. "You paid for my birthday present with Sid's money?"

"But like I told you, I went to see him to pay the money back. All of it, every last cent!" Alex struggled to get his mind working straight. Now becoming angry, his spine stiffened as he stepped forward. Jabbing his finger in Rick's shoulder, he spluttered, "And what have you got against Sid's money? He's been bankrolling you for years! It was his money you were giving me for the rent. And you didn't have any problem asking him to pay for the doctor you were so insistent I go see."

"That's completely different! I asked Sid to book the doctor because I was worried about you. And it was me giving you the money for the rent, not him! Don't you understand how going behind my back to Sid's such a betrayal? You've consistently lied to me! Jesus, you've ruined everything between us!" Rick's face crumpled, the rage left and despair took its place. "My life's never going to work. It's one endless series of lies and deceit. I just want to die and end this hell!" Rick took off and ran out onto the deck.

"Rick, come back! Don't run off like that ..." Alex heard the front door slam. In frustration, Alex raked his hands through his hair. He wondered if he should just let Rick blow off steam so they could discuss things rationally once he'd calmed down. But the last thing Rick said came back to him, "*I just want to die ...*" Alex dashed out to the deck and saw Rick racing to the cliffs. Not giving it a second thought, he jumped down to the beach and took off at full pelt in pursuit.

Gasping for breath when he reached the foot of the cliffs, Alex saw Rick scrambling upwards, shale and sand tumbling from his footfalls. The surf swirled around Alex's ankles waterlogging his deck shoes. Alex cupped his hands and yelled, "Rick, come down! There's nothing that can't be talked through!"

Rick stopped climbing and turned to shout down, "You're no different to the rest! Momma, Sid, Gina. None of you love me for me! I'm going to do what I should have when I came here months ago!" With that Rick carried on up the hillside.

Alex's instinct was to follow Rick and bring him down. He picked his way over the rocks, but anger checked him as a terrible fury rose from his guts. "You're one hell of a spoiled brat!" shouted Alex viciously. "You want everybody dancing to your tune and if things don't go your way then you pull this suicide shit. Well bucko, you're not blackmailing me! I've done everything I can do to make you happy. Yeah, I made a mistake taking money from Sid, but I recognized that mistake and tried to put it right. And you've no idea of the shit I had to take from your mother!"

Rick paused and cocked his head to listen.

"She came to the house when you were out and offered to pay me off to end our relationship. She accused me of terrible things and called me vile names. So if you think it's only money

I'm after, you're dead wrong. I could have named my price with her. But you know what I think now? I think I should have taken her money, because you don't trust me. Even though I've done nothing but my best for you! Go on, you selfish little shit! Go to the top of that cliff and throw yourself off! Put us all out of your misery!" With his heart pumping pure venom, Alex ran through the surf to the house without a backward glance.

Kicking off his sodden shoes, Alex hurled them across the deck and stomped in through the front door. Tearing off his wet t-shirt, he went directly to his studio. He had to channel his searing rage into art or else he'd destroy something. There was a blank canvas on the easel. Picking up the palette, he used his fingers to smear scarlet and cadmium red onto the canvas. His mind was not a part of this, this was a primal urge channeled directly through his body without interruption of brush or intellect. After he'd wiped the palette dry, Alex squirted vermillion from the tube onto his hands and daubed it across the canvas, creating blazing trails of red. He emptied one tube after another, venting his anger through color. But there wasn't enough paint in the world to express the pain that Rick couldn't see how much he truly loved him. As the canvas became a sea of maroons, crimsons and madders, its sanguinity triggered a memory ...

The sea of red filling his vision morphed into the blood filling his eyes that night his father had beat him so badly. The pain where the belt buckle struck his brow reignited. A blinding flash of clarity struck in its place. This was the moment his world turned red. Was this what he'd been unconsciously exploring in the red series? Was this pain the artistic block he'd unknowingly been trying to overcome? So many things in his life he hadn't confronted. He hadn't allowed himself to really mourn the loss of his mother, or acknowledged his father had tried to beat the gayness out of him, or after Dora's death had no blood relative who truly him. Alex paused, contemplating the red paint on his hands. In despair, he clapped them to his face. He'd been so angry with Rick that he'd said that terrible thing about suicide. He recognized those hateful words may have condemned to death the one person in the world he loved who may actually love him back. Praying it wasn't too late, that Rick hadn't already done anything dumb, he had to go to the cliffs and bring him home. He realized he'd acted exactly like his father, lashing out with violence. Alex fought back the tears he'd promised himself never to shed, terrified he was already too late to save Rick ... but then he heard Rick's voice.

"I'm sorry," said Rick from the doorway.

Exhausted from spent emotion, Alex laid his wet red palms on the canvas.

"Alex, look at me."

Letting his heartrate slow, Alex took a deep breath. "Never pull that shit with me again. I shouldn't have said what I did, but you shouldn't use the threat of suicide to punish people. It's too hurtful. Once a life's ended there's no way anything can be changed. Don't condemn yourself to the past."

"There's something off in my head, I know. Feelings take over and I can't stop myself. Forgive me, I shouldn't have gone off at you like that," Rick came towards Alex and reached out pleadingly.

Alex held out his wet red palms. "Whoa. I'm covered in paint. You'll get it all over you."

"That's okay." In a few deft moves Rick stripped off his t-shirt and shorts. Totally naked, he came to Alex.

A rush of adrenalin and lust coursed through Alex's body, his anger replaced by relief. Overjoyed, Alex grabbed Rick's waist and pulled him close. Kissing him, the red paint on his face smeared over Rick's. Running his hands over Rick's body, the red paint streaked Rick's neck and shoulders.

Rick dropped to his knees, his fingers urgently unzipping Alex's damp jeans then tugging them down to his ankles along with his undershorts. Once Rick had got back to his feet, and was making lip contact again, Alex stepped out of the puddle of his pants and kicked them aside. Breaking from their embrace, Alex grabbed a rag to wipe the paint off his hand. Reaching behind him, he snatched the bottle of linseed oil and poured a generous amount into his palm, letting the overrun trickle through his fingers. "Come here."

Alex roughly spun Rick about and smeared the oil over his butt. He parted Rick's cheeks and slid two oiled fingers inside him. Rick gasped. Momentarily he pulled away, but then pushed his ass into Alex's fingers, pulsing back and forth to get Alex's fingers in deeper. Rick then yanked Alex's hand out. Grabbing Alex's wrist, Rick dragged him toward the stairs. Alex's blood engorged cock was throbbing, desperate to plunge itself up Rick, desperate to plug the passage his fingers had primed for entry. Passion's need overwhelmed them. Unable to wait until they got upstairs, Alex bent Rick over the ugly mustard couch.

"Not here, Al, the paint will ruin it ..." murmured Rick.

"Good! I've never liked this fucking thing anyway." Alex authoritatively raised Rick to his feet and lifted his right leg onto the couch's arm, spreading his butt wide open. Alex trailed his oiled hand down Rick's back, then ran a finger between his ass cheeks to once more probe his willing passage, now loosened and receptive. After running his oiled hand up and down his own erect dick, he grasped it and eased its pulsing length inside Rick. He thrust his hips upwards. Daubs of red paint off Alex's hands and Rick's body left dark stains over the stylish couch. Neither of them cared. Alex restrained Rick's hips while rhythmically pounding him.

"Oh god, don't stop," moaned Rick.

"I don't plan to," grunted Alex. He grasped a handful of Rick's hair, yanking back his head. "I'm going to fuck you till morning."

"Oh yeah, yeah."

"I'm going to fuck you till you bleed."

"It'll be hard to tell with the red paint ..."

Alex slapped Rick's butt and rammed himself in deeper. "No humor."

"Aaah," Rick moaned.

Hearing Rick moan with pleasure made Alex want to fuck him harder. He slapped Rick's butt again. "Luisa asked why I do what I do for you," gasped Alex between grunts.

"What did you say? Ah, ah ..." groaned Rick.

"I told her, it's because I love you." As he spoke, Alex felt Rick's sphincter spasm around him. It was the most exquisite feeling he'd ever experienced. Without any manual stimulation, he felt Rick cumming. Rick's orgasm's pulses inside his ass caressing Alex's throbbing cock in waves more powerful than the ocean. A noise outside the house distracted him. On the verge of spurting his own climax, Alex opened his eyes a fraction and glimpsed a shadow on the deck. Opening his eyes fully and coming to his senses, he realized it was Gloria Waverly. "Shit!" Startled, Alex withdrew. He was so close to ejaculation the interruption made him lose control. His cum shot in viscid white gushes over the mustard couch. Panting to catch their breath, Alex and Rick both looked up.

Gloria Waverley stood on the verandah outside the window, staring in. She covered her mouth with her hand and stumbled down onto the beach.

"Oh, Jesus," muttered Alex. Running back to the studio he used the paint rag to wipe the paint off his face and cum dripping from his cock. He wriggled into his jeans.

Rick followed, agitatedly pulling on his shorts. "Maybe she didn't see anything?" reasoned Rick tugging down his t-shirt.

"She's not blind, Rick. She was right outside the window! Fuck, I forgot to move the car," said Alex, furious with himself. He realized he'd left it blocking the lane which was probably why Gloria had come around. Maybe she'd knocked on the back door and they hadn't heard and so she'd come around to try the front. He picked up the car keys, ready to move it when ...

Crash!

"What the hell was that?" asked Alex glancing out the kitchen window.

Crash!

"She's fucking lost it," spluttered Alex.

Gloria was picking up the pot plants from her back porch and hurling them at their house. "Pigs! You filthy pigs! What you were doing's against God! Filthy bastards!"

Alex opened the back door.

Crash!

A plant pot narrowly missed Alex's head and shattered on the door frame in an explosion of terracotta and earth. "Back off, Gloria! We were doing nothing wrong. We were in our own home, for fuck's sake."

Gloria ran towards him, her face expressing total disgust. "I thought you were nice young men!"

"We are, Gloria! This doesn't change that. We helped you when Harry ran out on you. I saved your life, remember?" reasoned Alex extending his hand to her.

"Get your faggot hands away from me," spat Gloria.

"What on earth's going on?" shouted Mrs. Piper coming out of her back door.

"I saw them!" Gloria pointed at Alex, while Rick cowered against the wall inside. "They were doing something unspeakable. Faggots!"

"Stop that, you stop that now!" For a frail old woman, Mrs. Piper sure had a powerful voice when required. "I won't allow that kind of talk here, Mrs. Waverley. Please show respect for your neighbors."

"Those faggy pigs don't deserve respect ..." Gloria was cut off mid-sentence as Mrs. Piper hauled back and slapped her across the face.

Harry had brought his car from the dunes. He was revving it, desperate to get past Alex's car.

"Move your car, Alex," said Mrs. Piper calmly.

Alex followed her orders.

Gloria wiped her mouth with the back of her hand, taking it away she saw a smear of blood. "I ought to call the cops on you," she muttered to Mrs. Piper. "And I should call the cops on them too," she said shooting a dark look at Rick.

"That's enough out of you, Gloria Waverley. Get in your car and be on your way," said Mrs. Piper forcibly.

Alex had reversed and Harry's path was clear.

Gloria tossed her head back with pride. She shouted defiantly to Harry in the car, "Looks like we did the right thing selling back the lease to this place. Sunset Cove isn't for the likes of us." Gloria swaggered to their car.

"And thank the Good Lord for that!" yelled Mrs. Piper after her. Moments later, the Waverleys' Cadillac shot off in a cloud of gravel. With the Waverleys out of the way, Alex drove up and parked in the dunes. "What on earth was all that about?" asked Mrs. Piper when he came back to the house.

"Rick and I were ..." Alex paused, then thought there was no point in lying. "We were having sex. Gloria saw something she shouldn't have. We were downstairs and the drapes were open. Rick, you okay buddy?"

"I need the bathroom," said Rick. He ducked off to the john, cupping his hand to his mouth.

Mrs. Piper followed Alex into the beach house. "You both look a mite shook up."

"That was unfortunate. Sorry for the disturbance"

"You've nothing to apologize for. That woman's off her rocker. Always has been."

"Even so. I hope we haven't shocked you too."

Mrs. Piper laughed and patted his bare shoulder. "I wish you could have seen this place back in the thirties. Everyone talks about sexual freedom and free love nowadays, but we had it back then too. That's why those of us who wanted to do our own thing in private came to Sunset Cove. In fact, it's why I bought your grandmother here."

"*You* brought her here?"

"You see, I loved your grandmother."

"Yeah, I know ..."

"No." Mrs. Piper fixed him squarely in the face. "I *loved* her. We were lovers."

Alex struggled to fit this new information into his brain. "What about Jim? You're married?"

"When you love someone, you carry on loving them. Sometimes relationships cool, or they become something else. And not all of us are wholly one thing or the other, totally gay, totally straight. Dora and I stopped being lovers, but we never stopped loving each other. And I carried on loving her right to the end."

Alex remembered the times Mrs. Piper had been around the house during Dora's last months. He'd always thought what a wonderful friend and neighbor she'd been, even helping Dora to the bathroom when she'd been struggling in her final weeks.

"I'll leave you boys to get on with your evening." Mrs. Piper patted Alex's bare arm again. "Some people mistake kindness and caring for weakness. But your grandmother always felt those were your two greatest strengths. She was very proud of you for that. I shouldn't have lashed out at Gloria like I did, but she got me so riled. I'll have to paint something very beautiful tomorrow to make up for it. You're a good man, Alex. This world needs more of your kind."

Alex accompanied Mrs. Piper to the back door. "I loved grandma very much. Not a day goes by that I don't think of her."

"Me too," said Mrs. Piper. As she left, she glanced at the Waverleys' house. "Let's hope some decent folk move in next."

Rick came out of the bathroom, still a little green around the gills. "What was all that about with Mrs. Piper?" he asked.

"Apparently she and grandma were lovers in the past. Funny how we forget old people were young like us once. Explains why my family were so dead set against Dora," said Alex sadly. He stood behind Rick and tenderly wrapped his arms around him. "What we had going on back then felt pretty great until Gloria interrupted my flow."

"Wanna pick up where we left off?" asked Rick twisting his head around to check Alex's face. "Are we okay again?"

"Yeah," Alex nodded. "We're okay."

"Why didn't you tell me what momma said to you?"

"I didn't want to drive an even bigger wedge between you two, and I guess I could see things from her point of view to some degree."

"Really, when you consider how nuts momma and dad are, it's amazing I've turned out as level headed as I have."

Alex burst out laughing. "Positively miraculous."

"Back to what I was saying, wanna rewind the clock?"

"Yeah, but we'd better go upstairs this time." Alex smiled knowingly at Rick, then added, "Just in case any Mormons come knocking on the door."

Rick stared at the mustard couch, stained with paint, oil and cum. "Looks like we need another new couch," he said regretfully.

"Good. Buy one we can actually sit on next time."

Taking it on the chin, Rick laughed as they climbed the stairs.

THE SHOOT

"That's nice! Rick, can you turn to Tina? Look at her like she's just said something funny, but it's made you angry too. Tina, pull away from Rick like he's trying to kiss you and you're not in the mood, but still smiling. Keep it feisty, Tina. But still vulnerable!" The photographer twittered on. Watching the photoshoot from a folding canvas chair by craft services, Alex struggled to hide his bemusement as Rick and Tina Mason did their best to comply with the photographer's contradictory demands.

The publicity shoot was taking place in front of a rust backdrop which rolled down the wall onto the floor giving a seamless backdrop of color. These photos would be the first images of N.B.C.'s new detective duo, destined to be distributed to the press and affiliated T.V. stations to generate interest in the show. The costume designer had dressed Rick in a navy jacket with blue button-down collar shirt and a red and white striped tie. Tina, in her role as Carol, was wearing a scarlet blouse, tan culottes, brown knee boots, blue eye shadow and red lipstick. Hair and make-up people hovered on the perimeter, rushing up to powder and titivate the stars whenever there was a break in shooting. Alex frankly couldn't see what difference they'd made after they'd titivated the stars, but their activity added to the sense of something important going on.

"Rick, Tina, back off and when I say 'go' walk towards me with determination. But keep smiling! Brad and Carol want to solve a gruesome murder but still have fun along the way! I need to see all that! Okay. Go!"

Rick and Tina were doing their best to deliver, but that was one heck of a lot of subtext to pack into eight steps towards the camera. Alex struggled to suppress an involuntary giggle as they backed up for another attempt.

"Hold it a mo." The photographer shoved his camera to the assistant by his side and snatched a freshly loaded one. "Do that again. Happy, but determined."

"Ron. Ron Payne. I'm the show's producer. You're Rick's friend, aren't you?" asked a handsome dark-haired man wearing a natty Prince of Wales checked suit and white open necked shirt as he poured himself a Perrier.

"Yeah, Alex Morgan. Hi," said Alex getting up from his chair, afraid he was going to be reprimanded for smirking.

"The painter, right?" asked Ron while taking a couple of grapes off the table.

"Yeah," answered Alex wondering where this was going.

"Rick mentioned he was living in an artist's colony down the coast." Ron popped a grape into his mouth, he fixed Alex with his brooding eyes as he chewed. Ron swallowed, then said, "I like the atmosphere around Laguna. Some nice bars there." Ron sipped his water and watched Tina and Rick walk towards the camera while the photographer clicked away. "They make a good-looking couple, don't you think?" whispered Ron moving closer to Alex.

Alex became aware of Ron's citrus cologne and Ron's shoulder pressing into his. "Sure do," replied Alex. It was true. Rick's pretty boy looks contrasted well with Tina Mason's angular face. Alex had heard Rick describe certain women in the industry as 'tough cookies', Tina seemed to fit this bill.

"This is an important shoot," said Ron in Alex's ear. "If the network gets behind the show one of these pictures could be a T.V. Guide cover."

"Fingers crossed," said Alex wondering why Ron practically had his arm around him.

"Look, I'd like to ask you something ..."

Alex felt Ron's bicep flex under his suit sleeve as he gripped his water glass. "You're an artist. Tell me, how do you think the shoot looks?" Ron left his eyes fixed on Rick and Tina but bent his head close to Alex for his response.

Being economical with the truth had got him into trouble recently, so Alex figured he'd give his honest opinion. "Brad and Carol are mean to be students."

"Huh?" Ron turned his full attention to Alex. "What're you saying?"

"The way they're dressed makes them look like somebody's parents."

"Bradley's a student, but he is a student of law," reasoned Ron, a little defensively.

"He looks like a fully-fledged lawyer in that get-up. And Carol's dressed like a secretary, combined with that make-up it makes her look closer to thirty than twenty. And the backdrop's gloomy. From what Rick's told me this show's meant to be fun and frothy. These visuals project neither of those elements."

Ron popped another grape in his mouth and chewed it as he digested what Alex just said. "Interesting. Good to talk with you. Maybe we can catch up down the coast one day?" Ron put down his empty glass and hurried onto the set.

Alex went back to mooching the craft services table. He poured another coffee and resisted the temptation of a donut. Returning to the sanctuary of his canvas chair, he realized the shoot had paused. Ron was conferencing with the photographer and a red-haired woman with a pair of spectacles dangling on a chain around her neck. Once the conflab had wound up, the woman put on her glasses and took Rick and Tina off the set. The photographer's assistants rolled up the rust paper. A few moments later the background was replaced by a sunny yellow one. Alex checked the time on Rick's gold watch, which he was wearing for safekeeping. This delay would make the shoot overrun, which in turn would make them late for Scotty's opening. He was about to find a pay phone to let Scotty know they'd be late when Rick and Tina returned to set. They'd had a costume change. Tina was now wearing white knee socks and tennis shoes, a plaid mini skirt and a cute short sleeved turtle neck. No longer in shirt and tie, Rick wore the same navy jacket but over a faded orange polo shirt teamed with khaki pants and scuffed sneakers. Both their hairstyles had been loosened and Tina's make-up toned down.

They repeated the same photo set ups, but this time everything played better. Rick and Tina appeared relaxed yet determined. Feisty yet compliant. In love yet at odds. Compared to the torture of the previous two hours, the shoot's final thirty minutes went swimmingly well. So well, in fact, that they wrapped only ten minutes over schedule with a round of applause and everybody congratulating each other on a job well done.

Rick ducked off to the dressing room and quickly changed into a black crew neck sweater and gray suit, the light layer of pancake left on his face giving him an ultra-perfect sheen. "How we doing for time?" Rick asked Alex after he'd said hasty goodbyes to Tina and Ron and thanked the photographer.

"Fine, we'll make it," said Alex handing back Rick's watch as they left the studio, jumped in the car and headed downtown.

"Thank God they changed those costumes," laughed Rick in the car. "Ron insisted the designer knew what she was doing, but I didn't think they were right to begin with. I don't know what made Ron change his mind, but it was a good call. Guess that's why he's a top producer."

"I guess so," said Alex wondering if he should call up Ron and ask for a job as an art director.

Pockets of construction were springing up around downtown as the city attempted to regenerate the district. Scaffolding towers around the new Bonaventure Hotel spiked into the graphite and watermelon dusk sky. Although the downtown area attracted rushes of business during the day when night fell the abandoned soap factories and boarded-up store fronts became a ghost town. That's when the area belonged to Skid Row's wandering homeless and helpless, their next meal at Hippie Kitchen the only thing to look forward to.

"Maybe LaFonte's made a brilliant business decision but opening a gallery here seems risky to me," said Rick as they pulled up on a gloomy street.

"But these are terrific old buildings," said Alex looking up. "They're big spaces. And I bet they'll be going cheap seeing as no-one wants to be here. Kind of reminds me of Venice Beach when we first squatted there. I may need somewhere big if Yumi's hotel commission comes through. You know, this area could be ideal for artists."

"Yeah, artists are hardly likely to get mugged for paint. But will LaFonte get high rollers to venture here?"

"He's not having any problems tonight," said Alex tilting his head at the Rolls-Royces, Cadillacs and Lincolns lining the street, although they all had chauffeurs sitting guard behind the wheel. Rick maintained his dubious expression as Alex reversed the red Mercedes into a vacant spot. Although Rick had given the Brentwood keys back to Sid, and told him he didn't need his allowance anymore, the Mercedes was a part of Sid's largesse Rick was hanging on to for now.

There was nothing ritzy or fancy about the LaFonte Gallery's exterior. Sandwiched between derelict tin warehouses, however, simply the fact the building was in good repair made it stick out like a sore thumb. Its windows onto the sidewalk were mirrored so no-one could see inside, and the entrance was through an unmarked black metal door. The gallery's only identification was '2701' in silver numerals.

"Don't you think it resembles a mausoleum?" hissed Rick as they entered.

Alex had to agree. The vestibule off the street had been painted dark green with a single stem of giant red anthurium in a slim black vase on a gold pedestal, a targeted spotlight lighting the waxy red bloom. The effect was dramatic and a good introduction to Scotty's work, but it did lend the entrance a funereal atmosphere. The hum of conversation inside the gallery was audible through the double doors. "This feels more like going to view the body than see an exhibition," muttered Rick pushing inside.

Guy LaFonte had been watching the door. As soon as he spotted Rick and Alex enter, he dropped his conversation to make a beeline for them. "Gentlemen! Isn't this spectacular?" Indeed, it was. The dark matt walls receded as focused spotlights targeted Scotty's glossy three-dimensional blooms, and boy did the contrast make her pieces pop. "Scotty's a visionary. These subfusc walls are perfect for her work." LaFonte rolled his eyes. "But if I ever get them back to white after this it will be a miracle. Still, that's the future. Please, allow Greta to serve you drinks and give you a catalog." LaFonte snapped his fingers at a girl with Cher like hair parted in curtains. Dressed in a slinky black catsuit, she appeared like a white face hovering in the dark as she came to them with a tray.

As Rick and Alex accepted glasses of champagne, Scotty hustled towards them, acknowledging people on her way. "How'd I do?" she asked nervously.

"Real great. Congratulations," said Alex raising his glass.

"I'm elated today's here. My heart couldn't take any more worrying. And Rick, I owe you bigtime for helping with painting the place," said Scotty warmly.

"I only did the twelve square yards behind the iris. And I got as much paint on me as I did on the wall."

"Yeah, getting covered with paint's becoming a habit with you," Alex said to Rick with a wry smile. His comment went over Scotty's head - as it should.

Scotty kept glancing at the entrance as more guests arrived. She smoothed down her black velvet pants which she'd combined with a severely cut white shirt and black tie. "Have you spoken with your mother lately?" Scotty asked Rick.

"Not recently," replied Rick.

"You're not aware if she's coming, then?"

"I don't think she'll show. I figure she's keeping a low profile after pulling out of the show."

Alex noticed Rick had told Scotty that Luisa pulled out of the show rather than saying she'd asked for too much money and been knocked out. That was kind of him.

"Here's my boys!" Bob's voice boomed out in the stygian gloom. In keeping with the evening's theme, Bob was wearing a black suit and black shirt but had punched it up with a jaunty yellow tie. This aided his visibility but also made him look like the Mafia. After they'd all said hi, Bob laughingly remarked, "If you take note of Scotty's outfit it's clear you guys aren't the only ones who can argue about who wears the pants in the relationship!"

"Very funny," said Alex, not totally appreciating the humor.

"Excuse me. Monica Aigner just arrived." Scotty instantly slipped away.

Rick, Alex and Bob moved deeper into the gallery.

"Scotty couldn't have done this without you guys," said Bob sincerely. "You're the professional actor in our merry band, Rick, but Scotty puts on an act. She gives the outward appearance of confidence and bravado, but underneath she's a quivering wreck. Believe me, I see the picture's other side. And I appreciate anyone who buoys her up. The mark of true friends is when they stick together through thick and thin. And Scotty tells me we'll be getting a houseguest when you start filming," said Bob draping his arm around Rick's shoulder.

"I've been at the shooting range taking lessons in preparation. I hear one has to know their way around firearms in your house," quipped Rick.

Bob wagged his finger at Rick, then patted the underarm of his oversized jacket. "We all need to be prepared. Take this jerk who blew up that bomb at the airport. The press are calling him the Alphabet Bomber. Guy's some immigrant from Yugoslavia or wherever. Part of a group called Aliens in America, and we're not talking *Star Trek* aliens here," laughed Bob sardonically. "This is the beginning, I warn you. World War Three's around the corner, and it's gonna be fought on our soil. These terrorists fund themselves through crime and drugs. Hard working Joes are too busy earning a crust to build bombs. It's the criminal unemployed and illegals who pose the real threat to our country's way of life."

Alex lifted his glass. "Let's do politics tomorrow. Tonight's for Scotty, here's to her."

Bob came down off his high horse and they clinked glasses.

"And to Rick too. They did the photo shoot for his new show today." Alex was aware that Bob's brain gravitated to showbiz gossip and knew this would make a great segue out of World War Three.

"Ah yes, you've got Tina Mason in the line-up. Nice girl, but one helluva tough cookie," said Bob.

Alex realized he was getting to know show business too well.

"Any news on who's replacing your mother?" asked Bob.

"Replacing's not quite the word as she hadn't actually signed for it," reasoned Rick. "However, it's looking like Rosemarie Rodgers will get it. She's contracted on another show, but they think they can juggle the schedule to let her do both. We're shooting at Universal and her current show is too, so if they can agree her deal it's looking good."

Bob grabbed the back of Rick's neck with a bear like paw and shook him. "Word is your segment's going to be a terrific season opener. You got the chops, kid, and you got this one happier than I've seen him in forever." Bob pawed Alex with his other hand. "You guys are more than friends, you know?"

Alex and Rick checked with each other, wondering what Bob was going to say next.

"You're family." Bob extended his arms.

"Bob, as well as looking like the Mafia now you sound like it too," laughed Rick.

Bob clicked his fingers at Rick. "Your *McMillan* airs Wednesday. Scotty and I are throwing a screening party for you at our place."

Rick began to say 'no'.

"And we will not let you say no! I'm inviting every big hitter I know. And you invite anyone you want too. As long as they're high up the ladder. Let's keep this purely A-list. I'll set T.V.s up all over the house. Ask your mother and Koenig, and make sure they come."

"That's swell of you Bob. I'll ask momma, but I can't guarantee anything," said Rick.

Bob was on a roll. "And Sid! Invite Sid! Oh, and Lavinia too."

"Letitia," corrected Alex.

Bob clapped his hands in satisfaction. "This party's going to make a big splash. I want to show the world you have the top men in Hollywood behind you."

Rick thanked Bob and made an excuse to break away. Alex caught up with Rick when he came to get another drink. Rick muttered, "Bob's party sounds like the night from hell. What if I'm lousy in the show? I pray I get struck down with beriberi. But I'm guessing any excuse that doesn't involve intensive care won't cut it with Bob."

"Fingers crossed on the beriberi front then," joked Alex blackly.

More people were cramming into the gallery. Scotty was everywhere at once. Explaining her work, making sure Greta got drinks to everyone, being charming. The red dots indicating sales were spreading faster than measles in a nursery. He was not a denizen of openings, but Alex had been to enough now to spot the familiar types - the true art aficionados, the financial speculators, the critics, the curious and those who'd go to the opening of an envelope. A barrage of flash bulbs went off outside, flashes bright enough to be visible through the tinted windows.

"It's Danielle. I'd no idea she was coming. The press must have had a tip off she'd be here," said Rick.

Danielle swept into the room. Her electrifying beauty made even more electrifying by the cobalt silk blouse and diamond necklace she had on. LaFonte was overwhelmed she'd turned up to his gallery. "Miss Brown, what a pleasure to meet you." He couldn't have greeted Garbo more humbly. Danielle thanked him with an extra dollop of southern added to her already very southern accent.

"Laying it on a bit thick, aren't you?" Alex joked quietly after she'd broken away from LaFonte and blended into the throng.

"Have to give the customers what they want," laughed Danielle.

Always one for accessories, Monica Aigner had put the finishing touch to her outfit with a small dog. She clutched it like a furry purse, which many people thought it was until it moved. "Darlings, you must meet Mimi!" LaFonte put his hand out to pat the dog, which immediately snapped at him. "Naughty, Mimi!" barked Monica, although chuckling indulgently as LaFonte surreptitiously checked his finger for blood.

"That dog's got taste," muttered Rick to Alex and Danielle.

"Alex," hissed Monica interrupting their illicit merriment. "May I have a private word with?"

"Sure. Excuse me." Alex allowed Monica to guide him to a secluded corner.

Monica clutched Mimi with one hand and her champagne in the other. "Rosemarie Rodgers is a dear old acquaintance of mine. God forbid I should ever say a word against her, but she can be a soupçon, how can I put this ... stifling. I shouldn't want you to feel that she's the only woman in L.A. with an eye for your talent." Monica fluttered her lashes unbecomingly.

"You surprise me. I was under the impression you weren't very fond of me. I heard you've been telling people I had a plan to increase my prices by having Rosemarie turn up to bid. I knew nothing about her being there that night, I assure you."

Monica placed her empty glass on a passing tray and fiddled nervously with her ugly emerald earring, "Oh, that terrible evening with the awful plane crash piece. It took my maid over a week to get the smoke out of my Chanel. I was very angry with Guy for dragging me to Venice Beach to have my eyebrows singed off. You were very lucky to miss that one, Mimi, weren't you, darling?" Mimi didn't seem to care one way or the other and was dozing off. "And, on reflection, I fear Luisa led me into saying things that could be misinterpreted. Anyway, Autumn Thayer let slip over lunch that Rosemarie's bought another of your pieces. She saw it in Malibu last week. I'm feeling terribly left out that I don't have you in my collection."

This was how it worked. Gossip, competition, smiling to your face when needed, daggers in the back when not. Giving Monica one of his most dazzling smiles, Alex responded, "And I'd love for you to have something of mine in your collection. Let's fix a time and date. I can either meet you at Yumi Mihara's gallery or bring my new pieces to you." Alex wondered if he was selling out. Perhaps, but to make money as an artist people had to want to buy your art – for whatever reason.

"Coming to me would be more intimate, don't you think, Mimi? Besides, I can never understand a single word dear Yumi says." Monica snuggled her little dog, then patted Alex's arm. "I'm so glad we've put this little misunderstanding behind us."

As Monica rejoined the party, Alex was aware Rick had been earwigging the last part of the conversation.

"Nice work," Rick whispered as they moved away.

"There's no point continuing a war that shouldn't have begun in the first place," said Alex.

Having fulfilled her quota of mingling, Danielle sidled up to them. "Rescue me," she whispered, while subtly glancing behind at the old man peering gummily through the crowd at her.

"That's John VanFleet Junior. Sixty-three and loaded. He'd set you up in your own production company if you asked him," explained Rick.

"I fear the price I'd have to pay is too high," laughed Danielle.

"We're grabbing a bite with Scotty and Bob afterwards," said Alex, "you're welcome to join us."

Danielle patted her diamonds. "I'm dressed more for uptown than downtown. Apart from that, I have an early call in the morning. I only wanted to drop by to get some publicity for Scotty. The press hounds me relentlessly, so someone may as well benefit from it. Rick, take my arm, let's grab Scotty and flaunt ourselves before the press."

Alex watched the flashbulbs pop around Danielle, Scotty and Rick as they moved through the room. They all looked great, which combined with Scotty's larger than life art works as background should make for some terrific photos.

After the photo opportunity, Scotty came back to Alex and squeezed his hand. "See all the sales! It's gone better than I'd dared hope."

Bob arrived beside them just in time to hear that. "Marvelous. You can buy the steaks next week."

Scotty scanned the gallery. "Shame R.J. and Natalie didn't make it."

"They already own one of your pieces, dear," said Bob.

"I know. But who other than them will see it hanging in their master suite? It would have been nice if they'd come," said Scotty with a pout.

The gallery was thinning. Everyone on their way out commented on the outstanding quality of Scotty's work and how the dramatically darkened décor of the LaFonte Gallery made her show a truly eye-popping event.

"Why's everyone leaving?" asked Scotty sadly.

"Because everything's been sold," added Bob. "And maybe they're as hungry as I am. Let's go eat."

"Around here?" questioned Scotty. "Can you give me my jacket, Greta?"

LaFonte's assistant took the last item off the rail in the coat check and handed Scotty her black jacket.

"There's a saloon a block away," said Bob.

Scotty made a baffled face as Bob helped her on with her jacket. "How on earth do you know about that?

"I get around. A man about town."

The final attendees spilled onto the sidewalk, LaFonte locked the doors behind them. Scotty went to get in Bob's black Mercedes. "Honey, it's a block away. We can walk it," said Bob.

"Walk? Around here?" asked Scotty incredulously.

"LaFonte lives above his gallery. Look, the streets are empty. No-one's around, good or bad."

Grudgingly, Scotty came away from the car and joined Bob. Together with Rick and Alex they walked down the street. The cars of the last departing guests overtook them as they turned the corner. Up ahead they saw a red neon sign with flashing yellow arrow pointing to the saloon's entrance at the end of the block. Alex felt everyone was relieved that the bar was as close as Bob had said. They all piled inside.

The saloon's dark wood paneling and etched glass interior was like stepping back forty years. Dim globe lights hung from a paneled tin ceiling. Behind the bar, a white aproned bartender was polishing glasses. A blousy waitress with purple rings under her eyes showed them to a table. Before she poured their water, she pointedly remarked the kitchen was near to closing. They took this as their cue to order a round of turkey dip sandwiches and beers without even perusing the menu.

"I don't feel dressed for this," muttered Scotty tucking a napkin over her pristine white shirt and black tie.

Their order arrived on the table like lightning. The staff was obviously keen to close up. While the waitress wiped tables around them and refilled ketchup bottles, Bob demonstrated how to eat the turkey dips. He spread a generous smear of mustard on his sandwich and dipped it into the side order of gravy before taking a big bite. The sandwiches were messy but delicious. As they ate, Rick filled them in on the photoshoot that afternoon.

Listening to them chattering away, Alex couldn't help his mind wandering while he munched his sandwich. He hadn't told Scotty about what had happened with Gloria Waverley. He guessed Rick was unlikely to bring it up either. Although he wasn't ashamed of what they'd been doing, he'd feel pretty raw if word of it got out. They'd been in their own home, but admittedly they had left the drapes open. Did that make them somehow culpable? Because the beach had such a laid-back vibe he'd never considered if people could see into the beach house. A queasy feeling overtook him, what if other people had seen them making love over the summer?

"Earth to Alex, are you receiving me, over?" Bob waved his hand before Alex's eyes.

"What?" Alex realized everyone was getting up to leave.

Bob tossed a couple of twenties on the table. "My shout. Don't say I don't show you the high life."

Barely disguising a yawn, the waitress saw them out. She flipped the sign on the door to 'closed' as she locked up. The lights inside went out before they'd gone up the small flight of steps to the sidewalk. Across the street, a lumpy shape in a dark doorway was either a derelict who'd bedded down for the night or a boozer who was the worse for wear. Caught by a sudden gust of wind, a tin can rattled along the sidewalk.

"Santa Anas are kicking up early this year," said Bob.

Feeling the hot dry air on his face, Alex agreed.

"LaFonte will be tucked up in bed by now," said Scotty glancing at the dark windows above the gallery once they'd turned the corner. "It's been a great night. Thanks for coming."

"See you Wednesday at our place," reminded Bob fumbling in his pocket for his keys.

"Sure thing," said Rick unsurely.

Alex guessed Rick was thinking up some way to get out of this event. They walked on to the Mercedes. "See you," called Alex over his shoulder. As he looked back to wave goodbye, a movement in the shadows behind Bob caught his eye. The wind might have been hot, but a cold shiver prickled his skin. "Bob!"

Bob looked up while unlocking the car.

A down at heel guy in a grimy windbreaker emerged from the darkness and approached Bob.

"Be careful," said Scotty coming around to Bob from her side of the car.

Alex walked towards Bob and Rick followed.

"I got no cash on me," Bob said conversationally to the guy while raising his hands.

The guy lifted his left hand and reached into his windbreaker's pocket.

After unbuttoning his suit jacket, Bob slipped his right hand inside and said to the street guy, "Move along, buddy. Let's all get on with our evenings. Scotty, get in the car."

Scotty went back to the passenger door while shooting an anxious glance at Alex and Rick who were going to Bob's aide. As Alex came up to Bob, the guy in the windbreaker withdraw his left hand. Bob went to draw his gun from his shoulder holster. The rough guy with the straggly moustache and limp hair reached out and handed Bob a crumpled piece of paper.

"He wants you to read something," said Alex figuring the guy didn't speak English and had written a begging note.

Relieved this wasn't a hold up, Bob removed his hand from his jacket without his gun.

In his peripheral vision, Alex saw the guy's right-hand move.

"Gimme your watches," growled the guy.

Rick's feet scuttled on the sidewalk as he shouted, "He's pulling a gun!"

The guy's right hand, with a gun in it, flew out of his windbreaker. "Gimme your watches and money and no-one gets hurt! Freeze!" The guy pointed his gun at Rick.

"Do what he says. Rick, give him your watch." Bob's voice was firm and cool.

Seeing Bob's eyes flick to Rick's, Alex knew he had a plan and could tell Rick had cottoned on to it.

"Here, have my watch. It's a good one. A Rolex. See, I'm taking it off. Give me a moment, the clasp's tricky," said Rick. Making a show of lifting his hand to undo the watch, Rick steadily approached the guy. Rick slid off his shiny gold watch. "Here, catch!" Rick tossed his watch to the guy.

It wasn't a great throw and the robber fumbled to catch the watch with his left hand.

Bob's shaking hand reached into his jacket again. "Drop, Rick!" barked Bob. This time Bob pulled his gun and aimed at the assailant.

Realizing Bob was now armed, the robber pointed his gun at Bob's head.

If Bob was going to shoot, Alex knew he had to do it immediately. The robber's finger moved to squeeze the trigger. But Bob didn't fire. Alex lurched forward and hurled himself at the robber.

Bang!

The assailant's gun fired a random shot as Alex tackled him to the ground. Falling under Alex's weight, the assailant lost grip of the gun and it clattered along the ground.

Scotty screamed.

Sprawled on the sidewalk, the mugger's fingers stretched out to his gun.

Rolling off the assailant, Alex kicked the gun out of his reach.

Stuffing Rick's Rolex in his windbreaker, the robber scrambled to his feet. Seeing his firearm was too far away to retrieve, the weasel faced assailant shot a menacing glare at Alex, then turned on his heels and scuttled off into the night.

A light came on upstairs at LaFonte's.

"Jesus Christ," muttered Bob holstering his gun and buttoning his jacket. "What the hell was that?" Gathering his wits, he checked around. "You okay, honey?"

Scotty came around the car, "I'm fine. That was scary."

"You all right, Alex?" asked Bob.

Dusting himself off, Alex got up. "Yep, good here."

The window above the gallery slid up and LaFonte's head poked out. "I've called the police!"

Almost immediately sirens were heard in the distance. Alex realized they hadn't checked Rick in the roll call. "Rick, you okay?" He looked around and saw Rick prone on the ground. "Rick!" Alex and Scotty rushed to him and knelt either side.

The gallery's front door rattled as LaFonte fumbled to unlock it.

"He's been hit," gasped Scotty.

Alex's heart was pounding so hard it was about to bust out of his chest. Together with Scotty they rolled Rick over. He was motionless.

That's when they saw dark red blood soaking through his pale gray jacket.

A BURIAL AT WESTWOOD

Over a hundred mourners were congregated around the grave.

Alex lifted his eyes as the pallbearers emerged from the chapel. Seeing the white casket strewn with yellow flowers borne on their shoulders, life once again took on the quality of an unending dream. Or rather nightmare. The fact he was at the funeral at all, sitting in the family section beside Letitia, Tyler and Tiffany, with Luisa breathing down his neck from the row behind, only added to the surreal quality of the past five days. A soprano began to sing ...

There's a place for us.

Letitia's emotion overwhelmed her. "He loved this song," she gasped covering her mouth with a lace handkerchief to stifle her sobs. Not because they had a total grip on the situation, but more because their mom was becoming upset, Tyler and Tiffany began sniveling. Alex heard Luisa's snort of annoyance. Letitia must have heard it too. "Shh," she whispered to the kids, "mustn't make noise. Listen to the nice lady sing." Letitia pulled Tiffany onto her lap and clasped Tyler's head to her chest. Maybe it was to comfort them, or maybe to keep them quiet thus avoiding Luisa's disapproval.

The song underscored the pallbearers' deliberate procession to the grave. The honorary pallbearers, a phalanx of old movie stars and technical crew, walked alongside

Somewhere.

The pallbearers lowered the casket onto the cradle above the open grave.

Somehow.

The pallbearers stepped back.

Someday ...

The minister approached the microphone, took a pause, then began, "Dearly beloved, we gather here today in the sight of God ..."

Hollywood's great and good, and not so great or good, had all turned out to pay their respects. Their display of genuine grief was touching, but there was only one face Alex wanted to see right now. Only one face could perhaps make this better. That was Rick's.

And he wasn't here.

Alex shifted uncomfortably as the priest continued the address. To take his mind off the service, and use his time more productively than listening to homilies he didn't believe in, Alex rewound to the night of Scotty's showing at the LaFonte Gallery. Perhaps running through the events of that fateful night again could make some sense out of the madness ...

The moment after the mugger had fled, leaving his gun behind, they'd collectively thanked their lucky stars that the danger had passed. Then they'd realized Rick was sprawled face down on the sidewalk. "Rick?" Alex had gasped, kneeling beside him. They rolled him over as gently as possible. That's when they'd seen the blood.

"Is he alive?" asked Scotty choking back tears.

After the jangling of keys being turned and bolts being pulled back, the gallery's heavy front door clanged open. LaFonte stepped onto the sidewalk. "Was that gunfire?" he asked wrapping a long black velour robe around himself.

"Yeah. Get back inside and call an ambulance. We need an ambulance here, damnit man!" Bob yelled at LaFonte.

Casting his eyes down to Rick, with Alex and Scotty ministering to him, LaFonte raised a trembling hand to his mouth. "This is terrible," he stuttered rushing back inside.

"Do you feel a pulse?" asked Scotty.

Alex pressed his fingers to the side of Rick's neck. "Yeah. Weak but there." He saw a lump on Rick's forehead and a streak of blood dribbling from his open mouth. "The fall must've knocked him out." The left side of Rick's gray jacket was wet with blood. "Rick. Rick, babe?" Alex patted Rick's face.

"Do you see where the bullet hit?" asked Bob peering down.

The street was dark, making it tough to see any detail. Getting his act together, Alex focused on the job in hand. Observing the blood soaking through Rick's pale gray jacket, he distinguished the darkest spot, the stain's epicenter. Running his hand over it, Alex's middle finger found the dent made by the bullet's entry. "Got it. We need to apply pressure. Get me a towel or something."

"I'll go find LaFonte." Scotty skittered into the gallery.

"How's he doing?" muttered Bob.

"He's breathing," responded Alex pressing his palms over the wound. "I hope I'm doing the right thing."

"This is so fucked up," murmured Bob under his breath.

"So very fucked up," agreed Alex.

"Before the cops show up, Al, we ought to get our stories straight," said Bob as he heard a siren's wail getting closer.

"What?" asked Alex distractedly.

"It would be better if we didn't say I pulled a gun."

"It was self-defense, Bob. The guy had a gun pointed at your head."

"I know that. But let's tell them I slipped my hand into my jacket for my wallet and he only assumed I was going for a gun. Tell them that when Rick threw his watch you took advantage of the distraction to tackle the guy."

"But that's not how it happened?"

"Jesus, Al. I've my reputation as a lawyer to consider. I can't afford to have my integrity questioned."

"I don't understand, Bob." They heard another set of sirens, slightly further away this time. "The guy's finger was about to squeeze the trigger."

"It'd just be better if no-one says I had a gun," said Bob insistently. A police car, siren wailing and lights blazing, crunched around the corner. Bob whispered forcibly in Alex's ear, "I'm still waiting on my application to carry a concealed weapon. Damn that Tom Bradley ..."

"Shit, Bob! If you're not licensed to carry, then why'd you bring the gun?"

"We're in a bad neighborhood," hissed Bob glancing over his shoulder. "And everyone carries from time to time. I figured just seeing I had a gun would scare him off."

"Is that why you didn't fire?"

"Jesus, you never think you're going to have to shoot someone. Carrying without a permit could get me a misdemeanor conviction. This could ruin me, Al," said Bob plaintively.

The police car's siren stopped, and two cops hauled themselves out of the vehicle.

"We need an ambulance. My friend's been shot!" barked Alex as the cops lumbered towards him.

"The call's in. They're on their way," growled the larger of the two uniformed men. "What's gone down here?"

"We were getting into our cars when some goon threatened us with a gun," said Bob rising to his feet.

The shorter of the two cops bent down to check on Rick and Alex.

Scotty dashed out of the gallery carrying several towels, LaFonte hard on her heels. He'd swapped his velour lounging robe for a cable knit sweater over his striped pajama pants. "Here," Scotty passed the towels to Alex.

"And the assailant shot the victim? He put up a fight or something?" asked the burly taller cop.

"No. I reached inside my jacket to give the guy my wallet, you know to placate him," said Bob, "but it must have spooked him because he went to pull the trigger. He had me in his sights. If it weren't for that guy there ..." Bob pointed to Alex, who was pressing wadded-up towels to Rick's bullet wound, "... I'd be dead. He tackled the guy before he could shoot. The gun misfired as the lowlife scum dropped it."

Both cops looked around. They spotted the gun on the sidewalk, the smaller of the two officers went to investigate it. "What happened to the assailant?" asked the burly cop.

"He hightailed it out of here," replied Bob.

"Which way?"

"That way." Bob pointed in the direction the robber fled.

"He get away empty handed?"

Bob scratched his head, then folded his arms across his chest. "Rick, the one who got shot, threw his watch to him in the hope it would see him off."

After a few brief questions to get a description of the assailant, the cop got on his walkie-talkie and alerted other units to be on the lookout for the mugger. An ambulance rounded the corner just as Bob went to his car. Two sets of flashing emergency lights were now sweeping around the dingy block. Scotty rested her head on Bob's shoulder as they watched the paramedics converse with the cops.

Keeping up pressure on the wound, Alex saw that Bob looked like he was comforting Scotty. But as Bob whispered to her, a momentary puzzlement crossed her face. It wouldn't have meant much to anybody else, but Alex knew exactly what Bob was telling her. Rick's eyes flickering open caught his attention. "Hey, you're back with us. You're going to be okay, the paramedics are here."

"Coming through. Give us room!" shouted the lead paramedic. "Step away, sir. We need to examine the patient."

"I'll be right here. These guys will look after you." Alex withdrew, wiping Rick's blood off his hands on one of the towels. He joined Scotty and Bob next to their car. "His eyes just opened."

"Thank God," sighed Scotty. "Is he going to be okay?"

"I hope so," said Alex.

The burly cop came over, flipping open his notepad. "Let's just run through a few details."

Alex gestured to the paramedics. "I need to go with him to the hospital. I can do that, right?"

"What's your relationship with the victim?" the cop asked Alex.

"Friend ... close personal friend," stammered Alex. "They can't take him away without me."

"No-one's going anyplace until I get a few things straight," muttered the burly cop. "And how do you two know the victim?" the cop turned his attention to Scotty and Bob.

"Likewise. A friend," said Bob, his voice tightening.

The hot dry wind grew stronger. The moon took on a dark red tinge as the Santa Anas kicked up a cloud of dust over the city. The smaller cop had bagged the gun and took it to the police car.

"Must we really do this now?" Bob gruffly asked the cop. "Some lowlife robbed us at gunpoint. If Alex hadn't thrown himself at the guy, I'd be dead. He was going to shoot me."

"Why was the alleged assailant going to shoot you, sir? Were you resisting giving him your valuables? You're not telling me you value your watches and trinkets more than your lives?" The cop rolled a wad of gum around his mouth, clicking it loudly as he waited for an answer.

"Let's not lose sight of the fact we're the victims here," said Bob tartly.

The cop shrugged. "I got three people, one gun and a shot guy. How'd I know one of you didn't shoot him?"

Scotty swept her hair back and stepped forward imperiously. "Do we look like the kind of people who go around shooting each other?"

"Just doing my job, lady. I need a quick round up of what happened. Let's take it one at a time. You, sir," he looked at Alex, "you're the close personal friend. You go first. Follow me." The cop led Alex aside. The smaller cop was now questioning

LaFonte, and the paramedics were loading Rick into the ambulance. "Tell me what happened," the cop said to Alex. The ambulance's siren rose to a wail as it sped off.

"Please, I should be going with him," Alex said, distress apparent in his voice.

"Yeah, yeah. Sooner we get this over with the sooner you get to Cedars," said the cop, a little kindlier this time.

Controlling his panic, Alex ran through the events after the robber had emerged from the shadows. Alex noticed Bob watching him intently as he said, "Anyway, the guy held out a piece of paper, like he wanted Bob to read it. Then he pulled a gun with his other hand. He waved the gun at us and told us to give him our wallets, watches, you know. That's when Rick took off his watch and threw it to him. While the mugger was distracted, Bob put his hand into his jacket to get his ..." Time slowed, the wind died. If Alex told the truth about the gun, Bob could face serious repercussions for carrying a concealed weapon without a license. If he lied, as Bob had begged him, it would make his tackling the gunman for no apparent reason seem like an act of reckless bravado that may have cost Rick his life.

"Please, carry on. You were telling me that while the gunman was distracted the guy over there by the car reached into his jacket to get his ... his what, sir?" The cop bore down on Alex.

"He reached inside his jacket for his gun. Bob aimed it at the guy and told him to drop his weapon. But the guy didn't lower his gun, instead he looked like he was going to fire. That's when I figured I had to knock the mugger down or else he'd shoot Bob."

"So that guy over there, the one by the car in the yellow tie, he drew a gun on the assailant but didn't fire?" asked the cop flicking his eyes at Bob. "Is that what you're telling me?"

"Correct," said Alex.

"Officer Lorenzo's gonna come over and take down some particulars from you, then you're free to go." The burly cop beckoned to his partner, who'd just finished interviewing LaFonte, then walked over to Bob and Scotty.

LaFonte came to Alex. "What a terrible end to a wonderful evening. I do hope this doesn't put people off coming downtown to my gallery."

At that moment, Officer Lorenzo interrupted to take down Alex's name, address and contact number. When Lorenzo had everything down, Alex said to LaFonte, "Excuse me, I need to get to the hospital."

LaFonte's hand fluttered to his throat. "Forgive me, that was an insensitive comment. I can't let you go off covered in blood like that. Come inside and let me find something for you to change into."

While not wanting any delay getting to the emergency room, spending hours in a blood-stained shirt and pants did not appeal, so Alex followed LaFonte inside. A door off the gallery's vestibule led to a narrow staircase up to LaFonte's private quarters. Expecting LaFonte's inner sanctum to be awash with chrome and black leather, Alex was surprised to find an interior décor more suited to a maiden aunt. Porcelain teapots with floral designs and crocheted throws accessorized a living room furnished with easy chairs and old newspapers.

After disappearing into a room at the back, LaFonte returned with an armful of clothes. "Here, these should fit," said LaFonte holding a lavender sweater in front of Alex.

Feeling a tad self-conscious, Alex stripped off his shirt. He used it to wipe off any remaining blood from his hands.

"I'll get you a washcloth." LaFonte hurried away.

While he was out of the room, Alex quickly removed his pants and changed into the ones LaFonte had brought in. They were cream gabardine with a slight flare. He was putting his shoes back on when LaFonte returned. "Hey, these actually fit," exclaimed Alex doing up the waist.

LaFonte dipped his head modestly and handed Alex the damp washcloth. "They belong to my business partner. I haven't been your waist size for twenty years." Alex nodded in understanding. After wiping the last spots of blood off his arms and throat, he pulled the lavender crew neck over his head. LaFonte picked up Alex's soiled shirt and pants. "Leave these with me. I've a wonderful Chinese laundress. She'll get them as good as new."

"Thanks." Alex went to leave.

"I sincerely hope Rick's alright. Please keep me informed." LaFonte gave Alex a sympathetic stroke on the arm as he left.

Out on the street, the cop had finished up with Bob and Scotty. Bob had opened his passenger door and Scotty was getting in. On his way past them to the Mercedes, Alex said softly, "Sorry Bob, I had to tell them the truth."

"Just leave it." Bob slammed the passenger door and walked around to the driver's side.

Alex tapped on the glass. Behind the window, Scotty struggled to meet his eyes. And when she did, for one brief moment, he knew things would never be the same between them ever again. There was no time to dwell on that, Alex jumped in the car and headed to Cedars Sinai.

Tracking Rick down in the E.R. wasn't a problem but getting any information on his condition was. The nurse politely informed Alex that 'close friend' wasn't sufficient to release information without consent of the patient or next of kin. Restraining the urge to slam his fist into the wall with frustration, Alex lingered in the waiting area hoping to wear the staff down with persistence. Every time a nurse or doctor passed, he pestered them for an update on Rick Stradman's condition. Desperately wondering what to do, after hours had passed and no-one would tell him anything, an idea struck him. Alex collared a nurse. "You won't tell me anything about Rick's condition, but you can tell me if you've contacted the next of kin, can't you? His father's Sid Stradman, he needs to know what's happened. His mother too. I know where she's staying if you need to call her."

"Everything's in hand, sir," said the nurse evasively before extricating herself from his grip.

That's when alarm bells started going off in Alex's head. Instead of dismissing further questions with polite answers, the staff completely avoided him. They huddled behind the nurses station, tossing concerned glances in his direction. At about six a.m. the sound of platform shoes on the tiled corridor roused him from a semi-slumber. In a phrase Alex never thought he'd hear in his own head, he was relieved to see Luisa striding in. "I don't know what's going on with him! They won't tell me anything," he said jumping up.

Luisa's face was free from makeup, her eyes were puffy, and her hair looked like she'd only run a brush through it once after getting out of bed. She tightened the belt on her tan jacket, as if Alex was a cold wind she needed protection from. "This is how you look after him? This is why Sid sang your praises?"

"Don't do this to me now, Luisa, please. I've been here for hours and I've no idea of how he is. How'd they find you? I was expecting they'd call Sid."

Luisa dropped her purse on the chrome and tan chair and said matter-of-factly, "Letitia got through to me and broke the news. He's dead."

The floor dropped from beneath Alex's feet. The combination of shock and fatigue buckled his knees and he sank onto the hard chair. Clenching his fists, he wanted to rail against Luisa's words to make them not true. "He was alive when the ambulance took him away! The bullet was in his shoulder, why the hell couldn't they save him?" Alex glared angrily at the nurses station.

Luisa shook her head in annoyance. "Not Rick. He's fine. The bullet only grazed his shoulder and he's got a concussion. No, it's Sid. It's Sid who's dead."

Although still shocked, Alex's brain got back into gear. "Sid? But how?"

"Rick had Sid's number in his wallet. The E.R. nurse called the house to let Sid know Rick had been admitted. He was getting dressed to come to the hospital when he collapsed. The paramedics tried to revive him on the spot, but they were too late. That's when Letitia called me at the hotel."

"Luisa, I'm so sorry," a hideous hollowness emptied Alex's chest. Sid was gone. What a terrible night. If Bob only had given the guy his wallet instead of pulling a gun all of this could have been avoided.

Luisa picked up her purse, took out a tissue and dabbed her eye. "There were times I wished that man dead, but not like this." Composing herself, Luisa put the tissue in her pocket, picked up her purse and headed to the nurses station. After a few moment's discussion with the nurse behind the counter, Luisa returned to Alex. "He's in recovery. They said you can see him briefly before they take him up to a room."

Alex couldn't quite believe her words. "Don't you want to see him?"

Luisa choked back a bitter laugh. "Naturally. But I can't imagine I'm the first face he'll want to see after this. I don't want to make the situation any worse. Don't tell him about Sid. Leave that until he's had some rest. Please," said Luisa.

Taking her point, Alex nodded. He got up dazedly and pushed through the double doors. A nurse led him through to Rick who was lying on a gurney. "The wound was superficial," explained the nurse as they walked. "He's stitched up and on antibiotics. We need to keep him in for observation because of the concussion, but other than that he should be a right as rain."

"Where the hell have you been?" was Rick's slurry response to Alex once the nurse had left.

"Next of kin shit. It's taken a while to get them to let me see you." Alex surreptitiously squeezed Rick's hand. "How's the shoulder? Does it hurt?"

"Oh, no. It feels like it's been licked by a kitten," said Rick sweetly, then snarled, "of course it fucking hurts. If we need an armed guard in the future remind me not to rely on Bob. Not exactly Frank Butler, is he?"

Alex hemmed and hawed, then said, "Bob didn't have a license to carry concealed. He begged me not to tell the cops he'd pulled a gun."

"What did you tell them then?"

"I couldn't lie."

Closing his eyes wearily, Rick adjusted himself on the gurney. "Bob's got money, power and influential friends. They tend to smooth over problems." Opening his eyes, Rick looked blearily at Alex. Trying to focus, he raised himself on one elbow and ran his eyes up and down Alex's outfit. "Did you go shopping? What are you wearing?"

"I had blood all over my shirt and pants so LaFonte lent me these."

Rick snorted a laugh. "And no silk neckerchief to finish off the ensemble?"

"Knock it off, he was being kind. Look, they'll be admitting you to a room in a few minutes."

"Just take me home. I'm fine."

"They need to keep you under observation for the concussion." Alex paused, "Look, I need to tell you something. But you must promise me first that you won't fly off the handle."

"I don't like the sound of this." Rick shifted uncomfortably. "Okay, shoot. If you pardon the expression."

"Your mother's outside."

"No way! I cannot deal with her now. Tell her to go away." Rick rolled away.

Alex rolled him back. "You have to see her. She's very upset."

"No, she's not ..."

"She is. And she sent me in first because she was afraid you wouldn't want to see her."

"I never credited her with that much perception."

"She's had a rough night too. I'll go fetch her." Leaving Rick, Alex went back to the waiting area.

"How is he?" asked Luisa rising to her feet.

"Irritable, complaining, sarcastic," replied Alex. "Pretty much back to normal."

Taken by surprise, Luisa fought to suppress an inadvertent smile. "That's our Ricardo."

Alex grinned in acknowledgment that they both had Rick's more challenging qualities nailed. "I told him you're here. He wants to see you."

Luisa asked, "He does?"

Alex nodded. He kept out of the way while Luisa visited with Rick in the recovery room. After that, she returned to the Beverly Wilshire while he hung around at the hospital. Once installed in his private room, Alex kept guard over Rick, ensuring he didn't turn on the T.V. in case Sid's death was reported on the news. When Luisa returned around lunchtime, she was restored to her fully made-up, coiffured glory, dressed in an immaculate taupe skirt and blouse with an ivory cape tossed over her shoulder. Rick was dozing in bed when Luisa beckoned to Alex from the doorway. In the corridor outside, she took a newspaper out of her bag and showed him the headline. It read 'Downtown Shooting of T.V. Actor Claims Unexpected Victim'. Under the banner were photos of Rick and Sid. Speed reading the report Alex saw nothing untoward in the story and said as much to Luisa.

"But did you read between the lines?" asked Luisa. "Listen to this part, 'Stradman had been partying at an avant-garde downtown gallery with an unidentified male companion prior to being shot in a bungled street robbery'." Luisa folded the paper and put it back in her bag. "This is how it begins." Steeling herself she then squared her shoulders. "I must break the news to Ricardo. The story is in the papers, soon it will be everywhere. We can keep it from him no longer."

Stepping aside, Alex let Luisa go into Rick's room. He heard a murmur of protest from Rick, which must have been him waking up and seeing his mother leaning over the bed. After Luisa had spoken to him in a low voice for a minute or two, Alex expected to hear an outburst from Rick. There was none. He peered around the doorframe. Luisa was sitting on the bed, cradling Rick in her arms and stroking his hair. Alex backed off, not wanting to intrude on the family grief. He took a seat down the corridor. After half an hour, Luisa emerged. "How'd he take it?" asked Alex.

Luisa clapped her hands together softly, then held them to her lips. "Not well."

"I didn't hear anything."

"Precisely. When that impenetrable wall of silence descends behind his eyes is when I fear most for his sanity. In times of crisis he retreats into a realm to which I have no claim. To which, I suspect, none of us has claim." She flicked her eyes towards Rick's room. "When we spoke that day at the beach, I was not truthful with you. I must confess there have been occasions when Ricardo has made attempts on his life." Luisa struggled to maintain her composure.

Alex reached out to Luisa, he knew how that felt.

Luisa snatched her arm away. "A close watch must be maintained. We must ensure he is not left alone until this crisis has passed. I cannot be with him all the time. We will need to share the duty."

"Okay, but I need to go back to Sunset Cove. I have to change my clothes."

Luisa thought this over for a moment, then declared, "It's too far for you to keep driving back and forth. You must be very tired too. I'll call my hotel and have them arrange a room. The hotel has a boutique. I'm sure they can find something to suit your style." Luisa ran her eyes over Alex's lavender sweater and gabardine flares.

Suddenly feeling terribly self-conscious, Alex said, "These aren't my clothes, they're Guy LaFonte's." Seeing Luisa's eyes widen, he elaborated, "Not actually LaFonte's. They belong to his business partner." Alex realized that sounded even worse. "LaFonte found them for me after I'd taken off my shirt and pants. I mean ..." Oh, what the fuck. Alex thought it was easier to just let people think what they wanted, they would anyway. And not having slept properly for over twenty-four hours, he didn't have the strength to argue about Luisa's offer or give an explanation about what he was wearing. "Fine, thank you, Luisa." While she went off to phone her hotel, Alex checked in on Rick, who had slipped into some kind of catatonic shock. Once Luisa returned to sit with Rick, Alex left the hospital.

Checking into the Beverly Wilshire with no luggage and his off-kilter outfit didn't raise an eyebrow. A quick peek into the hotel's boutique led Alex to the conclusion that any outfit from there would be more suited to LaFonte business partner's taste than his. So, before letting a bellman show him up to his room, he scooted over to Mr. Mike's jean store. He'd enough bucks on hand to buy a couple of black shirts, some indigo jeans and a navy linen safari jacket. After going up to his room, a well-appointed studio overlooking Rodeo Drive, he used the pit stop to shower and change. The king size bed was tempting, but he knew if he laid down to rest his eyes he was likely to doze off and not wake up until tomorrow. Wearing his fresh duds, he splashed his face with cold water and headed back to Cedars.

Luisa was sitting beside Rick's bed when he got back late afternoon. Rick appeared to be asleep and she took Alex to one side. "The police came. They wanted to ask him questions. I sent them away. He's in no fit state to talk to anyone."

Although Alex didn't care for the woman, there was no denying the trauma was weighing heavily on Luisa. Her posture wasn't as erect, her defiance not as fierce, her eyes not as bright. Her vital force usually lent her the illusion of a much younger woman. With that force diminished, the unflattering early evening light revealed her to be the late middle-aged woman she was. "Go back to the hotel and get some rest, Luisa. I'll watch over him."

Luisa gratefully nodded her acceptance. Picking up her purse, Luisa said to him sotto voce, "This does not change how I feel about your relationship with Ricardo. I do not approve of it and can never condone it." She looked over to Rick, ashen faced and asleep, an I.V. attached to his arm. "But he needs time to recover. And, although I don't understand why, I know he gains comfort from your presence. You've displayed your loyalty and I suspect you are, at heart, a decent man. That is why I'm blinding myself to certain things for the time being."

While not exactly a ringing endorsement, at least Luisa wasn't hurling brickbats at him, so Alex could live with this state of affairs.

Once Rick woke up, he was desperate to go home. However, the hospital insisted he remain under observation for an extra day as they were still concerned about his concussion. While changing their shifts in sitting with him, Alex overheard muted arguments between Rick and Luisa about where he would go after he was discharged. Luisa wanted him to move into the hotel with her, but Rick was insistent on going home to Sunset Cove. During her visits, Alex recognized something had changed within Luisa. Sid's death had knocked the fight out of her. Each time he saw her she'd aged slightly, gradually losing the willpower to keep those shoulders rolled back ready for combat. Oddly enough as Luisa's strength diminished, Rick's increased. Once the initial shock of Sid's death had passed, Rick didn't fall to pieces. Admittedly he was subdued, but the silence behind his eyes, the dark silence which Alex and Luisa had feared, did not materialize.

Satisfied that Rick wouldn't do anything stupid, like throw himself out of the hospital window, Luisa deemed it safe enough for them to leave him unattended. Taken off suicide watch and with no tangible reason to remain at Cedars until Rick was discharged, Alex swung by the florist, picked up some flowers and headed to lower Bel Air.

The house of mourning was easily identifiable. Daimlers, Rolls-Royces, Cadillacs and Lincoln Continentals lined Bellagio Road nose to tail. Alex squeezed the red Mercedes into a space several hundred yards away. Arriving at Sid's house, after a five-minute walk, Alex buzzed the house. Once he'd been granted access through the electric gates, he found the driveway rammed with cars too. The guy he'd met at the pool party, Blake, was standing sentry at the glossy front door.

"Hi," said Alex extending the flowers, expecting Blake to turn him away. "I came to leave these for Letitia and pass on my condolences."

"She's inside. Go on in." Blake cast a suspicious squint at the gate. "I'm keeping a look-out for the press. Already had some of them trying to tailgate people in. They're like vultures, the rancid smell of death attracts them," said Blake with a sneer.

Alex found the house awash with yellow flowers. Every room was crammed with people eating, drinking and smoking. The lively chatter was interspersed with occasional bursts of laughter. It was if a giant cocktail party had invaded the mansion. Passing through the busy rooms, briefly acknowledging familiar faces from the pool party. Alex made his way to the kitchen. He walked in and found Letitia overseeing the caterers and instructing the housekeeper to load the dishwasher yet again. "Hey, Letitia. Excuse me, I don't want to intrude. I just dropped by to say how sorry I am about Sid."

Letitia turned from the dishwasher. On seeing Alex, her eyes welled with tears. She broke away from what she was doing and took the flowers. "That's kind of you. Here, please put these in water. Use the Lalique vase and place them with the family flowers," instructed Letitia as she handed the bouquet of yellow and white roses to the housekeeper. "It's a mad house in here, I need a break. Come outside." Taking Alex's arm, she picked their way through the kitchen chaos. Out in the calm of the garden,

Letitia asked desperately, “You’re a smoker, aren’t you? I gave up years ago, but I could really use a cigarette.”

“You’re in luck.” Alex dug into his pocket. It was fortuitous he’d stocked up at the hotel. Flipping one from the pack, he offered it to Letitia. Taking one for himself too he clicked his lighter and lit them both. Letitia inhaled gratefully. They both took a few drags before Alex asked, “How’re Tiffany and Tyler doing?”

“I sent them to my parents. This zoo’s totally out of hand. The phone doesn’t stop ringing. It’s either the studio, the attorneys, Sid’s friends, Sid’s enemies or the press. And the funeral arrangements are like putting on a musical. You’ll come, won’t you? Will Rick be well enough to attend? He ought to be a pallbearer.”

“They plan on discharging him tomorrow, but he won’t be able to carry the casket. The bullet hit his shoulder.”

“He’ll be an honorary pallbearer then. I want you there too. You’ll sit with the family.”

Alex flicked ash off his cigarette. “I don’t think that’s a good idea.”

“You must be there. Sid was very fond of you.” Letitia took a couple of deeper drags on the cigarette. She glanced over her shoulder and regretfully surveyed the mansion. “It’ll be hard giving all of this up.”

“Why’d you have to give it up?”

“Haven’t you heard?” Letitia smiled ironically. “I forgot, you’re not on the Hollywood hotline. Sid was on the brink of going broke. He wasn’t even cold before the snakes were out.”

“How could Sid be broke? I mean, look at this place? Look at everything he had?”

“Exactly the problem. Leverage on leverage, Leo had been borrowing one thing against the other. The final straw was Sid guaranteeing the over run on *Tornado!* with his own money. The studio wanted all the special effects re-shot. It pushed him over the edge, that's what killed him. There's nothing left to borrow against."

"But I thought it was Rick being shot which caused his heart attack?"

"If it hadn't been the news about Rick, it would have been something else. Sid hadn't been himself for months. For a while I suspected he had another woman." Letitia couldn't help laughing at Alex's shocked response. "Sid possessed many great qualities, but resisting a pretty face was not one of them. He always said his heart couldn't take the strain. This time he was right." They smoked in silence for a few more minutes. Letitia took a final drag, then stubbed hers out. "It's lucky that Rick's career has taken off. I don't think he'll receive any legacy from Sid by the time the piranhas have picked the flesh from his corpse ..."

"... and so we commit his body to the ground." the Priest's words at the graveside jolted Alex back into the present.

"Brother Rick," blurted out Tyler. He pulled away from Letitia and pointed to Rick, who only now was walking towards the grave from the chapel.

The casket was lowered into the grave. "Earth to earth, ashes to ashes, dust to dust."

Rick arrived at the grave side, his arm in a sling. He hung back as Luisa, Blake, Shirley from the office, and about ten other people took their turn to toss a handful of dirt into the grave. Letitia kissed a yellow rose and cast it downwards. Rick was the last person to bend, gather his handful of earth and scatter it on the casket.

When Rick hadn't appeared with the rest of the honorary pallbearers, Alex feared he wasn't going to show up for the interment. However, it was fitting that Rick's should be the final farewell to Sid. And Alex was pleased he'd displayed the fortitude to do it. Over the past few days at the beach house Rick had displayed a new maturity. His show's producers had been solicitous and caring. Due to Rick's injury they'd delayed production on *The Brad and Carol Mysteries* for a month. They vehemently asserted they were one hundred and ten percent behind Rick and would make the schedule work for him. Scotty and Bob had sent flowers, but there'd been no phone call. Danielle had been the lone personal caller to Sunset Cove. She'd visited on her day off from shooting and was gracious and solicitous in her grief. She hadn't known Sid well, but he was part of Old Hollywood and she lamented the passing of a great showman such as he. Alex had expected Luisa to be pestering them, trying to assert her control over Rick, but she'd been so eerily quiet that Rick had started to worry about her and had actually begun calling the hotel daily to check she was okay.

Once Rick's last handful of soil had been thrown, the professionals took over to fill in the grave. The mourners began to make their way out of the enclosed memorial park, many of them pausing to pay their respects to a familiar name or two on the headstones they stepped around. While Alex let the crowd dissipate, a woman in dark glasses at the back of the mourners caught Alex's eye. Waiting in line to get out, she briefly took off her sunglasses and dabbed her eyes with a black lace hanky. Despite the broad brim of her black hat obscuring her face, he immediately recognized it was Julie. After putting her dark glasses back on, Julie walked unsteadily towards the exit. Picking his way through knots of people sharing memories of Sid, Alex caught up with her. "Julie!" he said breathlessly.

Pivoting, Julie dropped her glasses to discover who'd called her name. "Alex, it's you. I was hoping no-one would notice me." Julie hastily pushed her dark glasses up over her eyes.

"I was out at Fox the other week and came looking for you. I heard you'd got a job in the commissary. They said you were taking a day out to look after your mom. We miss you down at Sunset Cove, the Beachcomber's not the same without you."

"Maybe I'll come back. There's no reason for me to be at the studio anymore," Julie said with a sniff.

"Your mom's recovered then? That's great." Then Alex realized there could be another reason Julie no longer needed to be close to home, perhaps her mother had died. "Sorry, I hope you don't mean anything else to do with your mom."

"There was never anything wrong with mom. That was a cover story," said Julie with a bitter laugh. "Sid was planning to leave his wife, you see. He got me the job at the studio so we could see each other until he'd worked everything out ..." Julie kept talking, using the brim of her hat to shield her from unwanted scrutiny.

Alex watched Julie's lips move, but he'd stopped listening. After a minute he politely cut her off mid-sentence, wished her well and sent her on her way. Disillusioned with both Julie and Sid, Alex made his way back to Rick, still lingering by the graveside.

The beat of helicopter blades overhead startled the mourners. Women glared up and held on to their black hats as the chopper's downdraught scuttled loose blooms over the graves. Tapping Rick on the shoulder, Alex shouted over the helicopter's noise, "For a moment back then I thought you weren't going to show!"

"I didn't need to hear the service, I'd said goodbye to dad in the chapel. Let's get to the wake, I need a drink!"

They both squinted up and saw the chopper swing away to make another pass. Although the press had been barred from the funeral service, they had cameras directed at the cemetery from windows in the surrounding office buildings. The chop of another set of rotors indicated a second press helicopter was about to swoop. A television camera on top of a truck could be seen filming over the heads of the crowd outside the memorial park.

"For God's sake. Sid was broke, big deal. Worse things have happened in Hollywood. If *Tornado!*'s a hit, they'll all get their money back in the end!" said Rick angrily over the second chopper's noise as it swooped low. "What's with this all press interest in dad anyway? It's insane!"

The crush to get out of the cemetery was worsening. The circling helicopters and the press jostling in the car park led to a brewing sense of panic. The first inkling something was amiss came when Alex saw Letitia waving desperately, urging him and Rick to go back into the cemetery rather than come out. Grabbing one of Tiffany and Tyler's hands in each of hers, Letitia hustled the kids into her waiting black limo.

"I see him! There he is!"

Alex heard yells erupt from the press corps and the cry spread like hounds scenting the fox. Several news people and photographers broke loose from the press pack. Star reporters jostled through the exiting mourners, roughly pushing their way into the cemetery. Within moments, Rick was surrounded. Cameras and microphones were shoved in his face.

"Mr. Stradman! Did the shocking revelation about your lifestyle cause your father's death?" barked a harsh bottle blonde. She jabbed her orange foam-covered microphone at Rick, awaiting his response.

"What?" Rick shied away from the reporter.

"Do you regret being so open about your relationships with men?" A stringy brunette in coral lipstick bore into Rick while brandishing her pad and pen.

"Were you estranged from your father because he didn't approve of your sexual proclivities?" questioned a silver fox in a plaid jacket with his camera crew in tow.

"Back off!" Alex shouldered through, putting himself between the press and Rick.

Rick shielded his face as questions and flashes rained on him from all angles.

"Leave him alone! You stinking hacks!" Luisa launched herself into the fray. Cameras pulled away from Rick and zoomed in on Luisa as she used her purse to cosh any newshound within arm's length. Several of Sid's more agile pals set about forcibly ejecting the press from the cemetery, others surrounded Luisa to prevent her lashing out further.

With attention deflected from Rick, Alex shuffled him away from the reporters. Realizing the only refuge was the chapel, Alex whisked Rick through the rose garden, pulled open the double doors and dragged him inside. Safely installed in the vaulted chapel, Alex and Rick caught their breath. Hearing the doors fly open, they looked up in panic, fearing the press had followed. However, it was Blake wrestling Luisa inside. He pushed her towards the pews and slammed the doors shut.

"What the hell's going on?" gasped Rick in bewilderment.

Blake leaned on a pew and wiped his mouth with the back of his hand. "Sorry this had to hit you today, kid."

Taking off her veiled hat, which had been knocked askew in the fracas, Luisa fluffed out her hair and sat on a pew.

"I don't understand, why are the press after me?" stammered Rick.

Luisa put her hat down and gestured to Blake. "Show him."

"Shirley was on her way out. She rushed back when she saw the story had hit the stands. It's made the front page on all the evening papers," said Blake unrolling a newspaper.

Alex took the paper. Below the banner headline about the crash of a hijacked Air Vietnam passenger jet there was a photo of Rick with the tag line 'Was Sordid Sex Life of T.V.'s New Star the Cause of Sid Stradman's Death?'

Luisa leaned forward, as if in prayer, and rested her head momentarily. Shaking her head as she raised it again, she sadly smiled at Rick and declared, "This is what I wanted to protect you from. But it's too late. Once the genie is out of the bottle it can never be put back in."

Alex stared at Rick's ashen face. The four of them sat in the chapel silently listening to the mob outside, the press baying for Rick's blood.

CHIAROSCURO

Inky fingers of derelict factories probed the hot orange and purple sky. Undisclosed figures lurked in the shadows, only a toe cap's outline, or glint of an eye in the blackness lending a clue to hidden dangers about to pounce.

The new memory piece Alex was working on was as gloomy as hell. He felt it appropriate for his mood and continued to channel his depression onto the canvas. Working in the daytime with the electric lights on was an odd experience, but since the stories had broken in the press they'd had to keep the beach house's shutters and blinds closed to protect themselves from prying eyes.

Alex hadn't believed some of the things Danielle had told him about the press. He felt she must have been exaggerating the extent of their lurid curiosity about one's private life. The morning after Sid's funeral, however, he'd opened the kitchen blind only to come face to face with a photographer pointing his telephoto lens into the house. Alex barged out of the back door and gave the gutter hack a tongue lashing. Since he was only wearing his boxers and his morning hair was particularly wild, it wasn't the best look to present to the world to be portrayed as an upstanding citizen. While Alex had been screaming and yelling with flailing hands, the camera's speed wind had shot a roll of film before the photographer fled. Any one of those myriad photos would be a great addition to *The National Enquirer's* next installment in their expose of the Sodom and Gomorrah they equated Sunset Cove to. Alex wondered if the story of his and Rick's disgrace would get as far as Dayton, and if it did whether the news would kill his pop.

"This is fucking ridiculous," muttered Rick, bringing in a coffee and a pile of supermarket magazines. It's been over a week with no let up." Rick flicked through the papers, tossing each one onto the floor with a grunt of disgust after scanning it. "How'd they get this stuff on the newstands so fast?"

"Why keep torturing yourself by looking at that shit?"

"Because I can't believe they get away with what they write. None of it's true! Here, listen to this, 'Locals in Laguna Beach report spotting Stradman and various homosexual conquests dancing lasciviously in the locale's sleazy bars, many of them notorious gay pick up joints'."

"It'll blow over. It was very unfortunate Sid's death coincided with the T.V. show."

"This is no coincidence, someone timed releasing the story to the press for maximum impact. This was revenge and I've a pretty good idea of the narrow-minded bigot who wanted to ruin me." Rick scowled in the direction of the Waverleys' former summer residence. "It's a good job they moved out or I'd set their place on fire."

"Getting yourself arrested for arson would definitely deflect from the less savory stories about you in the press."

"It's okay for you, they're not trampling your name through the mud."

"Er? Don't you remember this fine piece of literature courtesy of the Evening Post, 'Alex Morgan, the bohemian artist whose sleazy beachfront shack served as the scene of lewd conduct and perverted acts in public view'? I considered having that embroidered on a scatter cushion."

"We were *inside* the house for fuck's sake. They make it sound like we were selling tickets for a sex show on the boardwalk. I'm amazed momma hasn't got her lawyers onto this and sued their asses off." Rick sighed in frustration.

"How's she doing? Spoken to her today?"

"I called first thing this morning. There was no answer from her suite, so I left a message with the front desk."

"She'd gone out that early?"

"I don't know if she was out, maybe she'd taken a sleeping pill?" Rick chewed it over in his head. "At least the new show will take my mind off this crap when we begin shooting. I guess my staying at Scotty's place is off the table now."

"I'd consider that a safe bet."

"Maybe I could stay at the hotel with momma during the shoot if she's in town any longer? The way things turned out with Sid I wouldn't have Brentwood now anyway. His attorneys called. By the time they wind up the Estate and divide it between his beneficiaries we could end up with as much as fifty bucks each."

"Don't spend it all at once. Which reminds me, I noticed your car was low on gas when I moved it."

"Maybe I should ask Mike for an advance on my fee when I see him today?" Rick checked his billfold. "You couldn't loan me fifty bucks until next week, could you?"

"Sure." Alex wiped his hand and dug in his pocket. "Why's he want to see you anyway?"

Rick shrugged. "Don't know. Maybe just a warning to keep my nose clean. The *McMillan* ratings were terrific, so that should keep everyone happy at least."

"Yeah, but the show screened the night before all this scandal broke. Here," said Alex handing Rick a few bills. "I've slipped you a little extra. Buy yourself something pretty."

Rick laughed as he counted the money, "Five bucks! Gee thanks, you're a swell boyfriend." Rick checked his watch. "I better get moving in case I have to wait in line for gas. I hope this oil crisis is over soon. I'll swing by the hotel to check on momma after the meeting, I should be home around seven."

"Cool, see you later." Once Rick had checked the coast was clear of reporters and left the house, Alex allowed himself the luxury of opening up the studio's shutters to let in some daylight and leaven the gloom. Getting back to his painting, he mulled over his friends' reactions to the past couple of weeks' events. Hank and Kaori had phoned to say the baby was due any second. Hank didn't pay much attention to the papers or T.V. news, so the story had pretty much gone over his head. Scotty and Bob had maintained radio silence, making their response hard to judge. Rosemarie Rodgers had signed to play the lead role on Rick's new show and was throwing a party to celebrate, to which she'd very publicly invited them both. Danielle had called him every day, and they'd spent a couple of hours on the phone each time. She'd become his sole confidante through the drama. He'd been totally truthful with her about his anger at Bob. In fact, he'd told Danielle everything about Sid and his disappointment in Julie's revelation they'd been having an affair. If anyone had a juicy story to sell to the press it was Danielle with all the behind the scenes secrets he'd spilled to her. But he knew she wouldn't breathe a word. Terrible things had happened, long term friendships shattered, but he'd made a new friend in Danielle and was grateful for that.

Around five, the phone rang. Dragging himself from his work, Alex answered it. Simply hearing Rick's tone of voice let him know that something was badly wrong. "Everything okay?"

"Not really. The network's requested some changes to the show."

"What kind of changes?"

"*The Brad and Carol Mysteries* is now *The Mysteries of Carol Carter*."

Alex immediately knew this meant Rick was off the show. "I'm so sorry."

"I wondered why Mike was being so evasive over why they hadn't sent the new script. Some secretary was busy with the Wite Out blanking all of Brad's lines. I guess my loss is Tina Mason's gain. I must send her flowers, something with poison ivy might be appropriate."

"There's no point being bitter, come on home. We'll get over this together."

Rick didn't answer immediately. "I still need to go see momma. It could take a while because she'll want to say 'I told you so' a few million times. Go ahead and eat dinner, I'll see you later."

Hanging up the phone, Alex had the feeling that wasn't going to be the case. Rick's call to say he wasn't coming home that night didn't come until nearly eleven. When Rick had gone up to Luisa's suite he found she'd fallen into a state of nervous collapse. Concerned about her unresponsive condition, he'd called for a doctor. Although the doctor diagnosed simple exhaustion, Rick was worried about leaving her alone and said he needed to stay over.

Rick stayed over at the hotel the next day too.

And the next.

Alex carried on painting. Each day Rick that didn't return, he opened up more windows. The house grew brighter and emptier with every pulled shutter and drape. Alex sensed the very thing he'd wanted most to avoid, the heartbreak of love, was stalking him.

On a lighter note, Yumi Mihara called to tell him she'd sold more of his work. "Ha," she said with glee, "you got notorious! Lots of interest. Now when I get a name fucker in the gallery, you got name I can sell. I got big interest from the gays. You folk hero. We need to find you a studio for the commission. They want big paintings so you need big space to work. I got a building downtown. I give you good price to rent it. Talk soon. Love you!"

Alex hung up and felt the earth shudder beneath his feet. Leaving the beach house to work someplace else had never crossed his mind.

The wind was changing.

When Rick hadn't come home by Saturday, Alex decided to jump in the car and swing by Luisa's hotel to find out what was going on. Maybe it was ridiculous, but he was concerned Luisa was holding Rick against his will. After enquiring at the

Beverly Wilshire's front desk, the receptionist made a phone call and then directed him up to Luisa's suite.

The hotel's gilded elevator glided up in total silence. A discrete 'ping' announced its arrival on the 8th floor. Alex stepped off the elevator and the plush apricot carpet cushioned his footfalls to the Presidential Suite. With trepidation, Alex rang the gold bell beside the double doors. A moment later, the suite's left-hand door opened and Rick peered around the corner. He appeared drained, dark circles under his eyes, his normally clear skin spotty and red. "Hey man, you look rough," said Alex. Not having seen Rick for several days, he was genuinely shocked by his appearance.

"Getting shot was a breeze compared to this. Come on in. You won't believe the past few days I've had." Rick led Alex down a dark corridor flanked by cream columns. Reaching the end of it, Rick flung back the doors to a sunlight drenched sitting room. The breeze fluttered the white gauze drapes over the patio doors onto the terrace. Once inside the room, Rick draped his arms around Alex and buried his head in his shoulder. Alex started to speak. "Don't talk," said Rick, "I need a moment to feel like everything's okay, that everything's like it was. Just hold me."

Doing as Rick asked, Alex held him tight and stroked his hair. While he did, he checked out the room. Steamer trunk wardrobes were dotted around, a couple of them were swung open. Cream, taupe, and white clothes were in the process of being packed - Luisa's wardrobe was apparently on the move. Finally releasing Rick from his arms and stepping back, Alex asked, "What's going on?"

"Can I get you a drink?"

"No, I'm fine."

"Momma's going back to Italy." Rick walked to the wet bar. He picked up a bottle of whiskey and poured himself a drink. "You sure?"

"Yeah."

Dropping in a couple of ice cubes, Rick swirled them in the glass. "I've never seen her like this, she's lost interest in everything. We've got the exhibition opening in Florence next month and building work on the Ca' dei Venti's about to commence. She's not talking to anyone. I'm having to field all her calls and make all her decisions."

"Why'd you have to do that? Surely she has assistants?"

"Momma never delegates, that's how she maintains complete power. There's a lot of money riding on these things, our family money." Rick slugged back his drink and shot Alex a weary smile. "I'm praying that once she's back in Italy she'll feel better. But until then I'm having to take the helm. If I don't, everything could fall apart."

Alex tilted his head suspiciously. "What does that mean?"

"I'm taking her back to Italy. And while I'm there I can do what needs to be done to maintain control of her empire. She's already dropped the ball on one deal. If I don't step in, her losses, well our losses, could be catastrophic." Rick looked away. "I should be able to wrap it up in six months."

"You coming back to the beach?" asked Alex as casually as possible.

"Oh, yeah. I'll be home tomorrow." Rick came over and stroked Alex's arm. "I need to pack up the stuff I have there. We fly to New York on Sunday and then take the Queen Elizabeth. God, this has been a nightmare. I'm scared momma's never going to be okay again. Now that dad's dead she's all I've left in the world. Sorry to run out on you like this."

"You must do whatever you think's best. She is your mother, after all," said Alex. They continued to chat a while longer, Alex telling Rick about the developments with Yumi and the hotel commission. As Alex talked, Rick carried on packing Luisa's clothes and accessories. "I'll leave you to it. See you back at the house." Alex kissed Rick softly on the cheek, then swept an errant strand of hair off his forehead. "I can find my own way out. I left a trail of breadcrumbs on the way in."

Rick laughed as he looked around the cavernous suite. "Yeah. Something she and dad had in common, they both think big. Thanks for coming, Al. This is so far from how I want things to be, you have to believe that."

Alex nodded manfully in response. Leaving Rick to carry on with his packing, Alex retraced his steps along the dark corridor to the double entrance doors. He was about to go leave when he heard another door off the corridor click open. Turning around, he saw Luisa appear behind the partially open door. Her face was haggard, her hair unkempt, she clutched a soiled hotel robe around herself. Alex's heart went out to her. He understood why Rick needed to do what he was doing, the woman looked so desperately unhappy. Alex was about to approach her to convey his concern, when a momentary flash of her old vitality sparked in Luisa's eyes. He watched her back straighten, her shoulders roll back, and a half smile cross her lips. The expression behind Luisa's stance said it all to him, it said, 'I win.' Looking away from him with distaste, she closed the door.

Alex turned and walked out of the suite, relieved that he'd never have to set eyes on Luisa D'Onofrio ever again. Although Luisa wasn't keeping Rick captive with ropes and chains, she had equally effective methods.

♦ ♦ ♦

Alex and Rick's time together at the beach house together was bitter sweet. By day, Rick filled packing boxes ready for the movers to take away to storage. By night, they clung to each other as the warm sun went down and the cold night air crept in. Although they lay entwined in the last glow of summer, fall was taking hold.

On their last day, after the movers had collected the final boxes and Rick's bags were all packed and waiting by the back door, he said to Alex, "Let's take a walk on the beach." Silently, they sloshed through the surf towards the cliffs. "I want to go up there one last time, I want to go back to where we began," said Rick suddenly.

Ignoring the warning sign, now fixed very firmly in place, they climbed to the cliff top. After reaching the peak, by the spot where the ground had crumbled beneath Alex's feet and Rick had saved him from falling, they sat on the rocks among the flaming red aloe vera blooms and stared out to sea.

"I'll miss you," said Alex summoning all his willpower to stop his voice trembling.

"I've never had anyone in my life like you. Or ever will again," said Rick, his bottom lip quivering.

"We don't know what's to come, but we do know what we had," said Alex, "we had one heck of a summer."

"That summer of seventy-four," laughed Rick. "One that changed everything for both of us."

"You sure you're doing the right thing, going back to Italy with Luisa? You're sure she's not manipulating you into it?"

"Who knows with momma? But there's no doubt she's a wreck, and she's not dealing with the business. It's not only our family's wealth at stake, we have employees to consider. I can't risk wrecking their lives too. I missed the chance to tell dad I loved him and be nice to him while he was alive. I can't make the same mistake with momma. Going back there's only temporary. I'll come home as soon as momma's her old self again."

Alex grimaced. "You sure you want that?"

"Actually I do. I used to have some idea of how she'd respond, but now I'm in uncharted waters. And who knows, after some time's passed maybe all this will be forgotten and I can work in Hollywood again."

"Maybe." Alex draped his arm around Rick and rubbed his shoulder.

"Or maybe times will change and no-one will care about any of this gay stuff anymore," said Rick softly.

"Let's hope."

"Look. A yacht!" Rick pointed out to sea, where a sloop with its sails raised was being blown towards the horizon. "Do you think the people on it are looking back at us here on shore?"

"Maybe," said Alex squinting into the sunlight shimmering on the water.

"I wonder who's on that boat?" mused Rick.

"It's two guys," answered Alex decisively.

Rick turned to Alex, a quizzical look on his face.

"Two guys who've had enough of all the bullshit in the world and have taken off on a whim. They're letting the wind take them where it will, drifting around the world like nomads."

"And what happens if they hit land and find a place they like?"

"Then they'll drop anchor and settle down. They'll build a big house, get a couple of dogs and become stalwarts of the community. They'll do good deeds and be kind to old ladies. The townsfolk will look up to them with respect, cherishing their integrity and rejoicing in their good humor. They'll have a wonderful life growing old together and loving each other more with every passing day."

"Sounds like a good place," said Rick with a sad smile. "What do you think will happen, you know, when the time comes? The time when one of them's gone and the other's left alone."

"The one who remains will treasure the memory of the good times. He'll live out his days content in the knowledge they'll be reunited when his time comes too."

Rick gave Alex a sly sidelong glance and nudged shoulders. "I thought you didn't believe in all that spiritual stuff?"

"No harm giving it a chance. Look, this isn't a ring, but maybe it'll do." Alex lifted his arms, wincing slightly from the pain in his shoulder, and grasped the cord around his neck. Shaking it free from his t-shirt, he took off the green soapstone pendant. "Lean forward."

Rick did as he was told.

With reverence, Alex draped the cord around Rick's neck, pulled Rick's shirt collar open and dropped the pendant inside. Letting it fall, he patted it in place over Rick's heart. "There you go, bud. Two souls linked for eternity. That's you and me, like it or not."

Rick rested his head on Alex's shoulder. "Look, the yacht's nearly out of sight. I hope those guys on it will be okay."

"They will. They're gonna be just fine."

Goodbyes were something neither of them wanted and so Rick made his way back alone while Alex remained on the cliff for another hour. When Alex got back to the house, Rick, and all trace of him, had gone.

Alex didn't feel like painting.

He didn't feel like smoking.

He sat in fugue like state.

The phone rang. He didn't want to answer and let it ring out.

He remained motionless as the daylight faded.

After a few hours had passed, a noise startled him. His stomach was growling. Remembering that he hadn't eaten today, he hauled himself back to life and went to the kitchen. Getting onions and garlic out of the refrigerator and pots and pans out of the cupboards, he attempted to re-enter the world of the living with the comforting procedure of feeding himself. The gloom was a welcome relief to his eyes. For some unknown reason they were tired and sore, so he carried on working in darkness. He was selecting a knife from the block when horizontal bands of light swept around the kitchen as headlights passed behind the house. He didn't allow false hope to enter his heart. It wasn't Rick. It was never going to be Rick again. He knew that.

A gentle knock on the back door. "Alex? You home?" asked a woman's voice from outside.

"Door's open," Alex called out.

The door swung open and a figure entered the kitchen. Alex couldn't quite make out who it was in the gloom.

"When no-one answered the phone, I got scared," said Danielle, "all sorts of crazy ideas ran through my head."

"Oh Danielle, it's you. Hi," said Alex. "I didn't feel like talking. Sorry to make you drive all the way down here to find out."

"No problem, honey. What you making?" asked Danielle coming up behind him.

"Something Italian. There's plenty. I've gotten used to catering for two. Wanna stay for dinner?"

"Sure." Danielle slipped off her jacket.

After smashing the garlic, Alex wiped down the chopping board and began to cut the onions.

"You must be able to make this with your eyes shut. My carrot intake must be low because I can't see a thing. Mind if I turn on some lamps?"

"Be my guest. I hadn't noticed."

After a few clicks, the warm glow of electric light filled the house. Danielle came back into the kitchen. "Can I do anything to help?"

"I'm fine. All under control."

Danielle leaned on the counter and watched him dice the onions. "Very professional. I'm impressed."

"I'll make someone a good little wife one day, huh?"

"I meant your knife skills, honey. If the art thing doesn't pan out, you can get work as a sous chef."

"Right," Alex laughed quietly. "Rick taught me this." Alex kept his head down and carried on chopping. "There's wine and beer in the refrigerator."

"Can I get you something?" asked Danielle going to the refrigerator.

"I'm fine." Alex struggled to restrain himself but let out an involuntary sob.

"You're not fine." Danielle rushed back and looked at him. "My Lord, Alex, don't cry. It'll be okay. Rick will come back. And I'm here for you until he does. All you have to do is call me if you get low or lonely."

"It's not that." Alex screwed up his eyes to restrain his tears. "It's these goddamn onions. Danielle, you can do something to help."

"Anything. Just ask me, honey," said Danielle gently.

Jerking his head to the counter behind, Alex said, "Rip off a hunk of that bread and bring it to me."

Slightly mystified, Danielle got him the bread.

"I learned this from Rick, it's a trick to stop your eyes watering when you chop onions." Tears rolled down Alex's cheeks. "Put it in my mouth."

Danielle placed the wafer of bread on Alex's tongue. She remained by his side until his eyes had stopped watering. And once his vision had cleared, Alex carried on making dinner.

UNTITLED / UNFINISHED – SEPTEMBER 2001

"... that's when I learned a blank canvas is the most intimidating thing in the world and ..." Alex paused, awkwardly hanging in mid-sentence, unable to recall what came next. Hovering in the moment, trying to make his mental struggle look like gravitas rather than forgetfulness, he feared he was losing his mind. He'd given this lecture many, many times before, how on earth could he forget a single word of it?

Staring at the sea of youthful faces expectantly waiting for him to continue, he imagined Danielle's face among them. His ploy of looking solemn to cover a moment of amnesia wouldn't have fooled her, she'd have immediately known he'd dried. To come to his aid, she'd have mouthed the next word, or given that little head wiggle, or done any one of those myriad other things she always came up with to help him along. But Danielle wasn't around anymore.

Beauty, kindness and grace are no match for cancer. He was on his own again now.

Alex summoned all his concentration to dig for the missing word. Aha! That was it, Teacher! "... and that's when I remember my old art teacher." Alex relaxed, he was back on track. "I remember his advice that if you're blocked, just get something on the page. It may not be great, but it will be something. You can't wait around for inspiration to strike or the moment to be right. Every single one of you has a unique perspective on the world. All of you out there looking at me see a similar thing - a man in his late fifties, whose hair's a bit longer than it should be and who's a bit heavier than he should be," cue appropriate laughter from the audience, "but no two of you can possibly see me exactly the same way due to your vision coming through the eyes in your head. Your view of me is dependent on your position in the room. And how you perceive your vision of me is colored by your life experience and your personal taste. For example, staring at a lilac wall all day long could be one person's idea of heaven and another's idea of hell. By the way …" Alex made eye contact with as many students as possible, "… I subscribe to neither of those concepts." Another small ripple of laughter. "Although I speak in this room, my words are actually happening inside of your head, their sounds and resonances triggering explosions of neurons in your brains. For those of you still awake, that is." Laughter. "Let's do an experiment. Close your eyes." Alex gave a moment for them to comply. "Now imagine something that makes you inordinately happy. It doesn't have to be a vision, it could be a smell, a sound, a memory, a person …" Alex waited, allowing a full minute to pass. "Open your eyes. I want you to consider how you'd communicate what you just experienced in your brain to an audience. Every one of you has a different joy or sadness. And every one of you has a different way of expressing it. I urge you to understand that when you paint, sculpt, write, or whatever creative art form you choose to express yourself by, you're not only sharing your unique vision, but also sharing your unique relationship with the Universe. I believe we artists are still cavemen. We go into our black cave with a flaming torch and paint our hopes, our fears, and our dreams. Imagine for a moment that I'm a caveman, with my long hair that's not such a hard ask …" Laughter. "My caveman didn't go to art school, and he won't make any money from his art, but he's been driven by a primal urge to arrange charcoal and pigments into shapes. Is my caveman painting the horses, bulls, bison, lions and deer to celebrate the beauty of creation? Or is he leaving a lesson for the hunters who follow about which animals to fear and which to eat? Or perhaps the animals vanished and my caveman's painting creatures he fears may never exist again? In that case, is my caveman casting a spell, creating images he believes will become real to make the animals return? We can't ask the cavemen why they painted their pictures, but you can ask yourself why you create. Is your passion to celebrate life, to exorcise demons, or shape the world to your desire? I've asked myself this very same question over the years. Today my answer is it's pain that has driven my creativity for the greater part of my life. I've used my art to either escape my pain or express it. My emotional pain has led to some of my most rewarding work and now ..." Alex raised his right hand, the knuckles enlarged and gnarled with arthritis. He winced as his flexed his misshapen fingers, "now physical pain's my muse. I consider my life lesson has been to find a way to embrace my pain. Maybe I've finally learned my lesson, for I've grown to love my pain. It's my constant companion, the dawn chorus which wakes me and the lullaby which rocks me to sleep. My pain draws me daily to the canvas, like a worthy adversary urging me to the ring for another round – always luring me with the tantalizing hope that my next artistic punch may land a knockout blow on that sucker. My pain inspires me to fill that blank page every day. I implore each and every one you not to run away from your lives. Use every experience, happy, painful, sad, passionate, whatever, and express your feelings in all their wonderful or shameful glory. Don't be apologetic, nor make your work acceptable or pleasant. Don't worry if no-one likes it or 'gets' it, be truthful and proud in your art. In that way the work you leave on your cave's wall will be a testament to your life. Who knows, after ten thousand years have passed maybe some traveler will discover it. They'll look at what you created and exclaim, 'I recognize that view. I know that feeling. I've had that same experience'. And although your mortal body will have disintegrated long, long ago, in that moment of sharing through art you'll be alive again. That's why I believe art transcends death, that's why I believe art is life!"

The audience, overwhelmed by the passion in his voice and the fire in his eyes, let his final words sink in. Then the students erupted in applause and rose to their feet as one.

A woman in a dark turtleneck stepped up to the microphone. "Thank you, Alex Morgan!" The woman gestured to the students to sit down. "Forgive me, Alex. I don't want to cut your ovation short, but we only have the lecture hall for another thirty minutes."

Alex smiled, relieved that she'd drawn a line under the ovation as he wanted to sit down too.

The woman continued, "May I say what a pleasure it is to welcome Alex Morgan back to Long Beach State University." Flipping her cue cards, the woman began to read from the first one. "I'm sure you don't need me to remind you all of the many awards and achievements in Alex Morgan's long career." The woman smiled at the audience, and then Alex, and continued, "However, I'm going to ..." The lights dimmed and a beam of light projected an image of his *Marooned on Red* painting onto a screen at the rear of the stage.

Alex settled back in his chair and modestly covered his eyes. "I'll take this opportunity to rest my eyes. I've seen most of these before," he said jokingly. He let the mistress of ceremonies reel off the accolades and turning points of his career, using the slide show of his art works to illustrate each chapter of his life. Alex didn't need to hear and see this, he'd lived it. Instead he drifted off into his thoughts, his memories ...

After Rick had taken Luisa back to Europe, Danielle had become his constant companion. The easy camaraderie they'd instantly enjoyed never waned. Their love hadn't been passionate, but it had been warm, genuine and deep. He'd never felt the same way about another man as he had Rick, and since he and Danielle spent every waking moment together, getting married had seemed the logical thing to do. They'd had a good life together. Danielle knew that she wasn't the love of his life, but she was happy to be the rock of his life. When he got that 'look' in his eye, she stepped aside and let him get it out of his system. She knew he'd always come back. Alex wondered why she'd settled for him, in fact he asked her that question once. "I didn't settle for you, sugar," Danielle drawled, "I chose you." And she had avoided any mention of the subject ever again.

A few years after they'd got married, and his career had really taken off, they'd bought a building on the edge of Venice and Santa Monica. The hotel commission Yumi secured for him had been a huge success, leading to critical acclaim and subsequent large projects which needed a big space to work in. They'd bought the Venice studio and house just before gentrification took hold. It was good timing for, despite his success, he wouldn't be able to afford to buy premises on such a scale there now.

Alex had held on to Dora's beach house until the lease expired. The landowner had been buying any leases that came up for sale so, combined with the expired leases, the landowner finally owned all the pieces of the puzzle. Just when it looked like the beach houses were going to be demolished and Sunset Cove turned into a luxury resort, local residents banded together to protest the destruction of such a treasure. They argued that Sunset Cove was an area of natural beauty and historical interest and should be preserved and remain accessible to the public. People power amazingly won out and big business was shooed off. The local council purchased the land and made the area into a State Park. The beach cottages had been lovingly restored and were now rented out as holiday homes. Although Alex steadfastly refused to allow himself to cry, a certain moisture had accumulated in his eyes when he and Danielle had gone to check out Sunset Cove after restoration. Dora's old house was listed as the *'Artist's Cottage'.* Once it became known that the great Alex Morgan had resided there in the seventies, his reputation made it the most desirable property.

Alex's relationship with Scotty and Bob had never recovered after the shooting at LaFonte's Gallery. Bob had called in some favors with the Sheriff's office, and they both granted and backdated his license to carry. In light of the Alphabet Bomber and other troubles around seventy-four, Bob had made a persuasive argument that as a prominent citizen and vocal Republican his life could be in danger, giving him a valid need to bear arms at all times. Scotty carried on working successfully as an artist, but she'd never been taken totally seriously. Bob had eventually married her. They'd retired to Palm Springs in the early nineties with several millions in the bank and spent their days playing golf and drinking (not always in that order and not always playing golf).

Hank and Kaori had become proud parents of five kids. Hank had taken a job in a motor repair shop around seventy-seven. He'd a natural aptitude for the work and took over the business when the owner retired. Kaori had retrained as an art teacher. She was extremely well liked and noted for her outlandish school art projects. So far she hadn't killed any of her students in an inferno of paper dolls, and for that everyone was truly grateful.

And as for Gina ... an article in the paper about tragic endings of famous lives had caught his eye. It said that the face of seventy-two, Gina Schiavello, had died of an A.I.D.S. related illness in Atlantic City in eighty-five. Reading further, the article stated that she'd lapsed into heroin addiction. That news made him very sad for several weeks.

And as for Rick. Well, Rick ...

After he'd taken Luisa back to Italy, there'd been phone calls and letters from him. But every time it sounded as though he was coming back to the U.S.A., Luisa would have a relapse of nervous exhaustion or face some major issue with one of her exhibitions, foundations or galleries which only Rick, now always known as Ricardo, could solve. The more Luisa stepped away from the business, the more Ricardo became entangled in the family fortune's labyrinthine web. And, after a few years, all communication ceased. Alex didn't blame Rick, when you had someone like Luisa for a mother resistance was futile.

Maybe it was losing Danielle, maybe it was the increasing weakness and pain he was experiencing in his arms and hands, but he'd become acutely aware of his mortality over the past few months. Having put Rick out of his mind for so many, many years, he'd recently found himself wasting time late at night on that handy invention called The Internet. After a few nights of searching, he'd discovered that Ricardo had married a plain but wealthy young woman called Giuliana Pessina. They'd had a daughter, Patrizia, and shortly after the child had been born the marriage was dissolved. Alex couldn't resist further exploration in the cyber world to see what else Ricardo had been up to. It was unsettling to see images of the man Rick had grown into superimposed on his memory of the boy he'd been. One late night internet search revealed Ricardo was in Boston for a gallery loan. On an impulse, triggered by too many whiskies and a maudlin bout of grief, Alex found himself picking up the phone and ringing around Boston's finest hotels. Ricardo was registered at the fifth one he tried. Alex put down the phone, thinking maybe it best to leave the past behind. But after filling half a glass with whiskey and slugging it down in one, he rashly called the hotel back and left a message with the front desk.

That was a week ago and he hadn't heard anything. Then again, Alex hadn't expected to. After so many years had passed, they were two different people. Alex suspected now Ricardo was an Internationally Respected Businessman he'd relegated that summer on the beach to history.

"...so once again, please show your appreciation for Alex Morgan! We thank him for illuminating and inspiring us all!" The mistress of ceremonies brought her speech to a close and extended a hand to Alex.

Alex unsteadily rose to his feet and the ovation reached a crescendo. He acknowledged it, raising a shaking hand as if to say, 'Enough already'. A young male student with spiky blue hair and a nose ring helped him down off the stage. The applause petered out as Alex shuffled into the backstage darkness.

In the administration corridor behind the lecture theater, a sound engineer unhooked the radio mic. While the sound guy was extricating the battery pac from Alex's pants pocket, an administrator poked her head around the main office's wire glass door and said, "Mr. Morgan, I've a call for you."

"What? For me? Here?" said Alex crossly. Wearily, he walked down the hall. Why on earth would anyone be calling him here? "Who the hell is it?" he barked to the administrator, holding out his hand for the receiver.

"They didn't say, sir," she replied sheepishly.

Alex grabbed the phone and snarled into it, "Y'ello."

Silence on the other end.

Alex was on the verge of hanging up.

"Alex?" came a voice over the line.

"Who is this?" Alex pressed the phone closer to his ear.

"It's me."

"That you, Rick?"

A quiet laugh. "Yeah ..."

"How the hell'd you track me down here?" growled Alex.

"I rang your studio. They said you were giving a lecture, so I asked the hotel operator to find the number for the University."

"You could have left a message with the studio. I'd have called you back."

"I know. But I needed to speak to you now."

"It's been twenty-six years, another couple of hours wouldn't have hurt," said Alex with annoyance while smiling inside. This was so Rick, he hadn't changed.

"I have wall to wall meetings booked for the rest of the day and I wasn't sure I'd get a chance to speak with you later. I've been in New York. I only just got back to the hotel here and they gave me your message. I was so sad to hear of Danielle's death. I'm so terribly sorry."

Alex swallowed his emotion, determined to keep it in check. "We had a lot of good years together. She spoke about you often. *We* spoke about you often. We never forgot you."

"I never forgot you either." After a pause, Rick said, "I was surprised to get your message. I thought you'd never want to speak to me again."

"Why on earth would you think that?"

"I was afraid you couldn't forgive me." Rick's voice wavered.

"Forgive you, for what?"

"For leaving like I did. Then I got caught up with momma's businesses and ... well, once she had me back in Italy everything kind of swallowed me up."

"I understand. You had your life to live."

Rick let out a loud laugh on the other end, "I don't know about that. I've discovered there are other ways to kill yourself than jumping off a cliff. My last twenty-six years have not been happy ones."

"I'm sorry," said Alex sincerely. "What happened to you back in seventy-four was unfair. You were a good actor. I always felt guilty that you lost out on being a star because of being with me."

"That wasn't your fault. Times have changed, thank goodness. It's practically desirable to be gay these days. Everything would be so different if we'd met like that today. Some things in the world get better at least."

"Hey, how long you in the States for? I'd like to see you."

"I go back to Italy next week." Rick left a long pause. "Alex, I want to see you too. Look, I'll try to re-arrange tomorrow's meetings and grab a flight to L.A. in the morning."

"Yeah? You sure."

"More than sure. I'm getting that flight even if I can't re-arrange the meetings."

"Still impetuous, huh? Okay, take down my cell, you got a pen?" Alex waited while Rick scrabbled around on the other end.

"Ready? It's 555 26809. Got that? Text me your flight number and I'll come meet you."

"God, it's so good to hear your voice again. Thanks for finding me, Al. You can't know how many times I've wanted to speak to you, but I was always too scared."

"Scared?"

"Scared you may hate me," said Rick, his voice breaking.

"Never, my love. I could never do that."

Rick took a moment on the other end to gather his breath.

"You still there?" asked Alex.

"Yeah. This is stupid, but I suddenly feel nervous about your seeing me again. I warn you, I got old."

"All of fifty-three! You're ancient!"

"God, you're quick at math."

"I warn you, too, I'm not the athlete I once was."

"Artist's don't need to lift weights."

"It helps if they can lift a brush," growled Alex.

"Well, if you can't lift a brush you can always use your hands. I recall you were quite good at that."

Alex let out a sound which was a mixture of a cough and a laugh. "Okay, you got my cell. Let me know your flight. I'll look out for the text."

"Alex, before you go there's something I need to tell you."

"What?"

"All the time we were together I never said it out loud, although I thought it all the time."

Alex held his breath.

Rick took a beat, then said, "I love you."

Alex's throat tightened. "I need to remember how those words sound." The University office's clatter and chatter dimmed into the background, Alex focused all his attention on the other end of the phone line. "Say it again."

"I love you."

"I love you too. Always have. Always will. See you tomorrow, kid."

"See you."

Alex hung up the phone, feeling like he'd been punched in the guts, but in a good way. Who knew what life would throw at you?

Alex's drive back to Venice Beach was slow due to the thick traffic, but for a change the congested freeway didn't make him mad. Back inside his tranquil bleached wood and white studio space, he exchanged words with his assistants. They were finishing up for the day. He checked over the shipping documents they'd prepared for the items leaving for the Philadelphia exhibit tomorrow. After he noticed someone had filled in tomorrow's date incorrectly as the 12th of September and he'd amended it to the 11th, he bid his staff goodnight. Once everyone had left, he savored being alone with his thoughts. Later that evening his phone buzzed. He picked it up and saw Rick's text. '*United 175. Arrives LA bout 10. R. xxx*' Alex set down his cell phone. Closing his eyes, he took a deep breath. Rick was coming home. Tomorrow they'd be re-united after all these years.

At pivotal points in his life he needed to put his feelings on canvas. Although it was late, and his hands ached like fuck, he rolled up his sleeves, picked up a palette, squeezed out some pigments, took a brush and mixed a wash of red. He regretted not making the effort to find Rick sooner. The memory of Rick on the beach that summer, running into the sun, full of conflict, full of laughter, full of life, reignited in his brain like it was yesterday.

The past held no surprises, it was complete. But the present was like this work in progress, incomplete and changeable. He carefully mixed the colors. He wanted this red to be different to those reds of anger and hurt in the past. This new red should be a red of love and reconciliation, a red of hope, a red of happiness, and a red of hearts mended. He controlled the brush and moved the paint into the shapes he wanted. He blended, he flicked, he swirled.

The endless possibilities in his work were now a comfort, no longer a confusion. Until a painting was finished everything could be changed. Like this messy, painful, joyous, silly, beautiful, gorgeous experience of being alive, each beat of our hearts taking us into the limitless eternity beyond.

ABOUT THE AUTHOR

Howard Rayner has worked extensively in theatre, film and television (both onstage and off), with nearly thirty years' experience behind him. As well as performing and designing, Howard has always loved writing and has now added this aspect of his creativity to his professional body of work. He has written several young adult novels and contributed to numerous text books published by Ernst Klett.

'The Summer of '74' is his first adult title and is a revised version of a novel called 'Running Out' which he originally wrote in 1978.

Printed in Poland
by Amazon Fulfillment
Poland Sp. z o.o., Wrocław